C000182079

Charles Heathcote has alw
very rarely leaves. A Creat
Cheshire and secretary t
Writing Group, he is a writer of radio plays, poetry and
prose. *Royally Doris* is the fourth and final book in a series
featuring Mrs Doris Copeland.

Also Available

Our Doris Series:

Our Doris
Indisputably Doris
Doris Ahoy

Valentine and Featherstone Series:

An Heir to Murder

ROYALLY DORIS

Charles Heathcote

ᴧ

VARIOUS ALTITUDES

Cheshire

Copyright © Charles Heathcote

Published by Various Altitudes, Cheshire

ISBN 13: 978-0-9932349-3-4

ISBN 10: 0993234934

All Rights Reserved

2022

The rights of the author have been asserted.

No part of this publication may be reproduced, stored on a retrieval system, or transmitted, in any form or by any means, electronic, mechanical, photocopying, recording or otherwise without the prior permission of the publisher or copyright owner.

All the characters in this book are fictitious, and any resemblance to actual persons, living or dead, is purely coincidental.

www.variousaltitudes.com

ONE

Our Doris has discovered that the Partridge Mews Women's Institute is no more.

We found out on the day when Alf was arrested. I were in the garden seeing what a mess he'd made of my geraniums when our Doris came over. She were as rosy-cheeked as a schoolgirl, her smile as wide as a football pitch. She scuttled over like the child-snatcher, all conspiratorial, with a mug of tea in her hand – something she never ordinarily does as she says that drinking from a mug in the garden is a habit for the proletariat – she handed it over and said to me, she said, 'You simply won't believe what I've just heard, our 'arold.'

I played along and said to her, I said, 'Your Mavis has died and left us her fortune.'

Our Doris sniffed at this. Her and that old crow Mavis are more like sisters than…well more than our Doris and her own sister. We haven't heard much from Bianca since she ran away with a clergyman in nineteen-ninety-three. They moved to Cleethorpes. No, Mavis is much more like our Doris – she's like a Yorkshire terrier with a perm and a catering license. If Mavis were to finally pop her clogs, our Doris would hold something like a Victorian memorial – curtains closed, black horses and atomic warfare. Grief does funny things to folk, and you don't get much funnier than our Doris.

Either way, I could tell our Doris were desperate to tell me her news, so I said, 'Go on then. What's got you hopping round my garden like an incontinent rabbit?'

That earned me the Look. Our Doris squinted her eyes so much I couldn't tell if she were trying to shoot laser beams from her pupils or thread a needle. 'This is *our* garden, our 'arold, and don't you forget it. I let you get away with that little comment about our Mavis because she can't stand you either, but I won't have people thinking this garden is anything but a joint enterprise.'

I slurped my tea. 'All right then, *our* garden. Still, what am I not going to believe?'

And that's when she came over all town crier. Her shoulder pads settled into place, she set both hands atop one another over her stomach and said to me, she said, all deep and free of inflection, 'The Partridge Mews Women's Institute is no more.'

Honestly, my wife is more dramatic than Margaret Rutherford. Fifty-six years we've been married, and she's never lost the tendency to go all theatrical, as though each day she's under some sort of spotlight, being observed, like The Truman Show with added Silvakrin.

I said to her, I said, 'What do you mean, it's no more?'

'Exactly what I said. Apparently, after I left, other members – and I mean longstanding members like Celia Cotton who entered a jam competition whilst fighting a lengthy battle with gout – upped and quit. Subscriptions were down. Fundraisers failed to raise funds and so the committee made the decision to shut up shop.'

Our Doris were gleeful, like the wicked stepmother after tearing up Cinderella's dress.

'Have you spoken to any of the ladies to see how they feel?'

'I've spoken to Erin and Edith, but apart from that, no. Those women held on to outdated ideas about morality that have no place in the twenty-first century, let alone a small-town WI. They brought this on themselves.'

I didn't say anything, but our Doris must have caught some hint of my thoughts. I'd been betrayed by my face again.

'You may very well look like that, 'arold Copeland. I'm aware of my own faux pas when it comes to societal obligations, but if I can make certain allowances and, dare I say, change my opinions, so can they.'

I said, 'You're right, our Doris.'

She went off to catch up on her correspondence. I couldn't imagine there'd be much. I supposed she could have had a letter from her sister, but Bianca has always been hit and miss when it comes to keeping in touch. Time was we thought she'd died, but she turned up two years later working down a scrap yard.

Our Doris stayed in contact with everyone whilst we were on our cruise. Even though they hadn't kept her updated on the state of the WI, I couldn't imagine they'd kept much else from her.

A few hours down the line, I received the phone call. I'd been prepared for a morning lazing about the house like a teenage layabout, binge-viewing Breaking Bad and munching on Maltesers, when I got called to the police station. I hadn't planned on answering the phone, but I decided I couldn't bear another lecture from our Doris on my abysmal telephone manner.

I hadn't been down to the station in a while, so I thanked the Lord for small mercies. At first, I thought that Alf might have mended his ways and gone on some sort of spiritual pilgrimage, accepting that at seventy-four, he ought to be calming down. Course, he still nicked pork pies from Tesco, but only the ones that had been reduced, and he always shared one with the security guard for his trouble.

I found my car keys, headed out the house and all but tripped over Mrs Cribbins, who was hobbling around the drive like a pigeon in search of breadcrumbs. She hasn't had a good life. You only have to look at her face and you can tell she hasn't had a good life. It's in all her wrinkles, the deep crevices in her forehead are threaded with woe and misery.

I stepped closer and said to her, I said, 'Morning Mrs Cribbins.'

She wagged a finger so as I'd bend my ear towards her mouth.

She's a fair bit shorter than me. It were like leaning down to give the hangman easy access. She said to me, her words a ticklish whisper, 'I've had a letter.'

I bolted upright at that. Moments earlier, I'd been planning to collect my best mate from the police station and heading down to the pub. Instead, I was stood listening to a woman who wanted to tell me about her mail.

'I don't know what that's got to do with anything, but I commend your postman for his early delivery.'

She wasn't happy with my response. Her lips pursed, looking like the anus of a constipated dachshund, and she said, 'I'm not senile, Mr. Copeland. I've had a letter. A very important letter. A letter of which Mrs Copeland needs to be made aware'

'You have our phone number, don't you, Mrs Cribbins?'

'I've been trying all morning, it's always engaged. I suppose Mrs Copeland is catching up on everything she's missed in her absence.'

Choosing not to think about the cost of our next phone bill, I said, 'Why don't you pop in now?'

'I could never call around unannounced.'

'If it's a matter of importance, I'm sure our Doris won't mind.'

Mrs Cribbins considered that before saying, 'That may be true. I will simply state you invited me around to discuss a letter of great urgency.'

For no reason known to man, I saluted Mrs Cribbins and replied, 'Godspeed, good woman.' Then I unlocked the car as she scuttled indoors.

I've been collecting Alf from the station since we were lads. It's not that he's malicious, he's just a bit dozy. Alf doesn't have it in him to be a career criminal.

The car park was full, and the disabled bay was taken, so I spent a fair few minutes waiting for someone to extricate their Ka from a spot by the side of the road. I don't think folk care about parallel parking anymore. It all went out the window with automatic cars and novelty condoms.

I traipsed to the police station, thinking about how being a frequent visitor should warrant some sort of priority parking. The number of times I've been down that station, you'd think they'd give me my own parking spot.

Alf rose to his feet like an ageing Labrador as I entered, a grin on his face the likes of which I hadn't seen since he found twenty quid under our table down the Hare and Horse.

I said to him, I said, 'What've you done this time?'

'Honestly, he doesn't see his best mate for three

months and then has nothing more to say than, "What've you done this time?"'

'Well?'

'Are the pubs open, 'arold? I could do with a drink.'

Geoff Pollock, the desk sergeant, piped up then, he said, 'You probably shouldn't be doing much drinking, Mr Simpson, not after what you've been up to.'

'I had no choice. This is the bleeding council's fault. I've said that enough already.'

'You say so, but that doesn't condone your actions.'

I said to Geoff, 'Is he free to go then?'

'Just make sure he doesn't get into any more trouble.' Geoff had a grim smile on his face. He's been at that desk for a few years now and he's so used to seeing Alf get up to mischief that he knows his warnings will probably fall on deaf ears. In any case, I think he appreciates a familiar face.

We left the station, and I took Alf to the Hare and Horse.

Not much had changed about the pub in the three months we'd been away. Apparently, my time on the cruise had lulled me into believing that all pubs had comfortable seating arrangements and played inoffensive, low-level muzak in the background. Instead, I entered the Hare and Horse only for my soles to squelch against the sticky carpet. It was a dark carpet, though I couldn't tell if it were blue, green or red. It was certainly a colour, and it was certainly stained to high heaven.

Linda still stood behind the bar, looking like a cross between Nora Batty and Olive from On the Buses. She greeted me with something like a smile and said, she said, 'How do, 'arold? Long time, no see. Good cruise, was it?'

'It were all right, but I'm glad to be home.'

I ordered two pints of bitter and took them over to the table. I'll admit it were nice to feel the perished cushion beneath my buttocks, the hard wood against the backs of my legs. I felt all nostalgic, nearing relaxation in a reverie about all the times I'd settled into that very seat.

And it hurt.

I was thrilled. I couldn't help grinning like a schoolboy who'd just seen his first garter belt. I supped my pint, smacked my lips and sighed that sigh that's common when enjoying life's little pleasures.

Alf said to me, he said, 'What's got you all happy?'

I said, 'You can never get a proper beer on a cruise ship. They don't want to offend any vegans.'

Alf eyed me warily, as though I'd been replaced by some form of artificial intelligence. 'What's veganism got to do with beer?'

I shrugged. I'm not supposed to shrug in public, but there wasn't much else I could do. When the situation calls for a shrug, you have to shrug. 'I've no idea. Something to do with sheep's bladder, apparently. The barmaid did tell me, but she had a great big hairy mole on her cheek.'

'What's that got to do with anything?'

'I got distracted.'

Alf were still bewildered. He took my pint off me, sniffed it with all the alacrity of a sniffer dog – they'd be glad of him at border control – then set my pint down, glanced from the bar to me and back again and checked his watch, an old Ingersoll thing he got when his Uncle Leadbetter died. I've no idea how it keeps running, but it's reliable, unlike Alf's Uncle Leadbetter. There's not many men would go to the trouble of bigamy. Maybe that's why he needed such a reliable watch; a man with two wives on the go is in sure need of a timepiece he can rely on.

Alf hadn't lost his look of trepidation. He were all wary, like a toddler approaching a heron, and he said to me, he said, 'Are you really all right, 'arold? Because you're acting a bit doolally tap.'

'There's nothing wrong. Can't a man just be glad to be home?'

'I'm not saying you can't be glad to be home. I'm glad you're home. Derek O'Malley can't handle his drink, and that Tom from the allotment never stops talking about marrow. But do you have to act so…'

'So what?'

'Weird.'

I inhaled a breath that were deep enough to render an asthmatic jealous and said to him, I said, 'I promise you, Alf, that this time next week, I'll be back to my old self.'

'Really?'

I nodded. 'So, what happened this morning, then?'

He shook his head and slurped his lager, before saying, 'Our Edith is going to kill me.'

'She might, but that's the point of wives. Each one of them comes with the in-built capability for homicide. It's in the Bible.'

'Really?'

'I mean, it's been a while since I read scripture, but I'm sure it's somewhere in the Gospel of our Doris.'

'But that's Doris. She's always been murderous. Our Edith didn't get murderous until I put the ring on her finger.'

I said to him, I said, 'Our wives have never been angels, Alf. It's part of the appeal, never knowing if your wife has put strychnine in the Bisto.'

'I thought you did the cooking,' he said.

'I do, but that doesn't mean our Doris doesn't have ample opportunity.' I supped my bitter for effect. I hadn't done much to earn a pint, but something told me it was going to be a long conversation. 'Forget the possibility of your Edith nobbling you when you get home. How did you end up down the coppers' yard this morning?'

'I had to pay a visit.'

'They arrested you, Alf. This isn't just turning up at somebody's front door because you haven't seen them in a while. People don't go down the police station for a friendly chat.'

Alf looked fit to brain me. 'Not that kind of visit. I had to *pay* a *visit*. Spend a penny. Urinate, 'arold, and you should know yourself that past seventy any trip to the lavatory is urgent business.'

'Oh.'

'Ever likely you should say oh,' he said.

Things started to slide into place. I said to him, I said, 'When you say it was urgent, where did you pay a visit?'

'I went to the public toilets on Chamberlain Rise, but the council has closed them. There was a sign on the door and everything. I were fit to bursting, 'arold, so I did what we all used to do when we were young. I went behind a hedge. There were no one around.'

'There must have been someone around for you to end up arrested.'

'They had me for indecent exposure. I tell you, the world's gone mad. A man can't pee on foliage anymore without being dragged down the police station.'

'Who saw you?'

He glared at me then, properly glared. He was getting into Doris territory with the ferocity of his look.

'Nobody saw me! Some young bobby happened to be walking past and guessed what I was doing. At first, I thought he was after some funny business, like George Michael and all that. I were ready to tell him I don't go in for cottaging when he started putting me in handcuffs and calling me a dirty old man. If I'd wet myself, he'd have had me in the back of his squad car and been sentencing me to Tena. I tell you, this is all because of that new detective inspector coming in and throwing his weight around. He's one of the main reasons the WI had to shut down.'

I said to him, I said, 'I were going to ask you about that. Our Doris has some of the ladies around.'

'You heard, then? Our Edith were ecstatic. I haven't seen her that happy since Martin broke my Cat Stevens CD.'

'How long's it been gone?'

'Only about a month. They gave our Edith the boot ages ago, though. Said as her behaviour towards their new chairwoman at the bake sale couldn't be condoned, or some such rubbish.'

'How did she take it?'

'She told them all that Pandra bought her home-made jam from Sainsbury's, soaked the labels off and put her own back on.'

'That's tame for Edith.'

It was. I've known Edith since she chewed her pigtails in literacy and she is renowned for her temper. She cut the head off Ethel Hobson's teddy bear in Form 6 when Ethel insulted her cross stitch. Sir made Edith sew the head back on, and she did. Backwards. So as, and I quote, 'He could see when someone tries to stab him in the back.'

Yes, Edith has always had anger issues. I couldn't

believe she stopped at telling Pandra's secret.

Alf had this mischievous glint in his eyes as he said to me, he said, 'She might have also taken Pandra a cake as a peace offering.'

'Why's that given you a face like Albert Steptoe?'

'She made it with laxative chocolate. Pandra didn't leave her house for three days.'

I've always said folk can't go around upsetting the WI, and when they fight amongst themselves it's like the Roundheads and the Cavaliers all over again. If the army had the women of Partridge Mews in their ranks, they'd have the entire world under their thumbs.

I used to have nightmares about the WI. With them disbanded, I'd no idea how my subconscious would react.

I said to Alf, I said, 'I'm going to need the full story here. What happened after they kicked Edith to the kerb?'

Alf smirked, he actually smirked. 'That'll take more than one pint, that will, 'arold.'

'All right then, I'll buy lunch. I don't exactly want to be at my house in any case. There's no knowing what Mrs Cribbins wants with our Doris, but I can't imagine it'll be anything good.'

Over lunch, Alf told me the tale of the WI's downfall. At least, I cobbled together the few snatches I could understand when he took a moment away from gobbling lasagne as though he hadn't seen food since the finale of Z Cars. Seeing Alf eat isn't for the faint-hearted; his jaw cracks, he chews with his mouth open – claims he can't breathe otherwise – meaning I got to see each chip squashed between his molars as tomato sauce and mince dribbled down his chin.

If there's one thing can be said of Alf, it's that he's messy.

He told me how after our Doris left the WI, Erin rescinded her membership. Some of the girls from the estate stayed on, but eventually found themselves forced out by Pandra's belief that they weren't the sort of people the National Federation of Women's Institutes wanted within their ranks. Others shared her belief, and with some careful coercion – raising subscription fees, taking trips to expensive locations on schooldays and writing letters to the Gazette – they left as well. Once the committee saw fit to remove Edith, all Hell broke loose – worse than when Magdalena Valentine upended a platter of tiramisu over Rupert Beauchamp at the Harrington's Greek Night in nineteen-eighty-seven. Others left in solidarity, saying as Pandra O'Malley were an over-the-top dictator with a sense of self-importance unseen since Doreen Leadworth came up with a new recipe for pear and stilton pastries whilst watching a particularly intense episode of All Creatures Great and Small.

Edith wrote to the Partridge Mews Gazette to inform them that Pandra had set up a JustGiving page for a chimpanzee with emphysema, only to use the money for a new haircut.

But Pandra needn't have worried about her hair because a lot worse was about to happen.

Two days before they were due to appear at the WI, a speaker pulled out of appearing due to the WI's stance towards underprivileged women. There'd been some backlash on social media, apparently. Alf and I couldn't make head nor tail of it, but it involved Erin, a group of students and placards and a viral video protesting the outdated organisation of the Partridge Mews Women's Institute.

Needless to say, Pandra had to book a new speaker. Fast.

She should have vetted her choice. If she'd learnt anything in her time as chairwoman, she would have vetted her choice. But she went with ease of booking over thinking about the particulars. The previous behaviour of a speaker, the perception of a speaker, and, indeed the social implications of booking such a speaker should all be considered when booking someone to speak to a select group of women.

And so it was that Gardenia Sprig, local independent author, led a talk on how octopus erotica was becoming the highest form of sexual liberation in North West England.

The WI met in the church hall. All performers, speakers and occasions were supposed to be respectful of that. Gardenia Sprig didn't get the message. She had a projector with censored depictions of scenes within her books and read it out alongside the pictures so as the WI could fully immerse themselves in her literature.

The members were well and truly gobsmacked. The vicar's wife were incensed. But the first member to speak up, looking as though she'd have no trouble wringing a chicken's neck – Alf's words not mine – was Heather Yearly.

Gardenia was only a quarter of an hour into her talk when Heather stood up and said, 'I'm sorry, but I really feel you should stop talking.'

Gardenia made to continue, trying to appear professional, but the ladies were having none of it.

Heather's words opened the floodgates.

Mrs McBride told Gardenia that she appreciated the need for sexual liberation as much as any woman, but that she preferred to read about octopuses in the menu of a sushi restaurant and not as a potential love interest.

Several ladies told her and her smut to push off.

Gardenia lingered long enough to collect her cheque and beggared off before the ladies could get properly offensive.

Not that they would. Turns out they were saving their wrath for Pandra. She was sitting in the front row, looking like she wished she were a hedgehog whilst the ladies bore down on her.

I said to Alf, I said, 'It sounds like the Ides of March all over again.'

He said, 'I've no idea what that is, but I bet it goes great with pudding.'

Once I ordered his treacle pudding and custard, Alf continued his story.

Mrs McBride nominated herself as spokeswoman and tore into Pandra. She said, 'What in the good Lord's name was that? You've had some thoughtless ideas before, Mrs O'Malley, but I for one am completely astounded that you thought it right to allow a purveyor of such sordid material to come and speak to us. I understand this event was arranged at short notice, but your predecessor was renowned for her ability to flourish in such circumstances. You, however, seem happy to lower yourself and invite sheer filth to our door just so you could say you did something.'

Pandra was sheepish. Despite this, she said, 'Do you believe that Mrs Copeland could have done better?'

Mrs McBride gave her no time to respond. 'We might have called Mrs Copeland before, but she never dragged us to the depths that you have. In less than two months, you've forced three quarters of our members out and made us a laughing stock.'

That was when Pandra found her backbone, saying, '*I* made us a laughing stock? You must have a short memory, because I seem to remember you getting us all into trouble when that news came out about you stealing from the donation plate at church!'

'We were a respected institution, Mrs O'Malley. Now we're seen as old biddies who know nothing of the modern world.'

'If people think you're old biddies, it's because you

are. You can't blame me for there being fewer members. Half of them have died off and the other half are well on their way. Let's not forget that there've been three chairwomen in as many years, and we've all had to contend with you. Mrs Valerie McBride, vice-chairwoman, and constant pain in the neck. Well, I tell you what. If you think you can handle the job, feel free, because I quit!'

'She never did,' I said to Alf. I was astonished. I was also mildly pie-eyed because we were three pints in and I'd just eaten a steak and ale pie with chips, vegetables and proper gravy, followed by rhubarb crumble and custard. I might have missed British food on the cruise. It's not that they didn't serve pie on board, it's just that there was no risk involved. Proper British food comes with enough dietary warnings to keep cardiovascular surgeons rubbing their hands with glee. If I ever have a proper day of baking, it's with the knowledge that I could keel over during an advert and never discover the culprit in Vera.

I tried to remain compos mentis to properly understand Alf's story.

'She did. After all she put you and Doris through, she quit.'

I couldn't believe I was finally interested in the WI. Granted, I'd only hoped for news of a bust-up, but still, it had happened. 'What did the ladies do?'

Mrs McBride said to Pandra, 'You can't quit. You have responsibilities.'

'Beggar the responsibilities. The WI is done, Val, and its members should see that sooner rather than later.'

And that's when Mrs Valerie McBride of Rowley Corner, former veterinary nurse and bellringer, slapped

Pandra O'Malley across the cheek.

In the echo of the church hall, the slap silenced everything. Pandra touched the visible handprint on her face whilst the remaining members looked on.

Pandra glowered at Mrs McBride and thumped her one right on the end of her nose. There's a lot of blood when it comes to a broken nose, and as Mrs McBride plummeted towards a table piled with jams, preserves and crafts, that's all the ladies saw: a fountain of blood.

Pandra launched herself at a dazed Mrs McBride, who was too stunned to fight back. She just lay there bleeding while the ladies tried to wrestle Pandra off her.

They succeeded.

And as the police arrived, Mrs McBride smashed a jar of gooseberry jam against the back of her opponent's head.

I'll admit I was flabbergasted, more so than when Lisa Faulkner got her face deep-fried in Spooks. I said to Alf, I said, 'That's worse than anything that went on between our Doris and Janice Dooley of Little Street, is that. What did the police do?'

'They arrested them.'

'All of them?'

'Just Pandra and Mrs McBride. They're both awaiting trial.'

I said, 'I never thought I'd see the day the WI would shut down.'

Alf grinned. 'Great, isn't it?'

We were well and truly bladdered by the time we'd finished drinking. Alf and I had three months to catch up on. Turns out that since Edith didn't have the WI and Alf didn't have me, they'd been spending more time with one another. I couldn't tell how Alf felt about that, but his collar was certainly cleaner than it had ever been.

Ordinarily, Alf would have rung his grandson, Martin, to come and drive us home, but he'd caught the travel bug as well and gone off gallivanting around Europe. He's a good lad is Martin, despite his tendency towards hoodies and French women. Anyway, it's the responsibility of grandsons to make sure their drunken grandparents and assorted friends make it home in one piece. Give it a couple of years and our Theo will be doing the same for me.

I considered ringing our Angela, but she would've been at work and I didn't want her first impression of me after three months away to be one where I was three sheets to the wind. No, we decided we'd walk back to Shakespeare Avenue, hoping it would sober us up on the way.

I can't say as our Doris and Edith were too happy to see us in the state we were in. They were chatting in the kitchen, but that soon stopped as we traipsed down the hall. I were a bit bleary-eyed, but I could tell they weren't happy. I said to them, I said, 'What's the matter?'

Our Doris gave me the Look and said, 'It's all well and good for you to go off carousing with your pal, our 'arold, whilst my world crumbles around me.'

I turned to Alf. He appealed to his Edith, 'I've told 'arold all about the WI, how Pandra and Mrs McBride knocked ten bells out of each other.'

Edith can have a proper glare when she tries and she was giving it her best go as she said, 'As you should, Alfred Simpson. However, we've received a letter today that changes our circumstances exponentially and we could have done with you two being here to help.'

I sobered up slightly in that moment. 'Is this the letter from Mrs Cribbins?'

Our Doris was in the middle of making a pot of tea. With a nod, she said, 'Mrs Cribbins has received a letter for the attention of the Partridge Mews Women's Institute.'

'About?'

'It's more of an invitation, really,' said Edith.

'So?' said Alf, 'the WI's finished. Tell that to whoever's invited you and get on with your lives.'

Our Doris set about finding the tea things. 'I'm afraid it's not as simple as that. Two representatives have been invited to a luncheon commemorating the great work of WIs across England.'

The mellow buzz of drunkenness had all but left me. I sat at the table and said to our Doris, I said, 'Who sent the invite?'

Dismayed, our Doris set the tea tray down and said, 'Buckingham Palace.'

Nothing was said whilst our Doris played mother and poured our drinks. She'd always had aspirations to be invited to Buckingham Palace, and with the opportunity in front of her, I'd no idea how she'd react.

The Queen and Prince Philip once passed through Partridge Mews to celebrate the silver jubilee. Our Doris waited behind a line of ribbon for six hours just to see the Queen giving the royal wave from a limousine. Rather than scream with merriment, our Doris tossed a notelet through the Queen's window, inviting her to a five-course meal with optional champagne – optional because Alf didn't know if any would fall off the back of his supplier's van. Either way, our Doris didn't think too much of the security, said as the fact they didn't wrestle her to the ground and ensure her note wasn't a letter bomb was the height of unprofessionalism and that they clearly weren't protective of the royal family. She went so far as to write a letter to the palace. She received no reply.

Alf spoke before anyone else, saying, 'The way I see it, that WI did the two of you wrong. RSVP and get yourselves down to that London.'

Edith offered Alf a smile but shook her head. 'It'd never work. Mrs Cribbins knows about the invite. She'll be sure to tell the others.'

'Norma Cribbins always was a gossip.' This was from our Doris, who went on to say, 'No, we can't simply up sticks and visit the palace. The Partridge Mews Women's Institute no longer exists. As such, I will write a letter informing the proper authorities and we can get on with our lives.'

I didn't want to point out the obvious. I'd only

received the best news in a long while that morning and I didn't plan on ruining it by verbalising the thought running through my head, but I couldn't help it. The words were on the tip of my tongue before I could wrangle them. I said to our Doris, I said, 'Why not restart the WI? It's only been gone a month.'

She looked at me all pitiful and said, 'I've spent most of my life worrying about that awful group, our 'arold. I am not prepared to continue doing so. The reputation of the WI has been completely ruined. These are words I never thought I'd say, but this town will be much better without its presence.'

As she sipped her tea, Edith, Alf, and I looked at one another. This had been a change I'd hoped for from our Doris since we'd wed, but when it arrived, I wondered just what she'd do if she didn't have the WI to worry about.

Some folk clearly didn't get the message.

Next morning, we'd barely been awake ten minutes when there came this almighty racket at the door, as though Ringo Starr thought it the perfect place to practice his percussion.

I said to our Doris, I said, 'I'm telling whoever that is to clear off.'

She gave me the Look and said to me, she said, 'You most certainly are not, 'arold Copeland. I've had three months of your uncouth behaviour and will remind you that you're not on holiday anymore.'

Our Doris didn't risk it, in any case. While I staggered and grumbled to get to my feet, she was halfway to the front door. She checked her hostess smile in the hall mirror (there's no teeth involved and it comes with a superior tilt of one's head). When our Doris does her hostess smile, she's not so much looking at a person with her eyes as with her nostrils.

She sorted out her posture – shoulders back, spine straight, knees not too far apart, a regular stand by your beds pose – removed some lint from her M&S dressing gown and answered the front door. She allowed the smile to slip into a querying glance for a moment until she realised who'd called unannounced.

It was hardly worth all our Doris's effort. Stood on our doorstep, looking as dishevelled as an umbrella in a hurricane, was Pandra O'Malley.

She didn't look good.

Her light pink raincoat had more creases and wrinkles than I don't know what. It looked like she'd slept in the thing. Her shoes – plimsolls, really – were completely unsuitable for walking around Partridge Mews on a cold September morning and were soaked through.

When I last saw Pandra O'Malley, she'd had bright red hair. It was so vivid that it made fire engines jealous. A few months later, she had greasy hair the colour of a rusty post box and her roots were showing.

Whatever I thought about Pandra, the last three months hadn't been good to her.

Our Doris hid a snarl behind a smile, all polite and vicious, and said to her, she said, 'I'm afraid you've caught us quite unawares, Mrs O'Malley. We don't usually entertain guests before eight AM.'

Pandra didn't cross the threshold. She didn't even say anything at first. She simply remained silent and sallow. Eventually, she said, and there was no mistaking the drunken drawl as she did so, 'I haven't been home yet. Couldn't face it. It's Derek. He hates me.'

I expected tears, some sort of soap opera moment where she'd fall to her knees in the rain as the credits rolled. Only she didn't cry and it wasn't raining, so I said, 'If you're coming in, come in. If you're not, push off. Whatever you're doing, put wood in th'ole. It's cold enough to freeze the beak off a brass budgerigar.'

Our Doris turned on me with a Look so evil I'm surprised I didn't turn into a pillar of salt. 'How dare you speak to our guest in such a manner, our 'arold?'

Cheeks boiling, I said, 'She's not a guest yet. She's still outside. If anything, she's a five-foot-seven obstruction on our doorstep.'

'Well, I never!' exclaimed our Doris. She turned back to speak to Pandra, but Pandra stepped inside and closed the door behind her. She still looked as meek as a hedgehog in a vicarage, but at least we weren't all in danger of freezing while she said whatever she'd come to say.

I'd pay for my comments later, but right then I was glad of the warmth. When I hit seventy-two, the cold started touching my arthritis in ways it had never touched it before. At the ripe age of seventy-six, I no longer care who I offend in my efforts to remain warm and pain-free.

Our Doris kept up the Look as she led Pandra down the hall towards the kitchen. She apologised for my words, though she knew I wasn't the least bit apologetic.

Pandra wasn't listening, either way. She stared off into space, eyes blank, taking nothing in.

I said to our Doris, I said, 'Can you tell me why we're being hospitable towards a woman who started a hate campaign against you?'

She poured Pandra a mug of tea, sweetened with four spoons of sugar, and said, 'Because, our 'arold, I was in the same position not too long ago. And I'm not prepared to make someone who feels bad enough already, feel worse.'

After a few minutes, and several long slurps of steaming tea, Pandra said to our Doris, 'Before I say anything, I just want to tell you I'm sorry, Mrs Copeland, for everything I put you through over the last eighteen months.'

Our Doris nodded. 'Apology accepted, though there's no need. We both allowed the competition to get the best of us.' She offered a wry chuckle. 'And the funny thing is there was no competition anyway.'

Pandra looked stricken. 'There wasn't?'

'Have you ever thought about how much easier life would have been if we hadn't allowed ourselves to be bogged down by social niceties and Darlington avocado dishes?'

'I haven't really given it much thought.'

'We gave our lives to the WI, and now look at us.' Our Doris went to make a fresh pot of tea.

'You heard, then?'

'Isn't that why you're here?'

Pandra gripped the empty mug in her hands with all the strength of a Jack Russell over a marrow bone. She said to our Doris, 'I came to apologise and to say that I've ruined my life and don't know what to do.'

Our Doris fetched the teapot over. 'Will you be staying for a spot of breakfast, Pandra?'

'Not "Mrs O'Malley"?'

'Since it appears you and Derek have had a falling out, I didn't think a reminder of him was appropriate.'

This was certainly a different Doris than I was used to, foregoing social niceties in favour of tact and not sniping at someone whose actions saw our Doris even further vilified by Partridge Mews and us spending a large amount of our savings on an around the world cruise. Admittedly, that probably hadn't been Pandra's intention when she stood against our Doris for the chairwoman's position in the WI, but I hadn't expected our Doris to forgive her so easily. Maybe the sea air had done our Doris some good after all.

When Sarah Entwistle beat her for the role of Fantine in an am-dram production of *Les Misérables*, our Doris didn't stop until Sarah fell through a trapdoor during a particularly off-pitch rendition of *I Dreamed a Dream*. Granted, it was nineteen-ninety-seven, and our Doris was suffering through the menopause. Sarah had recently spent a few months visiting the Ear, Nose and Throat Department at the hospital. Everyone thought she was having an affair. Nobody believed she was actually laid up with labyrinthitis.

I suggested that our Doris might send some flowers by way of apology, to which she responded, 'That part should have been mine, our 'arold. Everyone knows I'm the best soprano this side of the Pennines, but they chose to give the role to a woman whose musical career spans three years at the kitchen sink singing along to jingles on the radio.'

I said to her, I said, 'Fantine's supposed to be a young woman, our Doris.'

She gave me the Look and said, 'I should have known you'd be taken in by the ageism that's grown rampant in the theatrical community. The job of an actress is to embody any role sent their way. If Reg Varney can get away with playing someone many years his junior then so can I. Or would you like a wife who cowed, 'arold Copeland? Would you prefer me to submit to any ounce of sexism sent my way?'

I didn't argue.

Sarah Entwistle went on to gain a few bit parts in the soaps. Last time I saw her, she was a dead prostitute on Taggart. I always knew she'd go far, and it was nice to see her career go full circle.

Our Doris's treatment of Sarah was the reason why I was utterly flabbergasted by the way she spoke to Pandra O'Malley nearly two decades later.

'Now, why do you believe Derek dislikes you?'

Pandra gulped. That was when I noticed the tears in her eyes and thrust the kitchen roll in her direction. Our Doris intercepted it and handed over a fresh Kleenex from her pocket. She's like a Girl Guide is our Doris, well-prepared for every eventuality.

Pandra clutched the Kleenex as she spoke, occasionally dabbing her eyes. She said, 'Derek's hated me for a long time. You might know we were headed for divorce a while back. But when the committee came to me saying as I'd have more chance of being elected if we got back together, I split up with Linton and pretended things were fine back home.'

Our Doris made herself busy by putting out the breakfast things, but I caught a smile on her face. She wasn't as forgiving as she'd made out. She said to Pandra, she said, 'There's no shame in separating. Indeed, it's brave to admit when a relationship isn't working. It's highly disturbing that the committee suggested you reunite.'

'They said you were too sure of yourself. I heard from Mrs Patel that they thought I'd do exactly as they wanted.'

'They wanted all of the authority and none of the blame,' I said.

'That's exactly right, our 'arold,' our Doris said. 'The committee has always been the same. When your mother wanted to take us all on a bus trip to Prestatyn, the committee stepped in, saying they'd revoke her membership if she did because such an excursion wasn't really suited to the members of a provincial Women's

Institute.'

'I don't remember that,' I said.

'Because she told them to stick their membership where the sun doesn't shine and died a fortnight later.' Our Doris said this nonchalantly, as though she hadn't just revealed vital information about my mum's final weeks. She went on to say, 'I'm sorry I didn't tell you, but I thought you had enough to concentrate on with the funeral. I didn't think you could manage a vendetta against the committee of the WI.'

I didn't respond; I just drank my tea and thought about how our Doris was probably right, although she was more likely to get revenge than I ever was – I'd have only asked her to quit the WI in solidarity. Perhaps it was for the best that she didn't tell me sooner. Otherwise, we might have gone the same way as Pandra O'Malley and her Derek.

Pandra was sitting at the kitchen table, blowing her nose like an anteater playing a trombone. She said, 'Derek was seeing another woman when we split up for the first time. They were talking about moving to Carlisle once the divorce came through. She went herself when we got back together, and he's held it against me ever since.' She properly bawled then, a regular howl as she scrunched up her Kleenex and dropped her head in her hands.

I sat there with no idea what to do. Men aren't trained to cope with crying women; the most I can do for our Doris is to take her for coffee and give her a pat on the back. That's why I was glad of her crossing the room to console Pandra.

It's a good job we were in our own home, away from prying eyes, because she did something she wouldn't ordinarily do in public. She dragged her chair across the tiles, as close as she possibly could to Pandra without sitting on her lap, and put her arms around her shoulders. She said to her, she said, 'It's going to be all right. At least you can say as you gave it a proper try before calling it a day.'

If anything, that only made Pandra bawl louder. She practically wailed, 'That's just the thing, Mrs Copeland. We haven't. He goes to work before I wake up and doesn't come home until bedtime. He makes sure he never has to see me. I just wish he'd say he doesn't want to be with me anymore.'

Our Doris gave me a meaningful look. I wasn't sure what it meant, but I made myself scarce.

Forgetting my cup of tea, I went upstairs and got changed. When I left the house, our Doris was still consoling Pandra.

I got in the car and drove to the only place I could think of.

Derek O'Malley hadn't changed much since I last saw him. He was still an incorrigible git who dressed like he'd ram-raided a Cotton Traders.

He was bleary-eyed as he answered his front door. When he realised who I was, he said, 'How do, 'arold? Good cruise, was it?'

'I hear you've got a bird up in Carlisle.'

He visibly gulped, like a young lad who'd been caught with a dirty magazine. 'I'm just about to head off to work. I can't chat.'

'You're going in late today, Derek. I've got your missus at my house, breaking her heart to our Doris. If you're divorcing, that's fine, but you're coming with me right now and you're going to tell her, because I've spent three months on a cruise, I'm yet to have breakfast and your Pandra just put paid to any ideas I might have had about a good bacon sandwich.'

He locked his front door in response and made his way over to the car. There are a few things that will persuade another bloke to come to your aid, and unless they're of the vegan persuasion, any mention of bacon is usually the way to do it.

Derek didn't speak the entire way back. He just stared straight ahead, hands on his knees, looking as though he were on his way to be slaughtered.

I pulled into the drive and said, 'Strange, isn't it, Derek? Last time you were in this car, you thought your life was in danger.'

'There's no need to sound so happy about it.'

We went inside to find our Doris and Pandra where I'd left them.

Derek looked fit to flee, all prepared to pull his head beneath his shirt collar like an extraordinarily glum snail. He said, 'I think this is a bad idea.'

'I think you should get into that kitchen and speak to Pandra.' I nudged him in the back and he shuffled down the hall, head down, eyeing his feet.

Our Doris turned around and shared a glance with me. I didn't know if she was telling me I'd done a good job, but I did know we were both worried about how it would turn out.

Pandra met Derek's gaze, her eyes rimmed with that much red she looked like she was contending with a particularly nasty bout of conjunctivitis. She sniffed and gasped, all nasal as she said, 'I've been speaking to Mrs Copeland and I think it best if we go through with that divorce, Derek.'

He gave something of a shocked response. 'Um…if you think that would be for the best, love.'

'Georgina is waiting for you in Carlisle. I think

you've kept her waiting long enough.'

'Is there somebody else?'

And that's when Pandra O'Malley well and truly flipped her lid. She went from crying one moment to yelling like Peggy Mitchell the next. If she'd had a pub, he'd have been barred in a flash. She bellowed, 'Are you completely dense, Derek O'Malley? Did you honestly just ask me that? Did you honestly just ask me whether there was somebody else, moments after I mentioned Georgina?'

He said, 'But I didn't mean Georgie.'

'No, of course you didn't. You think that as a man, you automatically have the right to have a woman in every port, but if your wife should so much as talk to another man, it's grounds to have her shame paraded through the town centre like some medieval tart. There isn't another man in my life, Derek. I just don't love you. There's a train to Carlisle from Manchester Piccadilly at ten forty-five. If you hurry, you'll make it.'

Derek blinked a few times. I've never seen a man look more bewildered, and that includes the blokes down the pub when England were knocked out of the World Cup in two-thousand-and two. He said to Pandra, he said, 'And what about you?'

'You've no need to worry on that count. I'm following Doris's example and going away for a bit. Might go and visit my brothers. I haven't been back to Sligo in years.' She pulled herself together and stood up. 'Would you mind awfully giving us a lift back to ours, Harold? We've a fair bit of packing to be do between us.'

Derek said, 'But what about work?'

'I shouldn't worry,' Pandra said. 'You were never much good at your job anyway.'

I took them home.

When I got back, I headed straight for the kitchen and slumped down in my chair. Our Doris was clearing up a few things.

I said to her, I said, 'What did you say to Pandra?'

She had the beginnings of a smile on her face when she said to me, she said, 'I simply told her that we can't blame the WI for our behaviour. We didn't have to act as stupidly as we did, and all our mistakes are our own. I pointed out that any person who beat me in an election must have some wherewithal about them, so she shouldn't be moping but doing.'

'Can she really go to Ireland? Alf said her and Mrs McBride are awaiting trial.'

'I don't think it'll come to anything, our 'arold. I still have some influence in this town, and I think it's about time I used it for the benefit of other people.'

'What do you mean?'

'I'm going to write a letter to the Police Crime Commissioner saying as how I found it highly inappropriate for them to use their limited funds on a case of two older women bickering, and that while I understand the need to make an example of Pandra and Mrs McBride, I can't see how it will benefit the taxpayer. Nor is it in the public interest due to the fact that the public no longer cares about a now-defunct Women's Institute.'

I thought she'd gone completely 'round the twist. 'I don't know much about the law in this country, but I'm not sure it's legal to throw out a case based on the correspondence of a seventy-four-year-old criminal.'

'You'd be surprised at the power I have, our 'arold. Folk so often underestimate the place of letter writing in the modern world, but there's a lot to be said for a handwritten missive using an exceptional display of comprehension in the English language on specially selected Smythson's writing paper.'

I said to her, I said, 'If you're going to write a letter, do you think you could mention Alf's arrest?'

'I'm sorry, our 'arold, but Alf has been arrested that many times...which one in particular are you talking about?'

'He got taken in for indecent exposure the other day. He needed to use the toilet, but they've closed the public toilets in town. I just think of all the things he's done, this is one of those times when he might actually be a little bit innocent.'

Our Doris thought this over for a minute before saying to me, she said, 'I'll add a mention to my letter and see what I can do.'

I should've known our Doris knew what she was doing.

A few days down the line, she received a letter apologising for the stress caused by the local constabulary's error. Both women were meant to be let off with a caution, but due to an administrative error, they'd been incorrectly charged. In relation to Alf, he issued an apology for the over-zealousness of a young constable who, while fulfilling his role, should have taken full account of the situation before taking action. The Police Crime Commissioner for Partridge Mews wanted our Doris to know he appreciated her concern for her fellow man, something quite necessary in the modern world, and asked if she'd enjoyed her cruise.

She stood in front of me all gleeful, presenting her post like she'd found the golden ticket to Willy Wonka's factory. She said to me, she said, 'See, our 'arold. I knew as I could do some good.'

I said to her, I said, 'How do you know the PCC?'

'He's Eleanor Stockwell's lad. You'll remember her, no doubt.' She gave me a shrewd look that Helen Mirren would be glad to learn, and I became very intent upon my newspaper.

If our Doris had fixed it so that Pandra O'Malley would beggar off out the country, I didn't care who sent her letters. Instead, I said, 'I think I'll go and tell Alf the good news.'

I picked him up at his house and took him down the Hare and Horse.

We ordered our drinks and settled down at our usual table. I told him immediately, 'Our Doris has got you an apology from the Police Crime Commissioner.'

He gave a wary look. 'What do you mean?'

'He apologised for the overzealousness of a new constable.'

I didn't expect Alf's reaction. Every wrinkle in his forehead gained the depth of crevices as he widened his eyes, outraged. 'I shouldn't have been arrested in the first place! It's my right as a British citizen. If I was pregnant, I could've urinated in his cap. What's a man supposed to do if there's no other option? I suppose I should have gone in the bread aisle at Tesco. I could've asked if they'd let me dry my trousers by the ovens.'

'I shouldn't worry about it too much, Alf. You've had an apology.'

'That's not the point, 'arold. It's about the principle of the thing. If a person is caught short, there needs to be somewhere for them to take care of that need.'

'I agree with you, Alf, I do.'

'Those toilets on Chamberlain Rise are the only public toilets left in Partridge Mews. All the cafés were shut.'

'You're thinking too much about it.'

'I don't know if you realise, but people already think I'm a dirty old man. Now folk have an excuse to think I'm an old letch. It'll be all over the Gazette. Alfred Simpson, pork pie pincher and foliage flasher.'

Alf necked his pint and I realised I had no idea how to deal with the situation. So, I did something I can never remember doing in the history of being married. I rang our Doris and asked her to forego all her plans and come down to the pub.

She arrived half an hour later, dressed as though she were ready for the Conservative Party Conference in a pastel pink skirt, a cream silk blouse and her M&S houndstooth coat, an outfit that looked out of place in the Hare and Horse. She must have known I were serious because she took one look at the two of us and then went to the bar.

Linda greeted her. 'How do, Doris, what can I do you for?'

Our Doris nodded her head in our direction and said, 'I'll have another two pints of whatever concoction they're drinking today, a gin and slimline tonic for myself – ice and lemon, of course – and a sweet sherry for Edith. She'll be along any moment now. May I inquire as to the lunch specials?'

'I've a steak and kidney pie on today with chips, vegetables and proper gravy.'

Our Doris offered Linda a smile. 'That sounds like exactly the sort of thing we need this afternoon. We'll have four portions.' She came over to the table. 'Now, what is the trouble, Alf?'

That was when Alf started crying. He opened and closed his mouth a few times, trying to get the words out, and before I knew it, his chin fell to his chest and his shoulders shuddered with all the intensity of a jackhammer through tarmac. I'd never seen Alf cry before, not even when his Uncle Jim died and left a cockatiel in his care.

I won't lie, I'm no good with crying – especially men crying. I was brought up in the school of stiff upper lips and taking any frustrations out on a dartboard. I had no idea how to handle the situation. Me and Alf have been friends since our yo-yo years, and I don't remember him ever getting this tearful.

Luckily, our Doris was there. She plonked herself down next to him, handed him a fresh hankie and – foregoing all social niceties – pulled him into a hug she must've learned from a boa constrictor. She told him it was all right and let him press his face against her shoulder. She must have been worried about the state he was making of her coat, but she didn't stop consoling him.

Linda came over with the drinks. 'What's the matter, Alf? You haven't been mugged again, have you?' She forgot about the bar for a moment and pulled up a stool.

Edith arrived.

A hint of questioning at the empty bar caused her left eyebrow to quirk. The sight of Alf breaking his heart in our Doris's arms sent her flying across the pub faster than Superman after Lois Lane.

Our Doris let go of Alf and found herself replaced by Edith in an instant. That only made things worse. His sobbing reached new heights and his face turned this funny shade of purple I'd only ever seen associated with red cabbage.

'Can somebody tell me what the bleeding heck has happened to my husband?' Edith exclaimed. Her voice was filled with more fury than Boudica battling an entire army of Romans. While she held Alf in her arms, all comforting, her face couldn't relax. If she were the Hulk, she'd have been turning green.

Alf heaved a few breaths to calm himself down, sounding like a Hoover struggling to vacuum a dust bunny, and sat up straight. His eyes were still full of tears and he wouldn't meet my gaze, but he held onto Edith's hand for dear life. He repeated his story to the five of us, each word saturated in shame.

I could sense our Doris growing angrier as he spoke. She kept relaxing her shoulders, but inevitably they'd rise.

When Alf finished speaking, Linda said, 'That's a load of nonsense, that is, Alf. I'd write a complaint if I were you.'

I said to Linda, I said, 'Our Doris knows the PCC. She wrote to him and got an apology, but it seems to be beside the point.'

'I'll write to that bloody town council if I have to,' our Doris practically growled. 'In a world that so often shames the elderly, a policeman, no less, made a mockery of Alf, simply for performing a necessary bodily function. When I'm finished, that young man will be lucky to get a job as a traffic warden.'

Edith nodded her head in our Doris's direction. 'I'll have a few choice words for him as well. My Alf might be a rascal at times, but no one is going to make him out to be a dirty old man.' She downed her sherry and ordered another one.

Linda nodded.

Our Doris said, 'And please don't forget our food order, Linda. Times like these call for carbohydrates in abundance.'

We spent a few more hours at the Hare and Horse bringing Alf back around to himself. Our Doris didn't allow me any more bitter – not because she was domineering, but because she thought that after Alf's arrest, I shouldn't be seen drink-driving. She had me give Alf and Edith a lift back to theirs before we returned home. He still looked like someone had stolen his last cream cake, but he had Edith to take care of him, and that would have to be enough for the moment.

Later that week, our Doris had one of her ideas. I was in the living room catching up on NCIS: New Orleans. I'd been recording the series while on the cruise. I might have been stuck in the middle of the ocean with no way to escape, but I was safe in the knowledge that when I got home, I'd have enough proper telly to last me through to Christmas.

King was just about to enter a shootout with the perp when our Doris waltzed into the room like some great pantomime dame.

I grimaced – I can't deny I grimaced – and paused the television. I said to her, I said, 'What's got into you, our Doris?'

She had a glow about her that certainly wasn't the result of her Charlotte Tilbury – a recommendation from Mrs Veronica Ambrose – and that had more to do with her smile. She looked like a shark who'd been to the dentist for a scrape and polish, the way she was showing off them teeth.

She said to me, she said, 'I've had an idea, our 'arold.'

And that was where my interrogation started. I've learnt a lot from the police dramas I watch. If it hadn't been for my faithful viewing of Inspector Morse, I doubt I'd ever have found out our Doris's plans for the Harvest Festival in nineteen-ninety-eight. There's some who like to let the silence build and to make things so uncomfortable that the other person has no choice but to talk. I'm not like them. 'What sort of idea?'

Our Doris considered the Look. I saw it flicker briefly across her face before passing on by. Clearly, our Doris was excited. I've never known her too excited to forego a Look before, and that includes the time Robert Sandyshins bought her a lime and soda during New Years' celebrations that resulted in the destruction of the club's cricket pitch, a broken toe and the loss of an electric whisk.

Only, our Doris didn't tell me her idea. She came over all sheepish – a brave act on her part, because the most sheepish things about our Doris are her woolly jumpers. 'I'm afraid I can't give you that information currently, our 'arold, as I haven't sorted out the finer details.'

I went for the underhanded approach then. I let my thumb hover over the play button and said, 'I suppose after that debacle with the Hat Club, it's probably best you don't share your ideas.'

And I pressed play.

Our Doris was itching to tell me what was on her mind. She tried to appear composed but ended up looking like she'd got worms. Her eyes kept flicking from my face to the remote. She stopped still. I saw her begin to bristle. After fifty-six years of marriage, I'm aware when she's bristling.

I glanced over and saw the Look alight slowly in her

eyes, as though she were being possessed by some ghost of housewifery.

I pressed pause again and met her gaze. It's not often I return our Doris's looks, because I'm worried I'll melt, and our Doris's looks are usually enough to render any poor sod catatonic.

I suppose I felt mischievous.

She said, 'The Hat Club "debacle" was a coincidence of the worst kind, as well you know, Harold Copeland.'

'I don't disagree, our Doris. That's why I think it's best you say nothing about this idea.'

I pressed play, pausing again moments later when our Doris started looking fit to explode. I half expected static to fizz from her perm. 'You really don't want to hear about my idea, then?'

I said, 'Of course I want to hear all about your idea, our Doris, but what if someone's listening in? Mrs McBride could've had the house bugged while we were away.'

The Look became a proper glower. After a moment of uncertainty in which she glanced around the room, our Doris said to me, she said, 'Really, our 'arold, I find that idea quite preposterous. What could Mrs McBride hope to attain by bugging a house that would stand empty for three months? Maybe you forget that our Angela checked on the place while we were away. Or are you suggesting that our own daughter doesn't have the adequate knowledge to secure our home against would-be intruders? That could be perceived as a critique of my maternal teachings. Maybe you're saying I spent too much time helping her perfect her pastry as opposed to teaching her how to best dispose of a burglar.'

Our Doris knows all about subterfuge; she had to in that WI. She once tasted Seraphina Hollinshead's lime marmalade and remained stoic, despite the fact there wasn't enough sugar and it was as sour as if she'd bitten straight into the fruit itself. Our Doris didn't bat an eyelid, simply excused herself from the judges' tent and went to vomit in a Portakabin.

When I asked how she'd kept a straight face through it all, she told me she'd picked it up watching cookery shows. Ready, Steady, Cook had a lot to answer for.

That's how I know our Doris is a master of feigning stoicism. I'd have to tread carefully. I pressed play and watched my show before yawning and saying, 'Of course our Angela will have looked after the place properly, but there are plenty of new gadgets around nowadays. Mrs McBride could be outside with a drone as we speak. However, if you think I'm being too paranoid, I'd be more than happy to hear your idea.'

Our Doris mulled this over for a few more moments. Her spine straightened and she got this twinkle of recognition in her eyes. 'Were you trying to trick me into telling you my idea then, our 'arold?'

'I might have been,' I said.

'That was very good, but you'll never be able to pull the wool over my eyes. I knew all about Alan Bradley before Rita Sullivan even considered reporting him to that building society. Remember? I wrote a letter to ITV. However, I must say, I did appreciate your repartee just now. It simply wasn't enough to fool me.'

'I was close.'

'You were.'

'Go on then,' I said. 'What's your big idea?'

'If it's that important to you, our 'arold, I'm planning a party for the former members of the WI. Since we've all missed out on the opportunity to visit Buckingham Palace, I thought it only right.'

'It's not your responsibility to make them feel better, our Doris. The WI ended because of backbiting and infighting.'

'That I was part of. If we'd learnt to get along, there's every chance we wouldn't be in this mess.'

'You told me you weren't turning over a new leaf, and here you are, sounding all reasonable.'

'I've had plenty of chances to admit my faults over the years. I regret not doing it sooner.'

'Is this because of Pandra?'

Our Doris shook her head. 'It's a consequence of the way things ended with the WI. Your mother helped build it into a respectable institution and your wife contributed to its downfall.'

'Now, that just sounds dramatic.'

'In recent years, I've been prosecuted for assault, had a hip replacement, lost old friends and had my hair burned off by a would-be elf. Tell me, our 'arold, what part of that isn't dramatic?'

I said to her, I said, 'Aye, I'll give you that.' Then to change the subject, I went on, 'I think I'll make that shepherd's pie for tea. You know the one we saw in the James Martin book that Angela got us for Christmas?'

'I think that's an excellent idea, our 'arold. However, first, I require you to transport me to the Harrington. I wish to enquire as to the price of their function rooms.'

'Couldn't that be done over the phone?'

'It could, but I find that technology so often gets in the way of clear communication. It's the reason why so few people know how to hold a conversation nowadays. Quite honestly, I blame Star Trek.'

'Star Trek?'

'That show gave people aspirations, our 'arold. They stopped talking to one another just to find out whether

Pluto had acne scars.'

'You've lost me, our Doris.'

'And you'd be lost without me. Don't you forget it. Now, go and put your coat on. The Harrington awaits.'

It's only about a ten-minute drive to the Harrington from Shakespeare Avenue. When I were a lad, the Harrington was the place you went after a long summer's walk through the countryside. When I started courting, I learnt a lot more could be done in the countryside than making daisy chains and shooting at cans. Then they built the estate. No more could I go to the Harrington and look out across the fields that had provided the backdrop to my childhood. In nineteen-seventy-eight, they erected a bunch of pebble-dashed monstrosities and called it development.

I'm not against the idea of building affordable housing for folk, or council estates for that matter, but they were only put there because the council wanted them as far away from town as possible without losing their postcode.

Still, the Harrington is a nice enough hotel. The drive has been tarmacked and they try to make sure it's always free of litter, which I've come to appreciate at seventy-six with a new knee.

The hotel is a proper country house with bay windows and those ornate doors that leave you thinking Jacob Marley might be hiding in a knocker. It's one of those places that has me dreaming about a misspent youth. Of course, it's had Wi-Fi installed and a few games rooms for the kids, but the carpets are rich, thick and as scarlet as they come.

Our Doris admired the place as we parked up, keeping her smile fixed to hide her grin. She were like a debutante all set to have her first taste of champagne. Giddy, some might say. Though I don't know that I'm enough of a risk-taker to ever call our Doris giddy to her face.

We climbed the stone steps and went inside, entering the foyer. The air smelled clean. I swear it's manufactured cleanliness, not close enough to hospital ammonia, but there was definitely disinfectant in the air, along with an added note of fresh linen.

I followed our Doris over to the desk.

A young woman greeted us. Her navy-blue suit had been ironed to a military standard; her cuffs looked sharp enough to open envelopes. She had that false smile that's common in all customer-facing environments plastered across her face. They must teach it to them at school. Forget Chaucer, here's a rictus grin that will scare your customers halfway to Halifax. She said to us, 'Welcome to the Harrington Hotel, the premier guest house in Partridge Mews. My name is Kelly. How can I assist you today?'

Our Doris was impressed. She puffed up her shoulders a couple of times, like a hen trying to clear off ticks, and this wry smile settled on her lips so as she looked like she could have done with breaking wind.

She shook Kelly's hand.

That's how our Doris gets the measure of people. No matter their wealth, occupation or lifestyle, if a person has a limp handshake, our Doris doesn't give them the time of day.

Kelly's handshake must have made the grade.

Our Doris said to her, she said, 'Good afternoon to you, dear. I am Mrs Doris Copeland, local housewife, best soprano this side of the Pennines and former interim chairwoman of the Partridge Mews Women's Institute.'

Kelly didn't allow her smile to drop. Her cheeks looked as though they might split as she nodded with some vague understanding – telling the customer she's listening, but to everybody else she's thinking about last night's Emmerdale, wondering if Cain and Moira will ever make a proper go of things.

Either way, our Doris continued, 'You're perhaps aware that the WI has disbanded. As such, I thought I might hire one of your prestigious function rooms to hold a farewell party for the women who have dedicated their lives to upholding social niceties, being charitable in an uncharitable world.'

Kelly looked at our Doris all agog. It only lasted a moment, but she wasn't accustomed to being spoken to in such a fashion. Whilst the Harrington is the closest thing that Partridge Mews has to a Hilton, it's become renowned as a place for familial brawls and that time Jimmy Carson got his ankle caught in the cistern of a disabled toilet. The fire brigade was called and Jimmy's mother never spoke to Bertie again.

And our Doris wanted to book the place to show the WI a good time.

Kelly took a diary from beneath the desk and opened it to that day's date.

Our Doris looked down at the page. Her face contorted with a fury I hadn't seen since she heard they'd cancelled Peak Practice. She was livid, eyes as wild as a polecat's as she said to Kelly, she roared, 'Where is she?'

Kelly did her best to retain her composure but struggled with our Doris's instant transformation from demure septuagenarian into a Fury set down to torment Jason and his Argonauts. She said, 'I'm afraid I don't know what's caused you such upset, but do understand that I have the police on speed dial.'

'You're already allowing a criminal the use of your function rooms, unless the prison service has been privatised as well and this hotel is serving as Cheshire's answer to Holloway.'

'What're you talking about, our Doris?' I asked, more bewildered than I'd been at the end of Broadchurch.

She tore off across the foyer, leaving the reception desk in her wake. Kelly scurried after her, the managerial shape of her shoulders forgotten as she rushed after our Doris. She called, 'What's got you so upset, Mrs Copeland?'

Our Doris reached a set of stairs and began to climb them. She paid no attention to the Christmas-red carpet or the real oak banisters with Edwardian curlicues in her efforts to reach the function rooms.

Kelly lunged in front of our Doris and spread-eagled herself across the door. 'I can't let you in there. We've a rather big event going on. Should you wish to come back later and view the room, we can arrange something…if you'll just follow me back to reception.'

The air was thick with the scent of Febreze and sulphur. Our Doris was furious. She gripped her handbag that tight it looked less like a Radley and more like a forgotten aubergine. She coughed a very small cough, a mouse's cough, a cough with barely a breath to it, and said to Kelly, she said, 'Within the next two minutes, I will be in that function room, and you will be standing out here minding your own business. I don't wish to see an empty room to get a feel of the place because I know just the sort of people who use your rooms. Time was that the Harrington was a respectable establishment with traditional values and the best vegetable lasagne outside of Wren's Lea. Now, I realise it's a washed-up victim of the digital revolution. Uniform, classless and willing to open its rooms to anyone with a pittance to spare.'

Our Doris's eyes went as shrewd as darts. 'If you'll excuse me.' She pushed past Kelly and flung open the pair of white double doors.

There was a party in full swing, but when our Doris opened those doors, it were like a scene from a Western. The room went silent.

Our Doris stepped inside the brightly lit soiree and headed straight towards the woman in the centre of the room. The sound of her Dune heels against the lino punctuated her every step, like her very own funeral dirge. Our Doris stopped in front of the woman and said to her, she said, 'Janice Dooley of Little Street. It was such a surprise when I heard you'd hired the Harrington, I simply had to come and see it for myself. Aren't you more suited to alleys behind late night kebab shops?'

Janice grinned. 'All right, Doris? Here's hoping if that surprised you, this will kill you off. I'm a millionaire now.'

Our Doris went as white as sheep in snow. Her eyes nearly rolled back in her head, but she steadied herself. She gave herself some time before saying, she said, 'And which poor old so-and-so did you defraud to get your hands on that?'

Janice stepped aside to reveal a poster board of a man that old he was practically one giant liver spot. Then I saw the writing beneath his name and my heart sank.

I said something, not caring if I'd regret it later, I said, 'I think we should be going, our Doris.'

Janice frowned. 'You remember my dad then, 'arold? Good. Because it'd be pretty poor taste to gate-crash the wake of a man you didn't know.'

Our Doris had her gaze fixed on the portrait of Janice's father. She assessed the new information methodically, glancing around the room in silence. She'd taught herself a new trick to ease tension – tapping her fingers across her handbag, the sound like spiders over a leather sofa.

Meanwhile, I stood there with bated breath, unsure where to put myself. I'd never felt more awkward, and that includes the time I walked into the ladies' toilet at Leek Market and didn't realise until I was mid-stream.

Kelly appeared out of nowhere with a face like a gargoyle's. She placed a consoling hand on Janice's shoulder and said, 'On behalf of everyone here at the Harrington, I'd like to share my condolences once more and to apologise for the unexpected intrusion of Mrs Copeland.'

Our Doris gave Kelly a Look that powerful, it's a wonder she didn't turn to stone. She said to her, she said, 'Please don't presume to apologise for me. I've known Miss Dooley since our schooldays and whilst I lament the loss of her father and offer my most sincere condolences at this time, it doesn't change the fact that we haven't seen eye to eye since that business down the cenotaph with Billy Draper.'

Janice was going to say something, but Kelly stepped in, saying to our Doris, 'Whatever your history, to try and ruin the wake of a hundred-and-two-year-old man is about as disrespectful as it gets.'

Kelly achieved something that most people can only dream of; she made our Doris laugh. This wasn't her public titter, perfected to show amusement whilst retaining an air of class. Nor was it her secret laugh, the one she usually reserved for close friends and family. No, this laugh was practically demonic. This laugh said our Doris was furious and that anyone in the immediate vicinity should run for cover. She gave Kelly the Look, eyes as wide as saucers; they twinkled and raged with a fire from the deepest coals of Hell. The laugh was deep, full-bodied and terrifying.

Our Doris stopped laughing abruptly, leaving the room as silent as a mortuary. She said to Kelly, she said, 'When I arrived here, you greeted me in a professional manner that one doesn't see so often in this day and age. I was hopeful for our youth, but you very quickly ruined that. You saw me come in here, and I admit I was somewhat excitable. This does not excuse the way you have spoken to me. You failed to heed my advice to not make presumptions and made a fool of yourself by interfering. You have no knowledge of the history between Janice and I, yet you lecture me about disrespect. I'd like to say I've never been more insulted, but look at the woman you're working for. Janice's life is that offensive, they had to censor her birth certificate.'

Our Doris paused, seemingly to allow for rebuttal. There was none. Indeed, Janice smiled as though she enjoyed seeing our Doris give Kelly a tongue-lashing.

Since no one was talking, our Doris went on, 'You can call this a wake all you like, but I don't see any of your dad's pals. Granted, they were fortunate enough to die without seeing his daughter get hold of his wealth. Considering they're not here, I wonder why so many of your guests are from the council. Just what is this *wake* all about?'

That was when Janice's grin grew. Her dentures practically ran up to her ears as she said to our Doris, 'It's good to see you haven't lost it, Doris. I've heard it's difficult to recall names and faces as we get older.'

'You dare to call me senile? I never forgot about Sheena Utterthwaite's older brother.'

Janice went shifty then, rubbing her sweaty palms down the front of her blazer.

I said to her, I said, 'Do you mean Barry?'

Janice's eyes darted this way and that, like Hattie Jacques caught with her hand in a biscuit tin. 'I don't know what you're talking about, but if I did, I'd say I never knew Sheena was engaged, that Barry only accidentally broke Ged's wrist and that whatever happened ruined my best frock.'

'That's all well and good,' our Doris said, 'but that doesn't explain why half the town council is here.'

I noticed a smug grin exuding from Kelly. She was as proud as a Labrador with a tennis ball as she proclaimed, 'You clearly don't follow local news, Mrs Copeland. Miss Dooley is a saviour in Partridge Mews.'

Our Doris refused to acknowledge Kelly, saying to Janice, she said, 'What in the good Lord's name is this nitwit talking about?'

Janice beamed and held her head high. 'You might not have noticed, but there's a lack of affordable housing in town. I thought it only right to help find a solution, so that's what I'm going to do. You know that bit of land just outside Partridge Grove?'

Our Doris wasn't speaking; she'd tensed up, her face ashen.

I said to Janice, I said, 'Are you talking about Barraclough's Field?'

'The very one, 'arold,' Janice said. 'We've bought it. That's another reason why we're here celebrating. We're here today because we've just finalised plans to build three-hundred new homes.'

'It's going to help tons of people get on the property ladder,' Kelly said, grinning.

Our Doris said, 'And I'm sure you've been promised one of the new houses, have you?'

Kelly didn't respond.

Our Doris turned on Janice again. 'I don't imagine the council has given you any backing, so who's in on this with you? Who is "we"?'

Someone walked up behind me. A shiver ran down my spine as though my vertebrae had caught the frost. Soon enough, someone set their hand on my shoulder. 'Long time, no see, 'arold.'

'I should have known,' our Doris said. 'Douglas Grey. You always did land on your feet.'

Our Doris has decided to thwart the redevelopment of Barraclough's Field.

After the revelation that Janice and Doug Grey were in partnership with one another, our Doris said nothing. She simply turned on her heels and left them to their architectural machinations.

She didn't wait for me, mind.

I caught up with her beside the car five minutes later. I said to her, I said, 'You'd have torn strips off me if I'd left you like that, our Doris. What's going on?'

She said to me, she said, 'I didn't leave you anywhere, our 'arold. You're too slow, and you dawdle.'

'I don't dawdle.'

'You're a man, and if there's anything that men have excelled at over the centuries, it's dawdling. They should make it an Olympic sport.'

'They might do, eventually.'

We went home to find Alf, Edith and Erin waiting on the step. They looked as sheepish as lamb chops.

I hadn't seen Alf since he'd cried down the pub and

I still hadn't figured out how to talk to him. I couldn't help feeling as though I'd failed as a friend, and that's not something anyone wants to feel.

Especially not after nearly seventy years of knowing a person.

Our Doris was first out the car. 'Is there something the matter with the door? Only I *did* provide Erin with a key.'

She marched over, swiftly recovering her own keys from her handbag.

Erin said to her, reminiscent of Algy Thornton telling sir I had a frog hidden in my desk, she said, 'That's what told Mrs Simpson, but she was having none of it. She said as the place might not be at its most presentable.'

'Of course, that's only a supposition based on the fact you've only recently returned from your holiday,' Edith said. 'Whilst I've no doubt Miss Beaumont did her best to keep the house tidy, she simply doesn't have your eye for cleanliness.'

'Thanks a bunch. You came around enough whilst Mr and Mrs Copeland were away. Said as you were just checking in.'

'And give over talking all University Challenge, our Edie,' Alf said. 'You've been around since they came back.'

She frowned at him. 'That's as may be, Alfred Simpson, but one can't just break into a fellow woman's house without being thoroughly aware that she has her sideboard in order.'

Our Doris unlocked the door. Shaking her head, she said, 'Forget all that, let's get inside and you can tell us what you're doing here in the first place.'

We followed our Doris through into the kitchen.

Alf, Edith and Erin sat down at the table, settling themselves in, unprepared for what was about to happen.

I'd gone to make a brew. I'd only just filled the kettle when I became aware of a change in mood. I've been married to our Doris for fifty-six years. In that time, I've grown accustomed to the way her fury fills a room. I get this tingling in my chest – almost like an angina attack, but nowhere near as hopeful – and my ears start balancing on my shoulders as our Doris begins her pacing back and forth across the linoleum. I considered getting her a pedometer once, just so as we could appreciate the benefit of her pacing.

Usually, she directs her ire at me. I've got used to listening to our Doris's screeching with one ear and letting it fly straight out the other like a hurricane through a bus shelter. Sometimes I even allow my thoughts to wander, consider what life would have been like if our Doris had run away with one of The Beatles like she'd threatened. She could have had the world at her feet, like some poor man's Yoko Ono, and I could have spent my days at the allotment becoming a regular on Gardeners' Question Time, sharing the microphone with Clay Jones.

I shouldn't think our Doris ever really thought about running away with Ringo Starr – she preferred The Animals. There's also the language barrier to think about. Some dialects are just difficult to grasp, and our Doris has always had a problem with anything guttural.

Either way, she was pacing across the kitchen like an ostrich in search of a worm. I felt certain that her ears would pop off, the pressure of her anger too much for her skull to bear. I thought her anger had dimmed since the Harrington. Instead, it had been simmering away, waiting for this moment.

I focused on the kettle, listening to it heat up,

refusing to look at the others because I knew what they had coming.

For the first time since I'd married her, our Doris gave the Look to three people at once – her glaring and glowering as bad as it gets, her tone as imperious as a headmistress as she said, 'Can any of you enlighten me as to why I wasn't told about Janice Dooley's plans for Barraclough's Field?'

I was as grateful for the kettle boiling as Desperate Dan is for cow pies. I kept my head down and stuck to making the brews, ever the coward in the face of our Doris's wrath.

Edith spoke first, a tad tentative but nonetheless, she said, 'While I understand you're upset, there really is no need to take it out on us. We didn't tell you during the cruise because we didn't want to ruin your holiday.'

Our Doris thought over Edith's words. She mulled them as she continued pacing back and forth from the door to the table.

I nearly upended the tea tray when she did a swift about-face mid-thought. 'Watch where you're going!' I said, not thinking.

The others winced for me.

I set the tea things down, feeling their consoling gazes upon me. No matter how much they'd upset her, they hadn't yelled at our Doris in front of her granite worktops.

I expected the Look, expected her to take me by the collar and banish me to my shed.

She didn't.

She said to me, she said, 'My apologies, our 'arold. I simply wasn't paying attention due to the fact that our friends are lying to us.'

She sat beside me.

I must admit to looking all agog. 'What do you mean?'

'I understand not wanting to upset me when we were away. We removed ourselves from the petty squabbles of Partridge Mews, but we've been back well over a week, and I've heard nothing whatsoever about this.'

Edith bristled at that; her cheeks puffed out like a chinchilla with a murderous intent for sweetcorn. She said to our Doris, 'I couldn't flaming well tell you with Edna Cribbins in the room, could I? She'd be straight over to Mrs Patel telling her how you're out of the loop. Soon enough, the Gazette would be running stories saying as you're out of touch with the contemporary social news of the town.'

Erin stared at Edith, slack-jawed. 'Have you ever thought about Boxercise?'

'Boxercise?' It was Edith's turn to look bewildered.

'You seem to have some pent-up aggression. I thought it might help. Our Michelle hasn't broken nearly as many windscreens since she started.'

Alf said, 'I thought your Michelle had just been done for criminal damages.'

'Yeah, but that had nothing to do with aggression. Ryan pied her off for Tiffany Watkins.'

Me, Alf and our Doris eyed each other, hiding our sniggers behind our mugs.

Our Doris sipped her tea and said, she said, 'Boxercise is an excellent suggestion, Erin. Though let's return to the matter at hand. Edith, are you saying you came to tell me about Janice?'

Edith nodded. 'Only Mrs Cribbins turned up with that invitation. We'd been talking to your Angela about when best to tell you.'

Our Doris blushed, cheeks blooming as red as cherubs. 'That's most considerate, but you've known me since Miss Bell's class. Why ask our Angela?'

'Because we were worried about you, Mrs Copeland.' Erin groaned. 'I know I'm not the brightest tool at the picnic, but even I can tell you that we were worried. Theo was on the cruise with you, we didn't know what would be said and so we went to your Angela, and she told us to come around as soon as we heard you were back.'

Erin necked her tea in one long gulp and grabbed a few bourbons. I've noticed that about Erin: whenever she gets particularly emotional, she starts reaching for the sweets. I'm not sure how she'll manage in the workplace without a desk full of Kit-Kats and a visit from the Milk Tray Man.

Our Doris said to us, she said, 'I thought you were all too scared of me to say anything.'

Alf spoke then, saying, 'We've been through a lot together in the last year, Doris. We wouldn't keep something from you out of spite. We aren't scared of you, but we were worried about how the news would affect you.'

He poured himself another cup of tea.

And we all looked at him, gone out.

I said to him, I said, 'Since when did you start being the voice of reason?'

To which our Doris said, 'If that old tart can become a millionaire, our 'arold, then Alf can sure as damn it become the voice of reason. Now I need to know how far Janice and Doug have taken their plans.'

'There's going to be a public consultation next week,' Edith said. 'If you'd seen the Gazette at all over the last few weeks, you'd think it was a sure thing.'

'There's people that don't want it, though,' Erin said through a mouthful of crumbs. 'That elf and her cronies have set up an Instagram account to try and save the field.'

'Louise?'

'She was operating as Miss Moonflower when she burned off my hair, our 'arold.'

We didn't talk about our Doris's hair loss much. Most of it had grown back, giving her a bit of a pixie cut. She no longer looked like Wurzel Gummidge with an electric shock. There were something quite attractive about it, if I'm honest, a bit like being married to Partridge Mews' answer to Cilla Black.

Erin interrupted my reverie about our Doris's scalp when she said, 'Whatever she calls herself, she wants Barraclough's Field classified as a church.'

'A church?'

Alf nodded. 'That's right, 'arold. Says as it's a place of religious and cultural significance to her and her elfish brood. What was it she said about it, our Edie?'

'Something along the lines of the field being a gateway into the Otherworld and a shrine to her ancestors.'

'She set up a GoFundMe,' Erin said.

'That was all a ploy to get herself elf ears.'

It was our Doris's turn to look bewildered. 'Elf ears?'

That was when Alf got excitable, like a bumblebee trapped beneath a plant pot. 'They take a scalpel and cut–'

'Let's just call it surgery,' Edith said, cutting him off.

'I believe the correct term is body modification.' Alf slumped in his chair, defiantly glum after being stopped from giving us all the nitty-gritties about Miss

Moonflower's aspirations.

Our Doris pursed her lips. She purses her lips a lot, does our Doris, and has become renowned for the way in which she can say tons without having to open her mouth. Sometimes a pursed lip can mean she's angry; other times, it's that she's got the weight of the world on her shoulders, and once, after a particularly bad korma down Pakora Palace, trapped wind.

I hoped she hadn't pursed her lips because of the latter and said to her, I said, 'What's the matter, our Doris?'

'I'm worried, our 'arold. If the only person protesting the desecration of Barraclough's Field is Miss Moonflower, then I'm not sure we'll be able to put an end to this.'

'It can't just be Miss Moonflower though, surely.' I looked around the table for some sort of confirmation, but the three of them wouldn't meet my gaze. I went on, saying, I said, 'Are you telling me that folk in this town have completely lost their bottle? If this had happened three months ago, there'd have been Hell to pay.'

'If this had happened three months ago, our 'arold, the WI would have stepped in,' our Doris said, and it sounded every inch the lament. 'The fact of the matter is that while we might have had our fair share of backbiting, we had values. They don't count for much when all people ever hear about are the misdeeds of Mrs Doris Copeland.'

She sighed a sigh that she would never have shared in public.

'You can't blame yourself for the disassembly of the WI, Doris,' Edith said.

Our Doris reached for a biscuit and said to no one in particular, 'I don't believe it was all completely my fault, but I do think reparations should be made.' With that, she took a bite of her custard cream and put an end to the conversation.

Once the others had left, our Doris squirrelled herself away in her cubbyhole and started making phone calls. It took her a few hours of interrogating various sources throughout Partridge Mews, sounding like something out of Prime Suspect, before she eventually discovered that while Janice Dooley's plans had been finalised, they'd only just been submitted to the council and hadn't yet been approved. That was what the public consultation was all about.

Our Doris was thrilled.

She came into the living room with a smile on her face that I hadn't seen since Chastity Dingle tried to drown that girl off Downton Abbey in a pig trough.

When she told me what she'd learned, I said to her, I said, 'Does this mean we're in with a chance of stopping her, our Doris?'

She said to me, she said, 'There's a lot we have to think about, our 'arold.'

'What do you mean?'

'She's saying as she'll make twenty percent of the

new homes affordable. You heard that girl Kelly say that the town is crying out for that sort of thing. We need to be strategic about this.'

'You could really do with speaking to some of your ladies.'

'What do you mean, "my ladies"?'

'You know exactly what I mean, our Doris. There's no WI anymore, so what else am I supposed to call them?'

'Personally, I'd suggest the former members of the recently-defunct Partridge Mews Women's Institute, but I'm aware it's a mouthful.' She pondered my words for a moment before saying to me, she said, 'Whatever we call them, however, I think it's a splendid idea. The ladies might have their issues with me, but they'll know more than anyone else how things are looking.'

Next day, our Doris had me drive her down to Barraclough's Field to scope out the place. She'd had our Theo around the night before with his laptop. Apparently, any concerns about his A-Levels were thrown out the window in favour of helping her find out everything she needed to know.

I stayed in my chair, keeping an eye on ITV. Occasionally, there'd be a little squeal from our Doris that could have been either glee or incontinence – whatever it was, I hoped our Theo knew where we keep the mop bucket.

She had him looking up the legality of building on greenbelt land, TPOs and Paula Tilbrook – just in case.

We were standing in an empty field that didn't look like much. Sure, Barraclough's Field was the place to be when we were younger and in full control of our faculties, but once we realised there was a lot of funny business we could get up to down the cricket pavilion, a lot of us gave it up as a bad job.

Farmland never looks at its best in autumn,

especially farmland that's been left to go fallow. Old Barraclough must have been dead about twenty years, and his sons had never wanted to follow their father into the family business. Some men are built to farm, and some men are built to become international drag artists with a penchant for Kiki Dee. Granted, not all his children go around in high heels, but no one's heard anything about Sam since he moved to Milton Keynes.

The field was a mess. We avoided all manner of tyres as we trekked across the boggy ground – be it tractor, bicycle or motor home, Barraclough's Field had a tyre for it. Reeds came up to our waists, reaching beneath my anorak like some sort of skeletal security check. If they had reeds at Manchester Airport, folk'd think twice about smuggling.

I'd never been more grateful for my wellies. I had no idea what I was stepping in, just that it squelched and felt as though it might swallow my feet up to the ankles. I can't say as our Doris would mind having a bog man for a husband – she might enjoy the prestige that would come from saying she'd lost her husband of fifty-six years in a peat bog while campaigning to preserve our nation's natural history.

The place was cold, bleak and grey and ran on for enough acres to house three hundred new homes, once they tore up the place and made it look even more desolate.

I said to our Doris, I said, 'You should get Chris Packham down here. There's got to be all sorts of critters living amongst this muck.'

Our Doris gave me half a Look and said to me, she said, 'This isn't muck, it's nature.'

'Then what's all that stuff on your wellies?'

Our Doris looked down. Her face screwed up into

an approximation of a grimace, looking like Little Jimmy Krankie as she realised how much muck she'd managed to get all over her Joules wellington boots. She gave herself a moment and breathed deep before saying, 'These are issues one must deal with when one seeks to protect the environment.'

This from the woman who'd once complained about recycling because she didn't like the idea of her personal correspondence being transformed into toilet paper.

We wandered about the field for the best part of an hour. After we nearly got crippled sinking into the sodden earth, we checked the perimeter, following the path of a drystone wall until we came back on ourselves. We upset mites, rabbits and blackbirds and received a particularly grim stare from a heron who'd returned from wherever herons go to discover us trespassing on his land.

Then Janice Dooley of Little Street appeared. Some say money can't buy happiness, but it certainly helped to remove the nicotine stains from her hair. Janice has always had this look about her that folk like to call forlorn or bedraggled, and I like to call fifty years on ale down The Blind Cat. It's not that she's an alcoholic, she just appreciates the company that comes from knowing how to neck a yard of ale in under two minutes.

Either way, she had something like a look of triumph about her as she crossed the field towards us. She looked every inch the country housewife as she approached – Dublin River Boots and tweed. A lot of tweed. It's constraining, is tweed, but on someone as slight as Janice, it made her look all authoritarian, as though she'd have no problem showing us the right end of a shotgun.

She said to us, 'I thought you'd end up here eventually. 'Ow do 'arold?'

I felt like a schoolboy caught under the gaze of his headmistress. 'I'm all right, Janice. You?'

Our Doris gave me the Look before turning on Janice. 'I just thought I'd come and see the land before you start tearing it up.'

Janice did something I didn't expect. She smiled at our Doris, looking every inch the dominatrix, and said, 'You keep telling yourself that, Doris. The fact of the matter is that you're jealous.'

If anything, our Doris hadn't expected that. She stood flabbergasted, milling over her opponent's words. 'What do I have to be jealous of, Janice?'

'That I have money now. That I'll be using said money to build affordable houses, helping out the youth.' Janice shook her head. 'You've always been the same, unable to see me being successful.'

Our Doris sneered. 'I've seen you be very successful at dropping your knickers.'

'It's the loose elastic in cheap brands. I'm sure you know nothing about that. More rigid than a chalkboard, you are.'

'And you're wearing tweed,' I said.

She tugged on her lapels. 'I'm a businesswoman, didn't you hear? Saying that, what're you two doing here? This is private land. I can understand how you think it might be open to the public seeing as how it's been used over the years, but there never was a public right of way through these fields.'

Our Doris cut to the chase, 'We aren't going to sit back and let you do this, Janice.'

'I have no issue with you trying, but come along to the public consultation next Thursday. Trespassing on my land will do you no good.' Janice folded her arms and it sent chills through me, like being confronted by Kim Tate.

I said to our Doris, I said, 'Maybe she's right, love.'

Our Doris gave me the Look and said to me, she said, 'Don't you dare betray me at the first hurdle, 'arold Copeland.' She stormed across the field, towards a large oak tree that had seen better days.

'What's she doing now?' Janice rolled her eyes.

Our Doris pulled something shiny from her handbag and reached for a branch. In an instant, she'd handcuffed herself to the tree and we were left looking at her, bewildered.

I ran over – well, it was as close to a run as I could get, with my new knee and the wet ground – and said to her, I said, 'What the bleeding heck are you doing?'

Janice sauntered over to us, saying, 'Your wife has clearly discovered that this old oak tree has a TPO against it. Am I wrong?'

Our Doris had this uncertain look about her. She thrust the key to her handcuffs in my direction. I pocketed it without a second thought.

'From your personal collection are they, 'arold? I didn't think you had it in you.' She had this bawdy grin on her face as she folded her arms, stopping in her tracks. 'Whatever you found out about Tree Preservation Orders, you'll know that planning permission outweighs all that. We've already looked into replacing it. You really think I'd go into this half-heartedly when you're around, Doris?'

Our Doris gulped and looked from her handcuffed wrist to the tree and back at Janice. She pulled herself together as fast as she could and said, 'That's as may be, but this tree has been around for hundreds of years. How can you even consider felling it?'

'Sometimes sacrifices have to be made for progress to happen. There's a national housing crisis, and I'm doing my bit to solve it.' Janice met our Doris's scowl. 'When was the last time you visited Barraclough's Field? In fact, when was the last time you thought about it?'

Our Doris dropped her gaze, shamefaced. 'That's beside the point. This is about preserving our town's heritage.'

'This field has nothing to do with the town's heritage. It's literally disused farmland. No farmers are interested in renting it. I asked. I'm not so thick that I didn't research things first.'

I could see our Doris failing against Janice Dooley, something I never anticipated would happen. There had been occasions in the past when I thought she had us over a barrel, but our Doris had always managed to pull it out of the bag in the end. Still, she really seemed to be struggling.

After a moment, she said to Janice, she said, 'These new builds never match the architecture we already have in the town. They stick out worse than those new dentures of yours.'

Janice flinched. 'I wondered when you'd go for cheap insults. You needn't worry, Doris, the homes will be in keeping with other properties in town.'

'Ever likely, considering you have an intimate knowledge of seventy percent of the households in Partridge Mews.'

'Exactly. It's why I'm the perfect candidate for the job.'

'You should be ashamed of yourself, carrying on with married men.'

'Don't you think that says more about the men than

me? After all, I've always been notably unattached.'

'You've always been notably attached to other people's husbands.'

'Are you upset that I never took an interest in yours? Are you wondering just what it is about the great 'arold Copeland that I don't find particularly attractive?' She looked to me. 'No offence, 'arold.'

I shrugged and said, 'None taken. If anything, I'm glad of it. I've always thought you looked a bit too moth-eaten honestly.'

'Right.' She smacked her lips over her new dentures – she'd gone all in for the pearlescent white ones. When I got mine, I'd had them coloured so that they looked more like my actual teeth. Hers looked as though she'd had them constructed by Twyford's.

Our Doris said, 'The fact is –'

'The fact is,' Janice said, cutting her off, 'you've been trying to ruin me since we were in our teens, and now that I'm finally in a position where I might be able to make something of myself, to leave a legacy that isn't about my sex life, you still won't quit. Please tell me what I did to hurt you so deeply, Doris, because it's been nearly sixty years and I've still no idea.'

Our Doris's gripped my arm with all the intensity of that girl after Sylvester Stallone in Cliffhanger. I think her name was Sarah.

A haughty Janice said, 'Struck a chord, have I? I think it's only right. You go around town talking about making reparations, helping your friends get rid of charges against them, but me? What is it about me that gets you all riled up, Doris Copeland?'

Our Doris said to me, she said, 'Give me that key, 'arold.'

I reached into my pocket, but she whacked me

around the shoulder. 'Give me a second, for crying out loud.'

I handed the key over and she unlocked the handcuffs. She didn't look at Janice as she stomped back towards the gate, trying to get out of the field as fast as Road Runner escaping Wile E. Coyote.

Janice beamed at me. 'You best go after her. Can't have her facing the truth now, can we?'

I didn't know what to say. Janice hadn't said anything wrong, and for some reason that made the shame that bit worse. I felt her eyes on me as I walked back to the car. I could just imagine how she felt at winning.

Our Doris practically launched herself into the car when I unlocked it. I sat down in the driver's seat and said to her, I said, 'Are you all right, our Doris?'

'I'm not sure what I am, our 'arold. I need some time to think.'

I nodded and started the car.

Later that week, I was raking some leaves in the back garden when our Doris came to the back door and said, as posh as Prunella Scales on a bad day, she said, 'Do come in for a moment, our 'arold. I need your opinion on something vital.'

Her hair could have fizzed from her head, her eyes practically disembodied, all set to fire from their sockets like cannonballs.

I leant the rake against my shed and went inside.

Our Doris closed the door behind me and held onto the handle for dear life. She might have kept her anger subdued beneath her dignity, but I could tell that our Doris were ready to tear the door from its hinges and fling it at the nearest bystander. After nearly sixty years together, I've come to notice when even the merest twitch of a shoulder can mean our Doris is on track to give Atilla the Hun a run for his money.

I said to her, I said, 'Shall I make a cup of tea, our Doris?'

She said to me, she said, 'Since we can't have it

getting around that Mrs Doris Copeland uses brandy to solve any problem thrown her way, then I suppose tea will have to do, our 'arold.'

I went over to the kettle and started making the tea. 'What's the matter?'

'What's the matter? What's the matter? I'll tell you what the bleeding matter is,' our Doris said, each breath allowing more venom to build. 'Doug Grey. That man has been at the core of all my problems recently, and he continues to prove himself to be nothing short of an eighty-year-old villain with a penchant for filthy women and flat whites.'

She stopped to breathe.

'What's he done this time?'

'He's the one who got the toilets closed.'

I poured two mugs of tea. I didn't trust our Doris with bone china in her state and thought she'd manage with a dumpy Cath Kidston mug. I said to her, I said, 'I dislike Doug Grey as much as the next fella, but he didn't tell Alf to water the town's hedges.'

Our Doris gave me the Look and said to me, she said, 'Firstly, I'm aware that he didn't force Alf to do anything, but Doug is the reason that your *closest* friend broke his heart in public the other day. Secondly, I'm not angry because he closed the public toilets, it's the reason he closed the public toilets that has me wanting to tell this town just what he tried to get me to do in the Cricket Club's cloak room after the Christmas Party in nineteen-seventy-five.'

I blinked a few times and took her tea over. 'What did Doug try and get you to do?'

'Give it a rest, our 'arold. I don't need you trying to act all heroic. He simply tried something that women have been warned about since time immemorial.'

'You never told me,' I said. My fury were growing at this point, making the hairs on my arms stand on end.

Our Doris allowed the Look to go one step further. 'Forget about it. Doug made a few choice remarks, tried to unzip my dress, and I gave him a black eye.'

'And you've kept it quiet for forty years?'

'These were the seventies, our 'arold. I'd have got the blame. Someone would have said I'd been leading him on, and Doug has always had friends in high places.'

'Me and the lads could have sorted it, our Doris.'

She allowed me something like a smile, it were all sympathetic, and said to me, she said, 'I sorted it out myself. The women in this town are built of strong stuff, and we've all had our fair share of run-ins with men like Doug Grey.'

I shook my head. 'I'm too old for revelations like this.'

'I've one more for you, remember.'

'All right, then. Why did Doug have the toilets closed?'

'He's planning a development.'

'Of Barraclough's Field. I know.'

'That's just it, our 'arold. Barraclough's Field is there to draw our attention away from his big plans. Doug Grey has submitted plans to redevelop the entirety of Partridge Mews town centre, and this time, it looks as though they're going to be approved.'

'You're right. He's thick. I thought he had no money to be going on with.'

She slurped her tea like a builder, steam curling around her nostrils, and said to me, she said, 'He has Janice's money, our 'arold, Janice and Doug are planning on tearing apart our town, removing its individuality and turning it into a carbon copy of Manchester City Centre.'

I saw the gleam in her eye that I hadn't seen in a while, the one where I can never be sure if it is inspiration or glaucoma. I said to her, I said, 'What are you planning, our Doris?'

'I've got some redeveloping of my own to do, our 'arold. A few of the ladies will be visiting us for tea this afternoon. It's time to restart the Partridge Mews Women's Institute.'

The ladies assembled in the kitchen as though the last few years had never happened. I felt like Pam finding Bobby Ewing, only this wasn't a dream for me, this were the stuff of nightmares.

Me and Alf stood at the kitchen counter, holding mugs of tea like shields as we watched them.

Our Doris and Edith were sitting at the head of the table, alongside Erin. Mrs Cribbins was by the door, nibbling on a custard cream and looking every inch the hamster. I hadn't seen her since all that business with the letter from Buckingham Palace. I never did learn how that turned out. Mrs McBride was sitting with Mrs Patel; neither of them had removed their coats. It wasn't surprising. They're both so frosty that if we packed them off to the Arctic Circle, there'd be no mention of ice caps melting – there'd just be two hardnosed women teaching polar bears origami.

Mrs McBride took one introductory class at the Adult Learning Centre and thought of herself as an expert. Not one Christmas goes by without an attempt at a robin redbreast that looks like a hernia.

Who else should arrive fashionably late but Violet Grey?

I couldn't believe it. Mrs Cribbins gasped. We hadn't seen Violet Grey since she'd left town over a year earlier, but she entered the kitchen as though she'd only nipped down to the shops. She'd filled out a bit since we last saw her and looked less likely to get blown away by the slightest hint of a gale.

It was as though Mollie Sugden had just stepped through the door in her mauve overcoat and suede ankle boots. She'd had a go at styling her hair but just ended up reeking of hairspray. Her brunette wisps of hair emphasised that she can't do anything without someone else's intervention, and Violet Grey had missed her weekly hairdresser's appointment for the last two years.

It was a scandal.

It didn't matter that Violet had split from her husband and absconded Lord knew where; folk still wondered what her hairdresser must have done to warrant such behaviour.

Our Doris didn't question it. She'd been trying to get in Marc Carter's chair for years. She took Violet's slot and that was the end of the matter…until our Doris lost her hair in a freak firework accident.

No, the women of the former WI can't be trusted when it comes to regular hair maintenance. All hairdressers gossip, and the one with the most scandal is the most popular.

Violet certainly hadn't visited the hairdresser in a while. Separation must've taken its toll on her. She'd always looked like an anaemic beansprout, but she looked even more gaunt – cheeks hollower, no matter the amount of make-up she used to fill in the cracks.

Our Doris greeted her, 'How kind of you to join us, Violet. We haven't begun proceedings yet, but–'

'Where have you been?' Mrs McBride sniped across the table.

I'll give Violet her due. She's always remained impassive in the face of adversity, like a sommelier in an elephant house. She offered Mrs McBride a sneer to rival Judith Anderson and said, 'It's ever so lovely to see you again, Joyce. I'd quite forgotten how prompt you've always been. I'll never forget that time you announced the winner of the jam competition before the judges even finished their tasting. Your daughter-in-law was awarded the blue ribbon that year, if I'm not mistaken.'

Mrs McBride's face screwed up like she'd just ingested a ton of lemon sherbet. Her lips had this look of mouldy prunes, all dry and wrinkly. She said to Violet, 'I apologise if you misunderstood my tone as churlish, but–'

'Give over, will you?' Erin said. 'We all know you're posher than Downton Abbey, Mrs Grey. And yes, she's late, Mrs McBride, but if we want to get stuff done, we don't need to make snide remarks. I wouldn't try it anyway if I were you. You can look down on us all you like, but we've had to hide all the jam and marmalade because of you. Mrs Copeland sorted all this, we're in her kitchen, so sit down, shut up and have some cake.' Erin did just that, she grabbed a sliver of Battenberg and shoved it between her lips with the alacrity of a bulldog after steak. She looked at Violet with all the distaste folk show dog muck. If she held her cup of tea much tighter, she'd break off the handle.

We watched as Violet made a meal of disrobing – as in, she spent the better part of three minutes unbuttoning her coat. Buttons become a right issue when you refuse to wear your glasses. Eventually, Mrs Cribbins took pity on Violet and helped her out.

Once all the ladies were settled, our Doris coughed a cough so light that she could have been a chaffinch. I looked her way and she said to me, she said, 'Harold, dear, perhaps you and Alfred would like to make yourselves scarce. This is women's talk, after all. I don't wish for you both to grow wearisome.'

I said to her, I said, 'I had been meaning to go and check on the allotment.'

'That sounds like a splendid idea, I look forward to an update on the state of your petunias this evening. Goodbye, dear.'

As Alf and I walked out the front door, he said, 'Things must be serious, 'arold, if she's calling you dear.'

'Twice in as many minutes as well.'

'Are you growing petunias?'

I zipped my coat against the cold and said to him, I said, 'No, but I'm not about to correct our Doris in front of company. She might have mellowed out a bit on the cruise, but if I did that, she'd beat me with a newspaper and tell everyone what I did to her Lladro lady in nineteen-ninety-seven.'

'After Pete's barbeque?'

'She's never forgiven me. I found another one down the charity shop, but she were having none of it. She said as a proper Lladro lady gave an air of prestige to any living room on Shakespeare Avenue.'

'We're not really going to the allotment, are we?'

We got in the car as I said, 'Course not, but I can't tell our Doris's ladies that I'm heading off to the Hare and Horse with my best mate to get bladdered.'

Alf's eyes lit up like Charlie after he found that golden ticket. 'Your Doris is letting us get properly addled? What will we do with the car?'

'Not bladdered then. Merry.'

'Merry?'

'Merry.'

'My Aunty Ida used to get merry. We're men, 'arold. We're made to do better than merry.'

'Are you buying?'

Alf shrank down in the passenger seat as though he were testing to see if he could fit in the glovebox. 'Spoilsport,' he said.

Inside the Hare and Horse – after we'd got our drinks and sat down – I decided it were high time Alf and I had a proper chat. We hadn't spoken to each other since I last saw him at the pub, and I felt an uncomfortable sensation in my stomach like there were a millipede running around my intestines. I hadn't slept properly since and it was nothing to do with our Doris's snoring. All I could think about was Alf's tears and me sitting across from him like a regular lemon.

Once we'd settled in, Alf said, 'Go on then, tell me what's wrong.'

'What do you mean?'

His expression was a mixture of sympathy and constipation as he said, 'You've got this look on your face, like when they told me about Uncle Jim.'

'There's a few things, actually.'

He supped his beer. 'Why am I not surprised?'

'I think I need to say sorry.'

He eyed his pint and sniffed it before saying, 'It's not non-alcoholic, is it?'

'I'm not apologising for the lager, Alf. I'm apologising because you were in bits the other day and I did nothing.'

He shrugged and looked at his right thumb; he were

trying to use the grain of the table to scrape beneath his nail. His words were muffled when he said, 'I shouldn't have let it get to me. I felt a right tart.'

I swallowed a fair amount of bitter before I spoke, thinking about his words, because I could see the memory of the other day threatening to make him shrink back in on himself, and I said to him, I said, 'I think you were pretty brave, actually.'

'Brave? What're you talking about, 'arold?'

'Your waterworks.'

'The weeing or the crying?'

'I hadn't thought about that,' I admitted.

We allowed ourselves a snigger and I felt that uncomfortable feeling again. The conversation wasn't going the way I'd planned. I hadn't really planned anything, wasn't sure what I wanted to say, but still said to Alf, I said, 'It were brave to cry in public, Alf. I know we were taught different, that men aren't supposed to show any sort of emotion, but then I thought about your Uncle Jim.'

'My mum always said he were never the same after the war.'

'And he never talked about it. Us men never talk about the things that have upset us. Now, I'm not saying that what you went through were anywhere near close to what your Uncle Jim experienced. I don't know what I'm saying, actually, but I think if men weren't supposed to cry then God wouldn't have given us tear-ducts.'

Alf went quiet. I could tell he were thinking about my words, really mulling them over, because he didn't finish his pint in barely three minutes and start tapping the table. After a few minutes of silence, he said to me, he said, 'I think you're onto something there, 'arold, but why couldn't you have had this breakthrough last week?

I'm not holding this against you, so don't think I'm holding this against you, but those tears last week came from feeling ashamed and what made it worse were you sitting there, looking at me like I were something out of Doctor Who.'

'I've just never been good with tears.'

'That's as may be, but you didn't even ask what had got me into such a state. You just sat there and let Doris do the consoling.'

I felt trapped under Alf's stare, like a spider beneath a pint glass. He reminded me of sir when I'd hidden a copy of The Eagle in my desk, all impassive and ready with the slipper. But this were Alf and we've known each other since we used to get rulers out to see who had the biggest scab. He'd coached me through how to chat up our Doris, so in a way he's to blame for everything that's happened in my life in the last sixty years.

I had no choice.

I said to him, I said, 'I thought it were just the stress of seeing our Doris. She has that effect on folk, does my wife. She can reduce a man to misery in seconds.'

He shook his head but couldn't hide the smile on his face. 'You're the one who brought it up, so let's be serious here.'

'All right,' I said. 'What got you crying, Alf?'

He contemplated his half-drunk pint for a moment before saying, 'Sometimes I think it were a mistake getting old.'

'What do you mean?'

'I've always had a reputation for being a bit of a filthy sod, but when I were younger, actually contributing to society, folk had more time for me. I were a cheeky chap. They were more likely to forgive my antics, but now I can't do anything without it being related to my age.'

'That policeman nearly had you on a public indecency charge. I can't think that had anything to do with your age.'

'It did though, 'arold. If I hadn't been seventy-six, he'd have thrown the book at me. Some'll say as it's lucky to be old, because you get all this free time, but they don't see us. They're scared of getting old, don't want to contend with wrinkles, so avoid any reminder of it. We're invisible now.'

'I didn't know you felt like this.'

'I didn't until that copper stopped me for doing my business against a bush. Then I thought about the supermarket. Am I really getting away with nabbing food, or does the manager think I'm doddering? Is he putting the money in himself thinking it's one way of being charitable towards the senile old fella who keeps hiding pork pies in his coat pockets? It's put me right off nicking things.'

'It isn't all bad. Our Doris still managed to get a community order at the age of seventy-two and that's practically an ASBO is that.'

'You're not wrong there.'

'I'm not one for being optimistic, it isn't British, but getting old means we survived. Despite war, and illness and Mantovani, we're still going. There's something to be said for that.'

Something like a smile lit up Alf's face. He said to me, he said, 'I knew that cruise sent you funny.'

'This is nothing to do with the cruise.'

'You never used to sound like Miriam Stoppard before.'

'I told you, I've been thinking.'

'Much good that's done. Look, 'arold, I know what

I've been through. I know all the stupid things I've done or said, but at the end of the day, I am mad at the policeman. I'm not saying folk should respect their elders, that he should've reached over and shook it for me, but he made me feel like Tom Thumb.'

I were careful with what I said next, saying, 'I think we're getting mad at the wrong person. The policeman were only doing his job.'

Alf were affronted, eyes all set to burst from his head. He said, 'That policeman had me handcuffed that fast, I splashed my shoes.'

'I think you're fine with getting arrested, Alf. You're basically a professional at this point. I think it's the embarrassment that's really got to you.'

Alf smacked his lips and admired his empty glass, watching beads of foam slide down the inside. He were intent, as though this were the Grand National and he'd got good money on one of the bubbles of froth. He could have been thinking, I suppose, really dwelling on my words.

'You're right. I were more embarrassed than when Mallory Clutterbuck ran off with my Y-fronts down the public baths, but I'm still mad, 'arold.'

I said to him, I said, 'Be mad then, but try to think of it this way. You're still old enough to get arrested, and that's not to be sniffed at. Can you imagine what your Edith would've done if he'd carted you off to an old folks' home?'

'She wouldn't have been hugging me in here, I can tell thee.'

'That's right. Now, I'm getting another pint. All this serious talk meant I couldn't enjoy the last one.'

'That's the problem with serious conversation,' Alf said. 'It always gets in the way of ale.'

Once we'd finished our session, Alf went down the allotment – something about Tom and a load of farm machinery. I wasn't about to get involved in anything that had a sniff of illegality about it. I'd said my piece, apologised, and there was only one place I wanted to go.

The police station.

It were a mixture of Boddingtons and shame that made me visit. It probably wasn't the best idea to head to the local constabulary while mildly tipsy, but with any luck they'd label me a shaky geriatric like our Phil; we could never let him near a gravy boat.

I walked to the station in any case, hoping to sober myself up a bit with some fresh air. After several lorries passed by, covering me in dust and diesel fumes, I regretted that decision. There's nothing fresh about air anymore. Folk wonder why everyone stays home all the time; it isn't laziness, it's self-preservation.

I got to the station, ready to make a complaint on Alf's behalf, when I saw someone being escorted from the back of a squad car.

His cheeks were all splotchy, like Spam. He were angry all right. I couldn't help myself, I shouted across the car park, "Ow 'at, Doug?'

He let forth a great stream of expletives and directions on where to shove what. Another officer came to move me on.

Suddenly, the drunken giddiness disappeared. A sober thought went through my mind like a train through a bowl of rice pudding, and I said to the police officer, I said, 'Is Janice all right?'

'Friend of yours, is she?'

I didn't say either way, but the officer continued. She told me that the police had been called to a domestic disturbance and that after making a statement, Janice had been taken to A&E.

I thanked the officer for her information. I were a bit dumbfounded, to tell the truth. I couldn't very well turn up at A&E to visit Janice Dooley of Little Street – she and our Doris have always had it in for each other and it doesn't take much to get tongues wagging in Partridge Mews.

I went home.

All the ladies had disappeared. Erin was in the kitchen, clearing up a variety of crumbs and spills from the table – I thought induction into the WI came with lessons in how to properly dismantle a scone.

Our Doris was sitting in her cubbyhole, contemplating a cup of steaming tea. She was in the middle of some deep reverie, as though she were trying to remember who played Sexton Blake but couldn't quite put her finger on it.

I said to her, I said, 'What's the matter, our Doris?'

She didn't answer. Instead, Erin called, 'It's no good talking to Mrs Copeland. You'd best come through to the kitchen. I'll make you a brew.'

Over tea, Erin told me how the ladies had only showed up to talk about restarting the WI.

I said, 'Then why isn't our Doris talking?'

'I thought you might know.'

'You were here.'

'I was eating a bourbon. It's a difficult biscuit to eat when you don't want to make a mess.'

I gave that to Erin. Our Doris doesn't much care for crumbs. She's got better recently, but she still keeps a dustpan and brush beside the table. At least she's started waiting until we've finished our meals before she starts sweeping up.

Our Doris wandered into the kitchen and sat down. She sighed a sigh like a lawnmower in reverse and said to me, she said, 'The ladies are more than happy to restart the WI, our 'arold, but they categorically refuse to help me stop Doug Grey.'

I considered mentioning Janice, but instead I said, 'What about Violet?'

'After advice from her solicitor, Violet feels standing against Doug could mar divorce proceedings. I said to her, "He's been shacked up with Janice Dooley of Little Street since nineteen-seventy-three. I'm pretty sure he marred them years ago." I should have known I couldn't count on Violet. My mother always told me never to trust a woman who can't make pastry and Violet Grey's shortcrust is that tough you may as well be chewing on a headstone.'

'Did the other ladies speak up at all?'

'They were too interested in the WI. News has got around about the letter from Buckingham Palace.'

'Which you cancelled?'

Our Doris didn't look directly at me. She were up to

something, but she didn't give me time to question her, saying, 'The fact of the matter is that these women lead boring lives. Since the last meeting of the WI, Mrs Cribbins has knitted seven-hundred-and-thirty-four teddy bears for the hospital charity. Mrs McBride has taught herself Swedish and Yvonne Ackersly set up a podcast where she talks about her experience as a lesbian mycophagist in Partridge Mews.'

Our Doris necked her tea like it were a gallon of sweet sherry. She slammed her mug down. 'And then,' she said, 'they started talking about the committee, as though we're going back to normal. As though they're not the same women who tried to make me a pariah.'

'Mrs McBride said it would save an awful lot of fuss,' Erin said, eyeing up a Garibaldi. I don't mind that she's got a healthy appetite, but I wish she'd snack on the biscuits I don't like. She could do me a favour and gorge on ginger nuts – they play havoc with my dentures.

Our Doris handed Erin the biscuit. 'They don't see that I am trying to save this town from a man whose only claim to fame is appearing in the background of ITV News eating a cheese and onion pasty. The WI are supposed to be figureheads in this town. This isn't just the reformation of a WI, but our core values.'

'She gave that speech to the ladies and all,' Erin said.

I were certain our Doris wanted to give Erin the Look there and then, but she chose not to. She switched her grimace for a smile and said, 'I'm repeating myself because 'arold asked me what happened. I was quite fond of my speech, as it happens.'

'I know that, Mrs Copeland, but that's not the issue. Everyone wants to see something happen to the town centre. It's like a ghost town.'

'I don't think it's lowered itself to such levels just

yet.' Our Doris came over all authoritarian. She'd have made a great headmistress – Miss Trunchbull, eat your heart out.

The thing is, folk have wanted to see change in the town centre since the seventies. We thought there'd be a dramatic change when we got a Woolworths and look how that turned out.

Tabitha Quail once put a petition out calling for the council to do something about the lack of employment opportunities since the closure of Gadsden and Taylor. The council accepted Tabitha's petition, and promptly laid a new bypass through to Manchester. There's idiocy, and then there's the Partridge Mews Town Council.

Erin said to our Doris, 'It might not look like a ghost town to you, but the shops are empty because the council have set their rates too high. There are no job prospects unless you go out of town. And every other week there's a new charity shop or restaurant opening. I don't like that Doug Grey is the one in charge of the redevelopment, Mrs Copeland, but none of these schemes ever comes to anything. Every few years, the council gives one of its mates a pot of money to draw up plans. They go through all the procedures. The public makes comments, the council tells us how great it's going to be for the town, and then nothing. Everyone hangs their hopes on something good finally happening to this town. We don't just want to be a mini-Manchester, but those at the top are determined to keep us down.'

Our Doris looked at Erin, a little bit bewildered. She said to her, she said, 'Those are some excellent points, Erin, dear. Perhaps I'm fighting a losing battle.'

I said to her, I asked, 'What do you mean?'

'The WI want to return and while I'm the one who organised the meeting, I'm not sure if I want to return to their ranks. This town needs redeveloping. As much as it pains me that Doug Grey is the man in charge, perhaps I should shift my efforts into looking at how I could help influence the development, rather than oppose it.'

Erin said, 'I think that might be one way to help, Mrs Copeland.'

Our Doris looked all concerned, staring into her cup, every wrinkle in disarray. I said to her, I said, 'I don't think you want to do that, do you, our Doris?'

She shook her head and released another sigh. 'I don't, our 'arold, but as is commonly said, if I can't beat them, I must join them.'

'It's not a good idea, our Doris. I went down the police station earlier and saw Doug Grey. He's been arrested. I don't know what's gone on, but Janice is in hospital. You two aren't the best of friends, but–'

'What ward is she on?' Her spine jolted erect, taking on the pose of a general about to send her troops into Lidl for a warm pretzel.

'She was still in A&E.'

Our Doris nodded and looked to Erin. 'Can you get yourself to the hospital and check her condition?'

'Sure, but what are you going to do, Mrs Copeland?'

'Please telephone me to let me know how Janice is.' Our Doris stood up and straightened her blouse, saying, she said, 'She and I might not see eye to eye, but I know first-hand what an incorrigible so-and-so Douglas Grey is. We must speak to the Gazette before he has the opportunity.'

'Are you sure, our Doris?' I asked.

'We only have a few hours until he will undoubtedly be released. He has friends in high places and he will be working on smearing Janice's name.

'Erin, I need you to find out what happened.

Meanwhile, I must apologise for my previous misuse of garden implements.'

'You never mean my secateurs?'

'I can only hope that my apologising for a previous misdemeanour will get us a journalist who knows their way around an Oxford comma.'

Our Doris isn't one for apologising, so for her to enter the offices of the Partridge Mews Gazette and even consider speaking to the man she'd attacked with a pair of secateurs nearly two years earlier was a miracle.

We introduced ourselves to a girl on reception and before we knew it, we were being whisked into a side-office to chat to the reporter. There was this faint glimmer of fear in his eyes as we sat down across from him, like a rabbit peeking from his burrow, checking for buzzards. I suppose it must have been a slow news day if he had the time to chat.

Our Doris said to him, she said, 'I won't mince my words. I've come to apologise for the actions against you that took place in my home.'

Thus began a conversation in which our Doris told him everything. I mean *everything*. When she first talked about going down to the offices, I thought I'd be home in time for The Chase; the more she talked, the more I realised I'd struggle to even make it for the Ten O'Clock News. Our Doris told him about the court case and how she'd made reparations for her crimes against Janice Dooley of Little Street, and then she said to him, she said, '... the very same Janice Dooley who's currently in Partridge Mews District General Hospital after a dispute with former councillor Douglas Grey. He's been arrested, but we're unsure whether any charges will be pressed.'

That got the reporter interested. He'd been lolling about in his chair beforehand watching the clock. He leaned forward and asked our Doris to continue her tale.

She was only too happy to oblige.

Next day, we awoke to find a copy of the Partridge Mews Gazette on the doorstep.

When we saw the front page, it was no surprise.

Doug Grey said as he would no longer be pursuing redevelopment of the town centre so that he could help his fiancée – Janice Dooley – with her own redevelopment of Barraclough's Field.

I said to our Doris, I said, 'Does it mention the police at all?'

Both of us were in disbelief.

Erin had telephoned in the night before to say as Janice didn't want to see her. She'd only talk about Doug and say that the police were useless and had completely misunderstood what had happened. Janice had a split lip and a black eye, but when asked who'd given it to her, she didn't reply.

The newspaper didn't say anything about the "domestic disturbance". It just made light reference to a few injuries that Janice had received in pursuit of her redevelopment to help young folk get on the property ladder.

Our Doris said to me, she said, 'She might look like she's been brainwashed, but can we blame her, really? For nearly sixty years, this town has badmouthed her. I've been the main proponent of that. But the one constant throughout all of this has been Douglas Grey. We all know he's only after her money, but would she be thought of so badly if it wasn't for me?'

'Not many people would do what you did for a job, our Doris.'

She shook her head. 'This wasn't just about a job.'

'What was it then?'

'It doesn't matter. The fact remains that Doug has won again.'

'They still have to get the proposals approved. We can't give up yet. And I'm sure Janice will see the light eventually. We'll get the WI back on board.'

'This isn't just about Janice and Doug, our 'arold. This goes back decades, and a few letters in the Gazette and public meetings aren't going to help mend this town. Our council is rotten and if the WI is going to fight anybody, it's them.'

'If you can get the ladies back together then I've no doubt you'll manage it, but there's the public consultation to think about.'

Our Doris gave me the Look and said to me, she said, 'I certainly don't need you to remind me. All I wanted to do was to organise a party for the defunct Partridge Mews Women's Institute to get us all talking again. Instead, I found out that someone wants to destroy our town's heritage and that I'll have to fight it all on my own because most of those I thought I could trust have turned out to be bleeding useless.'

She cut to Erin here and said, 'Not you, dear, you've

worked incredibly hard and I am most grateful. No, while the town's redevelopment might not be going ahead, there is still a small chance that we are about to lose greenbelt land to line the pockets of Doug Grey and his friends on the council, and that is not something I'm prepared to allow without a heck of a war.'

With that, our Doris sped off to the back bedroom. She switched on the stereo and had Biffy Clyro blaring from the speakers before I'd had chance to close the front door.

I decided to leave her to her own devices and went to The Hare and Horse, stopping off to meet Alf on the way. His Edith was only too happy to have him out from under her feet – apparently, he's started to try and help her with the housekeeping, which she wouldn't mind if he had any idea as to her cleaning routine.

'You should see him with a mop,' she said. 'He leaves the lino looking like we've been flooded. If he can keep a firm grip on a pint, he has no business being looking so desultory with a mop, but that's just the sort of thing Ada Simpson instilled in her boys.'

'You shouldn't speak ill of the dead, our Edith.' Alf appeared behind her, pulling on his coat. 'There's every chance she'll start haunting us.'

'Well, if she does, I hope she's learning a thing or two. If there is a Heaven, I don't want to arrive to wet floorboards and poorly-ironed bed linen.' With that, she pushed Alf out the front door and slammed it behind him.

He grinned at me, waggling his tongue. 'I love it when she gets angry. She's been the same since we got back from Whitby.'

I said to him, I said, 'When did you go to Whitby?'

'A few weeks ago. It were our anniversary. Thought

it might be nice to treat the old girl.'

'And where did you find the money for Whitby?'

'You forget, 'arold. I'm not poor, just unkempt.'

'Unkempt?' I said, wondering where he'd learnt such a word.

'Yeah, you know, scruffy like.'

I rolled my eyes. When it comes to friends, I certainly know how to pick them.

At the Hare and Horse, I ordered two pints of Boddingtons Best and brought them over to our usual table.

'Right,' Alf said, 'what's wrong?'

'What do you mean?'

'You never usually come to pick me up, 'arold. I'll just wander in and you're sat here, having escaped the clutches of your Doris. Something must be wrong for you to make a house call.'

'It's to do with Janice Dooley.'

He supped his beer and said, 'Why am I not surprised?'

I told him the entire story, from our Doris's research to the handcuffs to her locking herself up in the back bedroom to listen to rock music.

The more I spoke, the more Alf looked aghast. His mouth hung open, corpse-like, and he held his half-finished pint like the Statue of Liberty holds her torch. Eventually, he said to me, he said, 'I suppose Janice has a point.'

I gulped back beer and nodded. 'That's what I thought as well.'

'Has your Doris really turned over a new leaf?'

'You can never really be sure, can you? Our Doris goes through phases. She's never been one for sympathy.'

'Especially when it comes to Janice Dooley of Little Street.'

'I've no idea what I'm supposed to do, Alf. No matter what Janice has said to her, our Doris will still want to protest the development.'

'I don't doubt that. You know her better than I do, 'arold, and I think there's every chance she'll be thinking about her next move. Your Doris was never one to fall at the first hurdle.'

'I said that, too, but this time she doesn't have the WI.'

'That's the problem. You all lay too much blame at the WI's door. She's Doris. She spent the last year fighting the beggars. Do you honestly believe she needs them?' He downed the rest of his pint to punctuate his sentence, slamming it down on the table. 'Now, go get the drinks in and let's see if I can't get you thinking straight.'

Alf might have been on to something.

I arrived home three hours later, a little worse for wear, with the remains of a fish supper down my jacket.

Our Doris was sitting in her cubbyhole, furiously flitting through the Yellow Pages. I don't see the point in it anymore – we usually use the iPad for finding out phone numbers, but there's something to be said for a physical object. Even slimmed down, the Yellow Pages can cause more damage to a would-be burglar than an iPad.

She gave me the Look and said to me, she said, 'Well, I've no need to question where you've been, Harold Copeland. I'm here in distress and you're off gallivanting down the pub with your friends.'

'Just the one, our Doris. Alf.' The fog of late afternoon drunkenness simmered in my head. I drawled my words as though my cheeks had forgotten how to move around syllables, sounding ever closer to Rocky Balboa after a few rounds against Mr T.

'I suppose you didn't think I'd want something

gluttonous from the chip shop?'

I'd been in the process of taking off my coat. I left the zip halfway down and said to her, I said, 'Do you want something from the chippy? Pete's is still open. If you want fish and chips, I'll head straight back out and grab you something.'

Our Doris shook her head. 'No, I need to keep my wits about me if I'm to stop Janice Dooley. The minute a proper chip passes my lips, I'll be more intent on shovelling fatty foods into my face than tackling our very own Anna Karenina.'

'Anna Karenina?' I asked, unsure if it were the beer or a genuine lack of what our Doris was getting at.

'Yes, Anna Karenina. An old tart who thinks she has a tragic backstory.'

'Is that the one with Sean Bean?'

'I don't know, our 'arold. I've never been one for foreign films. Either way, if you're not too drunk, would you mind making me some poached eggs? Yours always turn out better than mine.'

That much is true. Our Doris is one of the most nuclear of all housewives – could write entire dissertations on the subject of housewifery in the twenty-first century – but when it comes to poached eggs, she's about as much use as a bonfire in a monsoon.

I made her poached eggs on toast and a pot of tea to share between the both of us. We sat at the kitchen – our Doris intent on her food, and me focused on getting a couple of drinks down my throat before we attempted any conversation.

Once I was suitably sober, I said to our Doris, I said, 'Just why do you dislike Janice Dooley of Little Street?'

She'd finished her food and been staring out the window, reflecting. 'Quite honestly, I've completely forgotten.'

'I don't believe that for a second,' I said.

And I didn't. Our Doris doesn't forget her grudges. When Pauline Atkins was caught stepping out with Winston, our Doris didn't stop until they'd both moved to Leek, and even then, she'd kept an eye on them for so long she had their milk order memorised. One whole, one skimmed, and a yoghurt for the parrot.

That's how I knew for a fact that our Doris was hiding something from me.

There was also the fact that once I'd finished talking, she carried her plate over to the sink and began scrubbing at it with all the rage of Hulk Hogan in too-tight swimming trunks. She had the water running like a typhoon against the sink.

I reached over and turned off the tap. 'You need to tell me, our Doris. It'll make you feel better in the long run.'

'Don't you dare tell me what will make me feel better, our 'arold. I've known exactly the type of person Janice Dooley is since I was a child, and adding money doesn't change anything. You can put concealer over a spot, but there'll still be a great load of pus hiding beneath it.'

'What did she do to make you hate her so much?'

'You've gone fifty-six years without knowing, why should I tell you now?' And with that, our Doris left the room. A few seconds later, I heard the front door slamming shut.

Our Doris didn't come home that night.

I'd like to say I slept better in our bed without her snoring next to me, but the fact of the matter was that I stayed awake, staring at the wall until the first light of dawn started breaking through the curtains.

When our Doris has gone off in the past, I've waited in for the inevitable phone call from her Mavis where she tells me what a terrible husband I've been to her cousin, that our Doris should have waited and married John Nettles, and that my pastry would never be anything other than plasterboard.

Only she didn't.

I considered ringing Mavis myself, but if our Doris hadn't gone over to Wren's Lea then I'd be left answering questions about her disappearance and before I knew it, I'd be down the police station being arrested for murder and disposing of our Doris's body. It's just the type of thing that Mavis Thistlethwaite has wanted for decades. Sometimes I think she wouldn't mind me doing our Doris in, as long as it meant she got to see me behind bars.

I know why Mavis and I don't get on. She's always been too overprotective of our Doris, and no one will ever be good enough for her cousin. I understand it; I'd be the same if it was me. There's also the fact that she's a chain-smoking harridan with the temper of a chihuahua and a damaging right hook.

Yet another reason I know that our Doris remembers why she can't abide Janice Dooley of Little Street.

Eventually, I went down to the kitchen and made a coffee. A strong coffee with enough sugar to have dentists rubbing their hands – too bad I've got dentures. I sat down in my chair, staring down at my drink, all set to say something to our Doris before I remembered she wasn't there, and that's how I came to be in the kitchen at six o'clock in the morning. The newspaper hadn't even been delivered.

Once I'd finished my coffee, I made another and carried it into the living room. Then I started dusting. I don't usually dust – that's one of the jobs our Doris does, claims she appreciates the way it gets her heart rate up, but personally I think she enjoys sniffing the Mr Muscle.

I had the corner cupboard open, polishing the Lladro ladies our Doris had collected over the years, using cotton buds to get into all the nooks and crannies. I cleaned the cupboard doors and dusted under every coaster and magazine we had on the coffee table. I got the hoover out and had a quick whip around and I was still done before the newspaper arrived.

It was half past seven, and nothing I'd done took my mind off the fact that my wife was nowhere to be found.

Well, nowhere within the house.

A few hours down the line, I was sitting in front of

the television, watching a repeat of American Pickers. There's something thrilling about thinking that all the stuff you have hidden away in the attic might be worth something to somebody. They might not be worth anything at the minute, but one day my Ground Force VHS tapes might be worth hundreds.

The phone rang and I answered it.

It was our Doris. She said to me, she said, 'I haven't gone to Mavis's, our 'arold. I can't help but feel I might have returned to Partridge Mews too quickly.'

'Where are you, our Doris?'

'I didn't ring to tell you that. I just wanted to let you know that I'll be back for the public consultation, but until then I'll be remaining here. I will meet you at the council chambers next Thursday. I have spoken to Edith and our Angela. Don't think that this is permission for you to gad about behaving all reckless. You are my husband, 'arold Copeland, and you are expected to behave accordingly.'

I admit to being astounded. 'You're honestly telling me that rather than admitting what Janice Dooley did, you're going to run away?'

Our Doris chuckled down the phone. 'That's exactly right. She who fights and runs away lives to fight another day, and trust me, I have a lot of fighting planned. Janice Dooley of Little Street will wish she'd used her daddy's money to beggar right off.' With a final titter, our Doris said her goodbyes.

I held the phone against my ear, feeling like I did when Mrs Collins told me off for kicking my ball into her petunias – red-faced and terrified with a slight trace of something I'd only come to recognise when our Doris first showed me what went on beneath her Co-Op uniform.

I didn't really get up to much over the following week. I considered calling the lads around and making a night of it, but I was pining after our Doris. We'd spent nearly every second together on that cruise, and without her there, I struggled to figure out what I was supposed to do. In that moment, I wondered if that had been our Doris's plan all along – to make me entirely dependent on her so as I wouldn't resort to the drunkenness she'd always despised.

I pottered around the house, met Alf down the Hare and Horse and then visited the allotment. Our Doris's absence meant I could visit the allotment whenever I wanted. There's something about having all the time to do the things I want to do that also means I never have the time to do all the things I want to do. I arrived at the allotment only to realise that my shed was a disorganised shambles. I'd planned to pull up a few weeds, check the chicken wire and see if any of my carrots were ready. Instead, I spent three hours organising my screws by size. I found a Tiswas badge at one point, and I'm beggared if

117

I know how that got into my screw bucket.

By the time I'd finished sorting out my shed, I was thirsty and that meant another visit to the pub. Alf didn't show up, but I overheard a few councillors talking about Barraclough's Field. Of course, most of what they had to say was the regular arrogant nonsense I've come to expect from men who think wearing cufflinks automatically gives them the right to believe they're above everyone else. However, they did have one or two interesting things that made me slow down my beer drinking and take out my phone.

Our Theo had showed me how to use the Notes app when we were on the cruise, and it's come in quite handy. Admittedly, he only taught me how to use it because he thinks that being seventy-six automatically means I'm on the verge of senility, but still, it's a great tool for shopping lists.

I keyed in anything I thought might be useful later. Our Doris is known for her subterfuge, and being married as long as we have, I've learned a few things. Besides, those councillors were in their own little world. It were like hearing those trolls from The Hobbit, which I only got to watch because our Doris has a thing for Ian McKellen.

The day of the public consultation finally arrived. Thinking about seeing our Doris again, I was a bit like a kid at Christmas – filled with excitement and anticipating disappointment. I was thrilled, but there'd be tears by the day's end. I couldn't say for sure where they'd come from, but I put a box of Kleenex on the back seat of the car in any case.

The public consultation was held in the council chambers, a glorified meeting room with generic MDF tables, hard-backed plastic chairs – more rickety than a wooden leg with termites – and the astringent stench of Dettol mixed with mouthwash. A camera stood in the corner, its red light blinking, as though we were recording our very own episode of You've Been Framed. Someone had tried to make the place look more homely by placing a tea urn and mugs beside a plastic palm tree, but it still felt like we were trapped in an episode of The Office, waiting for Ricky Gervais to walk through the door and embarrass himself.

I arrived too early. That's one of the issues getting

older – as soon as I turned sixty-seven, I began arriving everywhere too early.

It all started when I got my new knee.

After the necessary physiotherapy and rehabilitation that had me going around looking like I was in a perpetual state of incontinence, I never knew how long it would take me to get somewhere. Wherever I'm going, I think about where I'll park, how near the disabled bays are to my destination and whether there will be stairs. They're a right beggar are stairs when you're in a rush and you have Herbie's hubcap in place of a patella.

I made myself a cup of tea and sat down, choosing a seat that had a view of the room but was close enough to the door that I'd be more than capable should I need to make a quick getaway.

The room slowly filled up.

I was there for a quarter of an hour before Doug Grey and Janice Dooley of Little Street walked in, looking like a right pair of hyenas. Those two could be a modern-day Punch and Judy, the way they go about – they never look happy to be together. They looked smug as they walked in, carrying their reusable Costa mugs like qualifications, but Doug had this look about him that I can only describe as being like a teenage boy who doesn't want to be seen shopping with his mother.

Alf and Edith soon joined me. I couldn't believe my eyes. I blinked a few times and said to Alf, I said, 'You've dressed up.'

Granted, he wasn't wearing a suit. He'd pulled out a pair of navy-blue chinos and wore a white polo shirt beneath a grey cardigan. He looked a regular grandfather, all set to tell a fireside tale. He'd showered, combed his hair, and sprayed himself liberally with what I could only imagine was Air Wick's Seasonal Spices.

Edith straightened his collar. 'I told him he had to show his support for Doris, and he couldn't very well do that looking like something an owl threw up.'

'It'd have to be a big owl,' I said.

'You should get yourself down Bulge Busters, 'arold,' he said. 'I hear the place is heaving with big birds.'

He earned a clout across the shoulder for that. Edith has always had great aim with her handbag. Alf grinned, a twinkle in his eye as bright as ever. Edith hid a smile behind her handkerchief as she scurried over to the tea urn.

Miss Moonflower and her posse of elves arrived next. They stood at the door, looking for a place to sit that could accommodate a host of capes and sceptres. I couldn't help myself; I felt this little tickle of fury gather in my chest and before I could stop, I called out to her, I said, 'I think you're in the wrong room. The crèche is downstairs.'

She turned to see who'd shouted and I gripped the edge of the table with all the intensity of that lad out of Titanic trying to keep hold of a door. Miss Moonflower had set fire to our Doris's head, and so she should flaming well remember me. I glowered at her, and I made sure it was a glower our Doris would be proud of – not quite a Look, but close enough to strike terror into her heart.

She said, 'Nice to see you, Mr Copeland.'

'Aren't you getting a bit old for all this, Louise? Dressing up like something out of Robin Hood.'

She didn't respond.

Not that it mattered. Edith placed a hand on my arm that clearly meant I needed to hold my tongue. I looked over to her, ready to tell her why I'd had to make comment, when she said to me, 'We all know what she did, 'arold, but she's one of only a few people who are protesting the development. For today only, we're on the same side.'

I let my shoulders relax and nodded, breathing through my nose like a dragon practicing yoga. I said to her, I said, 'You're not planning on throwing any carrot cake, are you?'

Edith offered a conciliatory smile and said, 'Alf wouldn't let me anywhere near the bakery. If we've got time after this, we should all go to Mrs Burr's for a lemon bun.'

Alf's face brightened at the mention of baked goods. His eyebrows were nearly lost in his hairline as he said, 'Did you hear that, 'arold? A lemon bun. A lemon bun! All that cream and icing. If she's letting us have messy food in public, it must be special.'

'There's no messy food, Alfred Simpson, only messy eaters.'

'It's not his fault, Edith,' I said. 'Alf was born with a lawnmower in place of a jaw.'

She chortled.

Edith was in the midst of a proper laugh when we heard this great thud from the other side of the room and a few gasps from the elves. Miss Moonflower had tripped and taken a few chairs with her. While everyone else was rushing over to rearrange furniture and check she hadn't done too much damage, I watched Janice Dooley edge her foot away from the hemline of Miss Moonflower's cloak.

For a moment, I thought it was in solidarity, before I realised Janice had simply seen an opportunity to embarrass an opponent and taken it. I met her gaze across the table, and she actually raised her Costa mug in a toast, complete with a bawdy grin. I'll say something for Janice Dooley of Little Street – she's never managed to find any class.

Soon enough, it was time for the consultation to start and our Doris still hadn't arrived. The councillors I'd heard talking at the Hare and Horse entered the room, carrying clipboards under their armpits like rifles at a drill show. They expressed every ounce of impartiality as they shook hands with Doug Grey and asked him to golf the following Wednesday to chat about starting work. That's always been an issue with Partridge Mews Town Council, has that; if you know the right palms to grease, you can get away without playing by the rulebook.

The councillors sat down at the head of the table, behind their name tags.

Ian Morris coughed to catch the attention of the room. He's a portly man is Ian – he's only in his mid-fifties, but he carries himself with the lumbering gait of a man twenty years his senior, like a hippopotamus with a limp.

'I think it best if we begin,' he said. 'My name is Ian Morris, and I'll chair proceedings this morning. Many thanks to all of you for attending this public consultation to discuss the proposed development of greenbelt land off the Partridge Grove Road, commonly referred to as Barraclough's Field. In the interests of full transparency, I wish to make it aware that this application has been submitted by former councillor Mr Douglas Grey and his business partner Ms Janice Dooley. I also wish to make it clear that we won't be granting or denying planning permission today. We're here to discuss opinions surrounding the development. You'll be aware that building on greenbelt land is a contentious issue in this day and age, and because of that, we understand that emotions might run high. However, we ask that you remain civil. Should you have something to say, you'll get the opportunity during our time together. This consultation is being recorded and streamed live across the internet. We ask that anyone who wishes to speak does so clearly. Now, I think we should allow Ms Dooley to say a few words about her planned proposal.'

Janice feigned confidence. She sat up straight in her chair and surveyed the room, curling the edges of her paperwork beneath her acrylic nails.

'Thank you, Mr Morris,' she said. 'Once again, I'd like to give thanks to everyone who's shown an interest in my plans for Barraclough's Field. When I heard about the legacy my father left behind, my immediate thoughts were how I could use the new-found finances to benefit our community. While Partridge Mews has proven to be a great home for many, the youth are finding it increasingly difficult to get on the property ladder due to increasing housing costs, meaning that they're unable to continue to inhabit the town they've lived in for their entire lives.'

I had to give it to Janice; she'd certainly rehearsed. I'd never heard her sound so eloquent. It was her Eliza Doolittle moment.

Then our Doris arrived and ruined it all.

She pushed the door open with all the aplomb of royalty. Our Doris had her shoulders straight and held her head tipped back, her nose to the air as though she were testing for unpleasant odours.

Janice stopped talking as our Doris entered, her steps as slow and confident as the evil queen ready to carve out Snow White's heart. She looked directly in Janice's direction and said to her, she said, 'Please accept my most sincere apologies for my late arrival, Ms Dooley.

I never expected you to be awake before noon.'

I saw Doug nudge Janice as our Doris sat down beside me.

Janice shot an anxious glance in our Doris's direction. 'That's fine, Mrs Copeland. I'm pleased you could make it.'

Our Doris offered a threatening smile. 'I wouldn't miss this for the world. Please continue as though nothing happened.'

I looked from Alf to Edith and back again. There was no avoiding it; we were impressed. We were also hopeful. I hadn't seen this side of our Doris in a while, and I was looking forward to seeing how things turned out.

Janice went on, 'When I recognised the lack of affordable housing in town, I knew I had to do something about it. I contacted my good friend Doug – Mr Grey –'

The door opened once again and the room collectively gasped. It was like being in the middle of one of those experimental theatre places where they make the audience part of the cast. I removed my gaze from our most recent interloper and turned to our Doris. I said to her, I said, 'Have you been with her for the last week?'

Stood in the doorway, looking more imposing than an office assistant with a fully-functioning stapler, was Violet Grey. She was dressed for war in her Marc Cain dress and court shoes. A thin string of pearls encircled her throat.

'Really, we must start locking the door if this sort of thing continues,' Ian said, in an attempt to -take back control of the meeting.

Violet shot Janice a glare that fierce, it was a wonder she didn't disintegrate on the spot. She said to her, 'I don't mean to be uncouth, but calling Douglas your good friend is a bit like calling the bubonic plague a sniffle. You spent that much time in his bed, I could never get the imprint of your buttocks out of the memory foam. But don't let that interrupt you. "Good friend," my aunt Fanny.'

Violet looked to Ian. 'It's good to see you again, Mr Morris. How is Nora? Is Jacob still doing well with his violin?' She came and sat down beside our Doris, greeting each of us on her way.

'I really can't allow any more interruptions,' Ian said, speaking to the room. 'There is a manner in which we must proceed, and I can't see that marred for late entrances and theatrics. Once Ms Dooley has said her piece, we will allow all present the opportunity to speak, as I said at the beginning.'

Violet said to him, 'Oh, I completely understand, Ian. However, I take great umbrage with the accusation of theatrics. I simply entered a room and pointed out an error on Ms Dooley's part. If we are to be transparent then surely she should have explained to the room that her relationship with Douglas doesn't stop at them simply being "business partners".'

I leaned over and whispered to our Doris, 'How do you two know everything that's been said?'

'Our Theo is in the corridor watching the live stream on his laptop. Don't question things, our 'arold. We know what we're doing.'

Ian gave Janice the opportunity to speak, but she looked completely floored. She slumped back in her seat, desultory; sweat beaded on her brow as though she'd just run ten laps around the building.

'It's true that Doug and I had a bit of a thing in the past,' she said. 'But that has nothing to do with all this. I went to him about building affordable houses and he recommended Barraclough's Field as a possible site. That's it. He's done this sort of thing before and thought he'd be just what I needed, so we went into partnership together. His company and my money will make this happen.'

'This would be DG Demolition, would it?' Our Doris asked. She kept her eyes firmly fixed on Janice Dooley, ignoring Ian's protestations that she wasn't following procedure.

Janice turned to Doug, who nodded his head furiously. He was popping the lid on and off his biro, his face as red as a beetroot with sunstroke.

'It is, yes,' Janice said.

I noticed the councillors looking shifty at the head of the table. They were glancing across at the camera in the corner, suddenly aware that everything they said was being seen by the few people in the community who cared about the way our council operated.

That was when our Doris pulled out her trump card, using the information I'd sent to her the evening before and that I'd gathered from a few careless councillors down the Hare and Horse.

She said to Janice, she said, 'Is this the same DG Demolition that lists several of the council members here today as shareholders? The same council members who are currently under investigation for deliberately falsifying air quality data in the area surrounding Barraclough's Field, as reported by the Partridge Mews Gazette in June? I have no issue with the development of greenbelt land if it truly is to build affordable homes. However, I am concerned that this is less about helping the younger members of the community get on the property ladder, and more about further lining the

127

pockets of dishonest members of the Partridge Mews Town Council.'

Janice gulped and slumped even further down in her seat, as though hoping that if she sank down far enough, she could crawl under the table and escape.

Doug looked apoplectic with rage. He loosened his tie and tapped his pen against his coffee mug.

Ian allowed himself a few moments of reflection. He surveyed the room, looking at the silently seething audience. He said to our Doris, trying to take control, he said, 'These are really excellent points to bring up, Mrs Copeland, and I'm sure they address the concerns of the community. However, I do not see how any of these matters have any bearing on the development of Barraclough's Field. It's certainly shameful that our air quality data has been misrepresented in such a fashion. Please note that this is all down to human error. We councillors have rather tough jobs at times, and that's why a few figures were entered incorrectly before the submission to DEFRA. Now, allow me to address your mention of councillors being shareholders in DG Demolition. Many councillors have interests outside of the council, and while a few of us may be involved in the monetary side of the company, it would be unethical for us to use our power to "force through" any proposed plans in an effort to "line our pockets".'

Our Doris allowed a moment for his words to settle before saying to him, she said, 'It pleases me that we have such a wordsmith on our town council. I am heartened to hear that there are still men who can be polite and honest while revealing themselves to be cunning businessmen with little thought to the community they're paid to help.'

She offered him a smile; it was slight, courteous and

came with a bobbing of the head that allowed him the floor.

Or it would have done if Violet hadn't chosen that moment to speak, 'I don't wish us to veer off-topic, but I feel that the following information is pertinent to these proceedings. Ms Dooley just said that she went into partnership with Mr Grey's company. However, that's not the case.'

'Don't you dare,' Doug growled, flinging himself to his feet. His chair flew back against the wall, marking the cream wallpaper with a thick, grey line. 'You just keep your mouth shut!'

Violet tittered before saying, 'I am the owner and CEO of DG Demolition. Douglas Grey has no standing in my company. I rescinded his employment before I left Partridge Mews and must admit I was rather concerned when I learned that he was operating under my name.

'Ms Dooley and Mr Grey might be in partnership, I don't deny that, but the fact of the matter remains that they cannot do so under the DG Demolition name. Therefore, I believe it is only right that the two of them take their plans away with them and resubmit them once they have a correct idea of the pollution levels surrounding the proposed development, and a proper knowledge of whether or not they have the funds to make this project happen.'

Ian stared at Violet, stunned – all pretence of this being official council business was thrown out the window. The Greys were in the middle of a divorce and Partridge Mews was at the centre. It was Batman versus the Joker. Kramer versus Kramer. Wurzel Gummidge versus a hairbrush.

Eventually, Miss Moonflower piped up, 'So what happens now?'

He looked like a blowfish on its way to becoming sushi. Ian said, 'I believe our best course of action is to adjourn this meeting early so as we can properly discuss with Mr Grey and Ms Dooley how they wish to continue.'

Our Doris beamed, saying, she said, 'That does sound like the best recourse in this instance. However, there are a few more people who had concerns unrelated to ours and perhaps it would prove helpful for Ms Dooley to hear them so as she can avoid any future issues.'

Ian considered our Doris's words. 'That actually sounds like a reasonable idea. What do you think, Ms Dooley?' He avoided looking at Doug, who'd returned to his seat, sitting beside the wall as though having a tantrum had been part of his plan.

Janice agreed to our Doris's idea and for the best part of an hour, we listened to the concerns of our fellow residents. Folk didn't like the idea of losing more greenbelt land to a housing development when so many council homes stood derelict. Others had environmental concerns. One woman got upset about the lack of a TK Maxx, only to realise she'd attended the wrong meeting and was supposed to be in Chester.

With every single person that voiced a concern, Janice Dooley sank further down into her seat, all traces of triumph erased from her face.

Once the final person had shared their thoughts, Ian called an end to the public consultation. Janice looked as downtrodden as Snoopy in a rainstorm. Doug was furious – he'd been insulted in front of all his mates on the council and there was a faint glimmer of worry in my chest about what he'd do next. He's always been one for retaliation, has Doug Grey – he's still not allowed back to Davenport Golf Club after what he did to their eighteenth hole.

As the room cleared out, I said to our Doris, I said, 'I can't believe it, our Doris. You actually did it. You beat them.'

She shook her head and said to me, she said, 'Now is not the time for complacency, our 'arold. We have simply postponed the inevitable. Doug Grey and his cronies have had these plans in the pipeline for years.'

Violet nodded. 'DG Demolition has never had the proper backing. There was also the small issue that Sam Barraclough wouldn't sell the land to Douglas, owing to the fact he thinks that my former husband is a no-good, two-faced scumbag with greasy palms and the integrity of a rotten banana.'

'Taken verbatim, was it?'

'I might have embellished slightly, but one mustn't swear in public.'

Alf was impatient. He practically rushed us from our seats and towards the door. 'Can we go to Mrs Burr's now? I don't want her to run out.'

'We'll ring ahead, Alf, and ask her Melanie to keep some aside.'

'What's he talking about?' Violet asked.

'We're going for a lemon bun to celebrate,' Edith said. 'Will you join us?'

Violet smirked. 'Oh no, I don't think I could do that at all, Mrs Simpson. See, I did not come here today as a favour to Mrs Copeland, as much as it might have seemed so. I do not wish to have any remaining ties with Douglas. He can submit his plans again for all I care, as long as my company isn't named anywhere on the paperwork.'

Edith's frown was as fixed as a gargoyle's as she said,

'You really are a self-serving, wretched, old cow, aren't you?'

'Moo,' Violet said, and with that, she walked out of the council chambers, her steps so pronounced that she looked as though she were mimicking an ostrich.

Our Doris stared after her before shrugging and saying, she said, 'Well, we always knew we couldn't rely on Violet Grey. Anyone who's ever attended one of her buffets knows that she's never been dedicated enough to put on a full spread.' She sighed. 'Now, lemon buns?'

TWO

Our Doris isn't having an affair.

At least, I don't think she's having an affair. There is the smallest possible chance that our Doris might have finally decided she's had enough of me and is about to embark upon a passionate romance with an accountant named Lars … but I'm not too certain.

I first had my suspicions about a fortnight ago. We'd just finished breakfast. I was loading the dishwasher and our Doris were examining herself in the hall mirror, debating whether she should go back for a perm or if Silvakrin would do the job.

Then the phone rang.

Being a perpetual office girl, our Doris answered it. She went about the usual business of giving the caller our surname, address and telephone number before going silent. Our Doris doesn't go in for humming at folk to let them know she's listening, tends to settle for a few choice sentences that would have Queen Victoria hiring her as a linguistic coach, but for that phone call, our Doris was humming like the best of them. There were even a few monosyllabic yeses, something she has always warned against because it's a mindless affirmation that can ultimately see a person agreeing to something they might later regret. That came after she ended up manning the sweet table at our Theo's school disco in two-thousand-and-seven. She's never forgiven herself.

I heard her replace the phone in its cradle. She called to me, and there were a crack in her voice as she said, all high-pitched, she said, 'I just need to pop out for a few hours. Perhaps you could make a start on that beef stew for supper.'

With that, she left.

If she were going somewhere important, our Doris would have had me drive her there. I wondered if she was considering our carbon footprint, if Violet Grey had decided to go green again and I'd end up back on a diet of chickpeas and bulgur wheat by Friday, but I put all those thoughts out of my head and had a cup of tea instead.

I supposed it could also have been to do with Doug Grey and his redevelopment. Our Doris had discovered that he'd rechristened his company DG Construction and set about recreating his plans for Barraclough's Field.

A beef stew was a small price to pay to have the house to myself. Our Doris had been spending a lot of time at home, and if fifty-six years of marriage has taught me anything, it's that we get on best when she's not here.

The WI was supposed to be getting back together, but after the debacle with Doug Grey, they'd all gone silent. Mrs Cribbins had been seen talking to Beverly Atkinson about her hydrangeas, but the conversation remained purely horticultural. There was no mention of how Bev's Seamus had been hospitalised after an accident with a nail gun. The doctors said he'll keep his big toe and he categorically refuses to help the WI with their trestle tables again.

It was supposed to be an impromptu jumble sale. It never happened.

I found all this out at the Hare and Horse. Business is booming with former WI husbands seeking refuge from their wives.

When they weren't being forced to do jobs around the house, the husbands of Partridge Mews were having to sample some of the most experimental foods ever created this side of the River Dane.

I'm lucky. Our Doris went through her culinary experimentation in nineteen-sixty-eight when avocado became the in-thing. We had it once at a dinner party. Next day, our Doris wrote a letter to the Gazette stating that avocado has no place in a respectable, middle-class household as it resembled something from Doctor Who and had all the appeal of a grass-fed slug.

There was also the moussaka for our Phil's fiftieth, but we don't talk about that. Whoever saw an aubergine and thought it were meant for eating had clearly never had a bacon sandwich.

I suppose they're all anyone eats nowadays: aubergines. There's that many vegans, the cows are starting to gain more confidence. Give them a decade and they'll be ram-raiding McDonalds.

No, I'm not one for funny food. Even after travelling around the world and sampling cuisine from all and sundry, I still prefer steak and kidney pie to paella. It has to have proper northern gravy as well – the sort that's as thick as tar, has enough fat to tempt a Weight Watcher and enough flavour that nothing stops the consumer licking their plate in polite company.

I shouldn't have bothered with the beef stew.

Our Doris didn't come home that day. I rang her mobile, but that was no use.

Our Angela was working late, so I invited Theo around for the evening. I hadn't seen him much since he started his A-Levels. He's very focused on his schoolwork is our Theo. 'Course, he could be partaking in enough underage drinking, sex and entry-level drugs to get his own documentary on Channel Four, but I don't think so. Not our Theo.

I'm not being a gullible, old Grandad in this. Our Doris taught Theo respectability and he's too fearful of his grandmother to ever go in for any serious debauchery.

I'd pottered around the house a bit without our Doris. I even took the hoover out and cleaned up any errant crumbs that might have come from my mid-afternoon croissant. That's something exotic that I don't mind is the croissant; with enough butter and jam, it's the only thing a person can have after seventy-five to feel truly sinful.

Either way, I removed all evidence before our Theo arrived in case he used it as a bit of blackmail at a later date. He's our Doris's grandson all right, is our Theo. I'm still concerned he'll one day tell our Doris what he saw at the Hare and Horse's New Year Party in two-thousand-and-five.

Then I saw something on the internet that filled me with equal parts joy and dread.

Before we went on the cruise, we created social media accounts. It was all our Doris's idea. Despite the fact that she claimed she wanted to get away from all the societal obligations that Partridge Mews forced upon her, there was a gossip page on there that she didn't want to miss. There we were, in our mid-seventies, signing up to find out things about folk that they'd never ordinarily tell you down the pub. I'll never get over seeing what Bob Seymour accidentally shared. It put me right off Angel Delight.

It's because of things like that happening that I rarely use it. I get the iPad out occasionally, do the odd Sudoku puzzle and look at which celebrities have died. I've been keeping an eye on Russ Abbot – he seems just the type to outlive me.

I were debating another chapter of my Andrea Camilleri when I got a notification. I saw something that would make our Doris heave. She'd be apoplectic. She would be running around the house like Audrey Hepburn at the end of Charade. She'd be on the phone to the Pope, wondering if he could pop around for an exorcism.

It were only a few photographs. I know that, but I didn't know what to do. Luckily, the subject of said images would arrive within the next half hour. I tried to settle down with my book, mulling over how best to manage the situation.

Our Theo turned up looking like Kenneth Williams in Carry on Screaming. He came into the kitchen with grey bags under his eyes and his skin all pale.

I said to him, I said, ''Ow 'at, our Theo. I can't say you look well.'

'This is what revision does to you, Grandad. A-Levels aren't what they used to be.'

I tapped the iPad as I set about making a brew. 'You're sure it's just revision? Only, some photos were shared on Facebook that suggest Captain Morgan might have had a hand in things.'

Theo slumped down at the table; face pressed against his arms. 'Wasn't it your responsibility as a grandfather to teach me that hangovers can last all day?'

'I've been showing you for years. You just haven't been paying attention.'

He said, voice all muffled as he spoke into his sleeves, he said, 'Fair point, well made.'

I took our drinks to the table and said, 'What do you say to a bowl of beef stew?'

'I don't know.'

'That bad, are you?'

He looked up from the comfort of his arms, his face contorted in a blend of confusion and steadily departing inebriation. 'I don't get it.'

'Get what?'

'The joke.'

'What joke?'

'"What do you say to a bowl of beef stew?"'

'That wasn't a joke. I wanted to know if you fancied some dinner.'

'Sounded like a joke to me. It was the perfect set-up for a joke, was that.' I could tell he must be poorly if he sounded more northern than usual. He usually mimics his grandmother and goes in for a posh tone usually confined to Alderley Edge, Prestbury and – at a push – Wilmslow.

I said to him, I said, 'Has anyone ever told you that you can be a bit gormless at times, our Theo?'

'They haven't, but then I suppose I had to inherit something from my grandfather.' He had this cheeky grin I couldn't help being proud of. I chuckled, if I'm being honest.

I'll give that to our Theo. He might've been worse for the wear, but he still turned the conversation around so that I looked thick. He definitely inherited that from our Doris.

I had a slurp of my tea. 'What are you going to tell your Nan when she sees the photos?'

Here he came over all political, ready to share a long diatribe about why a duck pond is a reasonable expense. He said, 'I'll inform my grandmother that I'm partaking in a social experiment, examining the increase in underage drinking amongst students in high-pressure A-Level courses. That's in the unlikely event she bothers to look.'

'What're you talking about? She's always on that gossip page.'

'Keep up, Grandad. She got banned last month for her outdated opinions regarding pleated skirts.'

'She's always on the iPad, in any case.'

'She's probably playing a game. They're highly addictive. Mark Deveraux got sent to rehab when his parents realised how much time he spent playing Minecraft.'

'Minecraft?'

Theo shrugged. 'Don't ask me. I've no time for video games. If I'm not doing homework, I'm down the gym.'

I said to him, I said, 'You kept up with the health kick then?'

'It's not a health kick, it's a new way of life.'

'Sounds like something only the truly indoctrinated would say.'

'You haven't done any extra exercise since the cruise, have you?'

'I haven't had chance.'

I haven't, if truth be told. Being our Doris's husband is a full-time job. It's not like one of these modern relationships where you can have as many partners as you like as long as they provide something different.

Madeleine Potter got her entire house renovated when she went polyamorous. I don't blame her, but I'm still more likely to hire a builder before inviting someone new into the bedroom. There's less fuss about figuring out who'll hold the hammer.

Our Theo looked at me in disbelief. 'I like to keep fit and I thought you'd like to as well. I don't want you turning into a sedentary grandfather at risk of a heart attack at every turn. I want you around as long as possible.'

There were something heart-warming in his words. Sentimental, even. I suppose it's nice to be thought of, like when our Doris gets Liquorice Allsorts and saves me the horsecakes.

I said to him, I said, 'I don't plan on going anywhere just yet, our Theo. And get off with your idea that I don't keep fit. You haven't seen me down the allotment. It's like a full body workout, is that.'

He nodded acceptance – he weren't happy, but he'd let me keep doing what I were doing – and said to me, 'Are we having this stew, then? I could do with some breakfast.'

'It's quarter to six at night, our Theo.'

'I woke up late.'

'Have a few biscuits out the tin. I'll warm something up.'

I were smiling as I got the dishes out the cupboard.

We chatted while I warmed up the stew. Our Theo stuck around afterwards to help me tidy up before claiming homework and heading off out.

I'll admit to some worry that our Doris hadn't returned. It wasn't the first time she'd gone out with little idea as to her location – she went missing for three days once when she got on the wrong bus and ended up in

Chester. That was before mobiles, and she refused to use a phone box because she didn't believe it would be to a sanitary standard worthy of a secretary from Cheshire's premier gnome manufacturers.

I were sat in bed reading when our Doris got home. I wondered if she were a thief, but there's a certain daintiness to the way our Doris closes the front door that no burglar could mimic.

She came up to the bedroom and I said to her, I said, 'Where were you, our Doris?'

She was looking a bit bedraggled; her blouse were creased and her hair were in disarray. She attempted the Look and said to me, she said, 'Give over, our 'arold. If that's your attempt at being a detective then Jim Bergerac can rest easy.'

I said nothing and went on reading.

I nodded off before she came to bed and when I got up in the morning she was already gone.

I met Alf at the Hare and Horse to discuss matters. I bought him a pint – he were happy because he'd had a win on the races – and said to him, I said, 'Our Doris is having an affair.'

That wiped the smile off his face. He took a gulp of bitter before saying, 'Have you gone completely off your rocker, 'arold?'

'I'm being serious,' I said.

'And clearly senile if you believe Doris would go after another fella.'

'He might have his own knee.'

'Your Doris is seventy-four. She's not got the time to train a new man to the levels she wants.'

I said to him, I said, 'I suppose.'

'What's got you thinking she's having it off with some other poor so-and-so?'

I told him about our Doris's phone call and how she'd disappeared for the day.

Alf looked at me like I'd got gravy all over my face. 'I never had you down as the insecure type. Your missus scarpers for one day and the only explanation that comes to mind is that she's having an affair? Where's the trust?'

I sank down in my seat, staring mournfully – well, as mournfully as a man in a pub can look – into my pint of Theakston's Old Peculiar. 'You're right.'

He was.

In fifty-six years of marriage, our Doris has never given me any reason to believe she's having an affair. Being quite honest, she's a master of subterfuge and trained in the art of housewifery; she can keep a secret. We've nearly been married for six decades, and she's never given me her Grandma Thistlethwaite's recipe for shortcrust pastry.

I suppose I should have been grateful for a Doris-free day. Ever since Doug Grey announced that he and Janice were resubmitting plans for Barraclough's Field, it's all I've heard about. Well, that and the WI.

A few of the ladies have been in touch to ask when our Doris plans on holding the first meeting. Falling short of telling them to go forth and multiply again, she's saying she has other obligations to attend to – obligations that look a lot like having an afternoon kip in front of Tipping Point. Maybe she's developed a thing for Ben Shepherd. Maybe there was a last-minute cancellation and they've had our Doris as a contestant on the show.

I don't think that's right, though. Our Doris wasn't built for quizzes – ask her any question you like about Laura Ashley home décor of the last seventy years, and she can tell you brand, texture and price, but ask her anything related to general knowledge and you're beggared. She once had to have a word with one of our Theo's teachers when it turned out Henry VIII didn't have a wife called Anne of Cleethorpes.

No, our Doris would most definitely not be

appearing on Tipping Point.

Dragging myself from a reverie involving our Doris, Ben Shepherd and a groundsheet at Dunelm Mill, I said to Alf, I said, 'Has your Edith said anything?'

'About Doris?'

'Who else?'

'No,' he said.

'No?'

'No.' And he nodded for emphasis.

I said, 'But it makes no sense. Our Doris never goes anywhere without having an outfit planned. Remember when I had to phone her an ambulance and she wouldn't let me until she'd put on her navy Pikolinos.'

'Didn't they have to cut them off her?'

I nodded. 'She'd sprained her ankle. Foot swelled and that's it. No more Pikolinos.'

'Expensive, weren't they?'

'She still hides the receipts,' I said.

'I were in all day yesterday waiting on a phone call. Gawky was supposed to be ringing about some pigeons he's got a hold of. If your Doris phoned, I'd have known about it.'

'What do you want to go getting involved with Gawky Cavendish for?'

'I won't be doing anything because he never rang. We'll be having words.'

'Mind your Edith doesn't find out.'

'This were for her in the first place.'

'What was?'

'Getting the pigeons off Gawky Cavendish.'

'What does Edith want with a load of pigeons?'

'Our anniversary is coming up.'

'And you think she wants a flock of pigeons?'

He shrugged. 'She might appreciate the

opportunity.'

'Has she said anything about liking pigeons?'

'Nobody likes pigeons, 'arold. They're just there. These are highly-trained homing pigeons. I thought our Edith could use them to send her letters, save money on stamps.'

'So, they're trained to deliver letters then?'

'Gawky says they can do anything they set their minds to.'

'And how did he come by these pigeons?'

'He says he picked them up here and there. Can you think of all the cash we'd save? You should think about getting some for Doris.'

'The day our budgie got loose was one of the best of our Doris's life. I don't think she'd be too happy about a lounge full of lice-infested pigeons.'

'They wouldn't be in the lounge, 'arold.'

'No?'

Alf shook his head, every inch a toddler outsmarting his parents. He said, 'You keep them in a loft.'

I didn't stick around for lunch with Alf. He wanted to get home in case there'd been any news about his newfound feathered friends.

Things didn't get much better when I arrived home. Violet Grey were waiting on the doorstep, looking particularly sallow in her mauve raincoat.

She didn't give me any time to greet her, saying, 'We must make haste indoors, Mr Copeland. I have a matter of great importance to discuss.'

I said to her, I said, 'Is this about the WI?'

'If this was about the WI, do you truly believe I'd come to you? I don't wish to besmirch your character, but you're as much use to the reformation of the WI as celery at a dinner party, and you have simply no idea as to the politics of jam competitions.'

I didn't bother telling her that our Doris has taught me well when it comes to the inner machinations of the Partridge Mews Women's Institute. Nor did I want to put my foot in it for our Doris's sake. I didn't know what she'd told the ladies about me, so I kept quiet and let Violet Grey into the house.

We went through to the kitchen and like every good host, I set about making a brew.

'There's no time for all that,' Violet snapped.

'There's nothing urgent enough to prevent a cup of tea. If you're feeling especially frantic, please help yourself to a custard cream.' I wouldn't ordinarily talk as though our Doris had her hand up my backside, but I wasn't giving Violet Grey the opportunity to leave me wrong-footed.

Violet plonked herself down at the table like a collapsing accordion. 'I'm sorry to inform you that Mrs Copeland has been spotted entering a high street bargain store.'

Violet delivered this news all solemn, as though she were telling me there'd been a freak accident and our Doris had been mown down by an ice cream man.

I said to her, I said, 'And?'

'She was seen purchasing off-brand denture adhesive.'

'Are you talking about my Fixadent?'

There were this faint glimmer of shock in Violet's eyes. The little wrinkles around her lips puckered, making her look every inch the mouldy grape. She was as outraged as Edith Evans as she said, 'Do you mean to tell me that this is a regular purchase?'

'Well, I need to regularly adhere my dentures. Otherwise, I end up looking like Wee Jimmy Krankie.'

'This is certainly news to me. Are you struggling for money?'

'And what business would that be of yours?'

She thought this over. 'You're right. Pardon me for my veritable misstep. Please know that it comes from a place of concern.'

I brought two mugs of tea to the table and said, 'That's all well and good, but why should my Fixadent cause any worry?'

'It's not the adhesive itself, but the store in which it was purchased. It simply isn't proper for an esteemed member of the community to frequent such an outlet.'

'Why does it bother you where we spend our money?'

'I have a friendship with Mrs Copeland. I am not the type of person to associate with those who purchase goods from bargain supermarkets.'

'Hang on a moment,' I said. 'One of your acquaintances must have seen our Doris go inside the shop and purchase the Fixadent, so does this mean you don't mind the association if it proves beneficial to you?'

Violet couldn't meet my eyes, like a suspect confronted on a police drama. She'd have probably found it easier to confess to murder. 'I didn't word that correctly.'

I said to her, I said, 'You forget that I know all you're about, Violet. You're trying to claim leadership of the WI before it's restarted. I suppose you've little else left after your failed marriage. We don't even know if our Doris wants to be part of the new group, so why don't you hold off dragging her name through the mud?'

'I can assure you that was never my intention.'

'Good, because she took the WI off you once. She could do it again without so much as blinking.'

'I seceded leadership of the WI to her. You were there.'

'Or was that always part of our Doris's plan and you went right along with it?' I slurped my tea, scalding my tongue, but it felt like the perfect way to punctuate my sentence. I wasn't about to let Violet Grey get back to her old tricks, not without our Doris there to defend herself.

Violet said, 'I'll leave the tea if you don't mind, Mr

Copeland. I did intimate that I didn't have the time to drink it. I have a pressing engagement to which I must attend.'

I thought I'd go in for a bit more of Doris language. I sounded like I'd swallowed a greengage whole as I said, 'I do apologise, Violet. I hope it had nothing to do with anything I said. Most spouses endeavour to look out for one another. I appreciate that your history with Doug means that you wouldn't know much on that front.'

She left and I heaved a breath that deep I'd have worried an asthmatic.

Our Doris is usually careful when it comes to buying my Fixadent – she has Erin or our Angela pick it up. Besides, I didn't need any more. I'd only just opened a new tube. Whoever our Doris was buying cut-price denture adhesive for, it wasn't me.

I wasn't about to let on to Violet Grey, though.

If I've learned anything from our Doris in fifty-six years, it's that we have to maintain a united front in the face of adversity.

I got straight on the phone to Alf. I said to him, I said, 'I've just had Violet Grey 'round.'

'And she told you that Doris has been caught buying Fixadent in the cheap shop. Edith told me.'

'How did she know?'

'They wire women differently in Partridge Mews, 'arold. She probably got an alert on her mobile. "Mrs Doris Copeland lowers herself for her husband."'

'That's just the thing, she wasn't buying it for me.'

'You're not going on with that affair rubbish again, are you?'

I said to him, I said, 'I'll take a different line of enquiry then. Who in this town has dentures?'

'You're serious, aren't you?'

'I think if we find a person who has dentures, who our Doris would want to keep away from me, then we'll know what's going on.'

'There's a lot of folk with dentures, 'arold, especially at our age. It's an occupational hazard after seventy-two, is dentures.'

'You don't have them.'

'I know,' he said, 'but I've had a lot of bread stuck to the roof of my mouth. I can empathise.'

'Just ask around, will you? See if Edith knows anything.'

'You're really worried about this, aren't you?'

'She's been that secretive, she could come home and say she's the next James Bond and I wouldn't be surprised.'

'Why don't you ask Mrs Patel what direction Doris went in after the shops?'

'It was never Edna Patel who dobbed our Doris in?'

'It was.'

'Violet never let on.' She clearly wanted to protect her source.

Alf was keen to get me off the line in case Gawky Cavendish rang, so I put the phone down, feeling as deflated as Ironside with a slow puncture.

Even though Alf suggested visiting Mrs Patel, I had ideas of my own. I left the house and decided to pay a visit to Mrs Cribbins. I went to her because I knew I'd have no luck with Mrs Patel; she's too much of a busybody – I'd only have to say 'good morning' to her and she'd be telling folk my marriage were in tatters. It's because she has too much time on her hands: she's retired, her kids absconded years back and her Amit spends all his days on the golf course.

Our Doris might call Mrs Cribbins a gossip, but she's nothing compared to Mrs Edna Patel. No, if anyone had answers, it would be her.

She answered the door with all the cowardice of a mole leaving its hill. Despite it being mid-morning, she squinted as though the sun had chosen to blind her specifically. She looked me up and down but didn't say anything. I were a bit disturbed, if I'm honest – there's something relaxing about a welcome. It lets you know that you're…well, welcome.

She said, 'Are the phone lines down, Mr Copeland?'

'I don't think so.'

'That is reassuring. I worried I might have missed the phone call in which you alerted me of your intention to visit.'

'Is it a bad time, Norma?'

'It's common courtesy to ring ahead and let the host know if you plan on popping over. I do believe we discussed this upon your return from the cruise.'

'Did we?'

She looked at me like a diminutive physician, trying to work out whether there were anything medically wrong with me or if I was just being obstreperous. She said, 'You've been married to Mrs Copeland for nearly sixty years. Have you learned nothing of social etiquette?'

I gulped. Fact was, she'd made me feel a shame I hadn't felt since my Mum found my collection of exotic postcards. They can do that, can old women. Even though I'm seventy-six years old myself, being chastised by a woman old enough to remember Mrs Dale's Diary makes me feel like a schoolboy caught with his hands in his pockets.

I said to her, I said, 'It's because of our Doris that I'm here.'

'Is this about Buckingham Palace?'

'No. Our Doris has been caught buying off-brand denture adhesive from Daily Bargains.'

Mrs Cribbins tutted and said, 'I told her she needed to be more careful, but did she listen to me? Did she heck. No, I'm just the former secretary of a disassembled WI.'

'You knew she shopped there?'

'We all do, but we have our ways of remaining inconspicuous. I have a lilac headscarf and a pair of tinted glasses. Not quite Diana Rigg, but close enough.'

'A veritable master of disguise, Mrs Cribbins. I can just see you being Partridge Mews' answer to Emma Peel.'

She gave me something of a look and said, 'Anyway, I saw Mrs Copeland last week getting on the bus, so I went over for a quiet word. There are a few things to discuss if she's serious about reforming the WI. I'm talking about membership fees, the Cheshire Show, this anniversary trip to Buckingham Palace. Well, when I mentioned Daily Bargains, she went off like a bottle of pop. She might be suffering, Mr Copeland, but that's no excuse to talk to me the way that she did. If I didn't know her already, I could have been hurt.'

'What do you mean "suffering"?'

'Is she not? I just assumed with her getting the bus to the hospital, something might be amiss. I was going to telephone later in the week to check on her.'

I had no words.

My head felt like someone had just crushed it between two paving stones and used my brain as cement. I were numb. A cold draught spilled from my scalp to my stomach. I said to Mrs Cribbins, I said, 'I must be going. Sorry to disturb you.'

She looked at me agog, rolled her eyes and disappeared back inside.

Meanwhile, I staggered down the garden path, grateful that I'd driven because I couldn't face walking – not past people. I couldn't breathe proper.

Our Doris was at the hospital. She'd been there all that time and I'd been none the wiser. It must've been serious and yet she'd kept it to herself; I'd no idea why.

I sat in the driver's seat, staring at my hands on the steering wheel, at my wedding ring. I'd said to our Doris that I didn't want it – they weren't for men, wedding rings. Not in our day. And she gave me this look – not quite *the* Look, but close enough – and she said to me, she said, 'A wedding ring is a physical representation of our commitment to one another. It signifies that our love has no end. Your refusal to wear one tells me that you see an end to our love. If that's the case, 'arold Copeland, tell me now. My Aunty Dru is coming up from Cockermouth and I don't want her forking out for a coach only to witness the beginning of a doomed courtship.'

It's been fifty-six years and I've only taken the ring off when I've been in for operations.

With our vows in my mind, I set off for the hospital.

Once again, there was a palaver with parking. Disabled badge holders get free parking but have to present their badge at the reception desk. It's not to be sniffed at, free parking, especially after the recent price hike, but I'd rather have a fully-functioning knee as opposed to one that feels like I've constantly got a rat gnawing at my patella.

After spending the best part of twenty minutes driving around the blithering car park in search of a space – all the while wondering just what illness my wife was laid up with – I got to the reception desk only to be faced with some sort of cross between a rhinoceros and a bodybuilder, looking at me as though I were a pile of freshly sown manure.

She said, 'I don't know what you expect me to do with this.'

Lord forbid that a receptionist should have manners in this day and age. I said to her, I said, 'Neither do I, but the sign outside says I have to present my disabled badge for free parking.'

'Does it?'

'It does,' I said.

She scrutinised my disabled badge – even got a magnifying glass out of a drawer to properly look at my photo. They should get her manning passport control; she'd never let anybody in. Eventually, she looked me up and down and said, 'Is this a recent photograph, Mr Copeland?'

'It's probably been about two years.'

She nodded. 'I thought as much. You've developed a few more wrinkles if you don't mind my saying. You're looking paler. Been ill recently?'

'If I had been, you'd probably have seen a lot more of me, don't you think?'

'That's a fair point. It's probably just that you're reaching the latter stages of life. Nothing to fear, death is perfectly natural. I'd recommend getting the coffin sorted now, you don't want to be buried in low quality wood. Imagine the splinters.'

'If I'm dead, it hardly matters, does it?'

She shrugged. 'It depends on what you believe. If you're one of them folk who's in for a bit of reincarnation, I'd say you'll be fine, but what if there's an afterlife and you're about to spend eternity pulling wood out of every orifice?'

I said to her, I said, 'I appreciate the thought, but I just want to find my wife.'

Her eyes brightened at this and she threw herself at her computer. 'All right, Mr Copeland, we'll just have to sort out the disabled badge. If you give me your registration, I can add it to the system and you'll be able to head straight to the wards without having to go through all this rigmarole next time.'

'Do you get much work on this desk?'

She whizzed through a few keys and handed me my badge back. 'There's not much to be going on with. Sure, I get to do the switchboard, but even that's gone south since everyone started video calls in the wards. I can think of nothing worse, being stuck sharing a room with a load of ill folk while getting to see all your family and friends at home, but that's just me, I've always been a pragmatist.'

My jaw were clenched as I asked, 'Can you tell me what ward Mrs Doris Copeland is on, please?' I were tense, scratching at the edge of my badge, my fingertips as white as extra-strong mints.

After a few mouse clicks and keyboard clatters, the receptionist said, 'I'm afraid I've no record of that name here. Was she admitted today?'

'She might not have been admitted at all. I just know she's here.'

The receptionist looked befuddled. She bit the tip of her tongue and tapped her fingernails on the desk. 'Did she come through A&E?'

'I've no idea.' I was about to give it up as a bad job, but then I remembered something about our Doris – she's one for subterfuge. Sure, she'd been caught shopping at the bargain shop, but that took a few years. I said to the receptionist, I said, 'Could you try Thistlethwaite?'

Another round of clicks and the receptionist had her eureka moment. She said, 'Ward Seven,' and I beggared off down the corridor.

I didn't run. After all the business on the cruise with our Theo having us running up and down everywhere for what he called daily exercise and what I called torture, I've steered clear of the enterprise. There's all these old fellas holding onto their youth, wanting to run half-marathons and emphasise that they haven't lost it, and I'm more than content to say that I never had it, never wanted it and that I've kept perfectly fit gardening.

One of the worst things about getting old is visiting hospitals. There's never a moment that you're not fearing for your life – even if you're not the one on the stretcher, an inner hypochondriac appears and starts taunting you, telling you that a specialist is going to come along and ask all these questions about your health, and before you know it, you'll be getting poked and prodded and scanned before inevitably being tossed in the mortuary as a precaution.

Then there's the scent of hospitals; it stinks to high heavens of disinfectant, so much so that it burns the nostrils of anyone unfortunate enough to breathe in. They expect it to make us feel at ease, peaceful in the knowledge that even with all the ill folk, it's still a pillar of cleanliness. I've seen enough Silent Witness; I know they're just trying to cover something up.

Death follows everyone down a hospital corridor, and you won't convince me otherwise.

I reached Ward Seven and stopped still for a moment. It was the cardiac ward.

Our Doris had never mentioned a problem with her heart before, hadn't looked in any sort of pain or discomfort, but then I'm not the best person to observe these things – she dyed her hair red in nineteen-sixty-three, and I didn't notice until sixty-five when we went to see Cilla Black at the Liverpool Empire.

I traipsed down another corridor and turned right. I don't wonder that folk had heart trouble on that ward with the amount of disinfectant they must have been inhaling – the stench was enough to make your eyes water.

The linoleum shone beneath halogen lights so that everywhere I looked was blinding. All I knew was that there were two medical bays on the ward filled with patients attached to an assortment of wires and machines that beeped incessantly – it were like a scene out of Doctor Who and I were about to see all these poor folk transformed into Cybermen. I don't know if our Doris could cope as a robot; she's never been a fan of stainless steel.

I collared a nurse and they led me in the right direction. Slowly and with great trepidation, I followed them towards the second medical bay.

The nurse went behind a set of blue curtains and moments later, the two of them crept out together.

Our Doris looked the picture of health in her tweed two-piece suit from Basler. She'd gone in for pink and cream, with a pair of shoes so sensible she'd paid extra for them. Naturally, she was all sweetness and light to the nurse, but as soon as they'd gone on their way, our Doris exclaimed, she positively growled, 'Did you follow me, 'arold Copeland?'

I tell you, her eyes looked fit to shoot flames in my direction.

I stammered, as nervous as Oliver Twist after another bowl of vittles, and said to her, I said, 'I were worried.'

And the Look changed, transformed from anger into this haughty, inquisitive gaze. She were hawk-like, with her nose in the air and eyebrows raised; a five-foot two generalissimo.

Her lips had been pursed the entire time. She said to me, she said, 'Can you tell me what caused you to worry?'

I couldn't answer, so our Doris barrelled forward, saying, 'Because my behaviour has been perfectly in keeping with that of a middle-class housewife from Partridge Mews with a Magnet kitchen and aspirations for a conservatory.'

I was shrinking in on myself worse than a slug in a salt bath. My mouth was dry, and I was still no closer to finding out who was behind the bed curtains.

I said to her, I said, 'You've not been home and you've been seen buying Fixadent from the discount shop.'

Our Doris's shoulder pads flew that high they were practically pillows for her ears. I hadn't seen her so angry since Morris Bellweather blew his nose during All Things Bright and Beautiful. He had to go Methodist after that.

She said to me, her face as red as a geranium, she said, 'Now we're getting to the bare bones of the matter. You don't trust me. After fifty-six years of marriage and several trips to Llandudno, for which I won't be blamed, you still don't trust that I could possibly leave the marital home without cavorting with every Tom, Dick and Harry on my way into town.'

I gulped. My shoulders hunched as a nurse approached. She was clearly accustomed to our Doris's outbursts because she said, 'Mrs Copeland, I've told you about shouting on the ward. It simply won't be tolerated.'

'And I've told you that if you don't want me to shout on the ward then you shouldn't admit such disagreeable patients.'

'This is a cardiac ward.'

'Then I know I'm in the right place if I need my blood pressure checked. Now, why don't you return to your desk, and I'll explain to my husband why I can't comprehend how he doesn't trust me after we just spent three months in confined quarters on a premier ocean cruise?'

I could tell the nurse wished I'd pushed our Doris overboard. She said, 'Well, perhaps you could take this conversation to the canteen? Or the day room. It's usually only for patients, but I'm sure I could make an exception.'

Our Doris exhaled. It was such an exhale that the patients were probably jealous of her breathing skills. She turned to face the nurse head on and said to her, she said, 'How would you feel if your husband stalked your every movement just because he couldn't trust you? Despite proclaiming differently in front of an audience of your friends and family nearly six decades ago?'

'I'm married to a woman.'

Our Doris nodded. 'My apologies, I should have said spouse. You'll never have my problem then. Women are much more trusting than men. Men judge everyone else by their own behaviour.' She fired another look in my direction, a look that can only be described as withering.

I could tell the nurse were softening towards our Doris. She looked between the two of us before saying, 'I think I'll leave you to it, but please try and keep it down.'

'Of course, dear. I'd never want to put a stranger's health in jeopardy.'

And I believe that our Doris would have calmed down as well, if it weren't for who appeared at the door in that moment. Janice Dooley of Little Street.

The colour rose in our Doris's cheeks again. She and Janice walked towards one another filled with the ire of a thousand Mrs Whitehouses.

The nurse stopped in her tracks, pretending to read the ECG results of a half-dead pensioner. She might not have liked shouting on the ward, but even she knew when we were in for a show.

Janice said to our Doris, 'I thought I could hear you, Doris. I was just down the corridor, and I says to Doug, I says, "It sounds like a whale giving birth down there. It must be Mrs Copeland."'

Our Doris said, she said, 'I forgot how witty you could be, Janice. I thought you'd had it all knocked out of you. What could you possibly be doing here? From the looks of you, you'd be better laid out in the chapel of rest.'

'Doug has a check-up for his angina.'

'Well, I knew it couldn't be you. You got rid of your heart in nineteen-fifty-six, just so Jack Smethwick would have farther to go.'

And that was another round of nightmares for me. I know our Doris can be offensive, but sometimes the images she creates are enough to leave me reaching for the Alka-Seltzer.

Then this voice called out from behind the curtains, a woman. She said, practically yelling, 'Open the curtains and let me get a look at her, our Doris.'

I hadn't heard that voice in nearly thirty years.

Since I was closest, I pulled back the curtains. She lay in that hospital bed looking all bedraggled. Our Doris's sister. Bianca Thistlethwaite has always been a big girl – stocky, muscular, a perpetual hockey player – and all I could think of when I looked at her was a submarine beneath a tea cosy.

''ow 'at, 'arold? Long time, no see.'

'What are you doing here?'

She scratched her head, dandruff flaking from her auburn hair onto her shoulders. 'What am I doing here? Doris, can you remember what I'm doing here? Ah, that's it. I'm dying, 'arold.'

'Dying?'

'Let's talk about this later, once I've had a gander at that old crow.' She glowered. 'How's the eye, Janice?'

It was the first time I'd ever seen Janice shrink away. She said to Bianca, 'It's all right, thanks, how are you doing?'

'It's a shame I had that heart attack, don't you think?'

Janice nodded. 'A right shame, Bianca, yeah.'

'Because then I could have laid you out good and proper.' Bianca chortled, as mischievous as a child pulling the wings off a moth. Her laughter descended into a coughing fit that sounded like a rattling, old motor.

I was clearly being left out of something. Janice couldn't look at our Doris, who displayed confidence I hadn't seen since the firework burnt her hair off.

I said to them, I said, 'Just what's going on here? What am I missing?'

Bianca said, 'Have you not told him, our Doris? Well, no wonder the lad's been feeling left out.' She looked my way. 'I'm the one who battered Janice.'

'You?' I couldn't help exclaiming, as surprised as Cilla Black.

She fell into a fit of laughter and coughing again. 'I wish I had a camera. You should see your face. That's made my day, that has. Reminds me of when you caught me and Barbara Blakeman.'

'You never said anything about Barbara Blakeman,' our Doris said to me.

I shrugged. 'I thought that was Bianca's business to tell you.'

I still shudder at the memory. I never looked at taramasalata the same after that.

'I thought that Doug beat her up. The police said it was a domestic disturbance.'

'It was!' Janice said. She sounded tremulous, and that's not a word I use often. 'She turned up at the house out of the blue, said she just wanted to chat.'

'I did.' Bianca had a grin on her face, several miles wide. She said, 'You see, 'arold, I decided that if I'm going to cark it, I don't want to leave any unfinished business. Suppose I should come back as a ghost? I've done an all right job of contacting folk, handed out a fair bit of justice. That shocked Marcus Fisher did that, him being a member of the clergy and all.'

'What unfinished business did you have with Janice?'

Bianca looked at our Doris, all aghast. 'You've really kept our 'arold in the dark, haven't you, duck?'

'Don't call me duck, Bianca. I've always hated being called duck.'

'Only because you think it's common.'

'It *is* common.'

'You never stopped Dad calling you duck.'

And Janice felt the need to pipe up here, saying, she said, 'Probably best not to mention your dad, Bianca. You know how it gets to Doris.'

Our Doris turned on Janice and said to her, she said, 'You might think you're safe because my sister is in a hospital bed, but I've already knocked seven bells out of you once, Janice Dooley, and I won't hesitate to do it again.'

Janice swallowed hard and became quite interested in the pattern on the ceiling tiles.

The nurse stepped in here, saying, she said, 'Mrs Copeland, I can't allow you to make threats on the ward.'

'Well, where can I go to make threats?'

Once again, Bianca guffawed. I'd forgotten what a force the two of them could be – they certainly must have been giving the hospital a fair run for their money.

The nurse hid a smirk and said to Janice, she said, 'Perhaps it would be best if you left. It seems like you only came to cause trouble.'

Janice pointed at our Doris. 'She just threatened me.'

'Yes, she did. That's who Mrs Copeland is.'

'You're a nurse!'

'I am. Now please beggar off because I don't need any more patients.' And with that, she led Janice from the ward.

I said to our Doris, I said, 'I think it's time I heard about this unfinished business.'

'Take him to the canteen,' Bianca said. 'After all that, I could do with a rest.'

'And I could do with a cuppa,' I said.

The hospital canteen smelled like cabbage. I don't know how, since they only sold coffee, sandwiches and cake, but that's hospital canteens for you; you think you're eating in a purpose-built eatery when in fact you're sipping your cappuccino in a repurposed morgue.

I approached the till, joining a queue of relatives, pregnant women and an unfortunate man who'd got his hand stuck in an empty Dolmio jar.

After about a quarter of an hour, in which jar-man performed a great balancing act with a hot chocolate and an apple strudel, I reached the counter and ordered two lattes.

It took a while for the volunteer in charge to figure out how to use the coffee machine. I'm pretty sure she went to school with my mother. She stood there in her tabard, clearly shaken by such a request.

Eventually, she gave me our drinks and I wandered back to our Doris. She'd picked the table closest to the door and sat so as she could see the entire canteen. She likes to people watch, does our Doris – she's a bit like

Miss Marple with her interest in human behaviour. She says you can tell a lot from the way a person eats a croissant.

When we'd been settled for a few minutes, I said to her, I said, 'Why did you keep this secret?'

She gave me the Look and said to me, she said, 'There's no need to confront me in a hospital canteen like that, our 'arold. This isn't an episode of Holby City. I didn't tell you about Bianca because I had other things on my mind. You heard her mention her impending demise, I expect?'

'All the more reason for you to tell me. That's a lot to try and handle on your own, our Doris.'

'I appreciate the concern, but I'm more than capable of sitting at my sister's bedside.'

'What about her children?'

'Graham is in Scarborough working on the fairground and Ruth has just set off on a three-month expedition on the Orkney Isles to find herself.'

'You told them about Bianca, though?'

'Graham, yes. I spoke to Ruth's neighbour. They weren't too happy about being left to care for a thirty-seven-year-old parrot with an addiction to celery.'

'Does Mavis know?'

'I'm not about to bother Mavis with all this. She has enough on her plate.'

I didn't know what to say to that. I don't pay much attention to what's happening in Mavis's life. It's not that our Doris doesn't tell me, I just don't listen. Mavis and I are civil because of our shared connection, but I'd have been quite content to bury her beneath the patio.

Eventually, I said to our Doris, 'You were seen buying Fixadent from Daily Bargains.'

'I should think so. This town is practically rife with

169

CCTV cameras. I'd say it's Orwellian, but that would suggest the council knows something about literature.'

I'll give it to our Doris. She might have been upset about her sister, but she still had that mischievous glint in her eyes that came from insulting the Partridge Mews Town Council.

'Aren't you worried what folk'll think, seeing you in the bargain shop?'

'If I thought it worth worrying about, our 'arold, I would, but when one is so assured of their social position, one can't worry about being seen in a shop that's commonly associated with the underclasses.'

I were agog. My mouth went haywire. My tongue didn't know what it were doing. I wanted to drink while simultaneously wanting to question our Doris. I stammered, saying to her, I said, 'Have you had an epiphany, our Doris?'

She gave me the Look, with a side of her smile, and said, 'There's not much else to do in a hospital waiting room.'

I never thought I'd see the day when our Doris admitted to shopping at Daily Bargains. It's always been an incognito operation, something she did because it's the only place they sell adhesive strong enough to keep my dentures intact. I once ruined a dinner party when my teeth fell into a tureen of mulligatawny soup.

I was serving at the time.

Next day, we discovered Fixadent and properly stuck my teeth in place. It became something of a Copeland family secret – it's probably on par with that story about my Uncle Jebediah and the parson's daughter.

And all of a sudden, our Doris was acting like there was no shame in shopping at Daily Bargains.

Until Doug Grey went and spoiled it all with a letter to the Gazette.

I'd just sat down at the kitchen table for my boiled egg and soldiers when our Doris stormed in looking as furious as Glenn Close after the Dalmatians.

Our Doris held the newspaper tight enough to make kindling in her hands. Her eyebrows had flown over her forehead and into her scalp, her eyes were that wide, and she said to me, she said, 'If they ever legalise murder, I am going straight after Doug Grey. I'll tear him limb from limb and sell him to Pedigree Chum. If he's even good enough for dog food, the slimy, cretinous letch.

'I don't know what these women see in him. He has all the appeal of a decomposing rat.'

Her face was purple as she slammed the Gazette on the table. She'd opened it at the letters page – I always hoped that with the advent of sex hotlines and social media, the letters page in local newspapers would cease to exist. Instead, it's become pettier and more gossip-filled than a school canteen; last week, a woman wrote in because her friend borrowed some Tupperware and returned it with 'stains of indeterminate origin, but most likely chicken tikka masala'.

It's always a wonder that there can be so many tragedies occurring in the world and people still get upset over yellowed plastic.

It beggars belief.

While our Doris poured herself a mug of coffee, I read Doug Grey's letter. He'd expressed concern that Mrs Doris Copeland of Shakespeare Avenue had been seen shopping at Daily Bargains. He mentioned our cruise, citing us as an example of people trying to live beyond their means in a society that tells them they must have everything in order to live a full and happy life.

Doug then went on to question if me and Doris weren't destitute, surviving in Shakespeare Avenue by the skin of our teeth – and dentures – and sponging off our daughter.

Then, to make everything worse, to add all the insults to all the injuries, he mentioned the redevelopment.

Doug claimed that those who used Daily Bargains were clearly struggling for money and might find it difficult to get on the property ladder. Which is where his redevelopment came in. Although he understood the controversy with building on green-belt land, twenty percent of the homes would be affordable, helping those who use bargain stores to make something of themselves.

The new-builds are right on the far-side of the field, beside a flood plain and a four-hundred-year-old tree, but that's all a person's worth if they buy cut-price denture adhesive from Daily Bargains. This was worse than when Sally Twemlow accused our Doris's egg mayonnaise of being the source of national salmonella fears. It were even worse than when our Doris left a child on a school coach in two-thousand-and-eight and nearly got arrested for trafficking.

I said to her, I yelled, 'What does he think he's playing at?'

Our Doris choked back her coffee like a lad trying to prove himself with a yard of ale. She slammed her mug on the counter and said to me, she said, 'Doug Grey is doing something he's always done, our 'arold. He's underestimating how much a woman can achieve.'

'He was married to Violet for fifty-odd years.'

'That's as may be, but she never had enough meat on her bones to be truly lethal. I'm a size fourteen, seventy-four-year-old woman from Partridge Mews. I've a certificate from secretarial college and a recipe for malt loaf that will send Doug packing.'

'You'll be replying, then?'

'Of course. I fought Janice Dooley of Little Street in a graveyard. They should know that if they sling mud my way, I'll throw headstones.'

Our Doris's rebuttal appeared in the Partridge Mews Gazette:

To the editor,

I write with reference to Mr Douglas Grey's letter featured in a recent edition of your once-esteemed newspaper.

In his correspondence, Mr Grey adopts the role of town gossip and chooses to question the social status of someone who takes their custom to our local discount store, Daily Bargains. I should think that at Mr Grey's late stage in life, he would have better things to concern himself with than how his acquaintances spend their money, but perhaps he has had good news concerning his angina. I, myself, was shocked to learn of Mr Grey's diagnosis, for I believed that one required a heart to be faced with such an affliction.

Perhaps Mr Grey thinks himself likely to be named a beneficiary in my will. If that is the case, he can be safe in the knowledge that in the unlikely event that I happen to leave this mortal coil before him – something that isn't likely, considering his propensity for steak pies – I've already portioned out my estate and am quite proud to say that he'll receive nothing. Nor was he ever in my thoughts when I penned my last will and testament.

Mr Grey drew attention to a recent cruise I embarked upon with my husband, suggesting that we're living beyond our means. I find it rather tasteless that he chose to discuss my financial situation in a public forum, rather than ask me his questions directly. However, Mr Grey is renowned for being tasteless – if we choose to cast aspersions, then let's not forget that he's currently in a relationship with Ms Janice Dooley of Little Street. The same Ms Dooley he cavorted with behind his wife's back for nearly forty years.

If I must discuss my finances publicly then your readers should take note: my husband and I worked for everything we have. We've saved our entire lives and dipped into said savings to realise a lifelong dream of travelling the world. Should anyone require financial advice then they should contact me before Mr Grey – this gentleman has seen the liquidation of at least four businesses in the last twenty years alone. The idea that certain individuals trust his promises of affordable housing baffles me, but I must admit that I'm pleased to hear there are still some daydreamers in the world.

The fact of the matter remains that Mr Grey wrote his letter in the hopes of besmirching my name – I'm but one of the many people who have protested his plans for Barraclough's Field – and he did so while I was absent, caring for my terminally-ill sister. It's for my sister that I visited Daily Bargains in the first place; she's partial to their denture adhesive.

I understand that some of your readers will also frequent the aforementioned discount store and I want them to know that there is no shame in being frugal. We live in uncertain times; finances might not be as secure as they once were, and certain shops make it easier to purchase essential items. I admit that in the past I've not had the best opinion of those who shop in such places; however, I am lucky enough to have had conversations with those of a less advantageous economic background than myself and have grown to recognise the importance of Daily Bargains in the growing accessibility of goods.

In future, I suggest that should Mr Grey wish to discuss finances, he visits a bank, where they can hopefully educate him in how to save money, stay out of business that does not concern him and ultimately lead a rich, fulfilling life.

Yours faithfully,

Mrs Doris Copeland, Shakespeare Avenue.

I closed the newspaper and said to her, I said, 'That's brilliant, our Doris.'

She smiled and said to me, she said, 'This is just the first step in my plan, our 'arold. I have dallied for too long; it is time to rebuild the Partridge Mews Women's Institute.'

Our Doris says that Bianca has to come and live with us.

She told me last week when I'd got back from the allotment – things are drawing to a close for winter, but I wanted to check on my geraniums and Art Mason is accepting Christmas orders for vegetables. I hadn't even had chance to remove my boots. My key was barely in the lock when the door swung open and our Doris stood there as impassive as Jabba the Hut in a tunnel.

I said to our Doris, I said, 'What do you mean, she has to live with us?'

'The specialist has said that our Bianca is allowed to leave the hospital.'

'And they specified she has to live with us?'

She seemed shifty, like when she's trying to avoid telling me the price of a pair of new plimsolls. She started checking her hair in the hall mirror and said, 'Not exactly, but our house is clearly the most suitable place for her.'

'She already has a house of her own.' I sat down on the front step and set about removing my boots.

'That may be, but–'

'I bet I can guess what you're going to say,' I said.

She gave me the Look and said, 'I'll have no gambling under my roof, our 'arold.'

'Your Bianca lives in an area you're not too fond of and you don't want to be traipsing back and forth every day to somewhere you associate with the social underclass.'

'I'd have perhaps employed more brevity, but it seems you've got the measure of things.'

'Despite everything going on with Daily Bargains, you're still a snob at heart,' I said. 'So, where's she living these days?'

Our Doris looked as though she'd eaten a funny vol-au-vent. Her face were like a repeat of Christmas Eve nineteen-eighty-two after the prawn starter. She swallowed hard and said to me, she said, 'Wren's Lea.'

I gave up the struggle with a bootlace and looked back to meet our Doris's gaze. She were a bit worrisome, but I wasn't about to rise to it; she's a very good actress when she wants to be is our Doris, and I've seen that worrisome gaze employed too many times with the Partridge Mews Amateur Dramatics Society. I asked, 'Wren's Lea? She'll have kept in touch with Mavis, then?'

Our Doris shook her head. 'She's been there since summer.'

'Didn't she want us to know she was here?' I used my right boot to kick my left off. It went flying down the drive like a goose after a toddler. I hopped down the cold paving after it – that'd definitely put me in our Doris's bad books, that would, kicking off my boot like a teenage boy with sinful intentions.

Once I were properly situated back on the front step, our Doris said to me, she said, 'Apparently, she tried to get in touch, but we were otherwise occupied.'

179

'We were on a cruise. Even then, we've been back three months.' I got my other boot off and stood up, making to step around our Doris. She wasn't for moving. My feet were freezing, but she wouldn't let me in. Our Doris wanted everyone to see how mournful she was looking – her at Number Forty-Two would probably be twitching the net curtains to figure out whether our Doris were giving me short shrift. Folk are always nosy when they think somebody else is getting an ear-bashing.

'None of that matters. The doctors want to discharge her, and I think she should come here.'

I saw a quick opening as our Doris leant against the doorframe, so I swept inside and said, 'I'm making a brew.'

Our Doris followed me into the kitchen.

I remained quiet while I made the drinks. It's a good way to get your head straight is making a cup of tea – watching the kettle boil can be hypnotic. If Paul McKenna got into making kettles, we'd all be non-smokers by elevenses.

I got the mugs out of the top cupboard; the plain blue ones our Doris reserves for guests she doesn't want to stick around. They might not be to her standard, but they're the biggest mugs we own and heavy topics require a lot of tea to aid digestion.

Once I'd sat down with our Doris, our teas, and a Wagon Wheel I'd found lurking, she said to me, she said, 'Do you dislike my sister?'

'Where do you get that idea from?

'You don't want her to come and live with us.'

I sliced the Wagon Wheel down the middle and gave half to our Doris – not something I'd ordinarily do, since I'm partial to a mid-morning sweet treat of marshmallow and biscuit encased in chocolate, but our Doris looked like she could do with cheering up and I've always found happiness in a biscuit tin.

I looked at our Doris with a gaze I hoped was conciliatory but could have come across as constipated – after seventy your face betrays you – and said to her, I said, 'I just think we're a bit old to be caring for your eighty-seven-year-old sister.'

Our Doris gave me the Look and said to me, she said, 'Of all the reasons you could have gone with, you chose our ages? I might be past seventy, but that doesn't mean I'm beyond capable of carrying a tea tray to the spare bedroom a few times a day.'

'I'm not saying you're incapable, our Doris, I just think that you'll struggle. You've got folk pestering you about the WI, there's something about Buckingham Palace I don't understand and then there's all this redevelopment business with Janice Dooley of Little Street.'

Our Doris sniffed. 'Thank you for reminding me of all my current engagements, our 'arold, but if I wanted a secretary, I'd hire someone who hasn't forgotten his wedding anniversary for thirty consecutive years.'

This had gone beyond the Look. Our Doris's eyes were as furious as a cat just awoken from its slumber – she were like that Maya in Coronation Street, all set to blow the place up.

I looked into my mug. I said to her, as though this were a hostage situation and I were hoping she'd make it a mercy killing, I said, 'I always get you a gift though, and I take you for dinner.'

'You and I both know that our Angela sorts everything in advance. Besides, this isn't about you being the world's most forgetful husband since Frank Spencer, this is about bringing my sister home to die.'

She stopped stock still.

That uncomfortable post-argument silence settled in the kitchen as our Doris clutched at the table edge. She had the grip of an eagle in its eyrie – the anger in her cheeks gave way as her skin paled; even beneath her foundation, I could tell she were paling.

'I'm sorry, our Doris.'

She nodded.

Her lower lip trembled, her chin were tightening up so much it looked like a golf ball.

As the tears started to trickle like rain through the gutters of her wrinkles, she said to me, she said, 'If you don't get over here and hug me, I won't be responsible for my actions.'

I practically launched myself to sit next to her. I wrapped her in my arms, and she pressed her face against my chest, trying to sob as gently as possible.

We stayed like that for a good half hour, saying nothing, neither of us knowing what to do next.

When I first met our Doris, I knew nothing about Bianca. Something had happened years before and our Doris had moved in with her aunty, uncle, and cousin. If anything, Mavis has been more of a sister to her than Bianca has ever been. A veritable minotaur of a woman, whenever I went to pick up our Doris, she'd be smoking her Silk Cut on the doorstep, ready with a new threat of what she'd do should I ever hurt her cousin. One week, she'd sell my carcass to the butcher and serve me as a special in her café; the next, she'd be for burying me beneath the new road. She's always had our Doris's best interests at heart, has Mavis.

But Bianca?

I first met Bianca the Wednesday before the wedding. She'd turned up at the Harrington with a load of bikers and got into a slanging match with Jill Hepworth about the price of a port and lemon. Things escalated, someone got hit with a barometer and the next thing we knew, the police were knocking on Aunty Phyllis's door.

Bianca always claimed that she was coming back to see her little sister wed, and we've always gone along with the story because it makes our Doris happy. I heard she were due to hitchhike down to Gloucestershire for a cheese festival, but the police told her not to skip town.

It didn't matter either way. When we arrived back from our honeymoon, Bianca was gone and our Doris set about choosing colours for the front bedroom.

Over the last fifty-six years, Bianca's visits have grown more sporadic. It started that we'd see her every three years. She'd come to town, stay with us, we'd have the regular chat about her maybe settling down – especially after her kids came along – and Bianca would say to us, she'd say, 'I move with the wind. I can't be confined by the societal machine, pressurised into a nuclear family by a government that searches for peace in nuclear bombs.'

We never let her smoke her special tobacco in the house, but I did wish she'd lend some to our Doris. It's not that I fancy drugging my wife, but she never stopped talking about new ways to revolutionise celery. I'll never forgive Rosemary Conley.

Even though Bianca hasn't played a major part in our Doris's life, she's still her sister. Rules don't apply when the relationship is sororal. Bianca can do what she likes; she set up a commune in the back garden, once. It was nineteen-seventy-six and there was a hose pipe ban, so our Doris didn't mind them sleeping beneath the stars if they cleaned up after themselves and used the lavatory at Number Forty-Two for all ablutions.

Bianca can do no wrong in our Doris's eyes.

Sometimes, I wish she showed such forgiveness to other people.

Our Doris had Erin over to discuss plans for a WI brunch. They were just getting onto the menu plans when there was a thud on the doormat.

I thanked the Lord for small mercies and went to fetch the Gazette. Doug Grey had been relatively quiet since our Doris's letter, so I was surprised to see a photograph of him on the front page. I was more surprised when I saw who was standing beside him.

What happened next was a mistake. I should have read the article, hidden it from our Doris and moved on, but outrage and general puzzlement got in the way.

I stormed into the kitchen and said to her, I said, 'So, Erin, you're working for the enemy?'

She looked like a rabbit in the shadow of a fox. Her eyes were as wide as flying saucers and I immediately regretted confronting her.

I handed the newspaper to our Doris.

She read the front page, fury rising to eliminate all thought as to whether beetroot was an acceptable replacement for bacon. Her lips pursed, her shoulders hunched, and she got that close to the paper she could near enough inhale the ink.

Then she took a deep breath and said to me, she said, 'I should have known how he'd spin things in the Gazette. They've really gone downhill since the advent of Instagram.'

'What're you talking about, our Doris? Erin is working for Doug Grey.' I were outraged – something warm surged through my veins like I'd just knocked back a double whisky.

Yet our Doris sat there like she had nothing to concern herself about. 'Give over, our 'arold. Although I've had fifty-six years to acclimatise, Erin hasn't yet had time to get used to your emotional outbursts.'

That put an abrupt end to the rant waiting to spout forth like an overfilled kettle. 'Did you know about this?'

'Of course, I knew about this. Who do you think told Erin to take the job in the first place?'

I looked to Erin and said, 'Our Doris has always been one for scheming, but what're you hoping to get out of this?'

Erin sat there, all set to shovel several garibaldis in her mouth to avoid having to speak. I'm always surprised at the levels she'll go to not have to share in any awkward conversation, but the fact she was considering gagging herself on a biscuit with the texture of sandpaper had me feeling ashamed; not to mention the fact that garibaldis look like the baker rolled crushed cockroaches into their dough. Our Doris stopped Erin's hand in its tracks and gave a delicate shake of her head. She said to her, she said, 'Those are just for show, dear. We'll treat ourselves to some more ideal refreshments in town.'

Erin simply nodded and averted her eyes, looking at her notes about the WI brunch.

'Why would Doug Grey give Erin a job? He knows that you two are friends.'

Then she decided to pipe up. I've no idea what spurred her on, but Erin said, 'That's precisely the point, Mr Copeland. He's too up his own nose. Mr Grey knows that to everyone else in Partridge Mews, it looks like I've betrayed Mrs Copeland by going to work for him, so he doesn't bother thinking that I'll report everything I find to her.'

Our Doris said, 'That's not strictly true. Doug will know that you're telling me all about his misdeeds, but he believes that there's no stopping him. That's why we must allow his behaviour to continue. It's through his arrogance that we'll put a stop to the redevelopment.'

'I suppose the money you'll have coming in will help as well?'

'One must never discuss finances at the breakfast table,' our Doris said. 'Especially with such paltry biscuits on display.' She eyed the garibaldis with disappointment.

I said to her, I said, 'You put them out.'

'That's as may be, our 'arold, but that's only because I believed I might receive a visit from Violet, and I had no intention of welcoming her with suitable confectionary. No, a garibaldi lets her know just where she stands.'

'And where's that?'

'About thirty miles south of the M6.'

'I've no idea why she came back,' Erin said.

'Apparently, she got fed up playing whist with her sister.'

I left them mulling over Violet Grey, the redevelopment and the most suitable sandwich for a WI brunch, then went into the lounge to read a Martina Cole.

Later that day, we went to meet Bianca's specialist to discuss the possibility of her returning home.

We met in Doctor Ezra's office – a porter wheeled Bianca in before us. He must've had the strength of Goliath, moving Bianca as though she were as light as a cream cracker. I tell you, it were like watching a bodybuilder push a transit van.

Some folk might class the office as spartan. There were nothing in the room to suggest that it ever got used, just a filing cabinet, a stretcher and a desk, upon which sat a shop-bought sandwich alongside a small bottle of Tropicana and a packet of McCoy's Ready Salted.

Doctor Ezra is in his mid-forties. If Annie Lennox swapped her microphone for a stethoscope, she'd be the spitting image of Doctor Ezra. He wore a dark red suit that our Doris would call burgundy and I'd leave on the hanger.

Back in my day, doctors never dressed fancy. Sure, they wore a suit, but it was usually brown corduroy. They were reliable for their fashion were doctors; even the young ones wore brown corduroy. Now they're free to wear whatever they like as long as it's somebody's definition of smart. I only hope the reason behind Ezra's suit was fashion and nothing to do with what the colour could hide.

He sat behind the desk, across from us, reading Bianca's notes. I've never seen a thicker folder of notes, bound with several elastic bands just to keep them all together. This were the Domesday Book of medical notes; a potted history of everything that had ever gone wrong with Bianca Thistlethwaite – including the mishap with a pipe-cleaner, Christmas nineteen-eighty-two.

After introducing himself and going through some details about Bianca's condition, Ezra said, 'Something I must emphasise is that today, we're discussing Bianca's end-of-life care.'

Bianca said, 'We've been through all of this, doctor. If I'm going to cark it, I'd rather cark it at home than in a hospital bed.'

Ezra nodded. 'I'm well aware of that. However, we do need to–'

'I'm not dying in here next to some poor sod with dementia. Now, I've got no problem with folk who're losing their memory. After sixty-four, most bikers have had it knocked out of them anyway. But can you imagine, lying there, waiting for the quiet touch of an angel to ease you away into whatever afterlife awaits, only for some poor so-and-so to whip his thing out and start windmilling it around like he's trying to curl a Cumberland sausage?'

Our Doris coughed and started rifling around in her handbag. She pulled out a paper bag and held it out towards Bianca. She said to her, she said, 'Have a cough drop, Bianca.'

'I don't want a cough drop.'

'You look like you need a cough drop.'

I said to her, I said, 'She says she doesn't want a cough drop, our Doris.'

She gave me the Look and said to me, she said, 'Don't you get involved.'

Bianca guffawed, throwing her head back and revealing just how well her cut-price denture adhesive worked. Her laughter descended into a raucous cough. She curled forwards, shoulders heaving beneath her tatty grey cardigan. Sitting up, she looked to the doctor and said, 'Our Doris doesn't like it when I talk about sex.'

'You weren't talking about sex,' our Doris said. She lowered her voice and added, 'Has someone done that to you?'

Bianca shrugged. 'It's one of the perils of being in a mixed ward.'

'What happened next?' Our Doris looked like a schoolgirl reading a particularly raunchy story in Bunty.

'I pressed my buzzer and a nurse came to collect the poor lad.' Bianca took a cough drop. She popped it in her mouth and said to our Doris, she said, 'If he was after getting amorous, he'd have been in for a disappointment. I haven't slept with a man since nineteen-ninety-three and even then, it was only out of a sense of obligation.'

'Obligation?' the doctor asked, clearly confused at the direction of our conversation.

'Front tyre came off my bike. He gave me a lift to the garage.'

Our Doris looked at her sister agog and said to her, she said, 'You could have just put some money towards his fuel.'

'There speaks the voice of the upper-classes. Some of us don't have cash we can just go throwing about whenever we end up in a sticky situation.'

Doctor Ezra decided to intervene here, saying, 'I don't wish to rush you along, but I do have other appointments to attend to.'

Our Doris looked to him and said, 'While I can only express gratitude at you for putting an end to that conversation, you should never rush someone, no matter the time constraints placed upon you by outside sources. We're here to discuss the end-of-life care necessary to make my sister comfortable during her final days upon this mortal coil. How do you expect it makes us feel when you don't have adequate time set aside in which to do so? Suppose I were to start crying? Would you have told me to take my tears elsewhere once thirty minutes had passed?'

Doctor Ezra gulped. 'I'm sorry, Mrs Copeland. That wasn't my intention.'

'Quite. What needs to be in place so that Bianca can return home?'

There, the tone of the conversation became more sombre, and we recognised the severity of the doctor's words. They talked about how Bianca's current living arrangements were unsustainable as she'd ideally always have someone with her. There was the mention of a care home, which our Doris threw out the window before Doctor Ezra could even finish his sentence. Honestly, I thought she were about to vaporise him with her nostrils, given how wide they flared.

Bianca would require someone to do most things for her – to take her to any appointments she had, to cook all her meals and to clean up after her. We could have done with borrowing Cinderella.

Our Doris threw the idea into the conversation. She hadn't mentioned anything to me beforehand. She said to Ezra, she said, 'Should it be all right with Bianca, then I'm quite content to move in with her and to see to her needs.'

Bianca looked at her sister, as dumbfounded as a swan faced with a pork pie. 'I can't have you hanging around the place, you'll cramp my style.'

'You haven't had style since nineteen-sixty-eight and even then, you stole it from Mary Tyler Moore.'

I didn't say anything. I wasn't about to question one of our Doris's ideas in public, not when she only had to nip down the corridor for a scalpel. Since she'd been visiting the hospital that much, I'd grown used to doing stuff on my own around the house; I'd even completed a jigsaw of a Robin Reliant. I said to Bianca, I said, 'Our Doris hasn't seen you for the best part of twenty years, Bianca. She might have a few funny ideas about artichokes, but she won't see you wrong.'

It were her turn to look shocked. The wrinkles around her eyes widened so that she looked less like a shrew and more like a lemur faced with its first papaya. She met Bianca's gaze and said to her, she said, 'Who would you rather, Bianca? Me, or some twenty-two-year-old who'll fly around that fast you won't notice you've been cared for?'

'I guess that settles it then,' Bianca said. 'Be prepared, our Doris, it's been nearly sixty years since we lived together. You've no idea what you're in for.'

After we'd finished at the hospital, our Doris had me drive over to Wren's Lea to get a better insight into her new living arrangements.

Bianca's bungalow is on Stoker Avenue. There's a row of them, red-bricked and solar-powered – kept by the council for all those over fifty-five or who are too doddery to be trusted with stairs.

A ramp led from a paved path to the front door, like our very own road to Hell.

I were filled with trepidation as we approached. Seeing the bungalows all lined up reminded me of my own mortality, as though I were about to enter the penultimate stop before the grave.

That's one of the worst things about getting older – the constant reminders that one day you'll stop.

Bianca's home didn't smell good. Someone had doused the place in Jeye's Fluid; the carpets were soaked in the stuff. It were like being in a beer garden after a stag do.

I said to our Doris, I said, 'I'll make us a brew while

you start looking around.'

She'd got her scarf held over her nose so just nodded her head and turned left into the sitting room.

I followed the hall into the kitchen. Not that it could really be called a hall. It were only about three steps from the front door – still, it's all about illusion when a person grows old, and even three steps can feel like a marathon when you've got arthritis.

The first thing I noticed about the kitchen was dust; a fine layer of grey coated every surface as though Bianca's kitchen were Pompeii and Vesuvius had erupted. Either that, or Bianca had a serious case of dandruff.

I supposed Bianca had been in hospital for a while, and apart from the dust it was tidy – it might not have pleased Kim and Aggie, but it was a good enough place to make a cuppa.

Or so I thought.

Once I cleaned the kettle, I popped it on and began searching for teabags. I opened a cupboard above my head. There was nothing in there, nor was there anything in the rest of the cupboards. I was every inch the Old Mother Hubbard as I tried to find myself the makings of a beverage.

Then I had a realisation. I stood up straight and called through to our Doris, 'There's no point in me making a drink.'

She didn't respond.

Ordinarily, she would have been telling me off for shouting in such close quarters.

I went through to find her, but the sitting room was empty. Once again, the room was tidy but dusty enough to unsettle an asthmatic.

Our Doris stood in a doorway to my right as still as

a pillar box.

I said to her, I said, 'What's the matter, our Doris?'

She glanced back at me, her face a mixture of confusion and sadness. She said to me, as morose as Eeyore, she said, 'I don't think I can stay here.'

'What do you mean?'

'There's only one bedroom, our 'arold, and from the looks of things, she's been living in it.'

I went to see what our Doris was talking about. I can't say as I've ever wondered what a witch's bedroom would look like before, but looking at Bianca's bedroom, I got a fairly good impression. The walls were all painted in this shade of green that put me in mind of The Creature from the Pit. There were dreamcatchers and garden gnomes and motorcycles and dragons on motorcycles, which I didn't think physically possible.

But that was just what she had on the walls.

The rest of Bianca's bedroom was in a state of disarray I'd come to expect from a scrapyard, not an older person's bungalow in East Cheshire. Clothes were strewn all over the place – well, night clothes, an assortment of stained and ragged pyjamas amongst ancient underclothes and socks in desperate need of darning. They were on the floor, on the bed, wound through the duvet and beneath the pillows.

Then there was the food. Aside from the empty crisp and chocolate wrappers, there were bread crusts and chocolate wrappers. A stack of mouldy crumpets sat on the bedside table besides a greasy, fat-spotted toaster, and I knew that somewhere amongst the mess, we'd find the remains of a pot of Utterly Butterly.

Our Doris was right. Bianca hadn't been making use of the entire bungalow – simply her bedroom. How she'd managed to get out of the place to batter Janice Dooley is beyond me.

I said to our Doris, I agreed, 'I don't think you can stay here.'

'Then what happens to Bianca?'

'Maybe we can get a few carers in.'

'She does get on well with strangers.'

'You could visit her every day to keep her company.'

'It's still not around-the-clock-care. That's what she needs.'

I took a deep breath and said to her, I said, 'Then maybe we should let her come home to Shakespeare Avenue.' I wasn't too fond of the idea, but the hopeful smile on our Doris's face was enough to soften the blow.

'In the past I'd have told you she was coming home regardless of your quarrels.'

'I know,' I said. 'You're going soft in your old age.'

She attempted the Look and said, 'I'm not a boiled egg, 'arold Copeland. I'm simply pre-empting the stages of grief by being kinder to my husband.'

'Are you sure about that?'

'Or I've recognised that you're getting more obstreperous and that I need to behave in a certain fashion to get my own way. I can't possibly allow you to find out.'

I didn't know how to respond to that so simply said, 'Shall we go home? We can sort this place out later.'

She said to me, she said, 'I always knew she wasn't the tidiest, but I expected more from our Bianca. And dragons? They really are the most common of fantastical creatures.'

My idea was to take our Doris home, put some lunch together and spend the afternoon figuring out how we'd make space for Bianca. I didn't expect to arrive home and find Violet Grey waiting on the doorstep.

Our Doris was first to speak to her, she said, 'Violet, I cannot say as this is a pleasant surprise. Still, it's best that you come inside.'

Once we'd settled ourselves in the kitchen, Violet said, 'I imagine you know why I'm here, Mrs Copeland.'

'Mrs Copeland, is it? Strange, how old-fashioned niceties are only employed when you wish to confront someone.'

'I'm concerned about the state of the Women's Institute.'

'The same Women's Institute that you abandoned?'

Violet's lips were pursed that tightly she looked as though she were chewing a dried apricot. She eyed our Doris with scorn saying, 'I wouldn't necessarily say as I abandoned it. Simply that I left due to the dissolution of my marriage and the subsequent media coverage.'

'There was one article in the local newspaper.'

'On the front page.'

'You really are quite assured of your own importance, aren't you?'

'I was chairwoman of the WI for decades.'

'Because the members were too scared to vote you out. Honestly, Violet, I'm worried about the state of your wellbeing. Over time, the WI became a cesspit of gossip and backbiting. The women of Partridge Mews have been at war with one another since you became chairwoman. We're supposed to uplift one another and–'

'Don't think to educate me on uplifting the community when you have always sought to set yourself above those you deem unworthy.'

Our Doris took a moment to compose herself. She shot a frown in Violet's direction, as imperious as Thora Hird, and said to Violet, she said, 'I admit to my past misdeeds, and had you been part of this community recently then you would have noticed as much. But let's move away from discussing whether or not we've proved ourselves to be upstanding members of the community and allow me to ask you one question. What the bleeding heck are you doing in my house?'

'You invited me in, Mrs Copeland.'

'Would you rather embarrass yourself on my front step?'

'I came to discuss your plans for the reformation of the WI.'

Our Doris offered Violet a smile – one of those smiles where she looks as though she could still swallow you whole in one fell swoop, but a smile nonetheless. She said, 'That's simple. I'm planning a brunch.'

'How quaint. Have you chosen a venue?'

'Have you received an invite?'

'No.'

'Then there's your answer.'

'I'm concerned because it's been a few months since you first brought the idea up and we're yet to see any results.'

'These things take time.'

'Still, you once organised a luncheon for thirty-seven people in three days with a budget of three-pounds-twenty-two per head.'

'Some things take more time than others. If you'd ever organised something *yourself* then perhaps you'd understand.'

'I organised plenty.'

'You organised people. If you hadn't got Mrs Cribbins and Mrs Patel wrapped so tightly around your little finger, your functions would have been as sub-par as your lemon drizzle cake.'

Violet's eyes flared; she looked like she'd just been hit in the face with a currant bun. She even gasped. 'And just what's wrong with my lemon drizzle?'

'Your sponge is the texture of sand, and the drizzle is that tart I'm surprised your husband didn't run off with it.'

'That's rich coming from the woman whose rock buns could have benefited the war effort as projectiles.'

'Rock buns are supposed to be hard, it's in the name.'

'They're still supposed to be edible.'

Our Doris seethed, all set to throw an entire pot of tea over Violet, and said to her, she said, 'We'll see how edible they are when I bake my next batch. They can have pride of place at your funeral.'

Violet offered our Doris a polite smile and said, 'I'm

growing tired of visiting this house just to be insulted.'

She was set to continue, but our Doris said to her, she said, 'Then don't visit. I can tell you that you're certainly not welcome.'

'Need I remind you that you came to me for help?'

'I needed help putting a stop to the redevelopment. You turned up to one council meeting before deciding that joining our protests might hinder divorce proceedings. Once your name was in the clear, you chose to rest easy. I asked for help because I thought the separation might have changed you, that you could be an ally. A friend, even. But you've proven time and time again to be as selfish and conceited as ever, and I simply do not wish to associate with you anymore.'

Violet hadn't expected those words; even I hadn't expected those words.

Violet sat there, the wind blown from her sails, as deflated as a school football. She reached for a garibaldi, still on the table from earlier, before letting her hand drop back to her lap. Her words were throaty as she asked, 'But what about the WI?'

'That isn't any of your concern, Mrs Grey. Now, I don't mean to rush you, but my husband and I have an appointment to keep.'

Violet swallowed hard, bolstered herself and said, 'I've been ejected from this house many times over the past few years, yet I've always returned in the hopes of guiding you towards more informed decisions about your behaviour. If you wish to wash your hands of me, Mrs Copeland, that's perfectly fine, but note that you'll lose any protections I've put in place.'

'Save your threats for the divorce court.'

'Goodbye, Mrs Copeland.'

'So long, Mrs Grey.'

Our Doris didn't escort Violet to the door. She watched her leave, shoulder-pads working overtime, as though they were jet-propelled.

When the front door closed behind Violet, our Doris breathed through her nose as deep as a bear sniffing for honey.

I said to her, I said, 'Are you all right, our Doris?'

'Who in the good Lord's name does that woman think she is? Coming here, acting as though she's the chair again and I'm nothing more than a lowly cake-baker wanting to prepare a sponge for the next bring and buy. She's always been one to blow her own trumpet, but that? She were practically a one-man-band, asking me about my plans for the WI. Why should I care about the WI?

'My sister is dying in a hospital bed and some geriatric old beggar is planning to ruin my hometown. I don't have the time to care about feeding the faces of forty assorted women from Partridge Mews.'

I said to her, I said, 'If you're that upset then maybe you should've let Violet take over organising the brunch.'

'She'd think she'd won then, our 'arold. I couldn't handle it. Besides, I'm doing this for Erin.'

'Erin doesn't strike me as the type to care about brunch.'

'I don't have time to tell you my plans.'

'You don't have time for anything, these days.'

She slumped forwards towards the table, staring desultory at the biscuits. 'I know. I'm starting to think our Bianca would be better off in a home.'

'You don't mean that,' I said.

'I do. I have too many obligations to make sure that she is provided with the adequate care necessary to make her comfortable. I think it best if Bianca spends her final days in a care home, away from me. I'll break it to her tomorrow. I've had enough conversation for one day.'

She took herself off into the living room with the plate of garibaldis and a Penny Vincenzi.

Next day, I went to visit Alf and Edith. At least, I planned to. I wandered down to their house, but Alf wasn't home.

Edith answered the door, the Daily Mail rolled under her arm, glasses perched on the tip of her nose, looking every inch the harassed housewife. She said, 'He's not here, but you'd best come in.'

At least at their house, I don't have to take my shoes off before entering. I followed Edith through to the kitchen as she went on, 'Before you ask me where he's gone off to, I've no idea. I'm not sure what funny business he's up to this time, but he's gone secretive. I just hope he hasn't got himself into more bother.'

I wasn't about to tell her about Gawky Cavendish and his pigeons so I said to her, I said, 'He's probably just getting you a Christmas present.'

She switched the kettle on. 'Alf hasn't given me a gift since he came home with a ferret and left with a concussion.'

He'd thought to start sending the ferret down rabbit

holes and that it'd be a companion for Edith that helped make money for the house. He'd barely opened its crate when a coyote in sausage skin lunged for his jugular. The way Alf tells the story, it were like a snake with sandpaper for fur, all sinuous and writhing as it flung itself around the room like a deadly Slinky looking to escape.

I'm not sure how much he really remembers because when the ferret went for his throat, Alf jumped and blacked out after he caught his head on a corner cabinet. Edith had to have the paramedics out – they helped to catch the ferret.

I said to Edith, I said, 'He only wanted to try and make some money.'

'Yes, and who'd be the one gutting rabbits and making pies if I'd let him keep it?'

I nodded. She had a fair point. I've been friends with Alf for the best part of seven decades and I've never tried his cooking. It's not that I don't trust him, it's the dirt under his fingernails. I said to Edith, 'Whatever did happen to the ferret?'

'Linda from the Hare and Horse had it. She rescues them.'

'Why would a ferret need rescuing?'

'Beats me, they've sharp enough teeth.' She fetched me a mug of tea and went on, saying, 'Do you need to speak to Alf, or will I do?'

'I'm worried about our Doris.'

Edith nodded, all solemn. 'Violet called around to visit and Doris gave her marching orders. You're concerned about Doris's reputation with the ladies.'

'That's about right.'

'Mrs Cribbins wanted to get me involved yesterday, but I was watching Dalziel and Pascoe.'

I said, 'And how did the other ladies react?'

'Doris is in luck. Nobody cares that she and Violet quarrelled.'

I'll admit to being bewildered. Time was that our Doris would only have to criticise the colour of Violet's blouse and the muckrakers in the WI wouldn't stop until she'd sufficiently apologised – with ten Hail Marys, a letter in the Gazette and tickets to see Daniel O'Donnell.

I said to Edith, I said, 'How's that happened, then?'

'Simply put, they're yesterday's news.'

'Our Doris won't be happy about that.'

Edith gave me a smile, one of those where she pities my ignorance, like when she had to explain to me that Alma Cogan wasn't a Scottish darts player. Edith said to me, she said, 'She's happy, says it frees up her obligations. It's one of the reasons she's taking so much time over this brunch for the WI. That and the recent discovery that Sheila Sedgwick has renounced solid food and refuses to eat anything that hasn't been approved by her nutritionist and spiritual advisor.'

'They're one and the same, are they?'

Edith nodded. 'Aleannah Gower's done another online course. She can advise you on the best food for your body type, commune with the dead and build a drystone wall. The only thing she won't do is vacuum.'

'And that's vital for drystone walling?'

'You can tell a lot about a person by the way they vacuum. She doesn't even do her hall carpet. What sort of welcome is that?'

'Forgetting Sheila, do the ladies really not give a fuss about our Doris and Violet?'

'It's too close to Christmas for them to worry. They've mincemeat to make,' Edith said, 'Speaking of which, I know that Doris has a lot on her plate with Bianca, so I made some extra. Do you think she'd be offended if I gave it to you?'

'She hasn't had chance to think about Christmas. It'd be a great help. Thanks, Edith.'

'You're most welcome. Just let me know if there's anything else I can help you with.'

I said to her, I said, 'I might actually have something in mind.'

'And what might that be?'

I told her.

She nodded, her smile growing into a beam and then a grin. Edith said, 'It sounds like I've got some work to do.'

That afternoon, I took our Doris to visit Bianca.

We didn't say much on the way to the hospital. I let Steve Wright go about his business on Radio 2 and kept quiet when our Doris turned the volume up high enough that every time Jon Bon Jovi took a shot to the heart, I thought my eardrums would burst from the recoil.

Bianca was sitting up when we arrived, reading an old copy of Take a Break. According to the front cover, someone spent three-hundred thousand on plastic surgery, wanting to look like Justin Bieber and ending up looking more like Engelbert Humperdinck.

As we sat beside her, Bianca said to us, she said, 'Well, I can honestly say I've never seen two more miserable beggars, and I've been camping with coeliacs.'

Our Doris kept her eyes on Bianca's bedsheets saying, she said, 'The thing is–'

'You've decided I'll be too much hassle and think I'd be better off in a home.' There were no malice in Bianca as she spoke. She were just being herself, straight to the point.

Our Doris had tears in her eyes. She reached for Bianca's hand, saying, 'I just have so many things going on that I wouldn't be able to care for you properly.'

Bianca nodded. 'I tried to warn you yesterday. I know you, our Doris. You're always chasing your tail, looking to impress folk. I understand. Besides, I've stayed in plenty of communes, and a care home will be just the same. At least with a care home, you can have a bunk-up whenever you like, as long as you let them test your blood pressure afterwards.'

I couldn't help myself. I said to her, I said, 'Well, you'll have to reschedule any planned "bunk-ups", because you're coming to stay with us.'

'I am?'

'She is?' Our Doris brightened up like a Weight Watcher faced with a loss. A smile bloomed on her face; she was happier than the time she found a Moncler jacket in the January sales.

'I can't be wasting all our petrol ferrying you to and fro when we've got a perfectly good spare bedroom. Either Bianca stays with us, or you're getting admitted as well.'

Bianca was wary. She closed her magazine and eyed me as though I were a tadpole and she were a toddler. She said, 'Are you sure about this, our 'arold? I can be demanding. I haven't lived with anyone for decades and I'm set in my ways.'

I shrugged. 'So's our Doris. I'm used to it.'

Our Doris piped up then and said to me, she said, 'But I've still got the WI brunch to organise, and I need to keep an eye on Doug Grey.'

'Edith is going to organise the brunch. She's got Erin on hand to help. Our Theo has an eye on Doug's activities online. Acting a proper Inspector Clouseau about it he is, as well. If Doug gets up to anything funny, Theo'll be straight on the phone.'

Bianca said, 'I could die at any time. Can you really cope with that? I'll be a burden.'

I said to her, as cheery as possible given the topic, I said, 'We could all die at any moment. Why should you get any special treatment? A care home? Have you considered how that would make our Doris look, putting you in a care home when we have a spare room and a clear diary?'

Our Doris's face switched between the Look and a smile that fast it were like seeing Bruce Banner transform, only less green and fully-clothed. 'It seems you'll be coming home with me after all, our Bianca.'

She said to our Doris, 'Let's hope we don't kill each other.'

We went to discuss logistics with Doctor Ezra after that. He'd arrange for someone to come and assess the house to see what Bianca would need. Our Doris wasn't impressed when I suggested bringing Bianca home in a coffin and playing the waiting game.

Our Doris was happier with Bianca at home.

We developed something of a routine. Our Doris woke Bianca up around quarter-past-nine with a cup of tea and a copy of The Sun – we had Alf sneak it in. He was the only one our Doris would let buy it, said as he'd already ruined his reputation and that folk expected nothing less from a man with a penchant for stealing pork pies. She only let Bianca have it because she were on her deathbed; she did try and convert her to the Daily Mail, but that resulted in some explicit language that hadn't been heard on Shakespeare Avenue since nineteen-seventy-six. She sounded just like a trucker did Bianca, at least she sounded like a trucker I once cut off on the M62 when our Doris couldn't find her Polo mints.

It was usually about midday by the time Bianca got out of bed, performed her morning ablutions, and traipsed downstairs. We'd have lunch. She'd tell a bawdy story about what she and Deborah Sharkey got up to in Prestatyn in nineteen-ninety-one, that descended into her coughing up a lung, and once she finished that, she went into the living room for a nap on the sofa. And Lord, she snored – they must breed it in the Thistlethwaite women, the innate ability to snore like a pneumatic drill. What with her and our Doris, I started wearing ear defenders to bed. I told our Doris I was listening to ambient music to help with my insomnia; I didn't want to upset her.

When Bianca awoke, she'd have more tea and biscuits whilst chatting life with our Doris. Then it were tea-time, evening television, and bed.

I never expected monotony living with our Doris, but I felt more at ease with it. Sure, I am never properly relaxed where she's concerned, but anyone would have difficulty in that area if they were married to Cheshire's own Attila the Hun.

Most of the time they were planning for Christmas – the first one they've spent together since nineteen-eighty-two. Bianca introduced our Angela to crème de menthe, before accidentally flambeeing her kaftan.

Our Doris was excited to be organising again. She didn't have so much passion for pulling the WI back together, but the thought of getting to spend the festive period with her sister lifted her spirits. She even started singing carols around the house; every morning there was a rendition of Ding Dong Merrily on High that might be all right for church when there's chance for her soprano to be drowned out, but in a semi-detached house on Shakespeare Avenue it was somewhere between ear-splitting and so high-pitched that only dogs can hear it.

They still had their fair share of arguments, but our Doris was more jovial about them. Besides, I don't think she'd ever throw a table lamp at Bianca – there would be every chance she'd throw it straight back.

With Bianca at home our Doris didn't really have much time for me, which suited me just fine.

I started spending more time down the allotment – not that there was much happening down there in the run up to Christmas, but it gave me some time to make sure my plot was tidy. I managed to get most of the rust out of an old pair of secateurs. Since our Doris used my new ones to batter a journalist, I felt like an accomplice in her crime whenever I clipped back any branches. I got my shed sorted out. After being left to Alf's devices, it looked a bit like something from Stig of the Dump – he just threw everything all over the place. He'd even opened some creosote. I've no idea what he used it for and I'm in no rush to ask him. Alf's business is Alf's business and the less I know, the better.

Our Doris and Bianca could get into some heavy conversations about what constitutes a proper Christmas dinner, and when they got onto talking about lardons for the fifteenth time in one afternoon, I disappeared down the coffee shop in town and set about reading a Michael Connelly.

I don't mind being a stranger in my own home. I'm not about to moan about only getting to see my wife at bedtime when none of us know how long her sister has left.

I brought it up with Bianca once. Our Doris left me and Bianca on our own in the living room and since the adverts were interrupting Emmerdale, we had no choice but to speak to one another.

I brought it up with Bianca once. Our Doris left me and Bianca on our own in the living room and since the adverts were interrupting Emmerdale, we had no choice but to speak to one another.

I hadn't spent much time alone with Bianca, so I'll

admit to feeling somewhat uncomfortable. I had no idea what to say to someone who was dying. The longer I live, the more conscious I am that I'm closer to not living anymore, and it leaves me feeling more uncomfortable than when I tie my laces too tight and nearly cut off blood flow to my ankles.

I sat across from her, wondering just how long it would take for our Doris to return from the back bedroom with her photograph albums.

Bianca munched on a chocolate digestive before saying to me, she said, 'You're not saying much, then?'

I shrugged and said to her, I said, 'I don't know what to say.'

'You've never had a problem before. I think you know very well what you want to say, our 'arold, you're just too scared to do so. It's one of those things that happens when you're about to slip off this mortal coil. Everyone thinks they've got to be nice to you. Time was, I could walk into a pub and if I fancied a fight, I'd have one. Now, if I go up to anyone and offend their mother, they'll agree and take her off for Botox.'

'Then you don't mind if I upset you?' I asked, feeling like a schoolboy given permission to admire a girl's collar bone.

She said, 'We're family. Give it your best shot.'

'All right then,' I said. 'How do you feel about all this?'

Bianca gave me a Look to rival our Doris and said to me, she said, 'Call it what it is, dying. I'm dying, our 'arold, and I don't have a problem with it.'

'Really?'

'When folk go through life fretting about death, they let it control their every flaming decision. I haven't fallen for all that rubbish. I've played the game, lived the way I wanted to live, done everything I wanted to do. Never really got a handle on scuba-diving, but that's labyrinthitis for you.'

'So, you don't mind dying?'

'How can I mind? None of us know if anything happens afterwards, but enough people have had a go and now it's my turn.'

'I've never met anyone with that attitude before.'

'That's because I've had eighty-seven years to get used to the idea. Being honest, I'm more worried about how it'll affect our Doris. I don't know if you've noticed, but she's fond of me for some reason.'

'You're her sister.'

'I've never been a good 'un. After everything that happened, I scarpered and left her behind. What sort of sister does that make me?'

I shrugged and said, 'There's no point wondering, is there? She loves you and that's something you'll have to learn to live with.'

Bianca smiled then. 'Not for long, our 'arold. My heart's made sure of that.'

One afternoon, I left our Doris and Bianca debating tinsel and went down the Hare and Horse. I hadn't had chance to properly talk to Alf, what with him chasing pigeons, so we'd agreed to meet for a Christmas knees-up – our own office party, minus the photocopier.

He were waiting at our table when I arrived. I were shocked because he'd got the drinks in. I were even more shocked by his appearance; he were wearing a tie. It was a festive tie with turkeys in bikinis, but it were a tie nonetheless.

I said to him, I said, 'You look clean.'

He got this cheeky grin on his face, reminiscent of the time he saw up Caroline Collins' skirt when she crossed Parsonage Bridge and he were fishing on the canal. He said that what he'd glimpsed would make good bait for her trout and she pushed him in. Of course, this were nineteen-fifty-five and that was practically a declaration of love back then. They were together for months, until she dumped him because he always picked her up in dirty wellies.

I were just about to ask him whatever happened to Caroline Collins when he said to me, he said, 'Do you want to hear my tie? It plays a tune.'

It did.

Alf pressed a button and this tinny racket started bleating from his chest, sounding like a bad attempt at Morse Code. I've never heard Jingle Bells sound so horrendous, even when our Angela were learning the penny whistle. I clenched my jaw, all set to stand-off against Clint Eastwood.

I told Alf, I said, 'That's terrible.'

'I know,' he said. 'I got it to upset Violet.'

For a moment, I wondered if he'd swapped bodies with our Doris. 'Why?'

'She made nasty comments about my clothing.'

'Doesn't she always make nasty comments about your clothing?'

He nodded, slurping his Boddingtons for inspiration. 'Aye, but our Edith's had enough.'

'What exactly did Violet say?'

'I've no idea. Since she got told never to darken your doorstep again, she's around ours every other day, bad-mouthing some poor so-and-so.'

'This time it was your turn?'

'No. Mrs Cribbins. Violet got turned away because she was watching Escape to the Country.'

'What's that got to do with your dress sense?'

'Nothing. Once she realised our Edith weren't listening to her, she started harping on about how whenever she comes over, I'm always in the same clothes. Told our Edith she wouldn't let her husband repeat his outfits so often. I said to her, "And look what happened there." She beggared off after that and Edith had me dig out this old tie.'

I took a handful of dry roasted from the middle of the table, saying to him, I said, 'The ladies have really had enough of her, then?'

'Look, 'arold. This is supposed to be some sort of catch up, isn't it? Do you really want to spend it talking about Violet Grey?'

He had me there. I said to him, I said, 'I've been spending too much time around our Doris.'

Alf grinned at that. 'I'll forgive you.'

'There's not been much else to do since you went searching for Gawky Cavendish.'

'Funny you should mention him.'

'Why's that?'

'He's gone off-grid.'

'Off-grid?'

'Turns out he was using a burner phone. He's had my money and beggared off Lord knows where.' Alf went desultory and planted his elbow on the table, chin on his hand. 'I'm beginning to think there never were any pigeons.'

I were that bewildered, I necked half my pint. I said to him, and I know my eyes were practically flying from my head as I said, 'You actually gave him money?'

Alf never spends money. It's one of the most reliable things about him – if he hasn't nicked it, he's usually got someone else to buy it. He's still not over the cost of taking his Martin to see Star Wars: The Phantom Menace. The fact that he actually forked out cash on the promise of pigeons was reason enough to be shocked.

'I wanted to get our Edith a proper present. Gawky said these pigeons were in high demand, so I gave him what I'd got as a deposit.'

'How much was that?'

He shrank into his collar. 'Twenty quid.'

I took a twenty-pound-note from my wallet and set it on the table. I said to him, I said, 'Take that and find something else.'

'But what about the pigeons?'

'If Gawky turns up with a load of pigeons then you can put it towards the full cost. I think I'd want at least a dozen pigeons for that amount, though.'

'You don't think Edith'll like the pigeons, do you?'

'I can't say as I do, no,' I said. 'Shall we have another round?'

We stayed for lunch. I had the steak and Alf went for one of those burgers that full of extras he'd have needed to be an anaconda to get his mouth around it. After a few more rounds, conversations about Christmas plans and some reminiscing – apparently Caroline Collins married a salmon farmer and moved to Tunbridge Wells – we went our separate ways. Alf wanted to get into town to see if his twenty pounds would stretch to a new hat for Edith.

The next morning, me and our Doris sat in the kitchen, staring into cold cups of coffee.

I'd arrived home from the Hare and Horse to find paramedics on the doorstep. I were a bit squiffy, if truth be told, not blinded by the blues and reds but far enough gone that it took me a moment to realise what was going on. When I did, my tonsils dropped to my ankles and the fog in my head cleared as though it been blown away by Pavarotti hitting a crescendo.

I walked slowly to the front door, staggering due to fear and not drunkenness. I'd barely crossed the threshold when our Doris bolted down the hall and into my arms, saying, she wailed, 'Why weren't you here, our 'arold?'

I had no answer for that. My brain hadn't had time to catch up with everything going on around me. I'd planned on going home, having a brew and snoozing through Tipping Point. I hadn't planned on getting back to find paramedics in the living room and our Doris frantic in the hall.

I said to her, I said, 'What happened?'

She sniffed hard, sounding as though she were slurping snot and trying to settle her breathing, all set to speak when the paramedics came barrelling down the hall with Bianca on a stretcher.

She didn't look well.

Our Doris went in the ambulance with them and I rang our Angela for a lift. Back in the day, I might have risked it, but the police will charge anyone nowadays regardless of age. Besides, I know only too well the perils of being three sheets to the wind in charge of an artificial knee.

It's funny how well-acquainted you get with hospitals when you pass seventy – you hit retirement and your body starts telling you about all the ills it's acquired after a life spent working hard. I question whether all that work was worth it, since I'm no longer fit enough to do all the fun things I had planned; all those years squirrelling money away, only to find out that I may as well have spent it because I'm more likely to buy a coffin than a canoe.

After the usual rigmarole with parking, we found our Doris in the A&E waiting room, coat like a blanket over her knees and her handbag swinging between her ankles. She looked like a lost child at a train station, trying to find patterns in the lino. We sat down on either side of her, and our Angela asked, 'What've they said, Mum?'

Our Doris inhaled, trying to steady her breathing as she sat up straight. She said to us, she said, 'They've taken her straight to intensive care. Never bothered telling me what they thought was wrong, just told me to wait here like I were some sort of criminal as opposed to a concerned sibling. I considered giving them a piece of my mind, but you can't say anything to an NHS professional without being accused of verbal abuse.'

I took our Doris's hand in mind and gave her a squeeze that I hoped was reassuring.

She offered me one of her smiles; it were shaky, but there were still some hope behind her eyes.

I almost wish she hadn't been so hopeful, because it might have made things easier when the nurse called us over a few hours later. We'd just finished a few of those awful vending machine coffees – they say cappuccino but mean milk soup, with an added aftertaste of disinfectant – when the nurse appeared from nowhere and said our names in a voice as sonorous as a beluga whale.

We bundled all our things up, pulled ourselves together and followed the nurse's lead.

There's an innate knowing when it comes to death; over time, you recognise what a certain type of silence means, and as a nurse led us into a side room, I knew what were coming.

Bianca is dead.

The specialist went all solemn when she told us, had that forward lean going on as though she were letting us in on a secret. In this case, I wish she'd kept it.

Our Doris gripped my hand like a crow trying to keep its balance on a telephone wire. She trembled from her shoulders to her toes as she held back her sobs, saying to the doctor, she said, 'Can I see her?'

I didn't really want to see the body of my dead sister-in-law. My Mum taught me to respect a person's dignity, and there's nothing more undignified than being a corpse – you've no control over how your body is displayed and have to wear whatever clothes your family think would be no use to a charity shop.

When my Aunty Emily died, her stepson had her

cremated wearing nothing but an old bedsheet. There were no wake either; apparently, the stepson didn't want to waste his inheritance disposing of a body. He sold her clothes to one of them rags traders, and anything of any worth were auctioned off. Our Phil went round to give the lad a piece of his mind and left with sore knuckles.

It didn't matter much anyway – the stepson had died himself within a year. There were no foul play. He were eighty-four himself and never figured out how to properly chew celery.

Forgetting all that, if our Doris wanted to see Bianca then I'd go with her.

We followed the specialist down to another side room. Me and Angela stood on either side of our Doris; I'm pretty sure we were the only thing keeping her upright. She could barely lift her feet, scuffing the soles of her Hotter plimsolls – something she warned against doing in everyday circumstances because of the lower-class association with shuffling. She nearly had a coronary when young girls started gadding about everywhere in Ugg boots.

She had trouble breathing as we headed down the corridors, heaving this great gust from her throat every now and then, determined to remain stoic. I kept asking her if she wanted to stop, to turn around, but she were having none of it. She kept her poise, shoulders back, nose in the air, even if her legs had turned to jelly.

The curtains were drawn in the side room. The specialist offered us all the time we needed and went on her merry way. I thanked her, but I'm not sure what I were expressing gratitude for. If she'd done her job properly, Bianca would be taking up too much room on our sofa, munching her way through Ritz crackers by the dozen.

I shouldn't blame the specialist. We all knew it was coming; we'd just expected some notice.

Our Doris took tentative steps towards the room. She let go of me and our Angela, straightened the lapels of her coat, tucked her handbag into her elbow and entered the room.

We followed.

I've no need to say what Bianca's body looked like without her in it. There's a sense of trespassing that comes from looking at a dead body. I can't really explain it – it's almost like when you visit an acquaintance and they leave you alone in a room and you don't want to move in case the host starts thinking you're on the rob.

We didn't stay with Bianca for too long, maybe twenty minutes. Our Doris said as we needed to get home and start ringing around, but it was no use. No one would see us without a death certificate and we couldn't get one of them without making an appointment. When we tried to make an appointment, we couldn't because the secretary had slipped on a corned beef sandwich at lunchtime and gone home to deal with the stress and embarrassment caused by her workplace accident.

Our Angela drove us home and checked we'd be all right, before heading off home herself.

It had gone dark by the time we got back. It's strange how everyday happenings suddenly feel out of place when someone dies. I thought about it while I rustled up some tea for the pair of us – nothing big, just a couple of sandwiches. Not that either of us was in the mood for eating, but I weren't really sure what else to do.

Our Doris didn't speak much that evening. She moved from the kitchen to her cubbyhole, from the cubbyhole to the living room, the only sound the hushing of her slippers against the carpet.

At one point I said to her, I said, 'Do you want me to ring her kids for you?'

She didn't bother with the Look as she said to me, she said, 'You can let me get used to the idea first, 'arold Copeland, before you go involving other people.'

We didn't sleep.

We went to bed at the usual time, but our Doris sat staring at nothing and I lay on my side, eyes closed, worrying about her. She hadn't seen Bianca in years, only for her to return and die.

That's how we found ourselves over cold cups of coffee in the kitchen, neither of us saying anything. Our Doris had drifted off, gazing into space, her eyes like marbles coated in fresh resin. It were like she'd visited Paul McKenna and he'd forgotten to pull her out of a trance.

I got too uncomfortable with the silence. Some might say I should count my blessings when our Doris is being quiet, but she was grieving and her silence saw us almost get arrested on our holiday to Skegness in nineteen-sixty-four. I never did find out if I were allergic to sunscreen.

No, I wanted our Doris to talk. Everywhere a person goes they're being told it's good to talk – better out than in and all that – so I said to her, I said, 'What're you thinking, our Doris?'

The sudden sound of my voice jolted her from her daze. She blinked a few times, acknowledged the skin on her coffee and said, 'Yesterday is all I can think about.'

I asked the question that I'd been delaying because I know only too well how grief can have you replaying events in your mind – how the death of a loved one brings back all the mistakes you made, leaving you wondering if their death could have been avoided had you not walked in on them using the toilet in nineteen-fifty-two. I asked, 'What happened?'

Our Doris looked into her cup as though she hoped it would swallow her up.

'We were going through photograph albums, having a joke and chatting about Christmas. She wanted me to get one of those five bird roasts and I was having none of it. I told her, I said, "You might be on your death bed, our Bianca, but I'm not going to allow you to bring the Frankenstein of the poultry world into this house. It's a creation that was only invented for the terminally common and those proletariats who want to give off the illusion of class without recognising what that actually means." She laughed at me and called me a snob to my face, but I let her off because she's spent a significant amount of time living in Rhyl with a golfer named Sue. I imagine that changes the way a person views the class system, does living in Rhyl. Anyway, we'd finally settled the argument. I'd buy a turkey and a duck and cook them separately. She had no problem with that.

'Well, all that planning made us thirsty. I said I'd make us a pot of tea, only Bianca had to be contentious as usual. I think it's because she's the older sister. She wanted cocoa. I never could say no to her, so I went off to make it.

'That was it, our 'arold. When I came back, she'd sort of slumped forward in the chair. I thought she were just dozing; I got the blanket to cover her up and it was only when I did, that I realised she wasn't breathing. I tried waking her up, gave her a good nudge, but it did nothing. She's dead, our 'arold. My sister is dead and the last words I said to her were, "Two sugars, is it?" She shouldn't have even been having sugar, not with her diabetes.'

Our Doris snatched the kitchen roll from the middle of the table, tore off a sheet and started mopping her cheeks. Her eyes looked sore when she said, 'Aren't you going to say something?'

'I'm sorry, our Doris, I don't know what to say.'

'Just console me, our 'arold, you just need to console me.' A moan rose from deep in her chest as the sound of her muffled sobbing filled the kitchen.

There were an ache in my throat as well; that's one of the things I don't particularly appreciate about crying is that ache in the throat that feels like I'm choking on an apricot. I pressed my hand against my neck, trying to rub any threat of tears away – it wouldn't do to join our Doris in her grief, I could always do that in the back bedroom later – and said to her, I said, 'You were never going to get a proper goodbye, our Doris. Bianca knew that you loved her...well, she said you were fond of her. And she knew you'd struggle after her death. She said I'd have to make sure to look after you when she did.'

'And how do you think you're doing?'

'I don't know what to do. Bianca wasn't supposed to die yet. I haven't got my head around it.'

Our Doris paused for a moment to consider my words. I could see the cogs whirring behind her eyes – she still had tears, but they were accompanied by a more contemplative look like Meryl Streep in Sophie's Choice – and she said to me, she said, 'I think our Bianca might have been the only family member of mine that you liked.'

'That goes without saying,' I said. 'I've never got on with your Mavis.'

'Is that it? You had two to choose from and you went with our Bianca.'

'There were nothing fake about her. She did what

she wanted to do, and she didn't care how other folk felt about that. It were like a breath of fresh air in these parts, I can tell you.'

Our Doris looked out at the back garden, clutching that scraggly piece of kitchen roll to her throat as though she were holding on for dear life, and she said, 'I just wish she'd been around more, our 'arold. She never got to see Theo grow up, and he's my only grandchild. She didn't get to see how proud I am of him.'

'That's true. And if she'd been around more, she might have stopped you wearing so many funny hats.'

'There's nothing wrong with my hats,' she said, attempting a Look but just coming off snotty.

'There were that one that made you look like you'd got a trumpet stuck on top of your head.'

'That was made by a reputable Cheshire designer, inspired by a fascinator Princess Margaret once wore. I'll have nothing said against it.'

'Trust me, it spoke for itself.'

I sighed and our Doris gave me something like a smile. 'She thought you calmed me down and stopped me getting too reckless.'

'If only she knew the truth.'

'She always said that I married well.'

'I can't say as I disagree.' I reached across the table at this point and took our Doris's hand in mine. 'I did pretty well myself.'

Our Doris's next smile were a bit shaky as she said, 'I think she was fond of you, our 'arold.'

'She made you happy, our Doris. Whenever Bianca appeared, you got more confident. Sometimes, you were even kinder to folk. If she were fond of me, the feeling was certainly mutual.'

Our Doris pressed her tongue against the back of

227

her front teeth and hissed. Every bone in her face was clenched as she tried to hold back another round of sobs; her entire body trembled with the effort, like Eddie Hall dragging a bus. She said to me, she said, 'How am I going to manage planning this funeral, our 'arold? I've no idea what she wanted.'

'I'm sure the undertakers will help us with all of that. Your job right now is to think of Bianca and remember all the good times you had. Have a proper cry. Everything that has to happen can happen on your terms.'

She sniffed and nodded her head, dabbing at her eyes some more. Then, to add a bit of levity – something completely unexpected from our Doris, who once cried at a burnt ratatouille – she said to me, she said, 'It's just like our Bianca to die so close to Christmas. I bet she didn't consider how it would ruin all my plans.'

'I imagine she did, our Doris. If there's one thing I know about your sister, it's that she always knew how to make an exit.'

Once we'd collected the death certificate, I took our Doris to the undertakers. Despite organising a few funerals in our time, it never gets any easier – there's a certain numbness that comes with discussing burials and cremations and what music will be played as the pallbearers enter; not Simon and Garfunkel, because our Brian once won a karaoke prize for his rendition of Bridge over Troubled Water.

I've been to some good funerals, and I've been to some terrible funerals. The worst are those for friends I'd lost touch with. We'd see each other in the street every few months, talk about going for a pint, and the next thing I knew there was a notice in the Gazette and I was digging out my navy suit. That's one of those things about life, I suppose – we always take advantage of time because we forget one day it'll stop. We take for granted that our friends will always be there, waiting with a pint in hand when we're ready.

The undertakers are hidden away on a back street. Take a right off the main road to town, right again and the car park's on your left. If you hit a tennis court, you've gone too far. I parked between a skip and a hearse. I should've taken that as a sign of how things would go.

If Albert Steptoe and Stig of the Dump ever collaborated in the funeral business, it would've been like

Backs, Whitlock & Co. They weren't our Doris's choice of undertakers. She'd have preferred to use Delaney's on the High Street, but Bianca had pre-paid for the funeral and so we had no choice but to enter a building that looked set to collapse. The roof had tiles missing, the gutters needed sorting and the windows hadn't been cleaned in about fifty years – they were filthy, and if it weren't mud, it were bird muck with an extra helping of cobwebs.

When I opened the front door, letting our Doris in before me, blue paint flaked off, dropping to join a growing pile on the welcome mat. The place smelt like a deli, like there were a ton of cheese refrigerating in the waiting room.

We made ourselves known to the receptionist and sat ourselves down. There were a coffee table in front of us, littered with magazines – none of them current. The earliest dated back to nineteen-ninety-one, and the cover were so faded that I couldn't tell if the week's celebrity was Pam Ferris or Sylvia Syms.

Not that I were in the mood to read a magazine, and I could guarantee our Doris certainly wasn't. She sat beside me, rigid, holding herself with all the dignity she could muster, handbag on her lap like she were cradling one of the Queen's corgis.

We didn't have much time to read in any case. I were in the midst of trying to identify the celebrity by their jowls when a young man stepped out of an office and called us in. He looked like he were just out of nappies. I could tell he weren't comfortable in his suit by the black finger marks along his collar; he kept tugging and fidgeting throughout our meeting. He'd have been much happier in the Superdry hoodie he had hanging on the back of his office door.

There's a time in every man's life when he grows comfortable wearing a suit. It usually happens around the mid-twenties, when he realises that it's his suit that helps him make five figures a year; it also helps that folk find a man in a suit attractive and it often makes it easier to find someone – whatever your persuasion – when you're wearing one. Our Doris says as men never get used to wearing suits, that we always act as though we'd rather be in jersey fabrics with elasticated waists. She also says that men can't be trusted to be sensible in a suit – that there used to be a certain responsibility that came from wearing a suit, but men will always find a way to be untidy. Granted, this was after Bhaskar Williams' wedding reception turned into a football match between the families of the grooms – our Doris never forgave that my blazer was used as a goalpost, nor the grass stains on my shirt. She'd have said differently had I been on the winning team.

No, our undertaker were uncomfortable, all right. He introduced himself as Tyler and led us back to his office. It stank to high heavens of Lynx Africa – I don't know what it is about young men trying to mask unpleasant odours with deodorant. Either air out the room or wait a few minutes before inviting your guests in; don't allow them to sit in a fug of artificial body spray and fresh flatulence.

We grimaced and sat ourselves down in leather chairs whose tears had been repaired with gaffer tape. I wondered if everything about the place weren't some sort of codge, if we weren't just in a glorified scrapyard with a few coffins scattered about the place.

Tyler sat across from us, paying no mind to his cluttered desk. He slurped coffee from a chipped Ozzy Osbourne mug and smacked his lips together. No matter what he did, it were like watching a lad playing at being an adult. He spoke to us as he clicked away on his computer. 'I were right sorry to hear about Mrs Thistlethwaite. She were a proper laugh, she was.'

Our Doris gritted her teeth and said to him, she said, 'Aren't you rather young to have known my sister for any sufficient length of time?'

He nodded enthusiastically, grinning at his screen. 'She had an account here for years, but only started making proper plans back in July. We've been meeting every week since. Did you know she once lost a swimsuit competition to Denise van Outen?'

Our Doris winced. There were this blend of grief and anger spreading throughout her wrinkles – those around her mouth looked fit to sob, but her eyes scowled, all set to knock nine bells out of someone. However, she remained diplomatic, saying, 'Perhaps you could tell us just what these plans entail.'

Tyler ballooned out his cheeks and leaned forward. 'Do you want the good or bad news first?'

'My sister just died. I think I've had the bad news.'

He scratched the back of his head. He actually looked hurt, glancing to me for some support, but I were having none of it. I kept my arms folded and tried my own version of the Look, though I probably looked like a poor man's Sid James. Tyler said to our Doris, 'I'm sorry, Mrs Copeland. Poor choice of words, was that. The bad news is that we can't find any doves for the funeral.'

'Doves?'

He nodded again. 'Bianca wanted a dozen doves to be released during her burial, only there aren't any around.'

'Did you try hard enough to locate them?'

'Course I did. There just weren't anyone who could lend us a few birds.'

Our Doris were set to throttle him, so I decided to intervene, saying to Tyler, I said, 'And what's the good news?'

He beamed here, grinning like a gardener with a new hoe, and said, 'I know how hard things can be when a person's gone and died, so I thought I'd ring the vicar on your behalf. She says it's difficult this close to Christmas, but she could fit you in next Thursday.'

Our Doris's voice went high-pitched as she said, 'Which vicar is this?'

'Adanya Weatherill at Saint Bartholomew's.'

She shook her head. 'We attend Saint Michael's.'

'Bianca explicitly stated Saint Bartholomew's. She's bought a plot and everything.'

'Can't you sell it on? People are dying all the time. Someone will soon snap it up.'

'I'm not an estate agent, Mrs Copeland.'

'With that tie? Certainly not.'

He looked down at his tie. It were light blue, shiny, with flamingos down it – he straightened it, leaving greasy streaks behind. He'd have been much more suited to being a mechanic, would Tyler – I could tell by the filth he left behind wherever he touched. 'She said your parents are buried there. That she wants to be close to them.'

Our Doris were set to burn him with her gaze. 'And

what if that goes against my wishes?'

'Did she speak to either of you about her plans?'

She'd spoken to me on one of those nights our Doris were out – something to do with how Mrs Cribbins had fallen asleep watching The Crown and got it into her head that our Doris were going to run off and become the next Camilla Parker-Bowles. She certainly has the hair for it.

Either way, I were reminiscing with Bianca about the size of Wagon Wheels when an advert for Four Weddings and a Funeral came on. I said to her, I said, 'Our Doris won't let us watch that.' She has a thing about the way Hugh Grant chews, says it looks like he can't decide if he's lost a molar or is trying to remember where he left his car.

And that's when Bianca said to me, she said, 'I don't want a sad funeral, our 'arold.'

I were a bit flabbergasted, truth be told. 'But that's what funerals are: sad. You don't see many folk switching on Lulu and dancing around the coffin like it's a bleeding Maypole, do you?'

'I wouldn't mind,' she said. 'Funerals can get boring. Everyone expects hymns and eulogies. They want to condense me down to a few funny stories and tell my friends and family why they should be sad I'm not around anymore. They know why they're sad. Why make it worse by reminding them of the time I tried to save a pigeon's life only to find out it had no ribcage?'

'Well, what do you want then?'

'I'll tell you one thing I don't want.'

'What's that?'

'*All Things Bright and Beautiful*. It's all you ever hear at these things. That, or *Morning Has Broken*. I want them struck from the set list. I refuse to let you celebrate my life with hymns so out of date that Aldi is about to start selling them.'

'That's taken six minutes off. I'll be able to fit in another pint at this rate.'

'You do that, if our Doris will let you.'

'So, how do you see this funeral going?'

'I'd be happy if they took me out to the woods and let nature have its way, but apparently that would constitute a crime scene. I've gone with what they call a humanist ceremony and spoken to some friends about carrying my coffin. I'm not shaped like most people, our 'arold, I've no illusions about that. It'll be hard work getting me through the church, so since I know a few bodybuilders, I've asked them.'

'What if they're not up to it?'

She smirked, all mischievous, and said, 'You'll have to carry me. I'd start training though, you haven't the biceps to be a pallbearer.'

Our Bianca went into greater detail about what she wanted at her funeral. Bon Jovi should play when we entered the church and the vicar would only be allowed to speak in a celebratory fashion, with nothing maudlin. She wanted readings from the works of Katherine Mansfield, and if anyone fancied reading from the Bible, that would be fine, but they had to steer clear of Exodus. No hymns, but everyone could sing along to Stevie Nicks.

She never mentioned any doves. She wanted her wake at the church hall to save on travel costs, but that was it. Not that all Bianca's conversation was light-hearted. We'd both got invested in an advert about carrots when she said, 'My two won't be at the funeral.'

'Graham and Ruth? They're your kids, of course they'll be there.'

She tapped my arm all comrade-like. 'I'm a terrible mother. We all know it. I had them, kept them around for three years and palmed them off on their fathers. I've had more committed relationships with Carte d'Or. No, I wanted to live my life and children got in the way. I don't have a bad word to say against them, but they won't be there, and I don't want our Doris creating ructions with them once I'm gone.'

'I'll tell her,' I said.

Granted, it were a few weeks later in an undertaker's office, but I told our Doris everything Bianca had said.

She took in all this information as calmly as possible. Underneath, she were seething. I could tell she were seething; it were all in the way she clutched her handbag, knuckles tense and white as meringue around the strap. Her lips were tightly pursed and all, looking like an old, dried grape.

Tyler sat there, smug, his eyes on our Doris, glinting with all the success of a toddler using the potty properly for the first time.

Our Doris said to me, she said, 'How long have you been keeping this from me, Harold Copeland?'

I felt defensive under the intensity of her gaze when I said to her, I said, 'I wasn't keeping it from you. I thought that Bianca would've told you her plans as well.'

She nodded once, curt. 'I see.'

Tyler interjected there, saying to us, he said, 'I can show you everything we've sorted already.'

He turned his monitor towards us.

Tyler had made a mistake. He tried to close the program, frantically stabbing the mouse to hide what he'd been doing. While we talked about the funeral plans, Tyler was playing solitaire.

He gave up, turned the screen back to himself and

attempted to hide behind his monitor, as apologetic as John Profumo.

Our Doris was having none of it. She fired the Look in Tyler's direction, her eyes like lasers, and she said, 'I'm aware that this is all a business transaction to you, that my sister's death has contributed to your wages and you're already planning your next holiday.' She paused to look Tyler up and down. 'From the look of your collar and cuffs, you're the type of man suited to Malaga. It's cheap, everyone's visited, and folk can only stomach you when they're pie-eyed.'

'I'm not sure what you mean,' Tyler said, his voice little more than a squeak, as meek as a mouse in a cattery.

'I bet you don't. I can't imagine one needs many qualifications to pop a bit of lippy on a corpse.'

Tyler shrank further, looking like he were trying to contort into the very folds of his office chair.

'Only this corpse is my sister, and it isn't too much to ask that you have the common bloody decency to hear what she wanted at her funeral, rather than spend the entire time playing a pointless little game on your computer.'

'You're quite right, Mrs Copeland.'

'I know I'm right. I certainly don't need you to tell me I'm right. I'll tell you something, though. Once this funeral is over, you'd better search for another job, because I'll be writing to your superiors. By the time I'm finished, you won't even be able to organise a funeral for a goldfish.'

Later, I met Alf down the Hare and Horse. He were surprised to see me. I didn't blame him – I hadn't planned on visiting the pub myself, but our Doris wanted me out from under her feet.

It didn't feel right to be back there. Not a day had passed since I'd been making merry with Alf, only to arrive home and discover that my sister-in-law had died. It's strange; Bianca weren't with us for long, but her absence left an impression. Perhaps it's because this time she isn't coming back – for every other departure, we've known that although we don't where or when, Bianca will turn up. She could be three sheets to the wind on a merry-go-round at the nineteen-ninety-eight summer fair or trying to drink a lorry driver under the table, but she'd be there.

Alf bought me a pint and sat down. ''ow do, 'arold?'

I shrugged, watching the bubbles rise in my bitter. I said to him, I said, 'Do you know the last words I said to my mother?'

'No,' he said. 'What were they?'

I sighed. It'd been a long time since I'd had a good, proper sigh. 'I can't remember. I can remember exactly what I said to her in May nineteen-seventy-four when we were arguing about vinyl flooring, but not my last words to her.'

Alf had this concerned look about him. It's one of those looks well known with men – a wariness of seeing another man express emotion; after what went on with the public toilets, I couldn't blame him.

He took a slurp of his pint and said, 'It don't matter.'

'What do you mean, "it don't matter"?'

'She's still dead.'

I'll admit that he had me angry, I were all set to explode like a bottle of pop left out in the sun. He must've seen that as well because he said to me, as calm as a heron, he said, 'If you know it's the final time you're going to see someone alive, you're not going to behave proper. You'll be too worried about what to say, making sure the dead 'un remembers happy days down the seaside and that you love them. It's not real, none of it. When I go, I don't want folk to tell me how they feel about me. I want one last blazing row with our Edith and then I'll be on my merry way.'

I blinked at him a few times. There weren't much else I could think to do. I eyed him up suspiciously, wondering if he'd got into the vicar's secret stash of Glenfiddich again – August nineteen-seventy-two, and they never got the smell out of the vestry.

I said to Alf, I said, 'You might be onto something there.'

He offered a smile I hadn't seen since Manchester City lost two-one to Crystal Palace, all conciliatory, as he said, 'I know I am. I've had over seventy years to think about it. Now, what have you got sorted?'

His face were a picture as I told him, like his nose were finally picking up the stench of beer and pickled onion crisps that filled the pub. He said, 'That's bleeding disgusting, that is. You two grieving and he's got nowt better to do than play computer games?'

'Our Doris wants his head on a platter.'

'I'd be the same. I might've been work-shy in my younger days, but this is different.'

'Forgetting all that though, have you found Gawky Cavendish?'

He shook his head. 'His mates are all saying they haven't seen him.'

'Have you any idea where he could be?'

'I were going to ask down The Blind Cat, but I haven't been there since that business with my wedding ring. Why?'

'Bianca wanted doves at her funeral.'

'Doves?'

'That's right. If Gawky found you some pigeons, do you think he could find us some doves? The undertakers are saying they can't get any.'

'He'd have your money off you, but I can't say you'd get anything back.'

'I thought you'd say that. Do you know anyone else I could ask?'

'Gawky was your best bet.'

'Then we'd better find him, hadn't we?'

'It's been over a month now, 'arold. I've given up hope.'

I slurped my bitter and said to him, I said, 'I'll give our Theo a ring. He's helped our Doris with research in the past. I'm sure he'll know how to find a poultry-pilfering pensioner.'

Our Theo came through the door twenty minutes

later, rucksack slung over his shoulder, looking as breezy as an A-Level student after a long school day. He ordered himself a bitter shandy and sat with us.

'How's Nan doing?' he asked, heaving off his rucksack and stretching his shoulders.

'As expected,' I said. 'She's grieving. One minute she's lamenting never finding out Bianca's favourite flavour of jam, the next, she's ready to destroy Blackpool.'

'Blackpool?'

'Bianca broke her wrist when she fell off a waltzer in nineteen-fifty-three.'

Theo said to me, drawling slowly, 'Right.' He gave me that look he reserves for when he thinks I'm well and truly plunging headfirst into senility and went on, saying, 'Maybe you should just tell me what help you need.'

'We need to find Gawky Cavendish,' said Alf.

'Should I know who that is?'

'If your Nan thought you knew Gawky, she'd have sent you to a nunnery.'

'Do you mean a monastery?'

'Whatever. Gawky isn't the type of person your grandmother wants you cavorting with.'

Our Theo slurped his shandy, staring incredulously at Alf. 'Why do you want to find him?'

'He owes me some pigeons.'

'And we need some doves for the funeral.'

Theo shook his head and said to me, he said, 'Does this mean you've got a date for the funeral, then?'

'Next Thursday.'

'So, I have just over a week to locate a man I've never heard of before and who my Nan doesn't want me to know?'

'That's about it.'

He considered things for a moment, before a grin bloomed on his face. I won't say he looked like a cherub, but he were jubilant as he said to me, he said, 'It's been ages since you involved me in one of your schemes.'

Next day, me and our Doris went to Bianca's to find an outfit for her to wear in her coffin.

Our Doris had been and tidied the bungalow since our first visit. It wasn't to her highest standard of cleaning where she takes a toothbrush to the skirting board, but we could have invited the vicar around and not worried about his cassock. She'd aired out the rooms and sprayed a bit of Estée Lauder Youth Dew so as the place didn't smell like a teenage boy's bedroom – all sweat and Monster Munch and other assorted, unmentionable odours.

The bedroom was the most improved. The clothes were in the wardrobe or in neat piles on the bed, and the kettle had been removed to the kitchen. We headed there directly.

Bianca wasn't renowned for dressing in a manner befitting her eternal resting place – not in our Doris's eyes, in any case. There was a lot of leather and denim in her wardrobe, alongside cheap t-shirts from Asda. She wasn't like our Doris; she was built for comfort, not the starched collars of the Partridge Mews Women's Institute.

Our Doris still hadn't recovered from her visit to the undertakers. On the way over, she said to me, she said, 'I'm beginning to think I didn't know our Bianca at all.'

I'd been waiting to pull out of a junction, so I didn't have much more to say than, 'You didn't.'

That didn't help matters. I wasn't facing in her direction, but I could tell that our Doris gave me the Look from the way my cheek burned, all the flesh set to melt from my jaw. I don't think there's another woman on this planet with a Look as nuclear as hers.

Once I'd got us onto the main road, I explained myself. I said to our Doris, I said, 'Bianca let you know what she wanted you to know. How would you have reacted if she'd told you about all she got up to as a biker, or when she became part of that commune, or when she was a librarian?'

'She only did that for three weeks. Even our Bianca couldn't deal with the sorts of reprobates that are welcome in a library.'

'She was sacked, our Doris.'

'That was a gross miscarriage of justice.'

'She battered a customer in the History section.'

'He was hiding pornography in a copy of The World at War.'

I didn't reiterate that it was a National Geographic; our Doris didn't need any more ammunition. Our conversation had done the job – she wasn't feeling as distant from her sister as she had been, and I was able to drive without the worry that our Doris would glare me into eternal damnation.

We stood amongst Bianca's clothes, unsure how she'd want to dress for her final journey into the Great

Beyond.

Our Doris held a wrinkled blouse in her hands, focused on the embroidery around the collar. She had her tongue pressed against the back of her teeth, looking fit to burst before she said, 'What in the good Lord's name is a humanist ceremony?'

'You know our Bianca weren't religious.'

'But I am, our 'arold. I am. Surely, she should have taken some account of my beliefs when she planned all of this.' She dropped the blouse onto the back of the sofa and pressed her hands against her face – she massaged her forehead as though she were trying to rid herself of wrinkles.

'She were thinking of you,' I said. 'If it were up to Bianca, there would be no funeral. She wouldn't have come back to Partridge Mews. She'd have quietly gone off somewhere and had her biker friends bring you her ashes. She came back and arranged all this for you.'

Our Doris said, wiping away a trickle of tears, she said, 'I know that. I *know*. But it doesn't stop me from wondering what will happen to her. If there is such a thing as an afterlife, where will she go?'   I went over and put my arms around our Doris. I'd properly assessed the situation beforehand, like, and it seemed like a moment when she'd accept something akin to a hug. I said to her, I said, 'Where do you plan on going when you eventually go?'

She sniffed. 'Heaven, I thought. If it's there, I always thought it'd be the place I'd meet my family again.'

'Then that's where Bianca will be.'

'Even if she never showed herself to be a good Christian?'

'What's one of them, anyways?'

'I should hope you know after all those decades at

Saint Michael's.'

'Even if they closed the gates to your Bianca, she'd find another way in. Remember when they told her she were too old for that new nightclub in town.'

'It were our Angela's first night out and I were worried about her.'

I nodded. 'What did Bianca do? She snuck in through the fire escape and made merry with the DJ. If you want to meet her again in Heaven, she'll be there.'

Our Doris offered me one of those smiles she saves for private. She said to me, she said, 'Sometimes, our 'arold, you know just the right thing to say. But don't you be getting your hopes up, I've no plans on going anywhere yet.'

'I should think not,' I said. 'I plan on you being around long enough to get a letter from the queen.'

'After all the work I've done for charity? I should expect more than a letter.' She had one last attempt at a smile and got back to work on finding an outfit for our Bianca.

We got home to find a swathe of post in the hall – cards offering condolences and a variety of verses telling our Doris not to fret about her dead sister because she still had her friends. She'd had cards from Mavis, Edith and Mrs Patel; even Violet Grey sent a missive, but it was the note from Mrs Cribbins that really seemed to cut her to the core.

Then something happened that affected her worse than any of the cards or their messages.

I'd just nipped into the kitchen to make a brew when the phone rang.

Our Doris answered with her customary greeting and then, dead silence. If I were her, I'd have developed a fear of telephones considering the amount of folk that contacted her with bad news. Instead, she listened to whatever the caller had to say, thanked them for relaying the information and put the phone down.

I could tell it were serious, so I went to her and said to her, I said, 'Who were that, our Doris?'

Her face were downturned, looking like a basset

hound in need of Botox, and she said to me, she said, 'That Tyler from the undertakers. He can't find any caterers for our Bianca's wake. We're too deep into the festive season, apparently. I should've said to him, I once organised a Christmas party for an entire factory in three days with no budget and several vegetarians after an administrative assistant developed gout and forgot to book anywhere.'

'He probably would've told you to do it yourself, then.'

'That's the problem with young people, they've got an answer for everything. Back in our day, you respected your elders. Now you just throw a jigsaw at them and rate their senility.'

'What're we going to do?'

She shook her head and looked at the cards in her hands. She said, 'I can't do this. Our Bianca was supposed to have everything organised, everything set in place for the funeral and the wake, and I don't have any space in my head at the moment to do it for her. No, she's the one who chose to die when she did. I certainly didn't want her heart to stop.'

'She didn't know it was going to happen when it did.'

'As far as I'm concerned, she's as much to blame as anyone else. What did she expect from a life of hard drinking and frivolity? You never see that behaviour in Catherine Cookson.'

'I doubt our Bianca did, either. She only read thrillers.'

'And look what good that did her.' Our Doris bundled the cards close to her chest and headed towards the stairs, saying to me, she said, 'Someone else can sort this because I certainly won't be. Why should I organise the funeral of a sister who only ever saw my home as a service station on the road to something better? Beggar this and beggar our Bianca. I'll never forgive her for what she's done.'

'She died, our Doris.'

'Don't remind me, Harold Copeland, don't you flaming dare.'

She sped to the back bedroom and slammed the door so hard that I swear the entire house shook. Within moments, she switched on her rock music and there were something in the pounding percussion full of sadness – our Doris wanted the entirety of Shakespeare Avenue to know she were grieving and that she lay the blame solely at the door of her sister.

I didn't linger to console our Doris.

When you've been together as long as us two, then you each get an idea of how the other operates. Our Doris needed some time alone to listen to assorted rock songs of the twenty-first century and sit in her sadness for a while, and I needed to help get the wake organised to a standard befitting of my wife.

Therefore, I went to a person who might just know her better than I do.

Our Theo.

I'd been planning on seeing him anyway to see if he'd managed to dig up anything on Gawky Cavendish. Since I didn't want his mother finding out that I'd got him fraternising with low-profile criminals, I picked him up from our Angela's and drove to the Hare and Horse.

We sat down with our drinks and he said to me, he said, 'From what I've seen, Mr Cavendish is currently staying in a cottage on Lyall Street.'

I said to our Theo, I said, 'How did you find that out?'

'I looked for anyone buying or selling poultry in Cheshire. He's been using some woman's account to chat with people. There were also some euphemisms involving ducks that would disturb Nan no end.'

I'll admit to being a bit agog. I hadn't expected our Theo to have found him so quickly, not when Alf said as he'd been trying for months. But that's the power of the internet for you – no one can have secrets when search engines exist.

'You've done a good job there, our Theo,' I said. 'Now I've got something else I need your help with.'

He looked as pleased as anything, like an over-eager puppy after another gravy bone. 'What is it?'

I told him about the situation with the caterers as he slurped his pint.

When I'd finished, he replied, saying, 'Grandad, you really need to get better at thinking things through beforehand. There are dozens of women eager to sink their teeth into organising something. Nan's been promising to bring back the WI. I don't imagine she thought they'd be planning her sister's funeral, but I'm sure they'd be happy to help.'

'Are you sure, our Theo? They didn't exactly end things on the best terms.'

'Which is why they'll want to help. They'll see it as an apology to Nan for how they treated her.'

'All right,' I said. 'How do we get them all together, though? I should hope you're not walking around with the contact details of every elderly woman in town on your phone.'

He grinned and said, 'Mrs Simpson does.'

Which is how we came to be stood in the church hall at seven o'clock in the evening, missing Emmerdale to chat with the disassembled Partridge Mews Women's Institute about organising a wake.

Our Theo was right. These women were thrilled to be out of the house.

Once we finished at the Hare and Horse, we went over to Alf and Edith's. Naturally, being Edith, she was aware that something might go wrong in terms of the funeral and had already got the ladies on standby, just in case. Whilst she went off to ring around, we told Alf about Gawky Cavendish.

His eyes went wide as tablespoons when we told him how easy it had been. He said to us, 'See, if our Martin hadn't gone off on his jollies, I could have got him to do all that.'

We arranged to visit Lyall Street the following day and said we'd see Edith down the church hall. The ladies sat nursing cups of lukewarm tea from an urn that had seen better days, chowing down on mince pies that Edith had been baking since October. Eunice Arbuckle chatted with Nancy Ramsbottom about the state of incontinence pants – a shock for me, considering I thought they'd carked it years ago. Meredith Weaver were there, bemoaning the arthritis in her hands whilst also planning her next piano recital; something Tchaikovsky, supposedly. Then there were the usual suspects; Mrs McBride, Mrs Patel, Mrs Cribbins and Violet Grey all sat along the back row, looking like something out of The Crucible.

It had been a while since I'd been out on a cold night to get to grips with a new WI scheme. Only, this time, I was the one with the scheme.

I let our Theo do the talking.

He stood in front of them, ever the orator, saying, he said, 'Good evening, ladies. First of all, let me thank you for turning out at short notice on such a bitterly cold night. I'm aware it's not the worst December weather you will have seen, but I know how these temperatures play havoc with a great many ailments. Therefore, I wished to express our gratitude.

'We have asked you here this evening on behalf of my grandmother, Mrs Doris Copeland. Some of you may be aware that my great-aunty Bianca passed away a few days ago from a long illness, and my Nan has taken it quite hard. Although plans were put in place before her death, now that we're so close to Christmas, the caterers are unable to fulfil their previous obligation to my Aunty Bianca and as such, we thought it best to speak to you all in the hopes that you'd be able to help us to celebrate her life.

'The funeral will take place next Thursday, and Mrs Simpson, my grandfather and I all hoped that, knowing your culinary prowess, you would be able to put together a spread that would rival the New Year's Buffet of two-thousand-and-nine – so acclaimed that they made mention of it for three years in a row in the Partridge Mews Gazette.

'I'm aware that we're asking a lot of you. Therefore, I'll give you a few minutes to talk amongst yourselves. If you come to a decision, we'll be waiting in the kitchen to hear from you.'

With that, our Theo and Edith walked off stage and I followed somewhat absent-mindedly after seeing my grandson perform a speech which would've made our Doris proud. I've said it before, and I'll say it again: that boy is terrifying when he's emulating his grandmother.

Less than quarter of an hour later, there was a knock at the kitchen door. Mrs Cribbins entered, notepad in hand. She said, 'We've worked it out and managed to put together, sixty-four sandwiches with assorted fillings, seven quiches, two-hundred miniature sausage rolls and various other pies and pastries, including Melton Mowbray pork pies for a certain friend of ours. Ida says that she will sort out the salads, Mrs Valentine says as her daughter can bake us some cakes and Mrs McBride is on the phone with Sandra Marsden to see if she can deliver any cooked meats. Eunice is going to see to it that there are refreshments, although we know that Saint Bartholomew's has an urn available, and I will seek out the gluten-free options, plus those foods necessary for anyone with specific dietary requirements. Mrs Grey says as she doesn't currently have the time to make anything, but she will happily purchase and donate a hamper or two for the occasion. And I think that's about everything.'

I'll admit to standing there open-mouthed. The level of organisation in the WI is such that I'm pretty confident they could conquer Sweden, and no one would notice they'd been invaded until they were out at eleven-thirty in the morning singing Jerusalem.

I said to Mrs Cribbins, I said, 'Thank you for this, Norma.'

She closed her notebook. 'You're quite welcome, Mr Copeland, but there's no need to thank us. We're the Partridge Mews Women's Institute. We always look out for our own.'

Next day, I took our Theo and Alf to find Gawky Cavendish.

When folk think of Partridge Mews, they don't think of Lyall Street. It's a row of terraced houses that lead to an old scrapyard. There's no tarmac on the road: it's all cobbles and thick paving stones that are only fit to crack your head open. That's not to mention the dandelions that riddle the pavement like some sort of horticultural uprising.

I parked and we knocked on the door of the house our Theo had found online.

A woman answered the door with a cigarette in hand and rollers in her hair. At least, I assumed they were rollers – they could've been cans of Budweiser, the state of her hair. I wouldn't have been surprised to hear a bevy of robin redbreasts calling out for help, trapped within a frizzy, blonde cage.

She scrutinised the three of us, lips set in such a way that she looked similar to a bulldog eyeing up a dormouse. She said to us, she said, 'If you're them

Jehovah's Witnesses, you can beggar off. I don't want no Watchtower and I don't want to know how you can save my soul. I want to go back inside and finish watching The Notebook.'

Alf said, 'We're after Gawky.'

'Then you can beggar off and all. Any friend of Gawky Cavendish is no friend of mine. Three weeks, he's been here. Our Verity said as I were wrong to take him back after last time, but he turns up at my door one day saying things will be different this time, that he's a changed man, that he hasn't touched another bird since July and that he's practically a monk.

'Well, our Verity told me so and I should've listened to her. There's not a week passed before he's back on the apps, taking phone calls at all hours of the day, and does he tell me who he's talking to? Does he heck as like. And then yesterday morning, I come into the kitchen and what do I see? There he is, fondling her like he hasn't even noticed I'm in the room. I told him, I said, "This is the last time you'll make a fool out of me, Gawky Cavendish." I threw them out there and then. I mean, how could he? He knows I'm allergic to feathers.'

Our Theo stepped in there, saying to her, he said, 'That must have been a terrible ordeal for you, and you're speaking to three people who know first-hand about the nefarious ways of Mr Cavendish. Indeed, the very reason we wish to find him is that he promised to source some doves for a family funeral, but we've heard nothing from him since he took our money.'

She considered what he said for a moment, straightened the wreath on her front door and said to us, she said, 'That sounds about right for Gawks, though he never mentioned any doves to me. Why would he?'

'Have you any idea where he might be?'

'He's probably at his mother's. If anything ever goes up the creek for Gawky, she's usually the one to jump in after him.'

We thanked her and she'd slammed the door in our faces before we'd even had chance to say our goodbyes.

'She must really be invested in that film,' I said.

'Have you seen it, 'arold?' Alf replied as we got into the car. 'She's not bothered about the film, she'll be watching for that kiss. I've no idea why, mind you. I don't think there's anything romantic about snogging in the middle of a downpour.'

Gawky wasn't at his mother's. She told us to try The Blind Cat.

He wasn't at The Blind Cat. After we ordered three pints of bitter, the barmaid told us to try the betting shop.

He wasn't there, either. Nor did the assistants have any idea where to find him, but they did know that our Theo wasn't old enough to be allowed over the threshold and so he was asked to kindly vacate the premises.

A man followed us out the door and advised us, he said, 'If you're looking for Gawky, I'd try South Park. He's usually messing about around the bandstand.'

The stranger was right.

We found Gawky in South Park, sitting on a bench with a bagful of bread beside him. He tore the crust off a loaf and held it out towards a pigeon who paid him no attention and pecked at the ground. Gawky swore and flung the bread at the bandstand, where it was unceremoniously caught by a German Shepherd who went haring across the park, chased by an owner who'd been staring at their phone.

Alf wasted no time. He sauntered straight over and said, 'All right, Gawky? I've been after you.'

He weren't happy to see Alf; he dropped his head into his hands. 'Not today, Alf. Any other day but today.'

Alf sat next to him, reached into the bag for a slice of bread and munched off a corner. He chewed it in his usual manner, mouth working overtime like he were Ozzy Osbourne with that bat, and he said to Gawky, he said, 'See, that doesn't work for me, and I'll tell thee why. I've no way of getting hold of you. Most people carry their mobiles everywhere with them, but you're not most people, are you? There's no answer when I call you, and whenever I go to your usual haunts, nobody knows if they've seen you. I've been around long enough to know when someone's avoiding me, and I wouldn't mind so much if that someone hadn't run off with my twenty quid.'

'If this is about them pigeons, there's been a delay in the production line.'

'Is that why you're hanging around here?' our Theo asked, eyeing Gawky as warily as a puppy approaching a hedgehog.

'Who's that?'

'This is Theo, 'arold's grandson. He's the one who helped track you down, and I think he asked a pretty good question. How many people have you promised pigeons?'

'Six or seven lads. Look, Alf, if it's money you're after then you'll be hard-pushed because Gary Leadbetter had it all off me when he found out that I didn't have any birds to sell.' Gawky shook his head. 'Audrey doesn't want me back and my mother's sick of finding droppings in her gravy boat. I needed some time to find some produce.'

'Why did you go around selling pigeons you didn't have?'

'I just needed a bit of money for Christmas. You know what it's like.'

'I never started offering pigeons around in the hope of making some easy money.' Alf set himself back against the bench and said to him, he said, 'Thing is, I knew I weren't getting any money back off you, but we had to find you for another reason. We need some doves for a funeral next Thursday. Sort that for us and we'll say no more about my twenty quid.'

We were all agog at Alf offering to clear a debt – he stole his Uncle Warwick's passport in nineteen-seventy-three because he was owed twenty pence.

Even Gawky were agog, saying to him, he said, 'Are you sure, Alf?'

'Do you remember Bianca Thistlethwaite?'

Gawky offered a small nod. There were some trepidation there as he wondered where this were going.

'She got you out of a spot of bother back in the day, and it's her funeral we're organising. She wanted doves, and she's having doves. I don't care how you find them but you'd better, because if you don't, I'll tell the whole town just what you got up to with Silas Muirhead.'

Gawky agreed and we left him to his own devices.

I said to Alf, I said, 'I'm not sure we should have resorted to threats.'

'That's the only thing folk like Gawky respond to.'

'That might be so, Mr Simpson,' our Theo said. 'But you played your trump card. I had a load of fake laws you could have used against him first.'

'You did?'

Our Theo affirmed himself, saying to us, he said, 'I planned an entire script last night, though I were heavily inspired by Legally Blonde.'

I couldn't believe my ears. I should have known by now the levels folk would go to just to get their hands on a few pigeons.

Things move at a strange pace after a death.

No sooner had we organised the funeral than it was upon us.

Our Doris didn't leave the back bedroom much. After three days of rock music, sobbing and gawping at old photograph albums like they were museum pieces, she took a bath that lasted about twelve hours and when she came downstairs, she headed directly to the kitchen and set about frying sausages.

I'd just come in from the garden – her next door said she'd seen a dead squirrel beneath our old apple tree, but it was just a pile of leaves frozen together; that's cataracts for you. She says that she's having them lasered in the new year. I don't know about that. She was supposed to be having a new conservatory in nineteen-ninety-six, and the foundations weren't even laid until two-thousand-and-five.

I'll admit to a warm feeling in the pit of my stomach when I saw our Doris stood at the stove. The sound of her sausages sizzling was a symphony to my ears. I said to her, I said, 'How're you feeling, our Doris?'

She were still a bit weepy, but nothing torrential when she said to me, she said, 'These sausages were about past their best, our 'arold. What have I told you about checking the dates on things before cooking?'

I didn't have much to say to that, so I simply smiled and made a brew.

After that, time sped up.

Our Doris had Erin over one day to discuss Doug Grey's machinations – apparently, he was a lot closer to submitting his new plans to the council and it was going to be difficult to oppose them. He'd even gone so far as to promise Erin first refusal on one of the homes once all of it was over.

Our Angela was around consoling her mother and helping with the tidying because I'd made a right pig's ear of things and our Doris had no idea where to start. I'd left a tin of baked beans in the fridge and forgotten about it, and so our Doris wanted the entire world to know how she couldn't rely on her husband in a crisis. I said to her, I said, 'I organised catering for the wake.'

She gave me the Look and said, 'From what I hear, our Theo did the talking, you simply stood around looking as gormless as a fruit cake.'

'A fruit cake?'

'If you weren't so gormless, you'd figure it out.' She went on with her ironing and I beggared off down the allotment to have some time alone in my shed.

Eventually, the day of the funeral arrived. Neither me nor our Doris got much sleep the night before – usually, I don't get much sleep because of her snoring like an air raid siren, but she wasn't snoring. She lay there, eyes wide open, staring into the darkness.

At about two in the morning, I said to her, I said,

'Do you want to talk, our Doris?'

She reached out to me and took her hand in mine, saying to me, she said, 'I've got nothing to say, our 'arold, I've just got a lot of thoughts.'

'You can tell me your thoughts if you'd like.'

She didn't respond; she just held my hand like she used to do when we first started courting and couldn't get enough of one another, simply holding on.

We were up at four, staring into mugs of coffee and thinking about the day ahead. Our Doris had hung our clothes up the night before; I was to go in my navy suit, and she'd be wearing a skirt and jacket in a complimentary shade. She's never been one for wearing black to funerals, has our Doris – says as it doesn't so much look like a day of mourning as an office worker's day out. I once said to her, I said, 'There's not many office workers who call a day out a visit to the crematorium.' Our Doris had responded, 'Try having a conversation with an office worker, our 'arold. They're only fit for chatting to the dead.'

The hearse arrived at half past ten, another car behind it for the pair of us. Our Bianca didn't want an entire cortege of vehicles blocking the roads – said there'd been nothing she despised more than getting stuck behind a funeral party. Her exact words went something along the lines of, 'You're off on your jollies, feeling all giddy about life, and there's a hearse to remind you it could all end tomorrow, something you certainly don't want when riding a motorcycle. No, I'll let our Doris have a car because she's a stickler for tradition, but anyone else who wants to come and watch me dropped into the ground can make their own way to the church.'

Our Doris chose not to have a wreath, saying, 'Our Bianca couldn't stand flowers. If they make a wreath of treacle toffee then she can have that, but she's beggared if she thinks I'm decorating her coffin in something she said were only good for hay fever and fornication.'

That had been the end of matters for our Doris, but the coffin did look bare, lying there in the back of the hearse, nothing more than a brass plaque to say that this wooden box held the remains of Bianca Thistlethwaite, biker and the first woman in Partridge Mews to win an arm wrestle against Bruce Hobson.

When the hearse rounded the corner at the bottom of the road, our Doris gripped my arm like a jackdaw on a telegraph pole. There were a tremor to her words as she said to me, she said, 'I don't think I'm built for this, our 'arold.'

'None of us are, our Doris, but just think about the sort of hat Mrs Patel will wear to the church. It'll get you through.'

She nodded and I wrapped an arm around her shoulder, pulling her as close to me as possible without absorbing her into my skin. I were a bit choked up myself. Our Bianca is dead. There won't be any more tales of debauchery over cheese on toast after our Doris has gone to bed. She won't be coming down the Hare and Horse to play dominoes with Alf. There won't be any more phone calls from Edinburgh to tell us that she might have accidentally joined a convent and asking if we could go and get her because she was never religious and she'd only gone for a fish supper.

I wiped my eyes on my handkerchief and led our Doris to the funeral car, both our legs shaking like goats over loose paving.

A motley crew waited for us outside the church.

The car park was filled by a horde of motorbikes, their leather-clad owners standing in two lines, creating a corridor for the hearse to drive through. There was another group, all women, all in floaty fabrics that had no place at a funeral in mid-December – if they died of hypothermia, we weren't paying for extra plots.

Most of the WI were there and as promised Mrs Patel wore a hat that looked like a necrotic jellyfish. Even though Edith were there, there was no sign of Alf – he were due for an ear-bashing when he got home. Edith looked murderous. Sure, she were keeping her composure, only grinding her shoes into the tarmac every few seconds as though she were scraping something unpleasant off her sole, but I could tell she weren't happy. It were all in her shoulders; Edith Simpson has very murderous shoulders.

I hadn't spoken to Alf much since we'd sorted out the dove debacle. He certainly hadn't contacted me to tell me that he planned on being late to the funeral – probably because he knew that if his Edith didn't slaughter him, our Doris would. At least, I thought she would – she was a bit too preoccupied to get any real sense of her homicidal intentions.

Our Doris quivered beside me and asked, 'Where did all these people come from?'

'I gave Bianca's address book to Mrs Cribbins and asked her to ring around. Our Theo sorted out an online obituary and contacted that commune just in case there were anyone who wanted to pay their final respects.'

We stopped and I gave our Doris a few moments to compose herself.

She held my wrist and said, 'Thank you, our 'arold.'

'You're welcome, our Doris. Now, shall we see how strong these bodybuilders actually are?'

There were thirty or forty muscular blokes and lasses crowding around the cemetery like extras on the set of Conan the Barbarian, just waiting for someone to slather them in vegetable oil and toss them out into the battlefield. They all wore suits tight enough to cut off circulation, emphasising every bicep, tricep and abdominal muscle they owned.

Our Bianca had picked out the four she wanted as her pallbearers. They stood chatting to the undertakers, learning the whys and wherefores of carrying a coffin – my only worry was that they'd take her down the aisle and start bench-pressing her.

I've carried a fair share of coffins in my lifetime, and I always thought it would be a good idea for the undertakers to show you a training video first. Sure, there's at least four of you hefting the box up on your shoulders, but then you've got to contend with balancing it and the weight of the corpse and the idea that there's only a sheet of wood keeping you from the decaying remains of a former loved one or acquaintance, all the while worrying that you might end up losing your footing and drop your side of the coffin and then the whole thing will topple to the ground and Aunty Ida will be left sprawling on the church floor like she'd had too many sherries down the Hare and Horse.

The lads didn't have much trouble carrying our Bianca into the church. We followed them alongside our Angela, her Neil and Theo, and as we entered the church, Bon Jovi's Wanted Dead or Alive played on the stereo.

I looked to our Doris and said to her, I said, 'Did our Bianca choose this?'

A small smile were on her face as she said to me, 'No, our 'arold, I did. She didn't want maudlin, did she? And I categorically refuse to have Eva Cassidy played at a funeral.'

From the looks of things, other folk were just as

mystified about the song choice as me.

We sat in the front pew, our Doris sitting herself as near to Bianca's coffin as she could without sitting on the thing, and after a quick word to check we were both all right, Reverend Adanya Weatherill started the proceedings.

She greeted us and began with a short introduction about the late Bianca Thistlethwaite – common funeral fare. I were worried when the reverend asked us all to rise and begin singing. I realised that I hadn't even bothered looking at the order of service. The first thing anyone does when attending a funeral is look at the order of service, but there were something in my head that had me hide the thing between me and our Doris. I picked it up and looked at the front, at Bianca's headshot and the year of her birth and death there in bold black font. It felt final – that familiar lump of grief lodged in my throat as I turned to the first page so as I could see the words to the hymn. Only it wasn't a hymn. Through the beginnings of tears, I raised my voice with the rest of them and sang along to Babushka by Kate Bush.

A couple of Bianca's friends got up to share readings from Adrienne Rich and Jeanette Winterson; even Wendy Cope got a brief mention. There was another song and then our Doris was called forward to share some words.

I said to her, I said, 'You never told me you were going to talk, our Doris.'

She gave me something like a Look, only more solemn and mildly tearful, before she said, 'Bianca is my sister and she's beggared if she's dying without letting me say something about it.'

Our Doris were a bit shaky as she made her way over to the lectern, taking the place of the reverend. She dabbed her eye with her handkerchief before addressing us all, she said, 'I didn't really know much about my sister. Our Bianca scarpered when I was a child. She always told me she ran off to work on the fairground, but that could have been a lie. Chances are, she moved to Scunthorpe to become an underwear model because she was just that type of person. She got on with anybody.

'To me, she will always remain a mystery, a woman that showed up every few years to make a mess of my back bedroom and regale me with tales about what she'd been doing. I won't repeat what happened on the London Eye in nineteen-ninety-seven, but needless to say it completely changed my opinion about lemon meringue pie.

'Protocol states that I should share a memory of our Bianca so as we can all remember her, and I know she wanted this to be a celebration of her life, but all that comes to mind is the first time she got arrested. Well, it was the first time I'd been contacted. She could have been arrested more times than Norman Stanley Fletcher and I'd be none the wiser. Still, I got this phone call, I'd just been putting together a cheese and tomato quiche if you must know, and it's our Bianca asking me to come down to the police station and collect her because she's been there all night and needs someone to fetch her bags and her moped. Now, I've never learned how to drive. I never saw the need. One doesn't when one has a husband who's perfectly adept behind a steering wheel, the same husband that knows if he wants a piece of rump steak on a Friday night then he can drive me about town as necessary. The only issue was that he was at work. This was the nineteen-seventies, and he had a very prestigious position at the garden centre. I couldn't very well telephone his office and ask them to release him for the afternoon so as we could go and rescue a felon. Do you know what I had to do? Me, a heterosexual, white woman renowned for my prawn cocktail and cross stitch? I had to ring for a taxi. Can you believe it? A taxi. Luckily, our good friend Alfred Simpson was the driver, but can you imagine what people must have thought, seeing me driven around town like something out of Coronation Street? I mean, I never was the type of woman to be driven around in taxis. One never knows what they might find on the back seat, and I certainly never planned on having an affair, so they just weren't a necessity for me.

'Either way, we picked up our Bianca and a rucksack that filthy it wouldn't have looked amiss in the Sahara Desert. We had to go back for the moped at a later date. And do you know, once we got back to my house, I had to pay for the taxi? She didn't even offer, told me she never kept any money on her. I said to her, I said, "You're an independent woman, our Bianca, you should keep your own purse." Well, I was very concerned about the state of affairs, especially with all of that going on in the back of a taxi. How was she paying for her food? Where was she living? Had she become one of those people who just navigate to the nearest bus shelter and doze off for a night? That was when she told me that folk were falling over themselves to pay for her meals and give her a bed for the night. It was only a few years later that she told me she was bisexual, but I'm not sure they'd been invented when she first got arrested. For that matter, I never did find out why she'd been picked up by the police. I suppose after forty-four years, I'm not likely to find out, either.'

Our Doris took a breath then and looked out across the church. There had been moments during her speech

271

where she'd smiled at the memory, as though she'd completely forgotten the reason we were there. She glanced across at the coffin and a moment of shock passed over her – she gathered herself and said, she said, 'Now, I look out across this church and see all of the people whose lives my sister has impacted, and I don't know their connections, or what they meant to our Bianca, and I can't deny that it hurts.

'It hurts because no matter where she was or what she did, I still loved my sister. I always counted on the fact that one day she would be back, turning up on my doorstep, getting filth all over my drive with that blasted motorcycle.

'I cannot deny that there have been many times in the last sixty years when I have felt angry towards our Bianca. We are two very different people, and that can lend itself to a certain type of sibling umbrage. When she missed important moments in my life, I wished she would stay in Partridge Mews so that I could share them with her. Now that she's doing so, I wish that she was back out there, traipsing down the country and getting into mischief.

'If there is such a thing as an afterlife then I hope that it is to her liking. And, if I may speak directly to her for a moment, I'm going to miss you, our Bianca, but I am pleased to have been your sister. No matter where you were in the world, you always lived life on your own terms. Thank you.'

Our Doris returned to her spot beside me.

I said to her, I said, 'It's a good job you taught me about the importance of a handkerchief.' I'd spent most of her speech dabbing at my eyes with the corners of a white cotton one she'd given me for my birthday.

She took my hand in hers and said to me, she said, 'I knew something good would come from this. Our Bianca's death has finally got you listening to me.'

There wasn't much left for the reverend to say. After we sang our final song and she invited everyone to the wake, the pallbearers returned to Bianca's side and hoisted her coffin up onto their shoulders. They followed Adanya through a side door towards the graveyard and we went soon after.

Our Doris didn't cling to me. She held her handbag in front of her like a shield and walked with all the aplomb of a poodle at Crufts.

Edith caught up with us and said, 'When I see that husband of mine, he'll be getting a firm talking to and no mistake. Fancy missing Bianca's funeral. I said to him this morning as he were heading out the front door, I said, "Are you sure you've time to be off gallivanting, Alf?" He said as he was off to sort something for this afternoon and that he'd see us here. Well, he's not flaming well turned up, has he?'

I said, 'He's been trying to sort out some doves.'

'Doves?'

'Bianca wanted them released as she was placed into the earth,' our Doris said. 'The undertakers said they couldn't get any. I had no idea that Alf was going to try and get his hands on them.'

We reached the plot that Bianca had picked; next to her parents, overlooking the rest of the churchyard, with a view of the hills – hills that a farmer was currently spreading muck all over. It was somehow fitting.

Bianca's coffin was waiting to be lowered into the ground and Adanya was all set to commit her into the ground – all ashes to ashes, Bob's your uncle, Fanny's his mistress – when there arose an almighty screech as a Volkswagen Golf came careening around the corner at top speed. The driver slammed on his brakes and the passenger door sprung open.

Alf jumped out screaming, yelling, 'Wait! Wait! I've got the doves!'

His face were red as a beetroot as he hefted a basket out of the footwell and came running towards us. He didn't bother coming through the church gates, he just climbed over the wall – not easy at his age – and scurried towards us at a pace that can be described as that of a squirrel with dynamite up its backside.

He were giving his best impression of the Big Bad Wolf on his way towards us.

His Edith gave him a Look to rival our Doris's, ready to vaporise him in an instant.

Then he fell.

Alf wasn't paying attention and banged straight into a headstone. His face was a picture as he plummeted to the ground. Both the basket and its handler dropped like a bag of fertiliser. The basket's door burst open, and out flew eight rather frazzled, rather grey pigeons.

We all stood watching as some of the birds headed off into the sky and others took a great interest in the ground, pecking at the grass, seemingly oblivious to their trauma.

I heard a recognisable snigger behind me. It gained more hissing and a dash of wheezing and when I turned to look at the culprit, I was as shocked as our Theo because his grandmother had unleashed her laugh upon the world – the laugh she keeps hidden, the one she says shows too much tooth. Tears sprung from her eyes and I didn't know if they were from grief or hysteria, but she couldn't stop her guffawing.

Well, that set me off and soon the laughter spread throughout the lot of us as we watched an incredibly dazed Alf stagger to his feet, surrounded by several pigeons.

Our Doris said, she said, 'That will have made Bianca's day, that will.'

'It certainly will,' I agreed.

'I'm proper sorry, Doris,' Alf said. 'It were a beggar to find Gawky, and I know that Bianca wanted doves to see her off.'

Edith were having none of it. She said to him, she said, 'Yes, doves, Alfred Simpson. Not a load of bleeding pigeons. If she'd wanted pigeons, she'd have had herself cremated in the town centre.'

We'd all descended on the church hall for the wake. The ladies of the former Partridge Mews Women's Institute had done themselves proud – trestle tables filled with typical buffet fare lined the furthest wall from the door, where an orderly queue had congregated. Our Bianca's biker friends had turned up crates of Guinness because she was partial to a pint or seven and they wanted to celebrate her in style. It turned out that the ladies in the flowing clothes came to represent the commune; although Bianca hadn't spent a great amount of time there, she'd helped them with funding for a proper sewage network and as such she was something of a legend in their community.

Our Theo had offered his Nan some words of condolence and she said to him, she said, 'Bianca wanted today to be a day of celebration, our Theo. I know that you want to make sure I'm all right, and I appreciate it. I'm grieving, but I'm perfectly fine, so please go and find yourself a quiet space to indulge in an alcoholic beverage where I can pretend I know nothing of your teenage alcoholism.'

'It's not alcoholism, Nan.'

I stepped in there and said, 'I reckon if your grandmother is telling you to beggar off and make merry, you should do so before she rescinds the offer and has you on pot washing duty.'

'Fair point, well made,' he said, and disappeared to cadge a beer off the bikers.

More folk came to offer their condolences with our Doris and to commend her on her speech. She took it all in her stride, aided by several large glasses of Courvoisier – she were happy to be hearing more tales of her sister, getting phone numbers and email addresses from Bianca's acquaintances so as she could bother them for more stories in the future.

One person our Doris hadn't anticipated approaching her was a woman named Dahlia. She was a wiry sort, all angles with cheekbones that looked like they could open beer bottles. She came over to our table, her purple dress swishing against her brown suede boots, and introduced herself.

Our Doris said to her, she said, 'I'm sorry, but I've not heard that name before.'

Dahlia nodded as a few tears strayed before she could catch them. She said, 'I don't know why I thought Bianca might have told you about me. She didn't tell me much about you, or any of her family, really. Always liked to keep us separate, did Bianca.'

'Well, who are you?'

'I'm Bianca's girlfriend.'

Our Doris absorbed the shock and said to Dahlia, she said, 'How long were you together?'

'Twenty-two years. Of course, she still had moments where she'd disappear for months at a time. I never knew when she was coming back until she turned up at the door with a few books she'd picked out for me on her journey.'

I couldn't believe it, how our Bianca had managed to keep a relationship secret for so long. I said to her, I said, 'When did you split up?'

This brought a fresh torrent of tears as Dahlia told us that they'd never split up. One morning, she'd awoken to find that Bianca had flown the coop, and believing it to be perfectly normal, she'd got on with things. She only started to worry as the days turned into weeks and then into more months than Bianca had been away before, but Bianca lived off the grid. She had no mobile, and no way to be contacted. If Mrs Cribbins hadn't called her, chances are that Dahlia wouldn't have known about the funeral.

Our Doris said, she said, 'I'm sorry that our Bianca did that to you. Had she told me about your existence, I would have come and collected you myself.'

'Well, you'd have got your husband to do it,' she said with a smile in my direction. 'I thought it a wonderful speech that you gave. No, it makes sense that Bianca wouldn't want me to see her dying. She never liked anything sad. I couldn't even watch Bambi. I'd have liked the chance to say a proper goodbye, especially after so long together, but I imagine she just couldn't bring herself to pick up the phone.'

Dahlia stood up then and said to our Doris, she said, 'Get Bianca's address book back and keep in touch.'

'Can't you stay a bit longer?' I asked, for our Doris's sake more than anything.

'I've got to get back, the spaniel has been left on her own too long.' And with that, Dahlia headed out of the church hall.

Me and our Doris stared at one another, agog. When our Angela came over to check on us, we had no idea what to say.

Once the buffet had been properly devastated, the bikers had booked themselves into the nearest Travelodge because our Doris wouldn't let them ride after all the Guinness they'd imbibed, and our Theo was located – dozing inside the church after a few too many – and Edith had finally forgiven Alf for the debacle with the pigeons, we returned home.

It was dark. An entire day had been spent toasting our Bianca's memory, learning more about just who she was outside of Partridge Mews. We always knew she had a large personality, and as I unlocked the front door, I became aware of her absence; the house felt too quiet. The television wasn't blaring with quiz show questions, and answers weren't being thrown out but were completely nonsensical. The kitchen wasn't filthy from when she'd attempted to make pancakes but had a coughing fit as she flipped them, and batter went all over the floor.

We ended up in the kitchen.

I said to our Doris, I said, 'That was a good turnout, wasn't it?'

'I knew that our Bianca must have meant a lot to people, but I hadn't realised just how much, or how many people that would be.' She shook her head and glanced down, all desultory, at her fingernails. She said to me, she said, 'She kept so much from us, our 'arold. I never minded because I thought it was only little things, but an entire relationship? We might not have seen her much in the last twenty-two years, but she had a relationship.'

'Maybe she thought you'd think differently of her.'

'Because she was in a relationship with a woman? If our Bianca was being treated well, I didn't mind with whom she had a relationship.'

I sat down at the table with our Doris, took her hands in mine and said to her, I said, 'We'll never know why she didn't tell us about Dahlia. We'll never know half of her stories. Look at everything we learned today. I hadn't heard those tales before, and I can guarantee our Bianca never planned on sharing them herself.'

'I just don't understand why.'

'She always said that she didn't like getting too attached to folk. Even Dahlia told us that Bianca would disappear for months at a time, and she lived with her.'

'Do you think Dahlia knew about the bungalow in Wren's Lea?'

'Let's just think about what we did know about our Bianca,' I said. 'We know that she loved you and for now, that's all we need.'

'I'm always stunned when you know the right thing to say, our 'arold. It's as though all that training is finally paying off.'

'Do I get a cuddle for it?'

Our Doris gave me a peck on the cheek and stood

up. 'I'm feeling a bit cold. How do you feel about a mug of cocoa?'

'If there's no cuddling on offer, then I guess a mug of cocoa will have to do.'

She opened the top cupboard and said to me, not thinking, she said, 'Two sugars, is it?'

The recollection floored her then. She slumped and grabbed hold of the edge of the counter, steadying herself as more tears eked from their ducts.

I crossed to her and led her back to the table. I wiped our Doris's tears and kissed her forehead, saying to her, I said, 'I'll make the cocoa, our Doris.'

THREE

Our Doris has had her name dragged through the mud by the Partridge Mews Gazette. It's reached the point that she can't leave the house without somebody shouting obscenities at her – it makes a change from the rag and bone men, in any case.

It all started about a fortnight ago, when our Doris was planning a do for the WI to say thank you for helping us with Bianca's wake. She'd invited Erin around to discuss arrangements. They were in the middle of a conversation about the benefits of tiramisu when a copy of the Gazette thudded through the letterbox.

I wish I hadn't bothered collecting it. I knew nothing good would be written within its pages when I saw our Doris on the front page. It wasn't a flattering photo. Our Doris were in her beige jacket from Bonmarché that she reserves for when she's trying to show sympathy for the underclasses, and the picture looked as though it had been take mid-sneeze. The photo came alongside a headline proclaiming that the newspaper would reveal the dark secrets of Partridge Mews' most renowned housewives.

I began reading as I walked back through to the kitchen. My entire body were trembling – I don't know if it were excitement, anger, or the poached eggs I'd had for breakfast, but I were trembling all right.

The Gazette claimed that in nineteen-fifty-five, our Doris's father had embarked on an affair with Janice Dooley of Little Street.

I dropped the paper on the table and said to our Doris, I said, 'I think you need to read this.'

She were about to give me the Look, but I must've looked something ferocious because she grabbed the Gazette and said nothing about my impoliteness.

Our Doris's shoulders bunched up, rising like fresh loaves towards her ears. Her brow furrowed, eyebrows knitting together like two caterpillars in the middle of a snog.

She sat absorbing the information for a minute or two before saying, she said, 'I wonder they're allowed to print such libel. This will all be Doug Grey, hoping to stop me protesting his redevelopment.'

Erin's face shifted at that, eyes wide, an expression between confusion and concern, like a three-year-old trying to figure out a toilet. She said to our Doris, she said, 'He's no need to stop you, Mrs Copeland. His plans have already been approved.'

Our Doris's rounded on Erin. 'When did this happen?'

'Last Thursday. I thought I was the last to know.'

'But you work for him.'

'He said nothing until the plans were put through. Right shady business it was, and all. They had the meeting in the council offices at three in the morning.'

'The rotten beggars,' our Doris said.

'I know,' Erin said. 'I can think of much better things to be doing at that time of day.'

Our Doris went as forlorn as a hen without an egg; her shoulders settled, and her face was a little less red. 'Then why choose to put this story in the Gazette and how was it found out?'

'So, it's true?' I asked. 'Your Dad was having an affair with Janice?'

Our Doris were incredulous when she said to me, she said, 'Have an affair? My father couldn't even read a bus timetable.'

'And why is it Mrs Copeland's fault even if he did?'

'Quite right, Erin. No, I will demand a retraction and an apology from the Gazette.'

'Do you think that will work?' I asked. 'You're not exactly their favourite person. Besides, you don't know if this is coming from them.'

Our Doris offered a smile and said, 'It will be another smear campaign, our 'arold. People forget that I'm one of twelve women who know what really happened at Mrs Winstanley's Tupperware party in nineteen-eighty-one. If I went to the Gazette with that knowledge, you'd never look the same way at an electric whisk.'

'You're going to fight back, then?' Erin asked.

Our Doris said, 'My sister just died. You can say anything you like when suitably bereaved and face no consequences.'

She said the first thing we would do was contact the writer of the article. I recognised his name immediately. My stomach sank as I said to our Doris, I said, 'It's him.'

'Who?'

'That lad you attacked with my secateurs.'

She blanched. 'I still maintain that it was a rather

287

inconsiderate place to hide a horticultural tool, our 'arold.'

Our Doris once beat a journalist with a pair of secateurs I'd ordered from a gardening catalogue. Granted, she'd planned on battering him with a copy of the Collins English Dictionary I'd been using to hide them. We hadn't heard anything from the lad since our Doris apologised – course, he occasionally made snide remarks in his column, but he'd received his fair share of flak for tormenting a septuagenarian to the point that she had no choice but to physically assault him with an implement intended to prune hedgerows. There was also that time he spoiled the finale of Line of Duty – he got relegated to ads for three months after that.

A couple of years down the line and he was after our Doris again. He'd clearly done some proper digging as well; I wouldn't call it investigative journalism, but I were surprised he didn't tell his readers what our Doris had for her breakfast on the ninth of April, nineteen-sixty-two.

I said to our Doris, I said, 'I'll meet Alf down the pub, see if he knows where this came from.'

She said to me, she said, 'If you're looking for an excuse to drink, our 'arold, then feel free to have one for me as well, but please don't insult my intelligence by suggesting that you're going on some sort of Scooby-Doo mystery solving business.'

'His Edith might have heard something.'

'I can't think of anyone who would sell this story, our 'arold. Have I hurt anyone so badly? I might not care for Eleanor Stockwell, but I still took her a cheese and onion quiche when she had that bother with her sinuses.'

I met Alf down the Hare and Horse.

Linda had put flyers up everywhere advertising the annual Burns Night celebration. It's an all right do, and one that I can usually get our Doris to avoid – it gets full up with ladies from the WI, and worse: poets. There's always some local lad with a pen who thinks himself the next John Cooper Clarke. No, it is one that we're always grateful to miss.

Alf had got the pints in – an unusual occurrence, but then this were unusual business. I couldn't imagine our Doris's Dad having an affair with Janice Dooley – not because of loyalty, Cyril Thistlethwaite was a twerp of colossal proportions – but because he always seemed too lazy to bother with women. He seemed too lazy to bother with a lot of things, actually – kept a diet of Woodbines and meat pies and died in nineteen-seventy-three during an episode of I'm Sorry I Haven't a Clue.

I sat across from Alf and asked, 'Who went to the Gazette, then?'

He shrugged, his face as perplexed as when he'd

heard the cost of wallpapering his front room, and said, 'Our Edith hasn't heard anything. She's ringing around, but folk are just as shocked as we are.'

'Our Doris says as there's no truth in it.'

Alf went shifty, closely examining the bubbles in his lager with all the intensity of Paul Hollywood over a Victoria sponge.

I said to him, I said, 'What do you know?'

He still avoided looking my way. 'This isn't the first time I've heard of Cyril and Janice getting together.'

I sagged in my seat like a deflating set of bagpipes and said, 'When did you hear about them?'

He thought for a moment, picking smoky bacon out of his molars, before saying, 'Must've been nineteen-fifty-six. A few months later, everyone were talking about Janice and old Gadsden down the factory and Cyril got forgotten, but I know it was one of the reasons why your Doris's parents split up.'

'Our Doris always said that was because her Mum got sent down.'

'There's some truth there,' Alf said. 'Elizabeth got pie-eyed and rowed with Cynthia Dooley in the middle of Little Street. Pushed her right in front of a passing cyclist.'

I gulped back my bitter, remaining silent as I considered what I'd learned. I've been married to our Doris for fifty-six years and she's never mentioned her father's extracurricular activities. I said to Alf, I said, 'I always thought she hated Janice because of their school nativity.'

'She has enough reasons to hate Janice. I always wondered if this tale were true, though.'

'About Cyril and Janice?'

He nodded. 'If it's true, why didn't Doris kill her?

Why did she wait fifty years and chuck a set of scales down Bulge Busters?'

'I came here for answers, Alf.'

'And I came here for lager. We do our best thinking when we're three sheets to the wind.'

In that moment, I agreed. I swallowed my pint with all the verve of a young lad out for his first night on the town and ordered another round.

I ended up having to ring our Angela to give me a lift home.

There was a struggle getting the front door open – a moment where I cursed our Doris for changing the locks while I were out – before our Angela took the key from me, opened the door, and I all but fell into the hall.

She helped me straighten up and said, 'Don't you think it's a bit early to be in such a state, Dad?'

'When you reach my age, our Angela, you have to take every opportunity you can to get inebriated because you never know when it'll be your last.'

'From the look of you, Harold Copeland, that time might have arrived,' our Doris said, as viperous as ever. She stood in the kitchen doorway looking as disapproving as Mary Whitehouse over The Magic Roundabout.

I managed to straighten myself and staggered towards her. 'I'll be all right with a brew, our Doris, just you watch.'

'I'm not letting you in charge of a kettle like that,'

she said, sitting me at the table. 'Suppose you scald yourself? The Gazette would have a field day. "Mrs Doris Copeland, child trafficker, assaults husband in fury at his drunken behaviour."'

'You have a point there, love.'

'Don't you "love" me, our 'arold. Have a custard cream and soak up some of that alcohol.'

I ate the biscuit as instructed. Drinking definitely gave me more courage than I thought capable because I said to our Doris, I said, 'I think it's time to tell me the truth. What happened between your dad and Janice Dooley of Little Street?'

She attempted the Look, but there was no heart in it. She ended up looking like she was trying to pass a gallstone.

Angela took over the tea-making and our Doris sat down across from me. Her voice trembled slightly as she said, 'They had an affair. Janice had just got her job at the factory, and he used to see her when he went to collect his wages.'

'How did you find out, Mum?'

Our Angela's question put paid to my joke about perks of the job. Quite honestly, she might have saved my life; if I'd made the joke, our Doris would have probably thrown a fish knife at me and pierced my eyebrow. That would have been fun to explain down the allotment.

'Violet told me about them,' she said. 'She saw them down The Blind Cat.'

That almost sobered me up. 'That doesn't sound right,' I said.

'What do you mean?' our Angela asked. She placed the tea tray on the table and sat down beside her mother. Our Doris gave me that enquiring look that's somewhere between Helen Mirren and a buzzard examining a carcass.

I said to them, I said, 'What was Violet doing there?'

'What does it matter, our 'arold? My father had an affair with a girl his daughter's age. Nobody cares about the details of where they met.'

'Perhaps you should. For one thing, they didn't let women into The Blind Cat in nineteen-fifty-five, especially underage women. That's forgetting that Violet Grey wouldn't be seen dead down those parts because she's an even bigger snob than you are.'

Our Angela snorted into her chocolate digestive. 'You pay her the best compliments, Dad.'

Our Doris shifted in her chair and said to me, she said, 'I am not a snob. I'm simply culturally discerning.'

'Whatever you call it, Violet's worse. The Blind Cat? She'd have bathed in Jeye's Fluid for months afterwards if she'd so much as put a foot down on the welcome mat.'

Our Doris's eyes widened that much she could've been ten years younger; her wrinkles retracted as realisation sped through her. She glanced from me to Angela and back again, before saying, 'Do you think they had an affair, our 'arold?'

'Janice has been seen with plenty of husbands through the years, but they were all minted. Look at Mr Gadsden.'

She looked behind me, staring out into the back garden, unable to meet my gaze.

'Mum, what is it?'

Our Doris shook her head. 'I made it all up.'

My brain was fogged by bitter, so I said, 'You made what up?'

'Janice never had an affair with Mr Gadsden.'

Something came over our Doris then; it were like she were sixteen years old again down the Co-Op, all set to throw broccoli at anyone who asked for something on the slate. She were furious as she said to us, she said, 'I don't know who else Violet told, but it was soon all anyone was talking about down our road. My Mum got sent down, Bianca beggared off who knows where, and I ended up moving in with my aunty and uncle. One day, I saw Janice having a laugh with Mr Gadsden. He must've given her a lift home or something. And that's when I started telling folk about trips to the supply closet.'

She slurped her tea, her body practically vibrating as though she'd stuck a fork into a toaster.

I said to her, I said, 'What if she never had an affair with Cyril?'

Our Doris shrugged and said, 'If they didn't have an affair, then all the hatred I've sent Janice's way has been for nothing.'

'I wouldn't say it's been for nothing, Mum. Whether they had an affair or not, Janice is still a horrible person.'

It's true. Janice might be the victim of a vicious rumour, but that hasn't stopped her from throwing sherry trifle at unsuspecting Methodists or impersonating a diabetic for free cake in town – and Nellie Klondike never got over her Matthew running off with Janice, leaving her with nothing but a faulty hostess trolley and a Cliff Richard LP. She never could listen to Summer Holiday after that.

I said to our Doris, I said, 'Besides, everyone knew there was a possibility that Janice wasn't going at it with Mr Gadsden.'

'They did?'

'You never cared for Janice, but you were always

good at getting folk on your side.'

Angela said, 'Thinking about this with Grandad Cyril though, Janice hasn't said anything in the last sixty years. Why wait until now?'

'She could have been playing the long game,' I suggested.

Our Doris said, she said, 'The long game, our 'arold? This is Janice Dooley we're talking about. Even her knickers drop at warp speed.'

'Well, I never expected you to make a Star Trek reference, Mum.'

'Your Neil has talked about nothing else since nineteen-ninety-six. You should've known I'd pick something up.'

'I'm just glad it isn't the Vulcan nerve pinch,' I said.

Within the half hour, our Theo were in the kitchen, sharing more bad news. The Gazette had shared its story online and folk were using it as a springboard to attack our Doris's character. Lisa Briginshaw wrote how she always knew not to trust a woman with such a tight perm. Marian Gradbach complained about the lack of imagination when it came to our Doris's dinner parties – apparently, serving coffee after pudding went out in two-thousand-and-twelve and she should have offered her guests matcha tea.

I said to our Theo, I said, 'What's matcha?'

'Green,' he said.

'It would be something eco-friendly. That's the only criticism these fools behind their keyboards have nowadays: be more friendly to the environment. Meanwhile, they're scarfing down bacon double cheeseburgers in a McDonalds drive-thru.'

He looked at me agog and said to me, he said, 'That was a great rant, Grandad, and probably true, but I just meant that it's green, as in the colour.'

'Still, great defence of Mum,' our Angela offered with a smile.

Our Doris looked to me and said, 'It's nice to know I've still got you in my corner, our 'arold.'

'Do you think I'd spend fifty-six years with you if you didn't?'

Our Theo said to me, he said, 'You might just fancy a woman with a tight perm and outdated views about beverage choices.'

'Shut up, Theo.' That came from our Angela as she handed him a chocolate digestive.

Next day, our Doris found herself on the local radio. A representative had telephoned the previous evening during a double bill of Coronation Street, asking if our Doris fancied telling her side of the story.

She hadn't liked the idea at first – said as local radio was a product of people too inept to have a conversation – then she found out that the presenter once interviewed Barbara Knox and agreed to be there at ten o'clock the following morning.

Despite dressing for the occasion – cream chinos, floral M&S top and Paver plimsolls – things didn't go well.

The interview took place in what the station called a studio but which were closer to a storage closet. There were all manner of forgotten pieces of technology: audio equipment, old keyboards and – for whatever reason – a wok.

The presenter – Rick Smethwick, his name were – looked more suited to being sat outside an off-licence with a bottle of White Lightning than interviewing a septuagenarian. By way of greeting, he tried to hug our Doris, who held him off with the offer of a handshake.

'You're right,' he said, 'you never know what you can and can't do anymore. I hug you and in five minutes you're down the cop shop telling them I've harassed you and you fancy your chances at compensation.'

Our Doris pursed her lips and said to him, she said, 'On the contrary, Mr Smethwick, I object to such physical contact when I've never met someone before. A handshake is an appropriate form of greeting and is often all I need to get the full measure of a person.'

'No problem there, love. I've been told I've got a firm handshake.'

'Have you?'

Rick told us how things would run. He'd introduce our Doris and offer her the chance to share her side of the story – he didn't want to blow things out of proportion, and she could have all the time she needed. I should have known he were lying. He looked just the type of person to be as accommodating as possible to get you onside, like an insurance salesman or a debt collector.

I had to stand outside the studio, watching the interview from a window in an adjoining office.

Our Doris sat across from him, headphones squashing the bulk of her perm, microphone dangling in front of her face.

Rick chatted to her as adverts played for the listeners at home, but once that was over, he spoke into his mic, saying, 'Good morning, Partridge Mews. In just a few minutes, I'll be chatting with Mrs Doris Copeland, a woman at the centre of a sex scandal that has shaken the town to its core. But first: Coldplay.'

Our Doris bolted upright in her seat. She gave him

the Look and said to him, she said, 'You assured me that you wouldn't sensationalise matters.'

To which he replied, 'My listeners are looking to be entertained.'

'At ten o'clock in the morning? You'll be lucky if she's got out of bed.'

'Who?'

'Your mother. I can't imagine anyone else willing to listen to your claptrap.'

'My mother lives in Holland.'

'Best place for her when her son speaks in double Dutch.'

They went silent until the song played out.

Our Doris composed herself; like a snake uncoiling from a wicker basket, she was preparing to attack. Her pupils became pins as she glared at Rick, more ferocious than a pigeon over a chicken tikka masala.

Rick addressed the listeners, welcoming them back before saying, 'How would you feel to discover that nearly sixty years ago, your father had an affair with one of your school friends? That's just what happened to Mrs Doris Copeland of Shakespeare Avenue this week when the Partridge Mews Gazette reported that Cyril Thistlethwaite entered into a relationship with Miss Janice Dooley, a name you'll recognise as she's set to build three-hundred new homes on the former Barraclough's Field. Welcome to the show, Mrs Copeland. What do you think of all this?'

Our Doris eyed him with a glance that was both inquisitive and sinister as she allowed the silence to build, dead air filling the studio like something out of a horror movie before the killer strikes. I were just waiting for Jason Voorhees to rise from beneath the desk and use a microphone for nefarious purposes.

Sweat built on Rick's brow. He opened and closed his mouth a few times, ever the goldfish, before he said to her, he pressed on, 'Mrs Copeland?'

Our Doris didn't respond. She reached for the headphones, removing them slowly, allowing the silence in the studio to speak volumes.

'Mrs Copeland, I know this must be hard to talk about.'

She stood up, clasped the strap of her Radley handbag tight and – without another word – headed for the door.

Rick apologised for technical difficulties, set some music to play and came haring after her. 'Mrs Copeland, stop!'

She ground her heel into the linoleum and spun around. She looked him up and down before saying to him, she said, 'Not today, thank you.'

'What if I say, please?'

At that moment, I realised Rick's colleagues were watching us. Some had their phones out, recording events.

Our Doris chuckled. She said to him, she said, 'Are you the type of man who believes the most basic of manners allows him permission to manipulate a woman to do as he wishes?'

He shoved his hands in his pockets. 'I don't know.'

'Perhaps it's worked in the past, but it won't wash with me. I have seventy-four years of experience. I can tell if a man is good to others by looking at his shoelaces, and what do I find with you, Mr Smethwick?'

'I don't tie them.'

'Exactly. Too lazy to tie a knot, but thinks he can interview me about such a serious matter. Take my advice and stick to fluff pieces about kittens stuck in ubends. You're not Jeremy Paxman, you're a man trapped in the worst midlife crisis I've ever seen, with your torn skinny jeans, overshadowed by that garish shirt that you would probably call Hawaiian, but which is stretched that tight across your belly the buttons look fit to jump ship to save themselves the strain. And then there's the hair. Do you use Brylcreem or Crisp 'n' Dry to style that? My Lord, hair like that is fit for a nature reserve. When you introduced yourself, I expected Chris Packham to appear in search of the great blithering cockatiel.'

Rick gulped.

He had every reason to, his colleagues chuckling, recording, or just staring as they watched our Doris tear him to shreds.

I hadn't seen her like this in a long time, and I won't deny, it made me fearful and proud in equal measure.

Rick said, 'There's no need to get personal, Mrs Copeland. I only wanted to interview you about what your dad did.'

'That's precisely where you went wrong. I'm not here to explain what he did. I came here to say that it had nothing to do with me. He was a grown man who made his own decisions, and I'm not responsible for his mistakes, no matter how you or your friends at the Gazette choose to paint things. You said it yourself just now, I was a schoolgirl as well when all of this was going on. What did you expect me to do as a teenager in nineteen-fifty-four?'

'You could have said that in the studio.'

Our Doris glowered at him further. 'I could not. You started by saying that I'm at the centre of this sex scandal. I'm not. This is between Cyril Thistlethwaite and Janice Dooley of Little Street–'

'– a woman you assaulted two years ago.'

'Say one more stupid thing and I will leave without educating you further, *Rick*. Let's discuss how you announced my presence. I have achieved many things in my lifetime. I am the former chairwoman of the Partridge Mews Women's Institute. I once climbed Mam Tor with a dozen Methodists and came out unscathed, and the Partridge Mews Players still talk about my role as Golde in Fiddler on the Roof. Tell me, why then did you choose to use the faults of my father as a representation of my character?'

'That's just the way it's done.'

'Buy a new shirt, Mr Smethwick. I'm going home.'

She flashed him the Look and we left.

Once I took our Doris home, I went around to Alf and Edith's. I might have been going round to ask if he fancied a trip down the Hare and Horse; I might also have been wondering about the extra-marital endeavours of my dead father-in-law and the implications for our Doris, but Alf wasn't home, so I had to contend with the latter.

Edith invited me into the kitchen, but she didn't switch the kettle on. She'd already got a mug of tea and had made no plans for guests. I sat down at the table and asked about Alf, but she had no idea where he was – that usually means he's off getting up to mischief and will roll in with a few Melton Mowbray pork pies stashed about his person, but we all thought he'd given up that game.

Edith said, 'That must be the first time I've heard Rick Smethwick go silent in decades. Doris should be proud of herself.'

I said to Edith, I said, 'She went to distance herself from all of this business with Cyril.'

'It's funny how we can never hide from these

things.'

'I understand that she has no part to play in all this, but I wish she'd mentioned it before.'

'Why should she? What business of ours is it if Cyril went round with a dozen women half his age?' She fixed me with a stern frown.

'I feel like I've been lied to.'

'Well, you haven't. Doris is being used as a fall guy for her father's misdeeds. She's done right to keep quiet.' Edith slurped her tea and went on, she said, 'Your job, 'arold, is to support her, not sit around in my kitchen after a free tutorial on the social machinations of small-town housewives.'

I said to her, I said, 'What do I do?'

'It's a marriage, not puff pastry. You've been at it for nearly sixty years, there's no need to act like it's difficult.'

'I'm married to our Doris, and this sort of thing has never happened before.'

'Pull the other one, 'arold. She's got you into plenty of scrapes over the years.'

'You're not going to side with me on this one, are you?'

Edith winced, shaking her head at me. 'If you were ever looking for a moment to prove you're a man, then that was it. There are no sides. This has nothing to do with Doris and everything to do with the way folk portion out blame. They'll soon decide that Doris should have kept Cyril home because everyone knows that Janice has tested more mattresses than Benson's for Beds.'

I sat and absorbed Edith's words. She wasn't wrong – some might be on the side of our Doris, maybe even Janice to some extent, but they wouldn't like to blame Cyril, even if he was a cider-drinking, chain-smoking gambler, more likely to siphon his money into the greyhound track than the family home.

I said to Edith, I said, 'I'd best be going, hadn't I?'

'That's one of the wisest things you've said today.'

I left, only to be met by Mrs Cribbins.

She was standing outside Alf and Edith's looking all mournful, like she were set to tell me that a litter of Dalmatian pups had been stolen. I asked her what the matter was, but all she said to me was, 'I'm sorry, Mr Copeland, I didn't mean for it to come out this way.' Then she dashed back towards her house with all the urgency of a weak bladder.

I didn't call after her, simply set off home wondering if she'd been the one to tell the Gazette about Cyril.

She hadn't.

I found out just what she meant the following morning when the Partridge Mews Gazette reported that our Doris had scammed the WI out of a trip to Buckingham Palace.

They were correct.

I looked at our Doris agog when she told me. I said to her, I said, 'How do you scam someone out of a visit to see the Queen?'

She said to me, she said, 'Give over, our 'arold. We would only have seen Camilla.'

'She's still a royal, our Doris.'

'And I could have been as well, if I didn't have an aversion to big ears and rapidly receding hairlines.'

According to the newspaper, Mrs Cribbins had received a letter inviting two representatives from the Partridge Mews Women's Institute to visit the Palace as a celebration of WIs across the country. Since the WI was no more, she'd contacted our Doris to inquire about the best form of action, only for my wife of fifty-six years to say as she'd write herself and inform them of the WI's dissolution, when in actual fact she'd accepted the invitation on behalf of herself and a guest.

Our Doris was slumped down at the kitchen table. 'This wasn't supposed to happen.'

'Well, what was?'

'When I found out about the redevelopment, I thought that if I could get the royals on side, they might help put a stop to it.'

'They don't get involved in things like that.'

'They would if they knew what's good for them,' she said. 'I've been a taxpayer for nearly sixty years, practically paying their electricity bills. The least they could do is visit and put a stop to the brutal desecration of our countryside.'

'That's a compelling argument, our Doris. Completely barmy, but compelling.'

'What would you have me do, our 'arold?'

'If you're really after saving the countryside then get John Craven on the blower, not the Duchess of Cornwall.'

'To tell the truth, when Bianca resurfaced, I thought I might take her.'

'Bianca hated the royals.'

'But she loved their gardens. I could just see her sipping Pimm's beneath the Queen's hydrangeas.'

I didn't point out that if Bianca went to Buckingham Palace, she'd pick a fight with Prince Charles and be in the Tower of London by mid-afternoon. Instead, I said to our Doris, I said, 'Did you consider contacting Veronica? I'm sure she'd be an acquaintance of the royals and it would have been less hassle than upsetting the entire WI.'

'I once upset them by bringing the wrong doily to a

bake sale in nineteen-seventy-four. Upsetting the WI is a strength of mine.'

'And it's one you keep training. What do we do now?'

'I've been summoned to the church hall this afternoon to meet the former members of the WI. I don't know what they expect of me. How can I be accused of scamming an organisation that doesn't exist anymore?'

Later that day, we entered the church hall as trepidatious as schoolchildren on their way to the headmistress. I felt just as I did when sir caught me with a gobstopper during "Music and Movement" and invited me to his classroom for the slipper.

What we found was reminiscent of an am-dram performance of The Crucible; a dozen or so ladies sat in a semi-circle of plastic chairs, cradling cups of instant coffee. As with all WI events, an urn took pride of place against the wall, beneath a Sunday school display on the topic of friendship.

Our Doris said to me, she said, 'Look, our 'arold, it's Partridge Mews' very own kangaroo court.'

Mrs McBride sat front and centre, as smarmy as an avocado in her burgundy jumper. She said to our Doris, she said, 'Thank you for finally choosing to grace us with your presence, Mrs Copeland. I suppose you were following the royal example and arriving fashionably late.'

'On the contrary, Mrs McBride, I didn't want to be

here.'

There were a few gasps and some chunnering from the ladies, as though they'd never watched television after nine o'clock at night. They were basically a chorus line at that point, there to make the proceedings appear more serious than they were – more often than not, it was how they got away from the endless monotony of housework and wondering how many times in one day they could buff a faux-marble countertop.

I checked the faces of folk, but the person I searched for wasn't there. I said to Mrs McBride, I said, 'Did Mrs Cribbins bottle it, then?'

'The whereabouts of Mrs Cribbins is none of your business. Besides, her absence has no bearing on today's proceedings.'

Our Doris removed her gloves and said, she said, 'I'd be quite interested to know what today's proceedings are. Since the WI doesn't exist anymore, I struggle to understand why we're here.'

Mrs McBride bristled at that. 'I'm not sure you understand the severity of what you've done, Mrs Copeland.'

When Mrs McBride started talking, our Doris started walking. She crossed the church hall to the urn and poured herself a cup of tea – as dull as dishwater, but she wanted to give off an aloof impression. I can always tell when our Doris wants to appear aloof – her steps become more pronounced, movements all slow and methodical. She makes sure that every clack of her heels can be heard against the linoleum in a staccato soundtrack.

Mrs McBride went on, saying to our Doris, 'That invite was meant to be seen by the entire WI, upon which we would have selected two members to best represent us to the royal family.'

'Once more, let me reiterate, since you can't be bothered to listen, that the Partridge Mews Women's Institute doesn't exist anymore. Your chairwoman has returned to Ireland. Prior to her, I was the interim chairwoman, therefore Mrs Cribbins came to me with the information and asked me to take it off her hands.'

'She didn't expect you to accept the invitation for yourself.'

'I had no intention of anyone finding out.' Our Doris took a sip of her tea before continuing – she always likes to punctuate her sentences with a beverage does our Doris, says as it raises anticipation. She said to Mrs McBride, she said, 'I provided the Palace with my details and asked them to contact me. Unfortunately, one letter slipped through the net and Mrs Cribbins discovered my faux pas.'

'It's a little more than a faux pas, Mrs Copeland.'

'Is this really because I accepted the invitation, or is it because you would have done the exact same thing in my position? I haven't embezzled money from the WI. I haven't said anything against the WI, not publicly anyway, and nor did I leave our tickets to the RHS Flower Show on the number thirty-eight to Crewe.'

'You and I both know that the members forgave me for that,' Mrs McBride said. 'What you did is another beast entirely.'

'Do you honestly believe that the royals care who turns up to their garden party? They asked for two representatives from the WI. As far as they're concerned, their job is done. They invited us. We accepted.'

'*You* accepted.'

Our Doris geared herself up. She walked back towards the front of the hall, staring over their heads with her shoulders back, her nose in the air and her eyes set in such a way that the women may as well have been slugs.

She said to them, she said, 'Let's not pretend to be shocked by my behaviour. I am Mrs Doris Copeland. I once single-handedly prepared a five-course meal for fourteen while my daughter was in labour. I know a thing or two about pressure. It's that, alongside my knowledge of WI procedure, that makes me the perfect candidate for chairwoman, or president, or whatever you decide to call it.

'Yes, I wrote to Buckingham Palace and said I'd attend a garden party hosted by the Duchess of Cornwall. I wasn't the reason the WI disbanded. The blame lies squarely at the door of Mrs McBride, a woman with her head so far up her own backside that if she went for a colonoscopy, she'd receive a complimentary brain scan.

'If anything, I've proven myself to be the most dedicated member of the WI, even though I have faced adversity at every turn. I won't apologise for feeling I deserved a reward. Should I tell everyone how I was practically run out of town by a WI that toxic it should be declared a nuclear hazard?

'We forgot that our core objective was to support one another as women. I don't deny being part of that, and if you need another apology, I am sorry, but I refuse to allow you to drag my name through the mud anymore.

'With that being said, there was a story about my father in the newspaper recently. Of course, I have some modicum of shame to know that someone would share my familial secrets to harm my reputation. It always seems such a risk in my opinion, especially considering the friends I've made over the years and the things they've confided in me. I can't say I'd ever do something as scandalous as to tell them, but who are we to suppose the future?

'I'll take my leave because I've quite frankly grown bored. I will just say, however, that my husband needs fertiliser for his allotment. If you're interested in spreading anymore manure, feel free to take it there.'

She handed her cup to some unsuspecting person in the front row and turned on her heel, ignoring any insults that Mrs McBride flung in her direction.

Our Doris contacted the Palace when we arrived home to inform them that she would no longer be attending Camilla's garden party, which she understood would be a major blow since our Doris best represents what it means to be a member of the WI, especially a WI from Cheshire. That's one thing about our Doris, she's always been sure of who she wants to be, even if that person is more cut-throat than Sweeney Todd.

After her phone call, she went to sulk in the living room. She said to me, she said, 'I'd found the perfect hat for the occasion as well.'

I said to her, I said, 'You didn't buy it, though?'

'Of course, I bought it, our 'arold. It's perfect for a garden party at Buckingham Palace; cerulean, avant-garde without being ridiculous, and subtle enough as to steer clear of upstaging any minor royals.'

'How much did it cost?'

'You can't put a price on perfection.'

'Well, somebody must have done.'

She gave me the Look and said to me, she said, 'As

my husband, you should support me in attaining the necessary goods to secure my happiness.'

I let her response linger before saying to her, I said, 'I suppose you'll just have to find somewhere else to wear the hat, then.'

'I won't get invited anywhere since I've thoroughly upset the ladies.' She looked me dead in the eyes and asked, 'What am I supposed to do? How do I make amends? Not just for my actions, but for those committed by my sod of a father as well.'

'You shouldn't have to apologise for Cyril.'

'Somebody has to, and why not his last remaining relative?' She sighed. 'I don't know where he found the energy for an affair, not with his gallstones.'

That's when it came to me. I don't know why Cyril's gallstones reminded me of the pub, but before I could properly think it over and consider how much we'd regret the experience with every fibre of our beings, I said, 'I might have an idea, our Doris.'

She set aside the television remote and said to me, she said, 'If this is an idea of a sexual nature, our 'arold, then I'm not in the mood. You can take it up with a copy of Woman's Weekly.'

'It's an idea for you to speak to the ladies.'

'At this point, I'll accept anything. I'd let Deborah Meaden flatten me beneath a steamroller if I thought it might help.'

'They're having a Burns Night celebration down the Hare and Horse. You know as well as I do that it's usually full of ladies from the WI. We go, and after the food, you get up and talk.'

Our Doris mulled – she looked like she were trying to dislodge a shard of toffee from her incisor, she was that deep in thought. Eventually, she said to me, she said,

315

'Will I have to eat haggis?'

'It is Burns Night.'

'Does that mean a horde of local poets getting up to read their doggerel?'

'You can call it penance for Buckingham Palace.'

'I think I'd rather have another shot at community service.'

I got on the phone before our Doris could protest and booked a table.

Burns Night arrived and I drove us down the Hare and Horse. We went with Alf and Edith to make the experience somewhat more bearable.

Linda had gone all out for the occasion; she'd draped tartan cloths on every table with centrepieces of fake thistles. Gerry Rafferty played on the stereo as the scent of over-boiled cabbage mingled with that of Boddington's Best and wended its way over to assault our nostrils.

Alf sniffed deeply and said, 'That's Burns Night, all right.'

I picked out the poets immediately, chatting raucously to one another, all scarves, blazers, and eyes like voles. They also happened to be the only people not glaring at us as though we'd just set fire to a cattery.

Our Doris had us wait a few minutes before arriving to let people settle down and calm themselves with the idea that they could bemoan her all they wanted. She always knows how to make an entrance and chose her moment specifically to make the most impact – it were like reaching the reduced aisle of Tesco only to see some greedy sod sweep a dozen rotisserie chickens into his trolley and claim an ill dog.

These folk were livid. They eyed our Doris with a malice I've only ever seen in cowboy films when someone is about to be shot – apart from the music, the pub was silent.

Our Doris offered a smile before focusing on one woman in particular – mousy hair, rosacea, mascara on her cheek – she said to her, she said, 'It's not often I see you quiet, Lavinia. I hope it's not laryngitis.'

Lavinia found her tongue and said to our Doris, 'I don't know how you can show your face around here after everything you've done.'

'I'm sure people said much the same when you had the Scouts' Legoland fund for your new conservatory, but here you are, clinging onto life even though everyone is desperately begging you to stop.'

Lavinia was gobsmacked. She reverted to silence and our Doris went to order our drinks.

When she sat down with us, I said to her, I said, 'Do you think you went a bit far there, our Doris?'

She gave me the Look and said, 'When I want advice on my conversational stylings, our 'arold, I will seek out an elocutionist, not a man who still struggles to pronounce Alnwick.'

Edith said, 'You're certainly gunning for everyone tonight, aren't you, Doris? Will you insult me now and get it over with, or do I need to book a slot?'

Our Doris attempted a glare in Edith's direction before breathing deep. She sipped her sauvignon blanc and said to us, she said, 'I'm sorry. There was no need for me to mention your linguistic disabilities, our 'arold, and it's not something I should use to attack you, not when you've so many other disappointing attributes to insult.'

I accepted her semblance of an apology and let the evening move on. Nobody else spoke to our Doris during the evening, although they certainly had much to say – I heard them chattering when I went to spend a penny – and the person fuelling the conversation was none other than Doug Grey.

I told our Doris.

Edith said to me, 'Of course he's talking nonsense about Doris. He's a mainstay of the community and has just announced how his development will help everyone's grandchildren progress further in life.'

Our Doris nodded. 'Exactly. Doug could announce he ran over a toddler in nineteen-seventy-seven and these people would lament a lack of education in the Green Cross Code.'

'It's just like old times,' Edith said. 'They're on his side because he has something they want, so they'll forget all about his past misdeeds. And yes, I do mean Janice Dooley of Little Street.'

Alf said, 'He ignores her now he's got her money.'

'He's no need for her,' I said. 'I wonder why she hasn't been over to accost you, our Doris.'

'Then you're more fool than I give you credit for, our 'arold. The town is calling me every name under the sun, so Janice has no need to. It's very much a horse-bolted-stable-door situation.'

Indeed, Janice didn't say much the entire night; she just sat in an alcove, checking her phone and sipping at a vodka tonic like it were holy communion. She'd had something done to her hair that left her looking like a cross between Bet Lynch and a tumbleweed. Janice were cowed – something I never imagine I'd say about the woman caught with Archie Butterworth in a portaloo during the under-twelves inter-county cricket match. Our Doris went on about it for weeks afterwards, not least because Janice wore a skirt from John Lewis that was well beyond her means, and she couldn't help but wonder who funded it – certainly not Archie with his paltry wage from the greengrocer. He's still at it is Archie – settled down a bit since his deep vein thrombosis, but that's to be expected.

Eventually we finished our meals – the typical neeps and tatties fare of such occasions – the lights dimmed, and Linda announced the poets.

I've never claimed to understand poetry – and at the age of seventy-six, with my literary tastes stretching just as far as Michael Connelly, I don't think I ever will – but I had absolutely no idea what that lot were on about. They're a different breed: poets. They look at the world, call a spade a metaphor for a broken heart and only garden when it's an allegory for sex, or death – there's not much else you can talk about in poetry, although one lass did have a go with a verse about a slug. That one really raised our Doris's hackles, did that.

Once the poets had finished their bit, Linda invited our Doris up to the microphone. There was a bit of chunnering amongst the crowd, but that had been going on since someone likened love to a sea anemone; Pam Ayres would be panicking.

Our Doris approached the microphone with as much dignity as she could muster, aided by her bottle-green ankle boots, purchased from a boutique, I'm told – making a statement without breaking the bank, she said. She stared at a bunch of folk with poor opinions of her – again. It happens that often I don't know why she bothers, but then I've never had to source an alternative to dairy only to feed a lactose-intolerant lass parmesan cheese when I thought she was making a political statement by going vegan. In all fairness, the girl did leave the lavatory eventually, and she was in time for the tombola, but that hasn't stopped her bringing it up every time our Doris gets put on sandwich duty.

Speaking of Alison, she was one of the people in the audience glaring at our Doris. However, she's also one of the only folk that our Doris has accidentally harmed physically – granted, it was only stomach pain that was cured with a dose of Buscopan.

After introducing herself, our Doris said, she said, 'While I'm aware that this isn't an event organised by the Partridge Mews Women's Institute, since there are enough of its former members here, I wish to make a statement with regards to my recent wrongdoing, and unfortunately that means taking up the time of an unsuspecting public. However, this will also be an education in decorum, so please do feel free to take notes. Especially you, Miss Dooley. You might now be a millionaire, but those shoes still scream Poundstretcher.

'I come to you first because I owe you an apology. Frankly, my father owes you an apology, but since he died forty years ago, I'll make it on his behalf. I'm sorry for the way you were treated all those years ago. I do not apologise for everything I have ever said to you, nor will I forgive your plans for Barraclough's Field, but for whatever went on between you and he, I apologise.

'Next, I owe an apology to the former members of the defunct Partridge Mews Women's Institute. Once more, I won't apologise for insulting Mrs McBride. Personal remarks are personal remarks, and I certainly wanted to bring her down a peg or two. But I will apologise for accepting an invitation to Buckingham

Palace in the hope of persuading the royals to get involved in putting a stop to Miss Dooley's development plans.'

'And look how well that worked!' This from Doug Grey, who had risen from his seat – even in the gloom of the pub, I could tell his face were practically purple, looking like some sort of drunken beetroot. He surged towards our Doris, face screwing up as he spoke, saying to her, he said, 'I've had about enough of you, Doris. When I were married to that old screw, Violet, all I heard about was Doris bloody Copeland, and then me and Janice get together and it's all I hear as well.'

Our Doris gave him the Look and said to him, she said, 'I never knew the power of my own celebrity, Mr Grey, but may I point out that throughout your marriage to Violet, you were also in a relationship with Miss Dooley. Quite honestly, I wonder if you were drawn to them not because of their personalities, but because of their obsession with me.'

'You wish, you old bat.'

'Old?' Our Doris grinned. 'Douglas, have you forgotten that you're older than my husband? And he's been old for the last twenty years. Besides, I've come to an even firmer conclusion as to how you came to be drawn to both Violet and Janice.'

'And what's that?'

'Money.'

Doug froze stock still in the middle of the pub, more aware than ever that there was an entire crowd of folk watching him and our Doris go at it. He said, 'Janice and I are due to be married.'

'This is true. Strange that it wasn't announced until she inherited all of her father's money. But then, she had no control of that.'

Doug looked as though he were about to say something more, but he stopped. Everyone remained silent as we grew more aware of the way he was clutching his left arm. There was enough sweat on his brow to fill a reservoir and his face looked set to explode. He howled and plummeted towards the ground.

Our Doris practically launched herself from the stage. It was like she'd forgotten she'd had a hip replacement as she rushed towards Doug. She dropped to her knees beside him, screaming for Linda to phone an ambulance.

She spoke to him, before removing something from the inside pocket of his jacket – a sort of spray that she fired beneath his tongue.

Janice joined her and they helped move Doug into some semblance of the recovery position, looking like a red kidney bean as he hunched there.

Our Doris continued to speak to Doug, ignoring all else going on around her, even the fact that she was holding hands with Janice Dooley of Little Street and working hard to calm her down.

After a few minutes, things eased for Doug. He sat up, looking older and as pale as a pork shoulder fresh from the freezer.

Our Doris wasn't looking much better herself. She waited with them until the paramedics arrived, at which point she headed straight towards the bar and ordered herself a large brandy. She downed it in one.

I went over and said to her, I said, 'Are you all right, our Doris?'

She shook her head and said, 'Of course I'm not all right, our 'arold. I just had to save the life of a man I can't stand.'

'If you hadn't, someone else would have stepped in.'

Our Doris said to me, she said, 'It suddenly came over me. I didn't mean to help him.'

'I never expected you to have an instinct to help folk.'

'I cared for you after you had your appendix removed.'

'You went to Chester for afternoon tea and I had to phone our Angela.'

'But I left the phone within reach. An uncaring person wouldn't have done that.' Our Doris downed a second brandy before saying to me, she said, 'No, our 'arold, as I saw Doug fall, I could only think about Bianca. If anyone could have saved her, I wouldn't have cared if they were my mortal enemy.'

I put my arms around our Doris and led her back towards our table.

Doug's angina scare put an end to the night. All around the Hare and Horse, folk tied their scarves and buttoned up their coats, setting themselves up for a walk home in the crisp January air.

We made for off ourselves.

The ambulance hadn't yet left when we got outside.

When Janice Dooley of Little Street saw us, she called out for our Doris and came running over – well, what septuagenarians call running, in any case. She reached us and said to our Doris, 'I just want to say that were right decent of you, what you did back there.'

'I'm surprised you have any concept of decency considering the length of your skirts.'

'I haven't caught a chill yet, Doris.' Janice smirked before swallowing hard and saying, 'You didn't have to help Doug. The way he is some days, I'm not sure I'd have helped him myself. But thanks, Doris.'

Our Doris nodded and said to Janice, she said,

'That's quite all right, Miss Dooley. I was merely performing my public duty. Although, as you say, it might have been kinder to let him croak. Alas, I might have disappointed the public once more.'

'That lot in there were all singing your praises, even Mrs McBride,' Janice said. 'But listen, there's something else I wanted to say. I didn't know how to tell you, because Doug thought all the publicity was good for the development, and well … it's Doug.'

'What is it, Janice?' I asked, feeling as though my eyelashes were due to freeze from the cold.

'It wasn't me who went to the Gazette about your dad and me. We might not get on, Doris, but I've always thought that was something that stayed between the two of us.' Janice's face was as earnest as I'd ever seen it, eyes wide and appealing to our Doris's better nature.

I said to them both, I said, 'There's nobody else it could have been?'

Janice looked knowingly to our Doris. 'There's only one other person that could have gone to the newspapers.' She breathed deep then, pulling the air from far beneath her ribcage, she said to our Doris, she said, 'The thing is, I never did have an affair with your dad.'

Our Doris's own breathing hitched. She pressed her fingernails into the leather of her handbag and said, 'What in the good Lord's name do you mean you never had an affair with him?'

'I know where you heard that there was something going on between us, but nothing happened.'

'Then why have you always teased me about it?'

'Because I could, it was an easy way to rile you up. We can't pretend that we like each other now, just because you stopped my Doug from carking it.'

Our Doris stared at Janice, disbelief etched into every pore, looking as though she'd just seen the inside of Doctor Who's TARDIS. She said to her, she said, 'You've had me thinking that you slept with my father for nearly sixty years! I thought he had some sort of shameful secret. My Mum ended up in prison for battering your mother.'

Janice nodded. 'Which just goes to show that we've never got on, Doris. One thing I've always wondered is how you found out about me and Mr Gadsden. I thought we kept that one well-hidden.'

She would have waited around for a response if the paramedics hadn't called her back to the ambulance. They slammed the doors behind her as she hopped into the back to go with Doug to the hospital. Meanwhile, I had to contend with a wife who looked as though she could go twenty rounds with Giant Haystacks and not stop for a breather.

We went straight into the kitchen when we got home. I switched on the kettle and our Doris slouched at the table, her coat still on, her face a blend of relief and consternation I hadn't seen since our Theo's fourth dance recital. It was two-thousand-and-eight, our Doris thought he could do with perking up and popped down to Starbucks. The dance hall never did get the stains out of the curtains; it's a good job they were brown.

Our Doris said to me, she said, 'All these years, I've held onto a shameful secret that isn't even true. Just imagine how things could have been.'

I took our drinks over, saying to her, I said, 'Janice told you herself, you two would never have been friends.'

'Exactly, our 'arold. Imagine all the things I could have said had I not felt guilty.'

'Did you ever feel guilty?'

She gave me the Look, appearing slightly less menacing in her lilac anorak. 'While I might not have felt guilt for my words, I've spent the best part of sixty years fearing that the secret would come out. Now I know it was all lies, it feels like a waste of perfectly good emotion. I could have directed all that anger towards breakfast television, excluding Lorraine Kelly.'

'At least you finally have the truth.'

She would have said more had it not been for a knock at the front door.

I answered to find Violet Grey hovering on the doorstep like the Bride of Frankenstein. She said, 'Good evening, Mr Copeland. I apologise for the late visit, but may I come in?'

I said to her, I said, 'I'm letting you in because you owe our Doris some answers, but I regret the day that she ever thought to call you for help.'

I led her into the kitchen.

With the strength of her glower, if our Doris had lasers for eyes then Violet wouldn't have made it past the hall mirror. She said to her, she said, 'Violet, how lovely to see you. I wondered why it suddenly smelled like a blocked drain.'

'Mrs McBride contacted me to tell me what you did for Douglas tonight, and I thought it only right that I visit.'

'Why?' I asked.

There was a flicker of shock at being asked such a question before she said, 'Whilst he and I may be in the process of divorcing, we've spent a considerable amount of our lives together and I wished to express how respectable it is that Mrs Copeland saved his life, even though Douglas has caused her much distress over the last few months.'

Our Doris stood up and said to her, she said, 'I don't believe that for a second, Violet. You have eyes all over this town, and perhaps you heard about how Janice Dooley of Little Street finally informed me that she never had an affair with my father.'

'Well, of course she'd say that.'

'She certainly took a long time to start defending herself. Who told me about the supposed affair in the first place? You. 'Arold told me how unlikely it was for you to have been near The Blind Cat to have seen the pair of them together, and the more I think about it, the more I realise how much you benefited from the rumour.'

Violet appeared shiftier, saying, 'You're thinking too much into things, Mrs Copeland.'

'Don't play dumb, Violet. While it might be your natural state, it's never suited you.'

She said nothing for a moment, then sighed. 'Douglas was courting Janice Dooley at the time. I knew how much you hated one another, so I simply said, and forgive me if I misremember, but I recall saying that your father and Janice had been seen in the same area. I never said that they'd been seen together.'

'I wouldn't call that misremembering. I'd call it a downright lie, but then, I suppose you're an expert. Can you imagine how it's been for me all these years? I thought less of my father, our family broke apart and I ended up having to go and live elsewhere.'

'I don't think that the lie can be blamed for that,' Violet said, as haughty as ever. 'If your parents hadn't separated because of the rumour, something else would have caused it, and we all know that Bianca was a flake, flitting about through life, never settling down, never making a home. You can call it my fault, Mrs Copeland, but I never cared where Bianca went, I think she just wanted to make sure she never had to spend time with an irksome little busybody like you.'

Our Doris clenched her fists and hissed through her

teeth. 'You ruined my family for a man so renowned for extra-marital activities that he was cited in forty-seven divorce cases. Douglas Grey is a sex pest, a philanderer...he is a worm. Only now do I begin to realise you're well-suited.'

'You once likened me to a slug.'

'I did.' Our Doris grinned. 'I do so enjoy when my estimations prove correct. Now, please don't take this the wrong way, but I'd quite appreciate if you were to buzz off.'

Violet had clearly expected more retaliation, something akin to when our Doris battered Janice Dooley of Little Street around that graveyard. She said, 'Don't you have more to say?'

Our Doris shrugged and said to her, she said, 'There is nothing left to say on the matter, Mrs Grey. I have the full measure of your character and I've no intention of stooping to the level of someone so far beneath me.'

I saw fear in Violet's eyes then; they were wide, and her skin seemed to have paled even further. She said to our Doris, 'But what will you do?'

Our Doris offered a polite smile, eyes filled with the fury of several-thousand seagulls, and said to Violet, she said, 'I am going to see about reforming the Partridge Mews Women's Institute, safe in the knowledge that you shan't have anything to do with it.'

'Those women are my friends.'

'Those women are your acquaintances. You've treated them like pawns since we were schoolgirls, manipulating them to bow to your demands. They will be far better off without you. Should you choose to worm your way back into our lives, then I will see to it that they find out everything you did. Not just how you led me to believe that my father debased himself with

Janice Dooley of Little Street, but just what went on in Barraclough's Field in nineteen-ninety.'

Our Doris had dealt the killer blow, Violet nodded, as meek as a hamster faced with an apricot, and without another word, she left.

After a few moments, I asked her, 'Did you mean all of that, our Doris? You're really not going to do anything?'

'For the moment, but if either Violet or Doug step out of line again, they won't know what's hit them.'

Our Doris picked up her cup of tea and necked it in one gulp. With the truth revealed, I couldn't help but wonder if she wasn't preparing one of her most nefarious schemes of the last seventy-four years.

Our Doris and Violet Grey are at it again.

It's been nearly two years since they last did battle and, once more, Partridge Mews is caught in the crossfire.

When she received the news that Violet was planning a tombola to raise funds for the reformation of the Partridge Mews Women's Institute, our Doris reached a level of fury I haven't seen since she heard about Patricia Pemberton's loft conversion.

She came into the living room and started pacing back and forth across the carpet as though she were desperate for the lavatory and the door was jammed, and she said to me, she said, 'I should have known that she wouldn't heed my warning. She's Violet Grey, for crying out loud. She practically fled the birth canal with a get out of jail free card. All this talk of a tombola to raise funds for the WI. A tombola? Everyone and their Chihuahua knows that they went out with stuffed aubergines and avocado dishes.'

I put aside my Dan Brown and said to her, I said,

'What are you going to do about it, our Doris?'

She could have been a jaguar after an iguana, her eyes were that wild. 'Erin and Edith are coming around. I warned Violet what would happen if she aligned herself with the ladies again.'

'She was chairwoman of the WI for decades. You know how much these women dislike change. Look how they reacted when Neighbours moved to Channel Five.'

'I don't think Margaret Belfield ever heard back from the Australian Embassy,' our Doris said. 'This means nothing right now, our 'arold. After everything that Violet Grey has done, the torment she's caused me over the years, I'm not prepared to stop until she leaves Partridge Mews for good.'

'You're the one who asked her to come back, our Doris.'

'And it proved to be nothing short of a mistake, even worse than when I served macaroni alongside salmon en croute.'

Erin and Edith arrived within a quarter of an hour. Erin had a Bag for Life slung over her elbow, crammed full of paperwork and plastic wallets, as though she were an ambulatory filing cabinet. I wouldn't be surprised if that were the case; Doug Grey would be thrilled to save money and storage space.

She huffed deeply as she headed into the kitchen, saying to me, she said, 'Mrs Copeland has had me making a few notes.'

'It looks like you've brought half of Doug Grey's private correspondence,' I said, looking over a few pages that had dropped to the floor.

'Well, Mrs Copeland needed evidence and I wasn't sure what to bring, so I just brought the lot.'

'The lot of what?'

She shrugged. 'Photocopies of confidential and highly classified files related to the business of DG Construction. You know how it is, Mr Copeland.'

I turned to our Doris then, practising a Look of my own. I said to her, I said, 'What're you thinking, our Doris? Erin could get in a lot of mither over this.'

Our Doris sighed the sigh of all aggrieved wives having to contend with their husband's temper tantrums and said, 'Erin isn't going to get into any trouble, our 'arold, you needn't worry.'

'What happens when Doug Grey finds out?'

She gave me the Look and said to me, she said, 'Firstly, Erin just told you that everything she has in that bag of hers is a copy. Secondly, Douglas Grey is still signed off sick due to ill health and very rarely went into the office anyway.'

'It's true, Mr Copeland. It's one of the reasons I was hired. Mr Grey only comes in to raid the petty cash, otherwise I'm pretty much on my own.' Erin spread the paperwork over the table. She went on, 'I've no idea why a man his age would want to get involved in a job like this. He should be at home with his feet up watching Dickinson's Real Deal.'

Edith said to Erin, 'I'll tell you what motivates men like Douglas Grey, Miss Beaumont. Greed. Men with money always want more money.'

I said to them, I said, 'I always thought it was a fear of dying. That he wanted to leave a legacy that didn't boil down to numerous affairs and poor cholesterol.'

Our Doris stepped in there, making sure everyone got a ginger nut before saying, she said, 'Whatever Douglas Grey's motivations are to be a colossal dimwit, we're not here to talk about him. Violet Grey is trying to get the ladies from the WI back on her side, and I intend to stop her.'

Erin said, 'I thought there wasn't a WI anymore.'

'There isn't. However, I have been making plans for the reformation of the WI and Violet is looking to take over.'

'And we're stopping her because?'

'She did not listen to my earlier warning about not interfering and remaining beneath the parapet. Now we teach her.'

'What are we teaching her?' Edith asked. 'It's not algebra, I can guarantee that much.'

Our Doris made a face that wouldn't have been misplaced in Fatal Attraction as she said to us, she said, 'I am going to teach her what happens when you betray the trust of Mrs Doris Copeland.'

'Just a minute, Mrs Copeland,' Erin said. 'Is this about the Easter egg hunt?'

Our Doris's jowls filled to the brim with fury. 'There's an Easter egg hunt?'

Erin nodded as excitable as a spaniel after a tennis ball and said to our Doris, 'Originally, she was going to hold a tombola, but I changed her mind.'

Our Doris were astonished. She said to her, she said, 'You changed Violet's mind?'

'It's just that tombolas are outdated, and nobody really cares about raising money for the WI. I said it should all be about community, and how some of the girls on the estate find it difficult to keep up with what the other Mums, the posher ones, all lip fillers and carrot sticks, are doing for their kids, so I asked Mrs Grey if it wouldn't be better to have something that benefited them. They might be more likely to join the WI then, if they felt they were being helped out.'

'So, this was your idea?' Our Doris looked

venomous, something Erin had clearly dealt with before, because she faced her as calm as a sausage roll at a vegan picnic.

'It might have been my idea, Mrs Copeland, but it's Mrs Grey's event. I wouldn't know anything about it if she hadn't been down to the office so much recently.'

'Is Janice there as well?'

'We haven't seen her or Mr Grey in weeks.'

'Then what's Violet doing there?'

I decided to intervene there, saying, 'Is it necessary for Erin to be here? She's onto a good thing with this job, whether we like Doug or not.'

Erin said to me, 'I don't do anything there anyway, Mr Copeland. I'm just a gopher for the old dears in the office. "Make us a coffee, Erin." and "Are you popping down the caff, Erin?" It's like the minute I step through the door, they lose the use of their legs.'

'Isn't that what you signed up for?'

Our Doris's Look was as fearsome as usual as she said to me, she said, 'Are you saying that Erin should accept her lot, our 'arold? A young woman set to have a good career in social work confined to doing the bidding of a few so-and-sos too lazy to get their own beverages?'

I said to her, I said, 'No, I'm saying that I'm going down the Hare and Horse. I'll pick up Alf on the way.'

Alf were happy to get out of the house. He'd been FaceTiming his grandson and had recalled how hard it was not having him around. Apparently, it was much easier to go on the rob with Martin about; he always had someone on hand to pick him up from the station. Otherwise, he had to wait for an officer to take him home, and while Edith turns a blind eye to petty theft, she draws the line at a squad car on her doorstep.

We arrived at the pub, ordered our drinks and sat down. I said to Alf, I said, 'How's your Martin doing on his big adventure?'

'He's having a great time. He made it to Paris a couple of weeks ago; don't know if he's met anyone yet. After all those French classes, it'd be a shame not to sow some wild oats.'

'I thought he went to see the world.'

'Aye,' Alf said, 'and to get some culture. But I hope he does more than chew a brie baguette under the Eiffel Tower.'

I supped my bitter and said, 'You must be missing

him.'

He nodded, all morose, chin on his chest, eyes on his beer. 'Sometimes, I wonder if Martin would have stayed if these new houses had been announced sooner.'

'Doug Grey's affordable housing?'

'It would be cheap enough for him in any case, and we would have helped him out.'

'You must be missing him, if you're prepared to give money away. You're the only man I know who once asked for change from a charity box.'

'Those things get full enough, 'arold, and I wasn't about to donate a fiver.' Alf sighed before continuing, 'No, I don't think our Martin would have stayed, even if the chance of a house came up. He needed to see more of the world, find out what it's really like. There's nowt much changes in Partridge Mews.'

I said to him, I said, 'There might be, soon. Our Doris has got Erin and your Edith around to plan the takedown of Violet Grey.'

'That sounds like them,' he said. 'You've said it before, if Winston Churchill had our wives, the war would have been over a heck of a lot faster and there'd have been time for supper, rations permitting.'

'I've said the same thing about Violet in the past as well.'

'What's she done this time?'

'She's decided to throw an Easter egg hunt.'

'An Easter egg hunt?' Alf were bewildered, wrinkles around his eyes like buckets as he said, 'What in the Lord's name is an Easter egg hunt?'

'It's exactly what it sounds like. Violet and co. hide Easter eggs around somewhere, probably the park, and then a bunch of parents let their kids go searching for them.'

'Is she charging them money?'

I shrugged. 'I've no idea. If our Doris has her way then it won't go ahead and Violet will flee town with her tail between her legs again.'

He shook his head. 'What's her problem with the hunt? It's hardly foxes, is it?'

'She's no problem with the hunt. It's the fact that it's Violet Grey arranging the hunting.'

'Would this be because Violet went to the Gazette and fed them that lie about her dad and Janice Dooley of Little Street?'

'Exactly,' I said.

'And since your Doris is planning the reformation of the WI, she sees this Easter egg hunt as an attempt to take it from her?'

'It's as though you understand my wife more than I do.'

He grinned and said, 'Your Doris has been doing stuff like this since we were at school together. I were surprised when you told me she was going to let Violet get away with having her think all that rubbish about Cyril. This actually sounds like she's back on form.'

I nodded. Alf was right. Folk say that revenge is sweet, and I know first-hand that our Doris has a heck of a sweet tooth.

When we left the pub, we saw something that had me reach for my phone and take a few photos. I drove home with Alf and presented my evidence to our Doris.

Edith saw the images and made such contortions with her face that it looked as though she were going for the blue ribbon in an international gurning competition. She said, 'I didn't think he'd be able to do that sort of thing. Not with his heart.'

I'd been walking to the car with Alf, only for him to grab my arm and drag me behind a Land Rover as though we were a young courting couple and he were after getting amorous. Either that, or a bloke after a fight. I said to him, I said, 'I'm not sure what you're after, Alf, but I'm not interested.'

He looked at me confused, bewildered, and I couldn't be sure if it were the beer or my words. He blinked a few times and said, 'I knew you hadn't seen them.'

'Who?'

And that's when I saw Doug and Violet Grey

snogging in a ginnel. She were giving it all that Ingrid Bergman in Casablanca and he were trying to be Humphrey Bogart but looked more like Pavarotti choking on a king prawn.

I took out my phone, snapped some photos and went home considering a new career as a paparazzo or a private investigator; I have just what it takes to be the next Columbo – I just have to get myself a raincoat and develop an interest in cigars.

Standing in the kitchen, all thoughts of changing jobs slipped from my mind as Erin took my phone and zoomed in on the faces of Doug and Violet. She said to us, 'Is this what people really look like when they're kissing?'

Our Doris nodded and said, 'It is when Doug Grey's part of it.'

'I don't think God blessed him with a tongue,' Edith said, 'just threw a walloping, great slug in his mouth and set him on his merry way.'

'Only you can't get rid of him by sprinkling salt on his head.'

Alf said, 'You could give it a go, for a laugh.'

'I could have our 'arold run him over for a laugh, but he's too concerned about his suspension.'

'And the murder charge,' I said.

'Don't be stupid, our 'arold, the PCC for Cheshire is an acquaintance of mine. We could have it all swept under the rug as a hit and run.'

'You've thought too much about this, our Doris.'

'I've watched a lot of Line of Duty, you pick these things up.'

Alf chimed in there, saying, 'I couldn't make head nor tail of that. There were too many acronyms. Spent half my time trying to figure out what they'd done to the

341

alphabet, only to hear them repeat fifty-thousand variations on BLT.'

'They're too skinny for bacon,' Erin said, 'I bet they're all on cottage cheese and celery juice.'

'Celery juice?' Edith asked.

A nod from Erin. 'It's the new thing to detox, apparently. My Mum's on another health kick, but it'll go the same way as kefir, you watch.'

'As much as I enjoy hearing about your mother's dietary regimes, may we please return to the matter at hand?'

I said to her, I said, 'Just a moment, our Doris, what about Janice?'

'We say nothing. For many years, Janice skulked around after Doug like a lovesick cockroach and we said nothing to Violet. We will extend the same courtesy to Janice.'

'But Violet knew what Doug was getting up to.'

'And she used it to her advantage. Until we're sure of everyone's motives, we say nothing.'

Edith said, 'Doris is right. Leave the Greys to it and we'll work on putting a stop to their plans.'

'It's only an Easter egg hunt, Edith.'

'For now,' she said.

I shook my head. I were completely oblivious to what the women in my kitchen had planned. I said, 'Honestly, this is like being in Churchill's war ministry.'

Our Doris said to me, she said, 'That's nonsense, our 'arold. Churchill wouldn't suit a perm.'

I said nothing and took Alf down the allotment. There's only so much support a husband can give to his wife's scheming.

Next day, we went to visit our Bianca's solicitor for the reading of her will. It was all fairly straightforward – she'd left money behind for her children and Dahlia, and everything else went to our Doris, including the bungalow. That surprised both of us. Bianca never seemed the type to own property, and we'd both thought the bungalow were council accommodation – it certainly had that utilitarian look that council houses have, all bleak and stinking of vanilla – but no, as well as a house on Shakespeare Avenue, our Doris had become the unsuspecting owner of a bungalow. She wasn't happy about it.

'A bungalow, our 'arold? What am I going to do with a bungalow?'

'You could sell it, our Doris,' I said.

She gave me the Look and said, 'I'm well-aware that I could sell the thing. However, our Bianca knew how much I had on my plate with the reformation of the WI and my other social obligations. Why would she think I had the time to sell a house as well?'

'It's only a little one.'

'That's beside the point. I've simply no time to get involved in such an ordeal.'

I pulled into our drive and what we saw put a stop to any conversation because Janice Dooley of Little Street was slumped in front of our door like a bag full of rubbish waiting for the bin men. Her hair had never seemed long enough to be unruly, but she looked as though she'd fallen headfirst into a bird's nest and been unable to untangle it from her roots. She were fit to play Fantine in a poor man's version of Les Misérables, her face were that sallow. And she'd clearly been crying – we could see from the car that she'd been crying – her eyes were in deep hollows and they were all red; if that weren't from tears, she had the worst case of conjunctivitis I'd ever seen.

Our Doris were first out of the car and headed straight for her. She said to Janice, she said, 'We might not care for one another, Miss Dooley, but to lounge about on my doorstep looking as uncouth as a drunk outside an off-licence might just be one of the worst insults you've ever thrown my way.'

Janice shook her head and, holding back sobs. 'I'm sorry, Doris, I am, but you're the only one I could think to come to.'

I'd got out of the car by this point and said to Janice, I said, 'Is this about Doug?'

Our Doris shot a Look in my direction before saying to Janice, 'Please forgive my husband for bringing up such matters in the street. Shall we go inside? Whilst I might not ordinarily allow you to cross my threshold, I think that this is one of those desperate times which call for desperate measures.'

Janice blinked a few times, trying to navigate the

confusion of our Doris's sentences, and said, 'You always did know what's going on before other folk.' She heaved herself to her feet, using the door handle to hold herself steady. 'I'll have a brew if you're offering.'

We went inside and settled in the kitchen. I set about making the tea while our Doris and Janice situated themselves at the table.

Our Doris said to her, she said, 'I think it only right that we begin by sharing what we already know with one another. What is it specifically that brings you to our home this morning?'

Janice sniffed deeply – from the sound of things, it left her with lungs full of snot – and said to our Doris, 'Last night it were, I were out in town and needed to pay a visit. Well, despite all that business with Alfred Simpson, the toilets were still closed, and since I had the office keys with me, I thought I'd nip in there. That's by the by. I sort myself out and think I'll give the place a quick tidy. It's not like me, but it's supposed to be a professional-looking place and the paperwork were strewn about like nobody's business. I start tidying, and the more that I tidy, the more I keep seeing the same name cropping up again and again. Violet Grey. Every application submitted to the council, every letter, she's included as one of the people in charge of the operation.'

Our Doris said, 'But we know that. That's how we got the first application withdrawn.'

Janice shook her head. 'That's what I thought as well. When that first came out, I were proper mad at Dougie, because I never knew that she owned the business. He said that he'd sort everything, that the D in DG Construction would mean Dooley. Well, he's been playing me like a fiddle, he has, because my name isn't mentioned on any of the documents. As far as this development is concerned, I'm nothing more than a money pit.'

She slumped down in her chair as our Doris straightened, spine erect. 'I'm afraid that's not the worst of things, Miss Dooley. Yesterday, we discovered that Violet and Doug show no signs of getting divorced.'

'What do you mean?'

'Show her, our 'arold.'

I set our drinks down on the table and took out my phone.

Janice blanched even further when I showed her the pictures, looking even more like an under-done poached egg, and said, 'What am I going to do? He's had me spend the better half of my inheritance on that land.'

I put my phone away. 'I'm sorry to have to show you those photos, Janice.'

I was – she might be nothing more than a goblin in a sausage skin, but nobody deserves to see the supposed love of their life getting amorous with his wife, especially when he's spent nearly fifty years shacking up with them behind said wife's back.

'It's all right, 'arold. I'm pleased to have it confirmed, actually. I thought there must have been something up when Violet kept popping up on the CCTV at our office.'

It was our Doris's turn to look shocked. She said to Janice, she said, 'I didn't expect you to check the cameras. I thought that with all the money Doug has, he'd have a private security firm.'

Janice grinned at our Doris then. 'Is this because I saw your little friend Erin photocopying our files?'

'Well, yes.'

'Why else do you think I'm here, Doris? You've clearly got some plans to take down Dougie, and I want in.'

Our Doris went uneasy, looking down into her cup of tea. She were considering her options, I could tell from the way she started chunnering under her breath, sounding like she were trying to summon someone from beyond the grave. Eventually, she said to Janice, she said, 'This had better not be a trick, Miss Dooley. I meant no harm in showing you those photographs. I merely wished to share all of the information we've obtained so far with you.'

'I'm not after hurting Erin in any way. She's an all right girl, despite the fact she calls you a mate.' Janice slurped her coffee and said to our Doris, she said, 'If Dougie wants Violet, he's welcome to her. I'll help you in any which way I can, but I'm going to ask one thing of you.'

'And what's that?'

'I want my money back,' she said. 'My name might not be on any of those plans, but I can guarantee that the land is in my name. Old Barraclough wouldn't sell it to anybody else.'

'How can you be sure of that?' I asked.

'Let's just say that I have an intimate knowledge of the upholstery in his back bedroom.'

Our Doris allowed herself a small smile. 'That's what I like to see: a woman putting her talents to good use.'

'Says the woman who always had a go at my extracurricular activities.'

'Oh, I've no issue with sex, Miss Dooley,' our Doris said. 'It's the fact that you never used it to your advantage that I always found unappealing.'

I chose not to point out our Doris's lie and sipped my tea in silence.

Janice said, 'Do you think we can help one another?'

Once more, our Doris considered Janice's words before saying, she said, 'I think we have our work cut out for us. The Greys have long been considered an upstanding couple within our community. He's a former mayor, and she's been at the forefront of the WI for decades. However, I've always enjoyed a challenge. I was one of the first women in Partridge Mews to attempt choux pastry. I'm sure that putting a stop to their plans is achievable.'

Again, I remained silent. Our Doris had attempted to make choux pastry after watching a Delia Smith Christmas special in nineteen-ninety-two; after several hours in the kitchen, she threw the mixture in the bin and had me pop to Tesco. Our Doris might always face a challenge, but even she knows when to accept her losses and take the easy way out.

Somehow, my photos of the Greys ended up in the Partridge Mews Gazette. I collected the newspaper from the letterbox, only to see the rather blurry images blown up to tabloid proportions with a headline about Doug Grey being a love-rat after announcing his engagement to Janice Dooley of Little Street.

I took the Gazette into the kitchen and left it on the table for our Doris, who was in the middle of doing her hair. She's always paid particular attention to her hair, has our Doris; she says that just one strand out of place can lead to certain ladies passing judgement on your health and welfare. It's one of the reasons she's always had a perm and Silvakrinned it to the high heavens. Since her hair has grown back to the point she can style it, she's started spending more time in front of the hall mirror in her effort to give off the impression that she's moved past having half of it burned off in a firework accident.

When she saw the front page of the newspaper, she poured herself a large mug of coffee. By the time she'd finished reading the article, she'd drunk the entire thing and were pouring herself another cup. She started pacing back and forth across the room, the soles of her Hotter plimsolls squeaking against the lino.

She said to me, she said, 'How in the good Lord's name did they get these photos, our 'arold?'

I said to her, I said, 'I've no idea, our Doris.'

She gave me the Look and said, 'I suppose this was your way of trying to help, was it? Send these photos off and let the Gazette do the work for you.'

'I didn't send anything to the Gazette.'

'Then how do you explain the photos you took being emblazoned across their blasted front page?' She were furious, her face getting redder by the second, looking like a gammon in need of roasting.

'I don't know. I were as shocked as you when I picked up the paper.'

The Look showed no sign of diminishing and with our Doris were that hyped up off caffeine, her pacing didn't look to be stopping, either.

After watching her for a few minutes, I said, 'What's the problem, our Doris?'

She stopped and turned to me, grabbing the back of a chair with such ferocity I thought she might splinter the wood – she were every inch the She-Hulk as she said to me, she said, 'The problem is that we have no idea whatsoever how the people of Partridge Mews will take this news. We've no idea of the general opinion surrounding the Greys. The last they heard, Doug was planning affordable housing and then he had an angina attack while getting accosted by Mrs Doris Copeland of Shakespeare Avenue. They've no idea what's been going on in the background, no conception of the fact that he's so genetically close to an amphibian that you'd be forgiven for thinking his father were Toad of Toad Hall.'

'I'll ring Theo, get him to check the internet for us.'

I would have done so had the doorbell not rung at that moment. Both our Doris and I knew exactly who it were before I went to answer it. Violet Grey. She stood on the doorway looking as haughty as ever, her nose in the air as prominent as the beak on a puffin, all set to tip backwards if she didn't get her angles right. She said, 'Good morning, Mr Copeland. I believe your wife and I have an important matter to discuss.'

Our Doris appeared behind me and said to her, she said, 'Certainly, Mrs Grey, please do come in. I despair to imagine what the neighbours would think were they to see such detritus on my doorstep.'

She followed us into the kitchen. I don't know why we don't invite folk into the living room – perhaps our Doris is concerned about someone throwing a drink in somebody's face, or crumbs on the carpet. She might even have an issue with showing guests what books we're reading. Perhaps Lee Child isn't as respectable as I once thought; perhaps our Doris would like a husband who reads Dostoevsky at every given opportunity. She's always had this hope that I'd become more cultured. She took me to see a foreign movie once – it were French, had subtitles and all that, but twenty minutes in they showed a woman's bare chest and suddenly culture no longer seemed to matter. Our Doris dragged me out of that cinema and had me buy her a Chinese takeaway – she's always had a thing for special fried rice.

Before I had chance to sit down at the table, the doorbell went again; this time, Erin lay in wait alongside Janice Dooley of Little Street.

I said to her, I said, 'This probably isn't the best time.'

Janice said, 'Violet's here, isn't she? I said as it were

her car on the corner. She never did learn how to flaming park.' With that, she pushed past me and stormed down the hall as determined as a pig after a banana peel.

They didn't give us chance to catch up before they started lambasting one another. First, Violet started proceedings, saying, 'Good morning, Miss Dooley. I wouldn't say as it's a pleasure to see my husband's side dish, especially when it spends so much of its time looking decidedly unappetising.'

'Nice to see you, too, Mrs Grey. I'd also use big words if I didn't have anything going for me in the looks department.'

Violet turned to our Doris then and said to her, she said, 'I must say I was rather surprised to see those photographs of me and Douglas in the newspaper, simply because it doesn't seem your usual style. Ordinarily, I'd have expected to be blackmailed with such images before finding something equally as tawdry about you. Of course, that's quite easy nowadays, Mrs Copeland. Especially when you choose to cavort with such as Miss Beaumont and Miss Dooley.'

'Although I would like nothing more than to take credit for those photos of you appearing in the Gazette, I'm afraid it wasn't me who sent them in.'

'Alas, I thought that might be the case. Naturally, I assumed it was you because you're threatened by my Easter egg hunt.'

Our Doris chuckled; it were sprightly, it were social and it were positively terrifying. Erin and I stood at the kitchen counter, watching the three of them, tense as anything. 'You demean me, Violet. While I warned you about trying to get the ladies on side, if I wished to drag your name through the dirt, I wouldn't have used pictures of you in flagrante delicto with your own blasted husband.'

'Does this mean you still plan to "drag my name through the dirt", as you so beautifully put it?' Violet straightened her handbag – she held it in the crook of her elbow as though preparing to use it as a weapon. Although I can't say as it looked like a weaponised handbag – they're usually cheap, faux-leather affairs – anyone carrying a Mulberry bag isn't looking for a fight.

Our Doris said to her, she said, 'It would be erroneous of me to admit to any plans, wouldn't it, Mrs Grey? I shouldn't like to think you believe me to be so foolish.'

'You were foolish enough to believe when I said as your father had an affair with that tart over there.' Those words were spoken with venom and aimed in Janice's direction.

'Be a big girl, Violet,' Janice said. 'If you're going to fling mud about the place, at least make sure to hit me directly.'

'The issue is, Miss Dooley, that I do not speak scum.'

'Yet you manage to talk to Dougie just fine.'

'If you have such a high opinion of Douglas, then why are you still chasing after him?'

I could tell Janice were doing her best to restrain herself – her arms were twitching and her shoulders vibrating, she were that full of anger. If we'd been down The Blind Cat, she'd have laid Violet out between the slot machines and been supping a pint of Stella Artois by then. She said to Violet, 'You might go after my sloppy seconds, Violet, but I'm not after yours. The fact is that me and Doug have been on and off since we were teenagers, and most of the time we were only on because he wasn't satisfied with a woman whose only action in bed was leaning over to switch the lamps off.'

'What went on in our bedroom is no business of yours, Miss Dooley.'

'It was when Doug used to come knocking on my door at three in the morning, complaining that he'd been breathing down your ear and you asked if he had pneumonia.'

That had Violet rattled. She was perfectly fine when the conversation were nothing more than trading insults, but the fact that Doug had been discussing his marital obligations with his mistress was clearly a step too far. The blood vessels on her cheeks looked to be popping. She were a lovely shade of puce as she said to Janice, she practically yelled, 'He only ever came after you because of your father's money.'

Strangely enough, Janice sagged slightly. She inhaled before saying to Violet, 'Do you think I haven't realised that? Your husband lost interest in me the minute Barraclough signed the land over. All Doug cares about is his redevelopment. Well, I suppose I should call it *your* redevelopment as well, since your name is on all the paperwork.'

Violet paused for a moment, shock settling into her wrinkles, the purple of her face appearing blotchier. She looked around at all of us, taking stock of our expressions before stopping on Erin and saying, 'I suppose you told them all about that, Miss Beaumont.'

Erin looked like she wished she had a biscuit to hand, something to munch on in her nervousness. She said, 'I wanted to know why you were spending so much time at the office if the company is supposed to be owned by Mr Grey and Miss Dooley.'

'That's none of your business.'

'Your name is on every scrap of paperwork in the

place, Mrs Grey,' Erin said, gaining some more composure. 'I can't help thinking that you always planned on taking Janice for every penny she's got and using it for your development. It's a big risk, and who better to lose everything than the woman who's been having an affair with your husband for your entire married life?'

Violet got angry; she started snarling like she belonged in The Lord of the Rings, and she said to Erin, 'That's the problem with girls like you. You always believe that you deserve better than you have when you've done nothing in life but lie on your back and infect the world with more of your spawn. I have worked for everything that I've got, and all Janice has done is lie in wait for her father to die before inheriting nothing short of a fortune. She deserves everything she has coming to her and then some.'

Our Doris stepped in there, saying to Violet, she said, 'Once more, you share falsehoods in my kitchen, Mrs Grey. I wouldn't mind if you'd come into my kitchen and chosen to offend me. Quite frankly, that's something you've been doing since time immemorial. However, I draw the line when you choose to come and speak to Miss Beaumont as though she's little more than dog muck under your kitten heels.

'You were born into money. That silver spoon in your mouth has always been gleaming, and we all know that the only reason Doug started hanging around with you in the first place was because of the size of your purse. It certainly wasn't your looks or your personality, both of which could be used as anaesthesia.

'Secondly, while Erin might have a child – his name is Reuben, and he'll undoubtedly become a delightful young man – she's also working to provide for him, which is more than can be said for your son. You just passed him from au pair to au pair and then sent him off to boarding school, and where is he now? He went the same way as Joanna Hollinshead, if memory serves me correctly.

'Sure, you might have your husband back, and some photos might have been shared in the newspaper that you didn't want people to see, but I refuse to allow you to expel such insults in front of my Magnet work tops.'

Violet seethed. She stared down at our Doris and said, 'Those photos have done us the world of good, actually. You should see the response online. People are thrilled to see that such a longstanding couple have combatted the stain of Douglas's fling with such a trollop and are working hard on their marriage.'

Our Doris said to her, she said, 'Well then, that is good news. Why don't you go back to him and share in each other's company once more? I've had enough of you in mine.'

'You do get a thrill out of attempting to offend me, don't you, Mrs Copeland?' Violet turned on her heel and headed for the front door. 'I'll see myself out. I honestly don't know how I've managed to cope with such a stench.'

I made no comments about her always holding her nose that high it were a wonder she could smell anything and just waited to hear the door slam behind her.

Janice slumped down at our kitchen table for the second time in as many days and said, 'Please can I stop for a brew, Doris? If I go after her now, I'm liable to get done for ABH.'

'I'll stick the kettle on,' I said.

Erin went over and sat beside Janice. 'I'm sorry about all of this. I thought that if people saw the pictures, they might end up on your side. I had no idea that they'd all think it were great that the Greys were back together again.'

Our Doris were gobsmacked. She said to Erin, she said, '*You* sent the photos to the Gazette?'

'How?' I asked.

'I texted Theo and asked if he still had your password for the Cloud. He did, and he sent the photos over to me. We both thought it would help the cause and kept Mrs Copeland's name out of it.'

'I appreciate the intent, Erin, but you really ought to have come to me first before following through with such an idea. One must always be aware of the way things could go.'

'Don't blame her too harshly,' Janice said. 'You weren't to know that folk would come out in support of Dougie and Violet.'

'All that anyone on social media is talking about is how you tried to ruin their marriage.'

'It's a good job I don't have social media, then,' Janice said. 'Look, Erin, I've had seventy-four years of this town looking down on me. I can cope with one newspaper article.'

Our Doris warned her then, saying, 'There may be more. If we're to put a stop to Doug and Violet, then there's every chance your name will be dragged into it again.'

Janice shook her head, a smile on her face. 'You once attacked me with a set of scales at Bulge Busters. You fought me in a graveyard after almost breaking my ribs, and I was the one who had to spend a night in a police cell. I'm pretty sure that I can cope with being public enemy number two.'

'I'm guessing that makes me public enemy number

one,' our Doris said.

'You're beginning to understand the way this town operates, Mrs Copeland.'

Our Doris wasted no time in putting the first phase of her plan into action.

She'd been scouring through the paperwork that Erin had stolen from DG Construction in the hopes of finding some incriminating evidence against Doug Grey. Naturally, she found such evidence at two o'clock in the morning when I'd been in the middle of a particularly steamy dream about Jane Fonda and sticky toffee pudding.

I awoke to her yelling in success. Bleary-eyed, I switched on my bedside lamp and said to our Doris, I said, 'What the bleeding heck are you going on about, our Doris?' At least, that's what I hoped it sounded like; I were a bit muffled with my face pressed against the pillow as though I were going to find some remnants of my subconscious dessert in the fabric.

Our Doris must've understood some of what I said because she replied, 'I've found just what I need to put a proper end to Doug Grey's plans.'

I pulled myself up into a seated position. 'That's all

well and good, our Doris, but it still makes no sense to me.'

'What doesn't?'

'You're supposed to be going after Violet. The whole reason you had Erin photocopy all of this "evidence" is because you wanted to stop her from getting the women onside. Or had you completely forgotten about the reformation of the WI?'

If I'd been able to see properly, I'd have said that our Doris looked shifty, but my eyes aren't the best when I've just woken up and so I couldn't say for certain. Either way, she said, 'Of course I haven't forgotten about the WI, our 'arold. Since Doug and Violet are attached to one another once more, I thought it much easier to go after both of them at once, rather than finding different ways to see that they both drift back to the swamps from which they originated.'

'You're very eloquent for two o'clock in the morning,' I said. 'Have you been at the coffee again?'

'I am working on pure adrenaline.'

'All right, then. What have you found that's going to help bring down the Greys?'

'They've been bribing the council.'

'That's common knowledge,' I said. 'Our council must be one of the most corrupt this side of the River Bollin.'

She said to me, she said, 'But here we have it all in black and white. I might just have to go and speak to one of the main beneficiaries of Douglas Grey's wallet.'

Then I said something I'd been waiting for a long while to say. I rubbed my eyes, cleared my throat and said to our Doris, I said, 'Why are you concerning yourself with the WI, our Doris? Only last year, you stepped down as chairwoman and told them where they could shove it. We went away for three months so you could forget about them. The group doesn't exist anymore, and you're that concerned about Violet taking it away from you that you're planning on not only ruining her reputation but also that of our town councillors.'

Our Doris heaved a sigh from deep within her lungs and set her papers on the bedside table. 'It's been a while since one of your outbursts, our 'arold, but I'm nothing if not a forgiving wife.'

I were definitely feeling my lack of sleep because I said to her, I said, 'Quit acting the lady of the manor and tell me what's going on.'

She gave me the Look and said, 'I will comport myself however I see fit, Harold Copeland, and don't you forget it. I am currently planning to resurrect the WI, not because I wish for things to return to how they once were, but because I recognise the opportunities it facilitated for me and I wish to offer such opportunities to the younger women in Partridge Mews. Now, I must also issue an apology for my actions last year and with regards to the Buckingham Palace debacle in a way that I see fit. By throwing a magnificent soiree that would make Andy Warhol jealous.'

She took a breath before continuing, 'Furthermore, need I remind you that it's no business of yours how I spend my time, just as it was no business of mine what you were doing in the ginnel behind Sterling's Hardware with Eleanor Stockwell in nineteen-fifty-four.'

'She had a flat tyre,' I protested.

'Yes, that was a common complaint when it came to Eleanor. It never put you off though, did it?'

I were too tired to have another conversation about what didn't happen with Eleanor Stockwell. I said to our Doris, I said, 'For the thousandth time, nothing happened with Eleanor Stockwell. I've been married to you for fifty-six years and I've seen that WI stress you out like nothing else. I simply don't understand why it appeals to you so much.'

'It isn't for you to understand, our 'arold,' she said. 'You're a man. Every inch of this blasted planet is a men's institute. The WI is one place I could go and not worry.'

I scowled at her then. 'That's a bare-faced lie, our Doris, and you know it. You worried all the time. You worried about baking and jam-making and committee elections. You worried more about that WI than you did when our Angela fell off Neil's motorbike.'

'She should've held on tighter.' Our Doris folded her arms and looked off in the other direction.

'If you send Violet packing and restart the WI, will you go back?'

Our Doris glanced back at me, her eyes full of sincerity as she shrugged and said, 'I don't know, our 'arold. I've spent a year without it, and that church hall gets bitter cold in winter.'

'I'll support you in whatever you decide.'

'No, you won't, but I appreciate the sentiment.' She offered me one of those smiles she saves for when we're in private and said, 'Now, will you come over here and help me work off some of this adrenaline? I don't see why the Greys should be the only ones having any fun.'

She took my hand as I switched off the bedside lamp and slid towards her side of the bed. There's always something about getting amorous that has my heart going as giddy as I was as a teenager, only I've more practice and a new knee. It also helps to have been with the same woman for fifty-six years. We know one another's likes and dislikes, I'm mindful of her hip replacement, and we've always made sure to fork out extra for a good mattress.

In the morning, over a breakfast of scrambled egg on toast, my wife of fifty-six years shocked me with a demand. Our Doris is known for her demands, and I'm known for agreeing to them, but what our Doris asked of me is one for the history books because she said to me, she said that she needed the day to herself. I can't deny that I were happy. Our Doris told me off for looking too smug, said as she could change her mind in an instant and have me as her driver.

She didn't; half an hour later, Edith turned up in her Corsa and they set off to do whatever meddling septuagenarians do when they're planning the downfall of the former head of the Partridge Mews Women's Institute. It would probably involve a break for coffee and cake. That's one of the reliable things about our Doris; if she's out for the day, she can never be more than ten feet away from a café just in case she wants to sample a slice of Victoria sponge. It's one of her favourite pastimes is criticising another baker's Victoria sponge.

With our Doris out of the way, I took myself into the living room with a copy of The Telegraph and a mug of tea. I had the radio on in the background, all set for Ken Bruce to get started with his quiz.

Our Doris never used to listen to Radio 2, called it a station developed for the anti-intellectual offspring of middle-class aspirants. Then she heard that Meredith Weaver had been a contestant on Popmaster – said hello to every Tom, Dick and Joan and all – and decided that if it was stimulating the mind then it can't be too bad. So, she listens every day in the hopes of scoring a thirty-nine. She won't. Our Doris's musical knowledge doesn't stretch much further than Billy Idol.

Not that I'm much better. Either way, once the quiz had finished and I'd drained my tea, I decided to visit our Angela.

She were in the garden when I arrived, fussing over a rose bush. Naturally, I went inside and brewed up first, before returning and asking if she needed my help. She handed me a pair of thick gloves and set me to work as though she'd anticipated my arrival. I wouldn't have been surprised if she had; the women of Partridge Mews always seem to get an alert when there's a husband with nothing to do, and that stretches to my daughter. She might be perfectly adept at dead-heading roses, but she'd be a fool not to get someone else to do it.

She hasn't learned anything about gardening from me. I offered to teach her the basics, lent her my VHS copies of Groundforce, but she prefers Monty Don to Charlie Dimmock. Besides, she took an evening course on horticulture. When I pointed out that I could have saved her money if she'd just listened to me, she hit me with that gaze that all daughters give to their fathers – that one where she's all superior, wondering how I couldn't understand something so simple. Our Angela started giving me that look when she was two years old and I questioned her need to wear a tutu to the swimming baths. The look comes with an added question as to whether I've hit that point of senility where she has to start worrying. I see it more in the way she purses her lips than in how she squints her eyes, that question. Either way, once she'd finished giving me that withering look, she said, 'Mum would much rather I have a formal qualification, no matter where it came from. Rather than say to her friends that I learned everything I know about gardening from my father – a man who came last in a best marrow competition when he entered a carrot that resembled Bob Mortimer.'

I'd misread the signs at the fete, the judges had a good laugh at my expense and our Doris had me down the opticians the next morning, regardless of whether they could see me or not. This means that I only lend a hand when I'm asked.

She was tossing leaves, bracken and other garden detritus into a green bin when she said, 'Where's Mum today, then?'

I said to her, I said, 'She's found evidence that Doug Grey has been bribing the council. I'm not sure what she's got planned, but she didn't want me to play a part in it.'

'She'll be thinking of damage limitation, Dad. If you're not around to witness anything then you can't be held accountable – she can be funny like that, can my mother.'

'I don't understand why she's gone after Doug when Violet is who she wants to stop.'

Our Angela gave another one of those looks where she questions if I really lack so much common sense.

'Mum has never been happy about Doug Grey's redevelopment. With Janice Dooley is on side, she's gone from housewife to war general.'

'Is that a thing?'

'I've no idea, but it's how Mum operates. She has free rein to do whatever she wants, and I'd hate to be on the wrong side of her. Remember when I cut my hair to resemble Toyah? I thought she was going to send me to a convent.'

'She were after having your hairdresser exiled to Guatemala.'

'And these are the Greys. She's disliked them for decades. Just imagine what she'll do to them.'

'I bet she regrets inviting Violet back to town.'

'Which is even more reason why she'll want to make sure that she flees town and doesn't come back.'

'You're right, love. Violet won't be able to scuttle off to her sister's this time. Your mother won't stop until she's chased her onto a ferry to Antarctica.'

'I don't know,' our Angela said. 'She might settle for Dunstable.'

We finished up in the garden and I took our Angela into town for a spot of lunch. It's not often that we get much time with one another, what with her job and me usually being involved in our Doris's schemes, so it was good to catch up, even if she does sometimes look at me as though I'm a poached egg and she's wary of salmonella.

Some days later, another edition of the Partridge Mews Gazette landed on the doorstep, and I chose to have a go at our Doris. It was all because the paper had a three-page spread on how Doug Grey had spent the last few decades bribing the local council.

I knew that I wasn't in the mood when the familiar sound of the Gazette thudding on the doorstep summoned a small amount of anger in me. Not clenched fists and breaking doors – this wasn't a Ken Barlow situation. I wasn't about to bash our Doris into the front door in the throes of anger, passion and some homoerotic tension that we didn't recognise until our Angela started going out in Manchester. No, this were anger that felt like butterflies were tickling my ribcage. As I headed into the kitchen, I read the article about Doug Grey and the ire rose in my chest like a terrier after an apple pie cooling in the window.

Our Doris stood unaware at the kitchen counter, spreading cream cheese on a bagel.

I sat down at the table and continued reading. The

article mentioned councillors by name – including Ian Morris, who'd been there at our first public consultation – and dove right into questioning every action the Greys had made, even going so far as to mention their new conservatory.

I clenched the paper in my hands as I finished reading, before slamming the Gazette down on the table and saying to our Doris, I said, 'What the bleeding heck do you mean by doing all of this, our Doris?'

She sat down across from me and said to me, she said, 'Please do tell me what I happen to have done this time, our 'arold.'

'You know what I mean. This article in the Gazette.'

'Here I was, believing that you would support my actions.' Our Doris bit into her bagel and crunched furiously. Once she swallowed, she gave me the Look and said, 'I did what was necessary to put a stop to the Greys, our 'arold, and I will thank you to modify your tone. That sort of language is not appropriate in front of Whittard's finest china.'

I said to her, I said, 'This doesn't just have a go at the Greys, our Doris. It has a go at the entirety of the Partridge Mews Town Council.'

'What else did you expect?' our Doris asked. 'Did you honestly believe that I'd forgiven them as well? They have allied themselves with Doug Grey. Their actions last year led to Alf's arrest and humiliation. They approved his plans for Barraclough's Field, knowing full well that we'd object.'

'What about you? The council aren't going to think too kindly of you raising this against them.'

'The council will have no idea where the Gazette got its information.'

'You can't be sure of that, our Doris.'

She smiled then, and this were an unnerving smile. It were a look of superiority I hadn't seen since she successfully baked a cheese soufflé in nineteen-seventy-six – she hasn't tried again since. Our Doris placed her hands on top of mine and began this stroking between my knuckles that were both conciliatory and threatening – the proper ministrations of any wife in the North West of England – and she said to me, she said, 'I understand your concerns, our 'arold, and I appreciate them, but there's no need to worry. I got our Theo involved. He and a group of his friends did some things on the computer and sent all the information we had to Edith's grandson in Paris. He then forwarded that information on to the Gazette. No matter what happens, it would be the Devil's own job working out just who blew the whistle on Doug Grey and the council.'

I'll admit to being flabbergasted. I sat there, terrified and impressed in equal measures. 'That's proper Spooks level stuff right there, our Doris.'

Her smile transformed into a grin, all dazzling – our dentist is clearly worth her money – and she said to me, our Doris said, 'This were my last chance to put a stop to things, our 'arold. I was determined to use every available resource.'

The Partridge Mews Town Council was quick to issue a press release stating that they'd hold an independent investigation into the claims made by our local newspaper, that they had a long-standing business relationship with Mr Douglas Grey – this included but wasn't confined to his work as a councillor – and that anyone concerned with the article could contact a town council representative who would be more than happy to assuage any fears they might have.

Doug Grey went so far as to organise a press conference for later that week to discuss the article. Clearly, neither the council nor the Greys planned on going down without a fight.

Of course, Doug Grey held his press conference at the church hall; it must be a cheap place to book.

It was a good day to a have a press conference, in any case. There was a touch of warmth in the air, but it weren't too hot. I still needed my thin M&S jumper – it's perfect for those days where we're headed towards spring and the sun has decided to make an appearance. Our Doris wore a navy-blue dress she'd bought from John Lewis in the sales. She wanted folk to understand that she has money but was frugal with it – although most of them know that we went on a three-month cruise around the world last year, so she won't be fooling too many people.

A large crowd had assembled inside the church hall, sitting in rows from the stage to the back wall. Some folk were forced to stand on the side-lines, unable to find a rigid plastic chair in which to situate themselves.

When we arrived, Doug and Violet were chatting to a reporter from the Gazette. I recognised them from the few times our Doris had visited their office. They were fitting a lapel mic to Doug's collar. I felt sorry for the reporter having to run their hands beneath Doug's shirt, but rather them than me.

Janice Dooley of Little Street was sitting in the front row, all desultory as she slurped from a polystyrene cup. Erin sat beside her, eyes staring straight ahead and focused on the back of the stage. Neither of them wanted to be there but had found themselves embroiled in Doug's machinations. I suppose that technically it was our Doris's fault that Erin had found herself there, but at least she were being paid for her time.

'Testing, testing, one, two three,' Doug barked into the microphone.

'You can speak normally, Mr Grey,' the reporter said. 'It'll pick you up.'

Doug said, 'I want to make sure that everyone hears what I have to say. I'm a respectable gentleman looking to improve life for the impoverished of Partridge Mews. Having these aspersions cast about me has been no good for my health.'

The reporter nodded. 'I understand that perfectly. If this one fails, there's always the microphone on stage.'

Doug pulled that obnoxious chortle from deep within his stomach and clapped the reporter on the back. 'All this technological stuff is beyond me, I still struggle with a calculator. Perhaps that's one of the reasons your newspaper thought I was bribing the council.'

'I'll just take my seat.' They left Doug and Violet and went to sit beside Janice Dooley.

Alf and Edith had saved a couple of seats for us. We headed over and I said to them, I said, 'He's putting on a good performance, isn't he?'

Edith bristled and said, 'I'm just glad I know about Janice Dooley's announcement because I'm likely to lamp Doug Grey given half the chance.'

'Our Doris still won't tell me what it is. I don't suppose you'd care to enlighten me.'

Our Doris didn't give Edith a chance to respond, saying to me, she said, 'The fewer people who know about Janice's announcement, the better, our 'arold. I might not particularly care for her, but if Doug were to find out what she's done then I fear what he might do.'

'I hope they get a move on then.' There wasn't much room left in the hall and I fancied getting down the allotment to check on my runner beans.

We didn't have to wait much longer. As Violet Grey climbed the steps up to the stage, Doug whispered something to Erin and she followed him out into the corridor – our Doris said as he probably wanted to make a grand entrance. Someone must have taught him how to turn his lapel mic down because we could no longer hear him heaving breath like a set of bagpipes with a puncture.

Violet clicked her tongue into the microphone, drawing attention to herself. She stood there in her mauve two-piece suit, looking as imperious as a gnat – she were going for this dowdy look in the hopes of looking like the stereotypical old woman: Doris Hare in On the Buses, that sort of thing. She clearly hoped that folk would have forgotten why they were there. She were using age how it's meant to be used – to make others feel guilty.

Her audience calmed themselves, and a hum of silence filled the place.

Violet thanked us all for coming, before saying, 'I wish that we were congregated here under better circumstances. Earlier this week, you'll have seen an article in the Partridge Mews Gazette that included a great many lies about myself and my husband. Since we've only just begun reconciling our relationship with one another, I won't deny that this felt as though a select few people, who are perhaps present here, sought to dampen our happiness at beating adversity and coming together to celebrate our ability to forgive one another.

'Please note that I don't feel any malice towards these individuals. I'm quite aware that there are people who are only happy when they're besmirching the reputation of others. If I've learned anything as an honest Christian woman, it's that forgiveness is key...'

She went on talking, but I turned to our Doris and whispered, saying, I said, 'Why does she keep going on about forgiveness?'

Our Doris hushed me. 'It's because she wants us all to forgive her. She knows that she's done wrong, so she's forgiving us in the hope that we'll offer her the same kindness. It's very calculated.'

Violet were still talking. 'Needless to say, I'll no longer be hosting an Easter egg hunt. I don't feel that it would be appropriate for me to take centre stage at this moment in time. I will admit to some wrongdoing on my part. There's clearly been a severe data breach at the council offices that has seen the discovery of money that Douglas and I donated to various causes throughout the years in the hopes of benefitting our local community. I believe that the Gazette labelled these donations as bribes, and I'd like to set the record straight that this is categorically untrue. My conservatory was approved through all the correct means, and we have already proved that we are an adequate distance away from the boundary line.'

She caught herself then. She'd been all set to get frantic, but she stopped, coughed lightly and straightened the buttons on her cardigan.

'Now, I think I'll hand the stage over to my husband Douglas, so as he can alleviate any further fears you might have and answer some questions before we hear from Miss Janice Dooley of Little Street who has so graciously appeared to reassure us of the redevelopment of Barraclough's Field.'

Heads turned towards the door. We had all expected Doug to come through it, acting the cock of the walk, gambolling towards the stage with all the tenacity of Humpty Dumpty on his way to the wall.

'Douglas?' Violet squeaked into the microphone.

Still nothing.

Janice stood up and said, 'Give us a moment, chaps. He's probably just draining his tank. I'll go and find him.'

She headed out of the double doors into the corridor.

A few seconds later, we heard the sound of static and Erin's voice could be heard from the speakers. She said, 'No, Mr Grey.'

'Come on, Miss Beaumont,' Doug said. 'Live a little. Once we've finished here, the council will issue a statement regarding the false claims made to besmirch my character and the redevelopment will go ahead. If you help me out, you can be first on the list for one of the two-bedrooms. Wouldn't you like a nice little semi?'

'But they're not false claims, Mr Grey. You *did* bribe the council.'

'Nobody will care if they get some nice new homes out of it,' he said. 'Now, what do you say to becoming employee of the month?'

A few of us rose from our seats at that point, me and our Doris included. She rushed straight for the corridor but stopped stock still when she saw another set of double doors in the centre of the room. They opened onto a cloak room where the plastic chairs were usually stashed when the hall wasn't in use.

Erin said to Doug, 'I won't slap you because I volunteer at a charity for older people and I think that'd see me sacked, but if you don't take your hands off my backside then I'll scream until your ear-drums bleed.'

We heard Doug laugh then; it were little more than a chuckle, but it were there. 'Do you think that you're the first girl to threaten me like that, Miss Beaumont? You're just a little tart from a council estate and I am a respected former councillor. All I have to say is that you were after one of my new houses and didn't like it when I said no and they'll run you out of town.'

'Mr Grey, I'm warning you.'

'If you didn't want my hands on you, you'd have moved by now.'

'You have me trapped in a cloakroom. There's nowhere for me to move.'

He heaved a deep breath and said, 'You can just slide right past me here.'

Our Doris headed towards the double doors at the back of the hall then, creeping as slowly as a leopard on the prowl.

Meanwhile, Erin were still trapped with Doug. She said to him, 'I knew you were an old lech, but I didn't think things were this bad. I am not interested in you. Frankly, I'm surprised that you've had two women falling over their feet for you, because you've about as much going for you as a slug in ketchup. But that's not what this is about, is it? I'll give you a bit of education since everyone else seems to have struggled. My son has managed to wrap his head around this, so it shouldn't be a struggle for you. Keep your hands, feet and other objects to yourself.'

'You're one of those modern women, are you? Well, let me tell you something, Miss Beaumont. Women only want equal rights because they don't have a man in control of them. I can teach you what I mean if you'd like.'

Erin screamed then, a bellow like nothing else.

Our Doris tore open the double doors.

Doug Grey froze on the spot. He'd wrapped his arms around Erin and was in the process of dragging her towards him; he blinked a few times, looking out at the hall, seemingly oblivious.

Our Doris's entire body vibrated; she clutched her handbag as though she were set to wield it as a weapon. She said to Doug, she said, 'I thought it best to come and find you, Mr Grey. You see, your microphone is on, and it wouldn't do for you to say anything incriminating, would it?'

He let Erin go and she stepped towards our Doris, saying, 'I would have hit him, Mrs Copeland, but I have Reuben to think about.'

Out of nowhere, we heard a loud thwack and Doug stumbled forwards into the hall. Our Doris and Erin jumped out of the way as he staggered towards the audience.

Doug grabbed hold of a chair to stop himself falling to the floor, looking like a drunk rhinoceros.

Janice Dooley of Little Street stepped out of the cloak room behind him. She put down the fire extinguisher she were holding and said to Erin, 'It's all right, duck, I've already got a criminal record. Folk expect this sort of thing from a woman brought up on Little Street.'

Doug's face might have been as pale as a swan's

feather in snow, but he said to her, he practically growled, 'I'll sue you for every penny you've got.'

'Good luck to you,' she said. Then, with all the poise she could muster, Janice walked towards the stage.

Violet stood there as she approached, looking as terrified as a dormouse beneath a barn owl. She said, 'Miss Dooley, I really don't think violence is the answer.'

'Shut your face, Violet, I've had enough of your claptrap to last a lifetime,' she said, pushing her away from the microphone so she could address the room. 'Now, I know that you were all looking forward to the redevelopment of Barraclough's Field, but it won't be going ahead. I've sold the land to Clementine Partridge, because I couldn't trust the Greys to have the town's best interests at heart. If you've any further questions, you can address them to someone who cares, because I'm off.'

She left. Janice Dooley of Little Street stepped down from the stage and walked straight out of the doors. We listened as she toddled off down the corridor, heels clacking on the linoleum like some staccato warning to the population.

The reporter from the Gazette couldn't scribble in their notebook fast enough.

Violet and Doug looked to one another from their respective spots in the hall – he rubbing his back while leaning over a plastic chair, she holding onto a ring-binder like a security blanket. She inched towards the microphone and said to the crowd, 'You will all be aware that Doug and I are in the process of getting a divorce.'

He yelled then, his words as sonorous as a lion's roar. 'You aren't saving yourself that easy, you blasted fool. They all saw the ruddy photo online!'

Violet stood there, mouth opening and closing as though she were auditioning for the part of a goldfish in

Dr. Doolittle, before running down the steps of the stage and out the side door, following Janice's trail.

We were all lost for words. The people of Partridge Mews had turned out for a show, and they'd received one; we hadn't expected Doug Grey's former mistress to wallop him with a fire extinguisher, and nor had we expected to see Violet Grey fleeing from the premises. She hadn't even walked out when she'd left the lavatory with toilet paper in her skirt after her sixtieth birthday celebrations, and she'd been as drunk as a bluebottle in a pint of Guinness then. Quite honestly, we were all stunned.

However, that wasn't the last of surprises.

Once she'd got her bearings, straightened out her blouse and rubbed away any marks Doug might have left on her, Erin held her head high, shoulders back – looking every inch as though she'd studied at the Doris Copeland School of Etiquette – and wandered over to the stage. She took to the microphone and addressed us all, saying, she said, 'Well, that were unexpected, wasn't it? A bunch of oldies going at it like this is the WWE. I suppose this means that I don't have a job with DG Construction anymore, so if anyone is hiring a young mum with a foundation degree in social care then keep me in mind.' She allowed herself a moment to breathe, before continuing, 'Although the redevelopment might not be going ahead, it doesn't mean we can't still come together as a community and support each other. Since Mrs Grey – Violet – has run off, you'll probably have some questions about the Easter egg hunt she was supposed to be holding. Since I had the idea in the first place, I'll make sure that it continues and see you all down the park on Easter Sunday. We could even have a picnic, if you fancy.'

That took folks' minds off things. They all started calling out to her, offering things that they could bring along – someone knew a DJ who might play a set as long as he was given a Kopparberg and a ham sandwich.

Whatever they organised, it gave me and Alf time to smuggle Doug out of the hall. I wasn't too happy to be dragging him down corridors, but our Doris wanted him out of the way before she committed homicide and I wasn't prepared to spend the next few years visiting her in Styal Prison.

He weren't too happy himself, chunnering about how he'd been wronged by some mad old bats who should have learned which way their bread is buttered, but he soon shut up when Alf threatened to deck him.

We got Doug to the car park and let him go. He were clearly still winded, but that didn't prevent him from saying to us, 'This has been a ruddy witch hunt since it started.'

I said to him, I said, 'You've done wrong, Doug, and you've been found out. Be a man about it and beggar off home.'

'Be a man? Be a man? I've been a man about all of this. It's men like you that give us a bad name. Pandering to every one of their wife's little whims, unable to grow a backbone. If you'd taught your wife her place then I wouldn't be having this problem.'

I did what anyone in a similar position would have done. I mustered all the force I could, clenched my fist and walloped him with all my strength. I thought I'd broken my flaming wrist when my knuckles connected with his jaw, but I hid my pain. I simply watched him fall to the ground like a sack of horse manure.

He lay there, all twenty-two-stone of him, and didn't respond.

I said to Doug, I said, 'Make no mistake, Doug. That weren't for today, that were for coming up to our Doris in nineteen-seventy-five. She can handle her own, and she'll be properly bothered when she finds out that I've hit you, but I'd never forgive myself if I let you gad about thinking you'd got one over on me. See, my wife knows her place, as I know mine. We support one another in achieving our goals. It's a partnership that's lasted over fifty years, and it seems to be going well for us. Perhaps we can get Violet over here and I'll give you some tips. Better yet, how about Janice? Or one of the other assorted women you've been associated with over the years?'

Alf took my arm and said, 'You can leave him now, 'arold, I think he's had enough for today. Anymore and folk'll think him a martyr.'

I let him lead me back towards the hall, where we found our Doris taking people's names and chatting to them about the proper way to iron a picnic blanket. Apparently, she had an Easter egg hunt to help organise.

We dropped Erin off on our way home and our Doris had me make one more stop before we returned to Shakespeare Avenue.

Janice Dooley had cleaned her front step since we'd last visited Little Street. She'd had her windowsills repainted and the front door no longer looked like it had been rammed by an elephant with poor peripheral vision.

She were stood on the front step when we arrived, smoking a cigarette with a suitcase beside her. She offered our Doris a smile as we got out of the car and said, 'I suppose I never did say thank you for helping me get rid of that land.'

Our Doris nodded and said to her, she said, 'You're quite welcome, Miss Dooley, but I didn't come here about that.'

'Let me guess, you came to see how I'm doing?'

'That's about the measure of things, yes.'

Janice took a long drag on her cigarette. 'I'll be fine, Mrs Copeland. I've always known that Doug is no good, but it hasn't stopped me going back to him again and again. Still, how's your Erin doing?'

'She's not my Erin.'

'We've all seen how you've taken her under your wing,' Janice said. 'She's been good for you, has that girl. Brought you to your senses a bit.'

Our Doris nodded and hid a smile. 'Thank you for looking out for her like you did.'

'Doug's had that coming for a long while, and then some. I won't be the last to whack him with a fire extinguisher, just you wait and see.' She dropped the cigarette and ground it beneath her heel.

A taxi pulled up in front of my car and the driver came to collect her suitcase.

Our Doris said to her, she said, 'What will you do?'

She shrugged. 'I've no idea, but this taxi is taking me to the airport.'

'I didn't intend to run you out of town. Not this time, in any case.'

Janice said to our Doris, 'I'm not leaving forever, Mrs Copeland. Little Street is my home, but I need some time away. I have my inheritance and I plan on squandering every penny.'

I chimed in there and said to Janice, I said, 'Have a good time then, wherever you end up, won't you?'

'You should get home and soak that hand. I saw the way you floored Dougie. Flaming marvellous, it was.'

Our Doris gave me one of her looks and said nothing about it.

'There's something I want to say before I go,' Janice said to our Doris. 'I won't pretend we'll ever be mates, Doris, but there's no one else I've disliked as much as you.'

'I can assure you that the feeling is mutual.'

'Don't I know, or have you forgotten the trial?'

'I still think it was a great miscarriage of justice.'

Janice got in the passenger seat of the taxi and said, 'Of course you do. Ta-ra, Doris.'

She slammed the door shut and the taxi pulled out, taking Janice Dooley of Little Street away to who-knows-where. I just hope that wherever she ends up has good insurance.

Our Doris kept her face averted away from me as she composed herself, sniffing a few times and dabbing at her eyes. Then she said to me, she said, 'Well, our 'arold, that just goes to show how skilled I am at modern warfare. I planned to send the Greys packing, and I sent Janice Dooley of Little Street on her merry way as well.'

'You should get a job with the Royal Mail,' I said. 'At least we know you always deliver.'

We went home. Since our Doris had put a stop to the redevelopment and made sure everyone had got the measure of the Greys, she just had to contend with the reformation of the Partridge Mews Women's Institute.

Our Doris has set about organising a party to celebrate the inaugural meeting of the reformed Partridge Mews Women's Institute, although she still hasn't decided if she wishes to re-join their folds.

The party has been a topic of discussion for so long that the ladies have begun to wonder whether it will ever take place, or whether it's just like Brenda Halliwell's new front porch – she kept purchasing brochures before eventually moving to Weston-Super-Mare.

Our Doris began making plans after Erin's Easter egg hunt. She used the event to gauge the ladies' interest in returning to the church hall once a week to debate the importance of quiche at a contemporary picnic. That one she soon decided was a waste of time – she were planning a menu for the party and said to me, she said, 'Nobody eats quiche anymore. They're all carb-avoiding, gluten-free vegans with tendencies towards acquiring badges in support of animal-rights charities, more likely to share a rant on the internet than ram-raid an abattoir.' Therefore, quiche is off the menu, and she still hasn't figured out what she's going to feed to her vegetarians.

She hit a snag as soon as she started making plans.

It was a nice enough day, so I'd taken our elevenses into the garden. I'd made our Doris a coffee with the posh blend she gets delivered – she doesn't need much by way of caffeine to get her going, but there's something about the aroma that reminds her of the coffee bars of our youth. I'd take her when we were young and more impressionable, when a cappuccino was all it took to get her to hold my hand – I'd stuck to my usual builder's brew and put a couple of fancy cakes on a saucer. They came from a new café in town. Our Doris always likes to be seen to support local businesses, even if their wares cost more than a return train ticket to Manchester.

She came into the garden with a look on her face that wouldn't have looked out of place on a gargoyle. It were a right royal grimace, were that look. She didn't come over to the table, just started pacing back and forth down the garden path as though she were intent on eroding the paving slabs.

I said to her, I said, 'What's the matter, our Doris?'

She stopped mid-stride and scowled at me, saying, 'I'll tell you what the matter is, our 'arold. That bleeding vicar.'

'Which vicar?'

'Our vicar.'

'Stephen?'

'Who else?'

'I thought you liked Stephen. You have him around here every Christmas, putting the star on the tree.'

Our Doris gave me the Look and said, 'That is because a tree is notably pagan, and I like to feel as though it's been properly blessed before I can even consider enjoying the festive season.'

'I always thought you just liked showing off your new decorations.'

'Is it a sin to be house-proud?'

I made no mention of pride and the deadly sins and said to her, I said, 'What has the vicar done to get you all riled?'

Our Doris came over to the garden table, grabbed her mug and glugged her coffee before saying, she said, 'I telephoned his secretary to enquire as to whether I'd be able to book the church hall for the party. Do you know what she said to me? Me, Mrs Doris Copeland? I have been an upstanding member of that church for my entire life, and his secretary – I say secretary, but she's more like a vole with a clipboard – she says that the hall has already been booked, but she can offer me the following Thursday. Well, then I get onto the vicar directly. I think if anyone can help me, it's the man who has a hotline to our noble Lord and Saviour. I was wrong. He tells me that when the WI disbanded, the Girl Guides took over our slot in the church hall, that it will likely remain like that for the foreseeable future, and that he hopes I can find an alternative venue. I told him, I said I'm not letting him get away with things that easily. We're going to see him this afternoon. I can't be my most persuasive over the phone. I'll bake him a cake and we'll take it with us. No one can say no to my lemon drizzle.'

'Why does it have to be the church hall?'

If anything, that made the Look even worse. 'It is tradition, our 'arold. The Partridge Mews Women's Institute has met at the church hall since nineteen-twenty-two, apart from those periods of renovation in which we met in one another's front rooms, and I refuse to allow a small society of knot-botherers to take it away from us.'

'Weren't you a Girl Guide, our Doris?'

She diverted her gaze to the garden fence and said, 'That's beside the point, our 'arold. We never aspired to take a historic building away from another group.'

'The WI disbanded,' I said. 'They didn't take it away from you.'

'I'd like to think that a husband would be on his wife's side.'

'I'm on your side, our Doris, I just don't believe that there's been any wrongdoing this time around.'

She sat down on the other side of the table. 'That bush needs pruning, our 'arold. You're supposed to have a knowledge of horticulture. I shouldn't have to tell you these things.'

I bit into my cake and looked over at the offending bush. Perhaps it could have done with a little trim, but I wasn't about to agree with her.

We visited the vicar that afternoon.

I hadn't seen the place since Alf's Edith threw so much cake at Pandra O'Malley that she could have opened her own bakery – the vicar had stepped in and ferried us into his living room like schoolchildren waiting for the headmistress. Back then, I'd been surprised by the number of doilies about the place, and it still looked as though he must spend every spare moment of his life crocheting. I suppose it could be the ladies of the WI still trying to curry favour; they all wanted their grandchildren to get the best part in the church nativity, or the choir at the Easter service, even serving drinks on the occasional coffee morning when Beryl Salisbury had played bridge the night before and couldn't trust her hands.

I took a seat on the sofa beside our Doris. A few minutes later, Vicar Stephen came back carrying a tray of tea and custard creams – not my favourite biscuit, but then I suppose you can't expect hobnobs from those of a religious persuasion.

Once we'd helped ourselves, the vicar asked us what

had brought us to his door.

Our Doris told him, 'We spoke on the phone regarding me booking the church hall to celebrate the reformation of the Partridge Mews Women's Institute.'

'I recall our phone call, Mrs Copeland. It only happened a few hours ago. I will, however, remind you that that Guides now hold that slot in the church hall and have booked ahead for the next eighteen months.'

That was where our Doris played her trump card. She reached into her crocheted shopping bag and removed a cake tin, setting it down in the middle of the coffee table.

'Are you trying to bribe me with cake, Mrs Copeland?'

She offered him a simpering smile. 'I simply thought it must have been a long time since you'd tasted home-baked goods, so I'd bring one along that I had going spare. One must maintain one's baking practice, if only to strengthen one's memory.'

Vicar Stephen patted his stomach. 'There has been a lack of cakes coming to my door, that's true, and it has done wonders for my waist-line.'

'All the more reason to sample some of my lemon drizzle.'

'No thank you, Mrs Copeland,' he said. 'I went gluten-free last year and wouldn't forgive myself if I broke the habit.'

'What about the custard creams?' I asked, eyeing them somewhat more tentatively than before. I've nothing against gluten-free products, but they do tend to taste like sand in biscuit form.

'Purchased from the free-from shelf at a well-known supermarket.'

Our Doris grimaced while reaching for the cake tin,

before trying another tactic. She said to the vicar, she said, 'Perhaps you could offer it around to the congregation at one of your prayer meetings.' She removed the lid so that the pang of lemony, sugary scent wafted through the living room.

'There's no issue there. Mrs Tunnicliffe sees to all refreshments.'

'The same Mrs Tunnicliffe who served spinach fritters at her last tea party?'

'I'm not sure what that has to do with anything. Either way, you're here to discuss rearranging the date of your party.'

'No,' our Doris said, plainly.

'No?'

'I'm not here to discuss, nor rearrange, nor am I holding a party. I must have that day for it's the day the WI has been meeting for decades.'

'Not for the last year.'

'This is also not just a party, but a celebration of the women in this town coming together to better the community.'

'The last I heard, you and the women within that particular group weren't on speaking terms. Indeed, I had a few come to me who were reticent about your continued involvement, especially after the Buckingham Palace debacle.'

'Many of the ladies have forgiven me since that event and this party is one of the ways in which I hope to make amends. Doesn't the good book say we should let bygones be bygones?'

He squinted at her, incredulous. 'While I believe in the phrase, I'm not sure you'll find it in any Biblical text.'

Our Doris scoffed. 'You clearly haven't studied the Bible as much as me.'

'I'm a vicar.'

'Yes, so your interpretation isn't your own. It's what the church tells you to preach. I credit my personal philosophy to a close and measured reading of John Chapter Three, Verse Twelve.'

Vicar Stephen's eyes widened in disbelief, his lips opening and closing as they tried to formulate the words necessary to argue with our Doris. 'I don't deny that you ought to sort things out with your friends, Mrs Copeland. I just question the need to force the Guides out of the church hall to do so.'

'They're Guides, they can go camping.'

'They've already hired the room. The WI will have to go elsewhere.'

Our Doris gave him the Look. After a moment, however, she reconsidered and settled for a sneer, saying to him, she said, 'It's a good job you're a man of the cloth, otherwise I'd question your deeply unsettling, un-Christian behaviour.'

He smiled and it were one of those smiles where a person has recognised that they've been challenged. He said to our Doris, 'You're quite right. It is a good job I'm a man of the cloth, otherwise I might say that you ought to recognise the un-Christian, considering the state of your buttercream.'

'It's never stopped you scarfing down my strawberry sponge like it was a competitive sport.'

'I'm a vicar. It's my job to be charitable.' He rose from his seat. 'I must ask you to leave. I have a pressing engagement to attend to.'

'Funeral, is it?' our Doris sniped. 'I can't imagine you get much call to engage with the living.'

'On the contrary, Mrs Copeland. It's date night. My boyfriend's taking me to the cinema.'

Our Doris stood up, a look of righteous fury on her face. She held her handbag close to her chest, angrier than the time Debra Lawler brought shop-bought sandwiches to the WI picnic. She said to Vicar Stephen, she said, 'I'll be telling my fellow parishioners about this.'

'Does this mean they're talking to you again?' he said. 'Fantastic. Then there's no need for your party. Goodbye, Mrs Copeland.'

Our Doris nearly chewed off her own lips, she was scowling that hard.

Our Doris had me take her to the Harrington, but they rejected her point blank. There was no arguing with the receptionist – she blamed our Doris for the cancellation of Doug Grey's redevelopment, meaning that she was stuck living in an end terrace on a congested main road, with three children under ten and a husband whose idea of a holiday was three weeks caravanning in Scotland in search of a Bohemian Waxwing.

The manager of Greenfields Hall wasn't as mean to our Doris, but we still couldn't be accommodated because they'd got a wedding booked for the same day.

Our Doris said to the manager, she said, 'You know these modern brides. They're forever leaving their grooms in the lurch to run off and find themselves in Peru with a Yoga instructor named Alessandro, only to return three months later with their tails between their legs when they discover that they weren't his only downward-facing dog. At least with my party for the WI, you're assured that it will definitely go ahead.'

The manager – Ingrid, her name were – looked our

Doris up and down before saying, 'I don't believe that's entirely true, Mrs Copeland. My mother is a member of the WI, and it's got to be nearly a year since she first mentioned that you were going to hold a party for the ladies.'

Our Doris went shifty. 'Unfortunately, I had a few obligations that required my full attention and as such I was unable to organise a celebration to my usual standards.'

Ingrid apologised for not being able to offer our Doris the date, but she did give her a voucher for a complimentary cupcake in Greenfields' tearoom.

After coffee, I dropped our Doris off at Mrs Cribbins' house – she had a meeting with the committee. I'd no idea what it was about. They could have been talking about the sudden influx of avocadoes on restaurant menus and I'd only find out when they were barricading themselves to benches, calling for a return to the cholesterol-drenched delicacies of nineteen-seventy-four.

I did what I always do when the occasion calls for it: I called on Alf and we went down the Hare and Horse.

Once we'd gone through the usual rigmarole of getting our drinks and sitting at the table, I said to him, I said, 'How's your Edith doing?'

He looked at me like I'd gone peculiar – eyes so far back in his head that they'd started to resemble pickled onions. 'What're you asking after our Edith for?'

I shrugged, supped my bitter and said, 'I just thought it might be a change of pace from talking about our Doris.'

'That's as may be, 'arold, but there's plenty of other

topics we could talk about other than our wives.'

I were dumbfounded. I sank back in my seat. 'I don't know what to say to that.'

'I don't blame you,' he said. 'You've been indoctrinated into the ways of your Doris. Other wives look at their spouses and wonder where they went wrong. They're all after an 'arold Copeland.'

'Why?'

'He doesn't talk back in public and takes his Doris, a woman we all know has a chronic case of housewifery, wherever she wants, including a three-month world cruise which they know she couldn't have afforded on her wage, being as she spent the better part of her life being a secretary for Mr Gadsden.'

'She was an administrative assistant.'

'Doesn't matter to them,' he said, nursing his pint. 'Mary Alcock is still mad at her Stan because they only went to Formby last year, and he was too tight to buy her a choc-ice.'

'The same Stan with the Mercedes?'

'That's the man. Says he was worried about leaving his tropical fish with their next-door neighbour. I mean, who has tropical fish in this day and age? The cost of electric is too high. I'd sooner watch Blue Planet and save my money.'

'You've always been good at that,' I said. Spending money is an alien concept to Alf – he's had plenty of well-paid jobs over the years and saved enough to buy a house. Yet, he still gads about like an extra from Oliver Twist.

He smiled at being complimented on his tight-fistedness. 'So why don't you want to talk about Doris?'

I'd drank a substantial amount of bitter at that point and looked down at my near-empty glass in disappointment. After signalling to Linda that we'd like another round, I said to Alf, I said, 'I never said that I didn't want to talk about our Doris. I were just being considerate. All she goes on about at the moment is that flaming party for the ladies of the former WI.'

'Well, they're a WI again, aren't they?' he said. 'Our Edith's already taken her hats out of the wardrobe for steaming. Some of them have got so squashed that they're practically new hats. She could pin them to her hair, and everyone would think she were going for something Ava Gardner.'

'Ava Gardner?'

'You know, all wonky, like they get on Bargain Hunt.'

'Avant garde?'

'You haven't got what?'

I didn't bother teaching Alf about the English language, never mind the French. He's seventy-five, he's learned all he needs to get by.

'They all want this party, but they don't have any intention of helping our Doris to sort the venue or the food.'

'I can get her some pork pies,' he said.

'I'm not sure she's after anything off the back of a lorry.'

He screwed up his face at that, like a potato that's just been mashed, and said, 'I'd get them from a proper shop. I'm not saying I'll pay for them, but I can get them.'

'There's no point getting food if she has nowhere to have the party.'

Alf looked around. He leaned out of his seat, eyes as wide as Gordon Ramsay's when he was served three-week-old potatoe skins. 'You could have it here.'

'I don't think our Doris will go for that,' I said.

Linda had just arrived at the table with our drinks. She set them down and I paid her, hoping that Alf would leave well-alone. Instead, he said, 'This isn't for me, duck, but for 'arold. His Doris is throwing a party for the WI and I were just thinking she could have it here.'

Linda asked the date and I told her. It turned out that the date were free, and Alf had Linda pencil us in. She said as she'd need to speak to our Doris about the food because she knows as well as anybody how particular my wife can be when it comes to organisation – Linda might still have traumatic memories of when our Doris caused a row at Frances Higginbotham's wake because they'd served egg mayonnaise sandwiches. She'd had me agree there and then that should she ever die before me – not very likely because she has regular conversations with our Lord and Saviour – that I'd make sure they didn't serve egg mayonnaise sandwiches.

She left us to our drinks, and I said to Alf, I said, 'I'm not sure what our Doris will say when I tell her.'

'Aye, I can see that she might be a bit fussy. That'll be your problem though, 'arold old chap. I've done my bit.'

We sat for a few moments then. I were looking around the pub, wondering how we'd get it to a standard that our Doris would approve of for a celebration of the Women's Institute she's been a part of for her entire adult life. To me, it's always been something of a second home so I can forgive its blemishes – the damp marks and scratches on the tables that are a poor imitation of mahogany, but not something I notice once I'm three drinks in talking about how Patsy Rowlands deserved better. Also, no matter the amount of Glade air freshener they use, the pub sometimes has an odour that folk associate with testosterone and poor hygiene.

No, it would be a right struggle explaining that to our Doris. Then another thing caught in my mind. I said to Alf, I said, 'Since you don't know "avant garde", where the devil did you learn a word like "indoctrinated" from?'

He shrugged like a teenager tired of being questioned about his performance in school. He said, 'It was in an episode of Homeland. Besides that, we were educated at the same school, some of us just choose not to show off.'

'Some of us actually showed up, you mean.'

He chuckled and knocked back some more of his pint. Meanwhile, I had to figure out how I'd tell our Doris that Alfred Simpson – renowned robber of baked goods from supermarket chain stores – had booked a venue for her and the Partridge Mews Women's Institute.

It was a good job that summer was on the way, because I had a strong feeling I'd be spending a fair few nights in my shed.

I didn't have to worry about telling our Doris when I got home. She were in the garden with an M. C. Beaton in her lap and a look of something between consternation and constipation on her face. She'd let her coffee go cold and a pigeon was picking over the remnants of a chocolate digestive a few feet away.

I sat down on the other garden chair and asked her what was wrong.

She said to me, she said, 'It transpires that Mrs Cribbins has received another letter from Buckingham Palace. They are still expecting two representatives from the WI to attend Camilla's garden party next month and wondered what exactly I had said in my letter. It's all Mrs McBride's fault – she's upset that she didn't know about the invitation first. Otherwise, she'd have done the exact same as me, but the less said about that the better – does she really believe that the Partridge Mews Women's Institute would want her representing us? I don't think so. Mrs McBride? Even if she improved the state of her wardrobe, we all know what her Peter got up to on the

Cricket Club's away day in nineteen-ninety-seven.

'I asked them what they thought would be the best idea, and do you know what they suggested? What the committee of the forthcoming reformed Partridge Mews Women's Institute considered an appropriate idea to decide who could best represent us to the royalty of our great nation?'

'Names in a hat,' I guessed.

She set her book down on the garden table, shaking her head. 'Names in a hat. I tell you, if I didn't laugh in their faces, I would have had to cry. Several women of a certain age in one living room and the best they could come up with is names in a hat? What's next, heads down thumbs up?'

'Maybe they thought it the most diplomatic way of choosing who gets the chance to go.'

She gave me the Look and said, 'I should've known you'd be on their side, our 'arold.'

'How would you choose a representative, our Doris?'

'If I knew that, I wouldn't be sitting in this garden watching a pigeon make light work of McVities best.' She huffed a sigh from deep within her lungs, as though she'd a great reserve of air she'd been withholding for such a moment. 'I simply believed that after so many years of upholding certain standards, the ladies would have developed the ability to think on their own without prompting from me. Instead, I raise a legitimate concern about picking names out of hats, knowing full well that Mrs McBride will put herself in there fifty times over, and they say to me, they say, "All right then, Mrs Copeland, you can choose who gets to go to the Palace." One of them, and I'll let you guess who, even has the cheek to suggest it'll be easier for me considering that

I've already had the gall to do it once before.

'The worst is that they don't believe I can recognise what they're doing. They know that by making me choose who gets to go, I cannot very well put my own name forward. Like I had any chance of going after what's happened. The reaction from the ladies wouldn't be dissimilar to sending a Dobermann into a butcher's.'

She stewed for a moment, before going on, 'Well, I'll make sure the right people get to enjoy the splendour of a garden party at Buckingham Palace, and I will tell you right now that it most certainly won't be Edna blasted McBride.'

She emptied her coffee cup on the grass and headed inside the house, practically fizzing with fury, like a bottle of lemonade that's just been dropped on the kitchen floor.

Next day, while Erin took our Doris and Edith off for a gin-tasting session in Wren's Lea – there was a chance they were off to visit her Mavis and I didn't fancy having my arm torn off by a pit-bull with a perm – I went to pick our Theo up from the gym. Credit where credit's due, he's kept up with his fitness. I'd thought it was just a fad, that there must have been someone who he fancied, and he'd picked up all these new training habits to impress them, like when I first saw our Doris down the Co-Op and kept going down to buy apples. There were a lot of crumbles going around my neighbourhood when I first started courting our Doris.

He came out to the car and got in the passenger seat, stinking of sweaty polyester and an overindulgence of Hugo Boss deodorant.

I said to him, I said, "ow 'at, our Theo?"

'It was leg day, Grandad. I'm suffering.'

'I'll take you for a coffee. Where are we going?'

'I'm guessing Thistlethwaite's is out of the question,' he said, grinning at me as cheekily as a Jack Russell who's just stolen a Cumberland sausage.

I took him to a coffee shop in the town centre. It had gone for more modern décor – white walls with touches of colour here and there on the wall, unlike those with lighting that dim there could be ants in the cocoa powder, and no one would know until their cappuccino started wriggling.

Despite only just leaving the gym, our Theo ordered himself a slab of cake. I can't be doing with all these modern baked goods – there's so much sugar in them that no matter the supposed flavour, they just taste sweet. Then the baker covers the sponge in too much buttercream and icing, hoping the consumer won't notice that they've created something dry enough to be used as loft insulation.

Still, our Theo didn't leave much chance to question the consistency of his cake. He guzzled it down as though he were worried someone would steal his slice if it were left on the plate too long. Then he leaned back in his chair, rubbed his stomach and said, 'Thanks for that, Grandad.'

I said to him, I said, 'Your grandmother will be glad you've kept your manners, even if you do eat cake like you've a Hoover for a mouth.'

He rolled his eyes. 'How is Nan?'

'She's finally putting that party together for the WI.'

'Then she'll be about as stressed as I am,' he said. 'I didn't think A-Level revision would be as hard since there are fewer subjects, but they feel more important than anything else.'

'Have you spoken to your Mum?'

He nodded. 'Course I have. She just says that there's nothing to worry about if I fail.'

'I should try that with your grandmother. How do

you think she'd react if I told her that life goes on?'

'She'd look at you like she was going to tear out your spleen and then you'd be sentenced to making her casserole for tea.'

'You're right, our Theo.'

'She's extremely predictable,' he said. 'What problems is she having with the party?'

'She won't budge from the date that she's chosen so she can't go to the church hall, and most venues in town have turned her away.' That's when I told him about booking the Hare and Horse behind our Doris's back and he gave me a Look to rival his grandmother's.

'You need to tell her, Grandad. You know what a control freak Nan is, she'll go ballistic. She thinks that the pub is an all-right place for you to go drinking with Alf, but not as a venue to host the best party ever experienced by the Partridge Mews Women's Institute. The carpet is too sticky, for a start.'

'I planned on telling her when Alf first brought it up, but she was upset about having to choose a new representative for Buckingham Palace.'

He took a deep slurp of his flat white before he said, 'This has been going on for too long. I thought she gave up on the WI last year. One cruise later and suddenly it's like nothing ever changed.'

'You're not telling me anything I don't know. What do you think I should do?'

Our Theo thought that over for a moment, looking as contemplative as a vicar over their sermon, and said, 'Tell Nan about the pub. I might be the grandson of Mrs Doris Copeland, but even I can't perform miracles.'

After this, the conversation switched to how our Theo was preparing for his exams and how his parents were getting on – our Angela had started working more hours and Neil had taken on the brunt of the housework. Apparently, the house wasn't worth living in when he used our Angela's guest towels to clean the bathroom and bleached the entire set.

He was in the middle of detailing Neil's rush to TK Maxx in the hopes of finding an appropriate replacement when my mobile rang.

It was Erin. She were fraught as she said, 'It's Mrs Copeland. You need to get home quick. Me and Edith don't know what to do.'

Next thing I knew, our Doris was wailing in the background. I disconnected the call and told Theo we needed to leave – his grandmother was drunk.

Our Doris came lumbering out from the front door when we pulled into the drive. Her perm was skew-whiff, her lipstick smeared so that she looked as though she'd filled her wrinkles with raspberry jam, and she was missing a turquoise Hotter plimsoll.

She staggered towards the car, caterwauling – Lord, she were loud – saying to me, she said, 'They kidnapped me, our 'arold.'

'Who?' I said.

She didn't answer me.

Our Theo climbed out of the passenger seat, and it were like a red rag to a bull.

Our Doris had been squinting when she left the house, but it became a squint of recognition. She lunged at our Theo, slumping over his body like a duvet, and said to him, she slurred, 'Why don't you visit me anymore, our Theo? I'm your grandmother.'

Our Theo stood with his arms spread-eagled, eyes wide and unsure what to do. 'Are you okay, Nan?'

'It was awful. They tricked me.'

'Where are Erin and Mrs Simpson?'

'I was defending myself.' She were using our Theo as a strut to hold herself up. She had her head cradled against his shoulder.

I helped our Theo lead her towards the house because both of us knew that a sober Doris wouldn't be happy to know that we'd allowed the neighbours to see her in such a state of drunkenness. Otherwise, I were filled with concern for Erin and Edith. Our Doris can be violent at the best of times, but when she's inebriated, she can be worse than Clint Eastwood in a bar brawl.

If an entire rugby team had just raced through our hallway, I wouldn't have been surprised. It was a mess – there were crooked photo frames all over the place, some broken on the floor. A copy of the Partridge Mews Gazette had been thrown at some point, its pages scattered everywhere as though we'd been set to re-decorate and needed to protect the carpet.

I said to our Doris, I said, 'What did you do?'

She said to me, she said, 'Don't shout at me, our 'arold, I can't bear it.'

Our Theo helped me escort our Doris into the kitchen. I sat her down, where she immediately slammed her head against the table. She exhaled loudly before groaning into the woodgrain.

That's when we heard a commotion in the garden. Erin and Edith were screaming and banging against the walls of my shed. I looked outside to see that a wheelbarrow had been wedged against the door, locking them inside.

Theo went out and released them and I set about making tea for five. I had a feeling there was a story behind it all.

They came inside. Edith took one look at our Doris

and shook her head before saying, 'I have to hand it to her, 'arold. She gives my Alf a run for his money, the way she can knock back a drink.'

I said to her, I said, 'I thought you were only supposed to be tasting the gin.'

Erin came over to the kitchen counter and took one of the mugs of tea off me. She added three sugars and an inordinate amount of milk before swilling it and tossing the scalding concoction down her gullet. After smacking her lips, she said, 'Mrs Copeland didn't get the memo. They had the gin in shot glasses for us to sip or mix with mixers. You know, tonics, sodas, that sort of thing. She didn't care for any of that and just knocked them back like they were Calpol.'

I gave Theo and Edith their drinks before putting one down in front of a comatose Doris. She let out a grunt, a curl of fringe wisping across her forehead. I said to Erin, I said, 'Didn't you say anything?'

Edith stepped in. 'You can't blame Miss Beaumont. Doris is her own person and for whatever reason, she went into that gin distillery with the intention of getting well and truly addled.'

'She's been on the sloe gin, the raspberry, the gingerbread, the hibiscus. Anything they put on the bar, she downed. She didn't care about the flavour, Mr Copeland. It could have been a shot of Domestos and she'd have necked it.'

'I don't particularly wish to say this in front of Theo, but we were concerned about her.' I looked at our Doris, slumped over the table like a common drunk, and shook my head. She'd wanted to visit the gin distillery ever since she'd found out that a local farmer had set up business in nearby woodland. It's an all-right place, if you don't mind meandering around winding country lanes through untold amounts of cow muck, always on the lookout for horse riders who've nothing better to do than trot.

Having visited for the first time she'd used it to get more drunk than she had on our fiftieth wedding anniversary, when folk kept refilling her champagne flute and no one realised until she was on stage singing "I'd Do Anything for Love" as though she were Meat Loaf himself.

I said to Erin, I said, 'Tell me what happened from start to finish.'

The host had given them a complimentary gin and tonic upon their arrival – except for Erin, who'd been given a glass of orange juice as she was driving. She really put emphasis on that orange juice. Then they proceeded on a tour of the distillery. Our Doris was interested at first, asking questions of their host about the creation of gin and why they'd opened a distillery in such an obscure location. Indeed, Erin said that anyone would have thought that our Doris and the host had known one another for decades.

Then came the gin tasting.

The three of them were led into a barn filled with folk who were all situated around wooden tables – birthday parties, work dos and even a young woman celebrating her divorce. Our Doris explained that she was looking for the appropriate drink to share with the ladies of the Partridge Mews Women's Institute, but she was always mindful of supporting local businesses. The host was thrilled and immediately began telling her about all the specialty gins.

Our Doris and Edith were supposed to take sips of each gin put before them before spitting it into a bucket. Our Doris said as she could never commit such an uncouth activity in public and vowed that she would simply swallow her samples, for she had fortified her stomach with a rather large breakfast and besides, she had a strong constitution coming from a long line of habitual drinkers.

Unfortunately, that hadn't been the case. She developed something of a facial tic after her fourth shot – lime-infused gin, she hadn't been a fan and proclaimed to the host that such a liquid should only be used for cleaning toilets – and by her seventh – raspberry gin, a firm favourite and one she would keep in mind for any future dinner parties – our Doris could no longer speak without slurring and her perm looked as though it had been run through with a salad fork.

While all this was going on, the host had been trying to get our Doris to stop, but she was having none of it, declaring that she was Mrs Doris Copeland of Shakespeare Avenue. She'd once drank enough Lambrusco Rosso to fell a rhinoceros and she'd still managed to lead a group of Girl Guides back to base camp.

Erin apologised to the host and left Edith to stand guard so as she could drive the car to the barn door and then bundle our Doris into the back seat. Believing that our Doris was too far gone to cause any real damage, Edith had decided to pop off to the ladies, only to return and find that she'd gone missing.

She can't have been on her own for more than five minutes. However, after having her demands for more drinks rejected by the staff members, our Doris nabbed a bottle of hibiscus gin from behind the bar and disappeared into the distillery.

They searched all over the place and couldn't find her – only the smashed remains of the gin bottle and most of its contents, having been shattered against the wall. A quick glance at the CCTV revealed that our Doris had taken a sip and thrown the bottle.

The CCTV had been the last resort.

Having looked over the security footage, they found that our Doris had traipsed throughout the distillery before making her way to the farm shop. Clearly, the shop assistants hadn't been warned about the possibility of a drunk septuagenarian housewife making her way there. They weren't aware that she'd been refused service.

'What are we going to do?' Erin asked me. 'Mrs Copeland has purchased six crates of gin from the distillery. It's being delivered here on Monday.'

'That's not the worst of it, though,' Edith added.

Erin gulped. 'She used the WI's debit card.'

I heaved a breath. Our Doris had been accused of not doing right by the WI many times over the last few months. She had already been blacklisted.

'Why didn't they cancel the card when they disbanded?' I asked.

Edith scoffed and said to me, she said, 'We've been having a few issues with the bank.'

'Such as?'

'There have been so many signatories over the years, some of whom have since passed on, but the bank maintains that they want permission from them to close the accounts as well. Not to mention how much paperwork they have "misplaced".'

My shoulders sank as I said, 'She doesn't even have a venue. What will she do with all that gin?'

'I don't know, Mr Copeland. When we found her, she ran off. We only managed to get her back in the car because I convinced her that there was a bottle waiting for her on the backseat. I had the child lock on so she couldn't get out. Then we brought her back here. She kept going on the entire way that we'd kidnapped her.'

Our Theo piped up and said, 'How did you end up inside the shed?'

'She went haring off as soon as we got her inside the house. We couldn't find her in the garden, but the shed door was open, so we thought as maybe Mr Copeland had a secret stash of booze in there. Mrs Simpson said as if Alf had a shed, that's where he'd keep it. Either way, we went in and the door slammed behind us. Mrs Copeland locked us in and ran off.'

I shook my head in disbelief. 'What the bleeding heck is going on with her?'

'Maybe she's really upset,' our Theo said. 'Her sister died, then she's had everything else going on with that redevelopment and this party. Maybe it all got to her.'

Our Theo had a point, and I can't believe that I hadn't considered it at first. Being married to our Doris, I always expect her to remain level-headed, especially since we're both in our seventies. When I was younger, I always thought that older people knew exactly what they were doing, that there were no tears and stresses because they'd figured everything out. I'd had that whole "if I don't mind, it doesn't matter" mentality. That's a load of codswallop.

I said to them, I said, 'What are we going to do with six crates of gin?'

'We could return them,' our Theo said.

Edith said, 'After all of the damage that she caused, I thought it right to leave the order in place lest the distillery owner went to the police.'

'That's some good thinking there, Edith.'

Erin said, 'We could always do a raffle. The WI will get some money back that way. Also, it's their stupid fault that Mrs Copeland had their card in any case. She's not the treasurer. How is she to know if she's spent too much money?'

I said to her, I said, 'She's done wrong, Erin, but that'll be a good argument to use against them if anything should happen.'

I considered phoning Linda immediately and asking if she minded us bringing our own booze to her pub, beggar the licensing laws, but I had an inebriated spouse to contend with first.

Theo helped me to get our Doris to the back bedroom, where we left her to sleep it off. I offered to give Edith a lift home but she declined, saying as she needed the walk after the day she'd had. I said to her, I said, 'I'm sorry that our Doris got herself into such a state. I didn't realise she felt this glum.'

Edith said, 'It's just one of those things, 'arold. There's no knowing if everything got on top of Doris or if she simply felt like being bloody-minded and getting pie-eyed. There's every chance she did this for some reason associated with organising the party for the WI. She's always considered the consequences of every action, and I hold no umbrage towards her behaviour today.'

She gave me a quick peck on the cheek and left.

Erin offered to stay and listen out for our Doris while I took Theo home.

When we arrived at our Angela's house, he sat in the passenger seat mulling over something before he said to me, our Theo said, 'Do you think that Nan got drunk because she misses me so much?'

I said to him, I said, 'No. There could be plenty of reasons or none at all, but I definitely don't believe that she got addled today because she hasn't seen you in a while.'

'But she thinks I don't visit enough?'

'She knows that you have your own life to live, our Theo,' I said. 'She just misses getting to see her favourite person on the planet.'

He looked down in the foot well then, all glum. 'Thanks for making me feel guilty, Grandad.'

'I didn't mean to,' I said. 'Don't worry about your grandmother. She's a grown woman who's had a bad year. It isn't your responsibility to make her feel better. You need to be out there living your life, our Theo, and she understands that.'

'It's not like I'm willingly avoiding the place. I have a lot on.'

'If she'd been sober then she wouldn't have said anything. You've done your bit for her. You helped organise your Aunty Bianca's wake. You're not a bad grandson, you're just growing up, and as much as it might upset your Nan not to see you as much, she'd be more upset if she thought she was keeping you from living your life. You'll be off to university within the next couple of years and she'll be just as supportive of your efforts as she's always been.'

He smiled. 'And you?'

'I'm just waiting for you to get old enough to buy me a pint. If you do that for me, I'll be happy.'

'Thanks, Grandad.'

He leaned over to give me a hug before heading into the house. He stood at the door, waving me off, and I went on my merry way.

A common complaint with grandchildren is that no matter how close you might have been, there comes a time when they no longer come around as much. They have exams to study for, friends to spend time with and relationships to ruin; with it comes the understanding as a grandparent that I did the same thing as a child, thinking that grandparents would always still be there for me to go back to, as faithful as the old jar of turmeric in the spice cupboard that I never figured out how to use. I can't hold it against our Theo – it's all part of growing up, and he probably hadn't even thought about how long it had been since I last saw him.

I'll admit that driving away, I did worry about how our Doris would react should he leave town, but that was nothing to concern him.

Our Doris didn't get out of bed that day. She remained unresponsive for the next day, although she popped downstairs to get herself a few strong coffees and meals full of starch and fat. On the third day, she awoke early and made us both proper Full English breakfasts and used the teapot that she usually saves for best.

I'd spent the previous days pottering about the house. I got a few things sorted in the garden – strained my back a bit, pulling up some of those weeds, but it was nowhere near the pain I'd experienced on the cruise when I'd been felled while trying to waltz around a dance hall. I visited the allotment to pick up some vegetables, but only when I heard our Doris snoring in the back bedroom. I didn't want to be out of the house if she took a turn for the worse. Her Bianca proved that the Thistlethwaite women are renowned for dying when I'm otherwise engaged.

Still, I was glad to hear our Doris up and clattering about in the kitchen. I took my time getting ready and went down to the kitchen to one of the best-looking meals I've had in a long while. I said to her, I said, 'How are you doing, our Doris?'

She handed me the salt and pepper to set down on the table. 'I fear I've done something unbelievably stupid, our 'arold.'

'You have,' I said.

Our Doris considered giving me the Look. I saw the familiar whirring of cogs in her brain before she nodded once and said, 'I'm not going to make any excuses for my actions. My behaviour was entirely unbecoming of a Partridge Mews housewife, and I can only ask my friends for their forgiveness.'

'I'm not trying to stoke any fires here, our Doris, but do you honestly believe that you're the first person to do something embarrassing while drunk? Erin blamed herself for not saying no, and Edith thinks that there is some grand plan related to the WI party. Nobody cares. There have been no reports in the Gazette and nobody has posted anything defamatory on social media. The world is not concerned with Mrs Doris Copeland.'

I took a bite of sausage to punctuate my sentence.

There were a bit of a smile on her face as she said to me, she said, 'Sometimes, I am astounded by you, our 'arold. Here I am, having prepared an excellent feast for my husband, only for him to turn around and say that he isn't concerned with me.'

'I said the world, our Doris. You're always a concern of mine.'

We sat in a comfortable silence, eating our breakfasts, and supping our tea – the kind of silence that only comes from a few decades of marriage.

Eventually though, I asked, 'Are you all right? Our Theo said as maybe you drank like that the other day because you were upset about everything going on.'

She smiled then. 'While I appreciate our grandson's concern for my wellbeing and will be contacting him forthwith to put his mind at ease – he is not a psychologist, nor is he attempting an AS-Level in psychology. I'm simply a seventy-four-year-old woman who didn't recognise her own limits.'

'So, you didn't do this because you're unbelievably sad?'

'I don't deny that I'm still grieving for our Bianca, but that's not what caused me to drink so heavily. I also don't need my family blaming my sister's death for my behaviour. I wanted to have fun, our 'arold. It really is as simple as that. I, Mrs Doris Copeland of Shakespeare Avenue, wanted to have fun.'

'You used the WI's debit card to order six crates of gin.'

The smile expanded, becoming a Cheshire cat of a grin, as she said to me, she said, 'Do you think I'd forget something as brilliant as that?'

'You meant to do it?'

'Of course, I meant to do it. The Partridge Mews Women's Institute is an organisation I hold dearly to my heart, but they can be a veritable thorn in my side at times. I acquired the crates, knowing that I could use them for my party, state that I thought it important to support a local business, and hit them where it hurts. They're always so concerned with making money that they've forgotten we have many members who can't afford such extravagances.'

'You're sharing the wealth, our Doris?'

'I am. I am sharing the wealth.' She raised her cup of tea and offered a toast to me. 'I intend on throwing the WI a party that they will never forget, and this is just one step in that plan.'

'And the venue?'

'There's always a hitch when it comes to you, 'arold Copeland. I've no idea why I married such a pessimist.'

'That's a shame, I know exactly why I married you.'

'Why's that?'

'It's an official secret,' I said.

Our Doris invited Erin around later that afternoon to apologise for barricading her in our shed. There was also the small matter of involving Erin in her scheme to charge six crates of assorted gins from a local forest distillery to the Partridge Mews Women's Institute, but I suppose we can't expect miracles when it comes to our Doris; she's never really got on with apologising. She sees it as an admission of being wrong and likes everyone to believe that she hasn't made a mistake since autumn nineteen-forty-four.

Once again, we took tea in the kitchen. Our Doris had taken the best biscuits out of the back of the cupboard – hexagonal shortbread, dipped in a thick layer of chocolate, usually saved for special occasions, or when our Doris gets angry at Coronation Street and needs an emergency biscuit to calm down. When they talked about turning the Rovers Return into a gastropub, she went through an entire pack.

Erin helped herself to a biscuit and said, 'There's no need to say sorry, Mrs Copeland, we've all been there.'

Our Doris thanked her for her kindness and said to her, she said, 'Ordinarily, I hold myself to a higher standard.'

'It's fine. Besides, I got to see the inside of Mr Copeland's shed. That was an experience.'

'What did you think?' I asked.

'I didn't expect it to be so neat. My stepdad's shed is a mess. You have to climb over the lawnmower if you want anything and even then, there's a chance you'll trip over his toolbox.'

I said to her, I said, 'If my shed were a mess, our Doris would spiflicate me.'

Our Doris gave me the Look and said, 'I bleeding well would and all, our 'arold. Can you imagine what the ladies would say should my husband keep an untidy work environment? It would be all over town that Mrs Doris Copeland might be able to keep a spotless skirting board but that she never taught her husband to keep his spanners in order. I think I'd die from shame.'

I looked over her head to Erin and said to her, I said, 'And that is exactly why I keep my shed tidy.'

'Didn't it used to be covered in those plastic bin covers? They were all floral?'

I nodded. 'That were another of our Doris's ideas. She wanted my shed camouflaged from view should her next door crane her neck over and have a coronary at seeing bare wood in all its glory.'

'What happened to them?'

'There were a storm, and they weren't built to be stretched over a shed. We came down one morning to see a shed that looked like a rainbow had melted on it. Our Doris let me keep the natural wood after that. I still had to re-paint it. though.'

'If you have quite finished talking about me like I'm

not in the room, there is something I'd like to say to Erin.' Our Doris's Look inched ever closer towards nuclear in her efforts to get me to shut up. I didn't mind – it had been a right palaver getting my shed back to normal after her insistence on making it look like a backdrop for a documentary on Alan Titchmarsh that wouldn't make it any further than Channel Five.

I said to our Doris, I said, 'By all means, feel free.'

Erin said, 'What's the matter, Mrs Copeland? I've told you that I don't need an apology. I've seen my other friends in much worse states than that. Shanice ended up on a coach to Scarborough when she decided to stow away.' She looked over to me and offered an explanation, saying, 'She thought it was for the Newcastle United team, but that was the next one over. This were for a retirement home. Still, she got free fish and chips and learned how to crochet, so it wasn't a wasted trip.'

Our Doris placed her hand on Erin's wrist. 'While I'm most pleased to hear that Shanice had such an edifying time upon her sojourn to Scarborough, I didn't wish to make another apology for my actions the other day.

'Over the last couple of years, you have proven to be a great friend to me. You helped my campaign for chairwoman of the WI – we know how that went, but you helped me – and you've helped me with a variety of small tragedies that would have kept Falcon's Crest going for another twelve years.'

'Falcon's Crest?' Erin gave me an enquiring look.

I shrugged and said, 'Before your time.'

She nodded and said to our Doris, 'I'm not trying to be mean, Mrs Copeland, but the last time someone reminded me of things that had happened between us, he gave me bad news. A boyfriend, actually. Kevin. He listed everything we'd done together, drive-in cinemas, Alton Towers, that short break where he took me to Manchester, and I said that twenty minutes on a train wasn't really my idea of a holiday and he said I'd soured the entire experience. I said to him, I said, "If you're posh enough to use the word soured, then you're posh enough to find an alternative to Wetherspoons." Anyway, he only went and left me for George Cartwright. I thought, you'll have your work cut out for you with George, he's never been one to settle for a pint of Stella and a half-eaten bag of pork scratchings. No, he expects at least two courses, and if you're not asking to look at the dessert menu then he's not interested.'

'It's not bad news, Erin,' our Doris said. 'In fact, it's a chance for you to take another step up in life.'

Erin eyed her warily. 'This isn't one of those pyramid schemes, is it? Because I've heard all about them from our Billy.'

'Nothing like that, Erin.'

I gave my twopenn'orth, saying to our Doris, I said, 'Where's this going, our Doris?'

She gave me the Look before turning back to Erin and saying, she said, 'Our Bianca left me a bungalow in her will, and I thought you might like it.'

I were stunned. A cold chill ran down my back and I bolted upright. I said to her, I said, 'You never mentioned this to me.'

If she had, I would have told her that it was a bad idea. Besides, I thought that we could sell the bungalow and use the money to help our Theo in future – either with university costs or with his own first home. It's not that I dislike Erin, but I'd prefer to help my own family out before some young woman who's only been in our lives for two years. Particularly one that our Doris hadn't initially liked.

Erin's eyes widened slightly. She met our Doris's gaze and scratched the back of her head before standing up and wandering over to the back door to look out over the garden. She thought hard over our Doris's words – a flush of red rose from her throat towards her cheeks like a steadily rising beetroot stain before she turned to our Doris and said to her, 'Sometimes I think that you don't see me as an equal, Mrs Copeland.'

Our Doris stood as well. 'This isn't about being equals, Erin. You've proven yourself to be a great support over the last couple of years and I wished to express my gratitude by helping you take your first step on the property ladder.'

'Listen to what I'm about to say, because I need you to know that I'm not mad at you. I get exactly where you're coming from, but this isn't okay.'

I said to our Doris, I said, 'You can't just give someone a house, our Doris.'

'Mr Copeland, I know you're trying to help, but please don't get involved.'

Our Doris gave me the Look and said to me, she said, 'See, you're upsetting her.'

Erin said, 'This is nothing to do with him. This is to do with the fact that you don't see me as an equal or a friend, but as some sort of charitable project that you've worked on. Why is it that all the old folk in this town think that I want a house? Doug Grey promised me a house before the development fell through, and you're trying to get me to take a bungalow because you've decided that I'm a worthy citizen.'

'You're thinking too much into this, Erin. Don't you think it might make you happy to get off that council estate?'

I've never seen Erin so upset. I could see the veins in her arms, she were that clenched up. 'I might come from a council estate, but my life doesn't need improving.'

Our Doris paused for a moment before saying, 'I wanted to help you.'

'You helped me get into college, Mrs Copeland. I didn't ask for any more help because I don't need it. Would you sell the bungalow and use any money raised towards helping other girls that are in the same place I was before I met you? From what I can see, you think you've made me into one of your model citizens and that you can reward me. I'm still the same person as the teenage girl whose name you dragged through the mud in the Partridge Mews Gazette. I couldn't walk down the street without some old biddy having a go at me because I hadn't been respectful. I admit that Red was a stupid name for a child, but I was a child myself, and you should have known better.'

Our Doris spoke into the table, saying, 'I thought that matter was in the past.'

'It is and I've forgiven you, but it's behaviour like this which reminds me that although I thought we'd moved past you thinking that I was part of the social underclasses, we haven't. You think that if I hadn't let you into my life then I'd still be worth less than dog muck beneath your shoes. Maybe I should remind you that I volunteered at the charity shop because I wanted to give back to the community. You wouldn't have set foot in there if it hadn't been for a court order.'

Our Doris nodded and sat back down. She stared down into her mug and no matter how much I tried to read what was going on with her face, I couldn't make sense of it. Not a single wrinkle twitched.

'Mrs Copeland?' Erin ventured.

Our Doris darted a glance in my direction and said, 'I need you to leave, our 'arold.'

I said to her, I said, 'What do you mean, our Doris?'

'I mean beggar off out of it because I need to have a private conversation with Erin and things will be said that I don't want you to hear.'

'All right then.' I shot Erin a sympathetic look and left the house. If our Doris wanted me to leave, then I'd grab Alf and head down the Hare and Horse. I was concerned for Erin though; I didn't think she'd ever stand up to my wife.

Down the pub, I told Alf what had happened.

He laughed. 'That sounds like Erin, does that.'

I said to him, I said, 'I always thought she was too nervous to properly stand up for herself.'

'Says the man who still hasn't told his wife that he's booked a venue for her party without her permission.' Alf supped his pint at that, giving me a superior glance over the top of his glass – that's the problem with mates who've known you since short trousers, they know too much. He still teases me about what happened down the Scout Hut with Albie Bickerstaff in nineteen-forty-eight. Snails were involved.

'How do you think it will go between our Doris and Erin, then?'

He shrugged. 'I don't think it'll be a grudge match to death, but Erin can hold her own when she's upset. She once locked a customer in the rag cupboard of the charity shop when he asked for a discount on a bit of Lladro.'

'That customer wouldn't have been you, would it?'

Alf went shifty there, saying, 'It's no Willow Tree.'

I took a sip of bitter. I was still terrified about our Doris's reaction were I to tell her that I'd booked the Hare and Horse for the WI's party. Admittedly, for a few days she wasn't worth approaching. I did consider telling her when she was three sheets to the wind but having already locked Edith and Erin in my shed, I feared what she might do when there was no one around to protect me.

Alongside the terror that is my wife, I was having to screen our phone calls as Linda kept ringing to speak to our Doris about what she'd like on the menu. Linda might be a qualified chef, but she's been serving pub grub since nineteen-ninety-two. I'm not sure she can contend with the dietary requirements of the Partridge Mews Women's Institute.

I said to Alf, I said, 'I will tell our Doris.'

'Good, because I've told our Edith and if word gets back to Doris before you tell her, we'll both be roasted like hogs for the WI's dinner.'

'I was going to tell her when we booked, but when I got home, she was ranting about the visit to Buckingham Palace.'

'I can tell you who categorically won't be going. Our Edith.'

'She doesn't fancy meeting the royals, then?'

'We're off to visit our Martin. He's told us the date that he plans on reaching Venice and we've said as we'll meet him out there. Might do a bit of travelling ourselves, like. You and Doris gave us the idea with your cruise last year, and we've got the savings there, just never liked the idea of a boat. I'm partial to lager, and our Edith would kill me if I were to drown on a luxury liner.'

'Funnily enough, I said the same thing about our

Doris.'

'Forget the open seas, 'arold. We're married to sharks.'

'You can't say fairer than that,' I said. 'Will you be flying out to visit Martin, then?'

'Well, we're not swimming there, are we? I don't know what you'll do with me out of town, though. You might have to start visiting one of those proper therapists.'

'What will you do without me, you mean,' I said. 'You'll have to actually pay for your own drinks for once.'

'I'll have our Martin around. He owes his Grandad a few drinks. He's the one who decided to gad about Europe without thinking about who would pick me up from the police station.'

'I don't think I've done too badly.'

'You've not done bad, I'll give you that,' he said. Then, with a sigh, he went on, 'I have missed our Martin though, 'arold. I raised that lad since he was two years old. I knew he'd always move on to find his place in the world, but the house doesn't half feel empty without him.'

'That's the problem with grandchildren, Alf. They always see us as some sort of fad. We're superheroes when they're children, taxi drivers when they're teenagers, and by the time they're in their twenties we're only good for a visit at Christmas.'

'We can't be bitter about it though, can we?'

'Like you say, they'll owe us a few drinks. I'm going to call it a guilt tax.'

He grinned and said to me, he said, 'I like the sound of that. Does this guilt tax only work for grandchildren? Because I've a friend who disappeared for three months on a world cruise and I think he owes me a few drinks.'

'I've been back since September.'

'Exactly. It's been nigh on a year and I'm still not over having to drink with Tom. He never stops going on about that bleeding marrow.'

'I'll order another round then, shall I?'

He necked the remaining mouthful of his lager, smacked his lips, and said, 'Look at that, the guilt tax is already paying its dividends.'

I don't believe Alf has ever had anything to do with dividends, but I didn't say anything, especially considering he was about to leave me for who knew how long while he went to visit his grandson. I couldn't blame him.

Erin had left by the time I got home.

I found our Doris in her cubby hole, scribbling notes in a notebook.

I took her a brew and said to her, I said, 'There's something I've been meaning to tell you, our Doris.'

She lowered her reading glasses to the end of her nose, looking at me as inquisitive as an owl over a struggling dormouse. She set down her biro and said to me, she said, 'Have you done something important enough to warrant interrupting me during a particularly stressful planning session, our 'arold? Because I've been on the phone for two hours trying to organise a party the likes of which the Partridge Mews Women's Institute has never experienced, and unless you've committed a particularly heinous crime, I'm not sure I have the capacity to manage.'

'I might have accidentally booked the Hare and Horse for your party.'

Our Doris froze. She sat up in her chair, removed her glasses and set them down on top of her notebook, picked up her mug of tea and took a glug – it was still so hot that steam flowed from her mouth, as though her throat were a kettle. She took a moment to exhale and said, 'While it's not my idea of a perfect location, I can't deny some relief that there's one less thing for me to concern myself with.'

'You don't mind then?' I asked, brightening.

'Of course not, our 'arold,' she said. 'It provides me with the perfect opportunity to show the Partridge Mews Women's Institute why I have permitted my husband to frequent the premises for the past fifty-plus years.'

'A lot of them went there to celebrate Burns Night as well.'

She smiled at that and said to me, she said, 'Exactly. I wish I'd considered it sooner. Since the ladies have already proven that they like the location, I could have saved myself a lot of trouble.'

'Linda says as you just need to contact her about organising the menu.'

'I should imagine so. She's been looking to exhibit her culinary prowess and this event will help her do just that.'

'You're not upset with me for booking the pub without asking, are you?'

'You showed initiative when you asked me to marry you, Harold Copeland, and I've been waiting for it to rear its head again for decades. I'm delighted to see it put to work.'

I leaned against the doorjamb and said, 'How did things go with Erin?'

'I'm not quite ready to discuss such matters just yet, but when I am, I can't guarantee you'll be the first person I tell.' She took another slurp of tea. 'Now, is there a biscuit to go with this brew? I've got a lot to be getting on with, you know?'

After telling our Doris about the Hare and Horse, things moved along as fast as Road Runner down a desert highway.

We had six crates of gin delivered the following Monday and stored them in my shed – there wasn't much room for them anywhere else. Linda had said as she didn't mind us offering it on the night, if we paid a bit extra and she could use it as a test for the customers; if they liked it, she might get in touch with the distillery herself.

She was particularly happy at the idea of being able to serve something more than pie and chips for once – she'd found a jackfruit recipe online that she wanted to try out on the vegans, and there was something gluten free that sounded like it would be more suited for filling cracks in walls, but I wasn't about to say anything that might offend a coeliac. I'd just watch their face on the night and see how they got on with a xanthan gum filled lasagne.

With the venue and catering sorted, our Doris

started sending out invitations to the former members of the Partridge Mews Women's Institute. I offered to deliver them for her, but she was determined to use Royal Mail – it also helped that she still had the WI's debit card, and no matter how dearly she held them to her heart, she still had some hard feelings.

She didn't let on as to whether she had made any decision about sending representatives to Buckingham Palace, but she did start having a lot of secret meetings with the committee. I were properly surprised when she had me drop her off in town, only to find Mrs McBride waiting for her outside Caffè Nero.

Still, if that was how our Doris wished to go about things then I wasn't about to start questioning her. There are a few things that I have learned about her after fifty-six years of marriage, and one is to never question her when she's dealing in subterfuge.

The day of the party arrived.

In that time, we'd seen neither hide nor hair of Erin at our house. To be fair, we saw little of anybody – our Doris made sure that all meetings took place in town. I wasn't sure why she wanted to keep me out of the loop. She hadn't resorted to full-blown secrecy in a long time; this felt as though she were three steps away from running off to her Mavis's and calling me to tell me to rendezvous in a layby on the way through Gawsworth.

Husbands had been invited to the party, too – a first in WI history, but our Doris wanted me there to heft the crates of gin, and she thought the ladies might appreciate the opportunity to put their husbands to work as well.

Our Doris acquired a new outfit for the occasion. We went to a retail park – she left me in the Waterstones café because she didn't believe I could offer an appropriate opinion about modern ladies' fashion. Personally, I think she wanted to keep me in the dark about how much she was spending, but that's always been the nature of our marriage: our Doris forks out money for designer gear, I don't question it, and she rewards me with a roast dinner.

She settled on a Basler dress that I called blue and she called cerulean. She had a matching pair of M&S shoes at home. A pair of tights and a white cardigan later and our Doris was ready for a party that she'd spent the better part of a year dithering over.

Our Doris considered buying a pair of trousers for me that would match her dress but said as the colour was too bright for my complexion – besides, she said as the colour was more youthful and I'd look as though I was having a mid-life crisis, something she believed I'd gone through in nineteen-eighty-six when I took our Angela to Knowsley Safari Park. Instead, our Doris had me wear black trousers and an orange-looking shirt she'd found in John Lewis. At least she let me choose my own socks.

We went to the Hare and Horse early to see how Linda had set things up. It was the first time since I'd started visiting the pub that it had closed for a private function – I shouldn't wonder that our Doris had paid extra for the privilege.

Linda had opened the doors to the function room so as we had more room to move. Trestle tables stood at the far end of the room, piled high with food – there was the usual buffet fare, sausage rolls, mini-quiches and Scotch eggs, alongside enough salad to appease a vegan. Linda said as she'd hidden the pork pies at the back in case Alf had any ideas about pocketing them. She'd have hot sandwich fillings as the party moved on, and the promise of that gluten free lasagne still hung in the air. I don't have a problem with the practise myself, but I wonder why those who've chosen such a diet won't simply sit in the corner quietly with a hardboiled egg.

Tables and chairs were arranged about the place so

there was still room for folk to dance when the opportunity arose. Our Doris hadn't arranged a DJ – not after the last debacle involving "Oops Upside Your Head" and some very arthritic older ladies stuck in the middle of the dancefloor like a pile of forgotten handbags. Instead, she and Linda had arranged a playlist to blare out over the sound system at the perfect time, once folk had worked through all their conversational topics, consumed a few too many carbohydrates and units of alcohol, and required a go at the twist to sober up.

Our Doris was particularly happy that Linda had opened the function room because it was bright, and there's nothing our Doris dislikes more than premises where the lighting is too dark to see what's going on with people's faces – she also spends a lot of time on moisturising, make-up and generally making her face look as presentable as the rest of her and she likes to show off. She's a habitual peacock, is our Doris.

Folk started to arrive soon enough and, after some polite suggestions from our Doris, chose to sample gin from a local distillery. It also helped that a rumour had circulated about the state of our Doris after one too many glasses, and they wanted to see what effect it would have on them – I really wouldn't be surprised if it turned out that our Doris had planned the entire thing. She can say she just wanted to have fun all she liked, but she didn't look displeased to have folk speculating about the possibility of her running about the distillery like Paula Radcliffe with a gammy hip.

The usual suspects came in: Mrs McBride brought Mrs Cribbins and Mrs Patel. Alf and Edith showed up with Erin in tow. They'd all dressed up for the occasion – Erin and Edith were in posh frocks, made-up as though they were about to set foot on a red carpet, and Alf, well he wore the shirt and trousers he's worn to every special event since two-thousand-and-three. He has the inexplicable ability to look scruffy even when he's wearing a tie.

I were glad to see Erin there. Our Doris still hadn't said how their private conversation had gone, but as soon as they set eyes on one another, Erin grinned and wandered over.

Up until that point, our Doris had greeted everyone who came through the door, but she let Erin take over and walked about the pub to chat with folk she hadn't seen in a long while – including Meredith Weaver, who we didn't know would be there as rumours were circulating that she'd run off with a church organist from Dumfries.

Alf came over to me and we ignored the gin in favour of ordering two pints from the bar. We stuck to our usual table rather than head into the function room where the ladies from the WI had congregated.

That's why we were the first to see Violet Grey enter the pub.

Nobody had heard from her since the church hall business. I considered getting up and offering to personally escort her from the premises – our Doris didn't need any trouble after all the planning she'd put in – but Alf stopped me in my tracks, saying, 'This is women's business, 'arold. Don't get involved.'

Erin said to Violet, 'Afternoon, Mrs Grey. Is your husband parking the car, or did he perhaps choose his bike today?'

Violet shot a deadly look in Erin's direction. 'I'll thank you to not mention Douglas in my presence. I haven't seen him in a few months, as you well know.'

441

'If there's anything that I've learned over the last year, it's that I can't trust a word that comes out of your mouth. Mrs Copeland told me she'd invited you today, but that's simply because you were a longstanding member of the Partridge Mews Women's Institute. Had it been up to me, you wouldn't be crossing that threshold. Should you so much as put a toe out of line today, I'm locking you in Linda's deep freeze and I won't let you out until Violet Grey is looking a little more blue, do you understand?'

Violet nodded, all meek.

Erin plastered a smile to her face and nodded. 'Good,' she said. 'There's gin behind the bar. Have a lovely afternoon.'

I looked to Alf and said to him, I said, 'You weren't wrong about Erin, were you?'

'She might have fallen out with your Doris, but they're mates. That counts a lot to Erin, does that.'

Throughout the afternoon, our Doris made cursory glances towards Violet to make sure that she was behaving herself; otherwise, she ignored the former chairwoman of the WI. Others attempted to make conversation, but Violet stuck beside Mrs McBride, who told a seemingly endless tale about what her nephew got up to on his trip to Thailand.

If anything, the day was a success.

I didn't get to see our Doris much as she was taking her position as hostess seriously. She was amenable to everyone, asking after their relatives – children and grandchildren who'd flown the coop and, in the case of Nancy Wainwright, currently occupied an old transit van on her front lawn where she used to grow geraniums. Our Doris made sure that they were all fed and watered. To my surprise, they ran out of gluten-free lasagne;

apparently there was an influx of toothless octogenarians who appreciated that it didn't take much chewing.

Everybody was catered for, and our Doris had proven that even though she hadn't organised such an event in a long time, she could still arrange a party that folk would be talking about for years afterward. She just had a disco and the small matter of speeches to get out of the way first.

Linda had a microphone behind the bar that she handed to our Doris.

The room silenced immediately. Our Doris always had the ability to command a room; I think it comes with the Look that could vaporise folk in an instant.

She said to us all, she said, 'Good afternoon, everyone. I am most pleased to see that we've all been able to put aside our differences to celebrate with one another today. Over the last few years, the Partridge Mews Women's Institute has experienced division in its ranks that has created something of a toxic environment and eventually led to its downfall. I appreciate that I contributed to that, and before I make any announcements, I wished to apologise.

'I thought that there was a way things ought to be done and refused to stray from that belief. In always aspiring to a better standard than was possible, I contributed towards growing resentments within a group that I have always seen as a vital part of my identity. That isn't to say you've all been saints, but credit where credit's due, I was a bit of an ogre.

'That is all I wish to say on the matter. I hope that you can find the strength to forgive my past actions – indeed, for how I left the WI – and while I do have some regrets, ultimately, I'm making no promises to change.

'I put this soirée together for a number of reasons.

Firstly, because I wished to make my apology. I wanted to bring the WI back together for us to celebrate and converse again without trying to outdo each other, and to remind ourselves that it's possible for us to have a laugh and a chinwag. I also think that the Partridge Mews Women's Institute is a necessary social group for the women in this town, and we don't want to return to regular meetings with feelings of disdain and misery.

'This is why the committee thought it best to make a few changes to the way things are run around here. Since the most recent chairwoman no longer lives in this country, the previous chairwoman no longer wishes to hold the role, and I've proven that I'm a bit of a tyrant when given a position of power, we thought it best to choose someone with modern sensibilities, who has exhibited that she is able to organise splendour at a moment's notice, is community-spirited, and has a charitable heart the likes of which I don't think we will ever truly understand.

'This person has taught me many things in the short time we've known each other. She reminds me every day of the girl I once was, whilst growing into a woman I wish I could have been. Our new chairwoman, or should I say president, is Miss Erin Beaumont.'

The silence was broken by a few gasps throughout the Hare and Horse.

Our Doris grinned in Erin's direction, who returned her smile, a few tears in her eyes.

I looked across to Alf and we did what two elderly gentlemen in such a position ought to do. We started applauding and cheering for Erin – that, in turn, led to the other husbands mimicking us, before a veritable storm of clapping and hooraying filled the pub. It were like the sound of Manchester United going three nil up against Liverpool, the way we went at it.

Once we'd settled down, our Doris said to us, she said, 'Miss Beaumont…oh, beggar that outdated nonsense.' She took a moment to breathe before she went on, saying, 'Erin's first duty will be to visit Buckingham Palace as one of our representatives, alongside Norma Cribbins, who's shown herself to be a capable secretary in the decades we've had her on the committee, and one we look forward to keeping in our ranks for many years to come.

'That about covers all I have to say, so once more, eat, drink and be merry, for we return to the church hall in three weeks, and I have a feeling there will be an influx of new members we ought to impress.'

There was another outpouring of applause for our Doris as she handed the microphone back to Linda and grabbed herself a glass of Pinot Grigio. She came over and said, 'We can discuss my speech later. For now, I need a moment of calm.'

'All right, our Doris,' I said, but I wasn't prepared to give it to her.

I don't know what came over me – it were this blend of pride and adoration that had filled my chest and for some reason, I decided that the only way to express it was by asking Linda for the microphone.

I don't have the same gift for commanding a room as our Doris. Folk weren't as prepared to give me their attention as they had been for her. Eventually, Linda got them to settle down – I'll admit, some of my courage were diminishing a bit at that point – and they all looked in my direction.

I said to them, I said, 'I'm sorry for interrupting your party yet again, but I just wanted to say a few words about my wife. Our Doris probably won't be too happy with me for saying this, because I haven't planned it and she'll say that I am doomed to failure, but–'

'Get on with it, 'arold, you've a pint growing warm,' Alf called from our table.

When I looked, he were sat there with a cheeky grin on his face and I said, 'I'll have to make this quick because for the first time since nineteen-seventy-one, Alfred Simpson has bought me a drink and hasn't called it a Christmas present.

'Our Doris has organised many events in the past fifty-six years. Anniversaries, dinner parties, theatre productions. She has done it all, and she's done it well. I don't need to tell you this. I don't need to tell you that she can be an insufferable tyrant. I've even described her as a harridan myself, and she's admitted her behaviour to you all. A few of you have even gone so far as to say I require a medal for taking her off the market in nineteen-fifty-eight. She was sixteen, I was eighteen, and Coronation Street hadn't been invented yet.

'Some people ask why I've stuck with our Doris. They wonder at my tenacity at being faced by a veritable bulldog with a perm, who constantly gnaws at my shins, every day. But, in the moments when she's being herself, organising parties for several-hundred so-and-sos with little more than a chunk of brie and a packet of cream crackers, whilst trying to accommodate all manner of dietary requirements, I get this tingle in my chest reminding me that although she is an unutterable pain at times and I will never understand her every foible, she is indisputably, royally, our Doris, and I think I might love her a little bit.'

I looked across the room, found our Doris's gaze – it were a mixture of teary and furious – and said to her, I said, 'I love you, our Doris, and seeing all that you've accomplished in bringing this WI back together, no matter how much aggro it's caused me over the years, has me remembering the girl who married me in nineteen-sixty. You were the first person to drop the "h" in my name, and I haven't been the same since.'

I addressed the pub again, saying to them, I said, 'You've done it once, but I would really like it if we could give our biggest cheers to our Doris, because there's nobody deserves it more at this moment.'

Everyone did as I asked and there was a cacophony of applause as I headed back over to the table.

Our Doris was letting her smile show in all its glory, no more that polite, diminutive one that she usually reserves for polite society. Then she did something she hasn't done in public in years. She kissed me. She actually grabbed my tie – I weren't sure if she were going to throttle me – and planted a firm kiss, smack-bang, on my lips.

She released me from her grasp, and I said to her, I said, 'You liked my speech then, our Doris?'

'I think that you're an indisputable, right royal pain in the backside at times as well, our 'arold, but I'm glad I took you off the market. There's not many would settle for such a cheap cut of meat.' Our Doris gave me another grin, pulled me in for another kiss and shouted across the Hare and Horse, she yelled, 'Linda, get that music playing, I've a husband here who owes me a couple of dances.'

'At least let me finish my pint first, our Doris.'

Alf said to me, 'You'll have to clean some lipstick off first, 'arold. Otherwise, folk'll start thinking you're part of a drag act.'

Edith interjected, 'It's also not your colour at all. You haven't the complexion for such a bright shade.'

'I think it suits you, Mr Copeland,' Erin said. 'Some people might even call it kissable.'

'I suppose that's just the comment I should expect from the new president of the Partridge Mews Women's Institute.'

'The power's not gone to my head just yet.'

'Something tells me it never will.' Edith lent me her compact mirror and I used a napkin to wipe the lipstick from my face – they were right, it definitely wasn't my colour.

After finishing our drinks, the five of us made our way into the function room to dance. There, our Doris didn't mind the lights being dimmed so as disco lights could flare across the dancefloor and illuminate us all, frolicking like a group of schoolkids with all our old favourites playing. She'd stopped caring what folk thought about her love of rock music, so I held our Doris close when Bon Jovi came on. It wasn't our song, but we've been together too many years for just one song. I was glad to be among friends again, slow dancing with my wife, without her worrying about who saw or how we were perceived.

Acknowledgements

It is somewhat surreal to have finished writing tales about Mrs Doris Copeland but, after a decade, I feel as though her story has been told and hope that *Royally Doris* proved to be a suitable last hurrah.

Seeds of this idea were planted by Barbara Walton many years ago, who had the opportunity to visit a garden party like the one referenced in this book. This led to me thinking what our Doris would do given the opportunity, and here we are.

I am thankful to Lindsey Watson for our friendship and continuing to support my writing. It has been seventeen years and we've yet to have that picnic, but I'm sure that it will happen one day – dietary requirements permitting.

Thanks are due to my beta-readers, Charlie Brook, Emily Novelle, who provided invaluable advice and support.

I wish to express gratitude to my mother, Cathryn Heathcote, who was the first person to cry at this book, and has also been driver, promotor, and assistant since I first released *Our Doris* all that time ago.

Furthermore, Dane Cobain agreed to be my editor once again. Thank you for your understanding and help in making Doris's final outing the best that it could possibly be. You were one of the first people to introduce my works to YouTube, and I appreciate the understanding you have when it comes to my writing, even if I have had to explain some Northern terminology over the years.

I am forever grateful to Joy Winkler for offering writerly insight. Thank you for the many conversations we have had about writing over the years, for your friendship, and for steering me in the right direction when it comes to my work. You have provided me with many opportunities since I started on this journey, and if you hadn't spurred me on all those years ago, then *Our Doris* might never have existed.

Thank you to the readers, audience members, librarians and to the entire community of bookish folk online who have read and supported my books over the years, meaning that more people have learned about them.

For those of you who have been here since the beginning, until next time, that is all.

Printed in Great Britain
by Amazon

38861615R10260